They walked out into the dark, the gunman trailing a few feet behind.

Of course there ████████████████████. Of course the ubiquitous Captain Brouillard was nowhere to be seen.

"You're driving," the man said quietly. "I'm in back, with this gun pointed at the place where your spine meets your head. Turn right at the end of the driveway."

They retraced the coastal route. Only this time, the moon was out, and, rather than impersonating a wealthy astrophysicist, Vermeer was playing himself, counting off his last minutes.

"Left here. Up the hill. Stop when I tell you."

And sooner than he wanted to, Vermeer knew where they were going. The failed children's athletic complex. Which, by the light of the half-moon, would be a terrible place to die.

—From MURDER AT THE B-SCHOOL

A+ ACCLAIM FOR *MURDER AT THE B-SCHOOL*

"Like the best academic mysteries . . . Cruikshank has come up with some wry, subtly fascinating insights into one of the world's most pervasive institutions, as well as an intriguing mystery with a surprisingly effective hero."

—*Chicago Tribune*

more . . .

"Compelling."

"Enjoyable and well paced . . . The author has the skill to keep it moving."

"Impressive . . . rings true . . . engagingly entertaining."

"Absorbing . . . Wonderfully crafted . . . a tight and suspenseful plot."

"A well-written, exciting tale . . . Cruikshank will keep his fans satisfied with this winning whodunit."

"Entertaining."

"A delightful page-turner."

"Cruikshank exhibits the finesse of a seasoned novelist, with well-defined characters and a plot that will keep you guessing right to the final page."

MURDER
AT THE B-SCHOOL

Jeffrey Cruikshank

WARNER BOOKS

NEW YORK   BOSTON

The events and characters in this book are fictitious. Certain real locations and public figures are mentioned, but all other characters and events described in the book are totally imaginary.

Cover art and design by Jesse Sanchez

The Mysterious Press name and logo are registered trademarks of Warner Books.

Warner Books

Time Warner Book Group
1271 Avenue of the Americas, New York, NY 10020
Visit our Web site at www.twbookmark.com.

Printed in the United States of America

Originally published in hardcover by Mysterious Press
First Paperback Printing: September 2005

10 9 8 7 6 5 4 3 2 1

ACKNOWLEDGMENTS

I want to acknowledge the contributions of a number of people to this book.

First, of course, is my agent, Helen Rees, who overcame her prejudice against works of fiction and agreed to represent me on this venture.

Next is my old pal Bob Rodat, who charged me up at a critical juncture.

Next is the late Sara Ann Freed, my first editor at Mysterious Press, who took a chance on an unfinished manuscript and an unproven mystery writer—thereby breaking her own two cardinal rules, as she told me one day. I was very lucky to have had the benefit of her help. Godspeed, Sara Ann.

Next is Colin Fox, who picked up where Sara Ann left off. Thanks, Colin. I know I presented some unusual challenges.

Next is my wife, Ann, and the entire Bryan clan, who passed the manuscript around and came back with encouragement and good ideas.

And last are all my friends at the B-School: good people at a great institution.

MURDER
AT THE B-SCHOOL

1

SOMETHING LIKE A BUZZING FLY GRADUALLY COMING into his consciousness: It took Patrolman Mattola a few minutes to pin down exactly what was irritating him about the death scene.

It was the noise of the shower. Or actually, just a piece of that noise. Some trick of the water rushing out, and air rushing in to replace it, creating a high-pitched whine like a liquid drill, boring into those little delicate ear bones he remembered only in a hazy kind of way from the anatomy course he had taken a few years back, when he was working toward a master's degree on the Quinn Bill—the great, sacred gravy train for Massachusetts police officers—and, of course, the raise that came with the advanced degree. Tympany bones, or some such.

Plus, it was *wasteful*. Mattola was a frugal man. The thought of the Quabbin Reservoir, out in the drowned hinterlands of western Massachusetts, slowly being drained by this unplugged hole rubbed his nerves raw. He was tempted, very tempted, to reach behind the half-closed shower curtain and snap the water off.

But Mattola knew better. If the prints showed that someone other than the dead kid had turned it on, the dusting crew would have earned their keep on this particular assignment. Finding some Boston Police prints on the knob couldn't help.

And as corpse-sitting details went, this wasn't such a bad one.

Indoors; no gawkers. No flies. No smells, other than the thick industrial perfume of chlorine in the wet air. In fact, if you had to be called in too early on a Monday morning to babysit a stiff, this was the duty you'd pick. The kid was floating facedown in the whirlpool, naked, suspended at forty-five degrees in a limp, looming bird-of-prey pose. The whirlpool's circle of underwater seats had caught his toes. That, and maybe some foul bubble trapped inside the corpse, prevented the body from sinking any farther.

As far as Mattola could see—and no one had invited him to get up close—there was very little damage on the kid. Some black-and-blue marks just below the bottom of his hair, where his neck met his shoulders. No blood in or around the pool. No debris. Just a forlorn bottle of Maker's Mark on the tiled edge of the pool, with that signature cork sitting next to the bottle, red plastic melted down its sides in a pretty good approximation of wax, extending a last mute invitation. Mattola remembered peeling the plastic off one such cork and nibbling on it—perhaps actually *eating* it, come to think of it—back in his drinking days.

He sighed, just audibly: Now, *there* was a bottle of good juice bound for a bad end.

———————

"Thank you, Sergeant. Nothing's been touched?"
"No, ma'am. Just as they found him."

Mattola, a shy man, not normally an ogler of women, allowed himself a few furtive once-overs of Captain Barbara Brouillard, known throughout the Boston Police Department as "Ms. Biz"—not necessarily a flattering nickname. First female to make detective. Credited with several high-profile busts, ranging from low-life shenanigans over in East Boston to some genuinely slick white-collar stings. Rumored to make up her own rules from time to time.

To Mattola's jaded eyes, she was nothing special. A pile of tangled brown curls, stacked carelessly on top of and behind her head. A blunt, businesslike nose and deep-set eyes, wrinkled at the corners, which looked as if they had seen through way too many people. Probably on the skinny side, although it was hard to tell with all the layers of clothes she was wearing to fend off the Boston winter. *A local,* Mattola reflected, *and we locals naturally look like lumps of dough six or seven months a year, squirreling away whatever heat we come across.* Brouillard hadn't even taken off her heavy trench coat, despite the warm and damp atmosphere.

This room was designed to be naked in. Idly Mattola imagined everyone in the increasingly cramped whirlpool room—the dusters, the photographers, Brouillard, himself—nude, going about their business, sweating slightly in the damp air. He didn't get much mileage out of it.

"All right," Captain Brouillard said crisply, breaking into Mattola's low-voltage reveries. "We have our water shots. Let's get our friend out for some close-ups. And, gentlemen, I want him coming out of the water hole nice and clean—no bruises, please."

Mattola caught the eye of his partner, Joe Linehan.

Linehan looked heavenward almost imperceptibly and then bent down to untie his shoes. Mattola, grumbling sourly, did the same. There were only two ways to get the meat out of the marsh: the sloppy way and the careful way. The careful way meant you had to get into the marsh with the meat.

Together, shoes and socks off, pant legs and shirt-sleeves rolled up, the two uniformed policemen, who were well into the out-of-shape phase of life, eased themselves down the steps, knee-deep into the surprisingly hot water. *A good detail gone bad,* sighed Mattola. This was the sort of thing that led to strained lower backs and, sooner or later, to self-righteous stories in the newspapers about deadbeat cops abusing the city's generous disability policies. They rolled the body over, hand over hand—just another log in the water, although nicely warmed by the water. Nice face, peach-fuzz body hair, modest endowments. Mattola reached under the corpse's armpits and maneuvered the dead weight slowly around so that its feet docked in Linehan's hands. Silently, with purposeful nods and jerks of the head left and right, the two policemen alley-ooped their way up the Jacuzzi's too-tall and slippery steps: *one,* pause, *two.* Water first streamed and then trickled off the body. Its face stared up, vacant and openmouthed, as if it had lost its train of thought in midsentence.

Gently, gently. But then, as they were easing it down onto the tiled floor, Mattola lost his grip under the right armpit, and the last four inches to the floor closed up instantly. The corpse's head bumped once, silently, and expelled a small gush of water from its mouth as it settled down for its last photographs, ever.

Mattola looked up into Brouillard's weary-looking

eyes at precisely that moment. She glided her head left-right, left-right, just perceptibly, as if it rode on ball bearings. It registered every bit of her disapproval of the world's clumsiness.

Or more specifically, of *his* clumsiness.

2

Wim Vermeer received large volumes of e-mail at his Baker Library office. Anyone monitoring this flow might have mistaken Vermeer for an important person.

But he wasn't. The e-mail was mostly academic spam: broadcast junk from professional societies, job hunters, publishers of dubious reputation, TIAA-CREF, credit unions, and so on.

The truth was, Vermeer was fairly insignificant. He was in his third year as an assistant professor of finance at the Harvard Business School. Three years earlier, brand-new to the campus, he had heard a colleague talking through gritted teeth about his job prospects. "That old tenure train won't be stopping at *my* station," his colleague had said. At the time, Vermeer had resolved that when his own time came, whatever his fate, he wouldn't impose it on the people around him. But now he was sorely tempted. He knew it was time to get comfortable with the notion of watching the tenure express roar right through the station, leaving him on the platform. Unemployed. And in the rarefied world of high-end business academics, maybe even tainted: *If Harvard didn't think he was worth hanging on to, why should we snap him up?*

The hard fact was, he wasn't quite good enough. A

very good but not great teacher. But he was improving slowly in that department. His student ratings had crept up, semester by semester.

No, it was his research that would doom him. Looking back, aiming to become the world's leading authority on the financing of corporate defined-benefit plans was a bad, bad bet, like becoming an expert in carburetors just as fuel injectors were becoming standard equipment in Detroit. Yes, some of the blame for that could be laid at the feet of his thesis adviser, who should have known better. (In retrospect, he should have picked a more mainstream character to guide his work.) Beyond that, though, the hard, simple fact remained: *He wasn't good enough.* Even a played-out mine gave up gems to a skilled prospector. He wasn't finding any gems.

A well-intentioned senior member of the faculty had tried to offer him comfort a few weeks back. "The fact is," the old fellow had said, a little wistfully, "you're exactly the kind of fellow we *used* to hire. The kind of fellow who used to do very well here."

Voice mail was less common. Occasionally, a friend from grad school, now safely ensconced in some second-tier college in the Midwest, would drop an acerbic gibe in his box: *Come on out where the land is flat and your chances are better.* Or his teaching-group head would phone in, asking for a clarification of some arcane aspect of Vermeer's recent classroom work. Early in his time at the school, back in the days of unbridled optimism, back when he was still lashing himself to his desk twelve hours per day, six days a week, it would have been difficult even to deposit such a message, because Vermeer would have jumped to pick up the phone whenever his secretary wasn't there.

Now he was far less interested in racking up the hours and showing good citizenship skills. And at the same time, fewer people were much inclined to call. That invisible but dense cloud, the cloud of failure, was settling down around his shoulders, he knew, and even once-friendly colleagues on the faculty were trying to open up a little distance between themselves and him. The tenured knew that he'd be gone soon and, except for bonds of affection, really wasn't worth investing any more time in. The untenured—roughly, people his age and younger—clearly feared contagion. *Whatever you've got, Wim, we sure don't want it.*

Pushing the overhanging shelf of blond hair out of his eyes, he sifted through the pile of junk in his in-box. Further clarifications of various Harvard benefits, for which he qualified. *But not for much longer.* The new Lands' End catalog, carefully crafted to disguise that company's acquisition by Sears. What was Thoreau's famous line? *Beware of enterprises that require new clothes.* At least he had a closet full of clothes. If he kept an eye on his weight, he thought, reflexively patting his still trim waistline, it might be years before he became noticeably shabby.

Picking up the entire pile, he put a rubber band around its middle, like a belt. Then he took a half sheet of his letterhead, on which he scrawled, "Make it all go away!" Then he signed the note with a flourish, slipped it under the rubber band, and dumped the whole package into his out-box. Closure, of a sort.

The phone churbled electronically: once, twice. Vermeer wondered only briefly if the temp outside his office had already gone home—5:25, his watch read—and picked up the handset midway through the third blurp.

"Vermeer here."

"Oh, hello, Wim," said the receiver. "I'm glad to catch you in."

"Uh-huh. Who's this?"

"Sorry. Jim Bishop."

"Oh. Hello, Dean Bishop."

"Got a minute to come over and chat?"

"Sure."

———————

Walking across Peterson Park to Morgan Hall, the seat of power, Vermeer tried to recall the speech he had rehearsed for the next time he had a private session with the dean of the Harvard Business School. He had never worked all the way through this oration, brave and self-exculpatory, because he didn't really think he'd ever get a chance to deliver it. Now the summons had come.

But it was still too early in the year for the Bad News: *How can we help you make plans for the future, Wim?* And the coup de grâce wouldn't come from Bishop, anyway. It would come from some senior functionary in the Finance area. Someone with gray hair and a brow deeply furrowed with concern. Probably Pirle, Vermeer thought, wincing and pulling his jacket a little more tightly around his chest.

So what was on Bishop's mind?

Whatever it was, it was not likely to be uncomplicated, because Bishop was rarely uncomplicated. Balding, angular, highly cerebral, and thoroughly understated, the dean of the Harvard Business School remained an enigma even to his closest advisers on the faculty, and even after many years in the post. (Vermeer, of course, only knew this from snatches of conversations overheard in the Faculty Club or in the hallways of Morgan Hall.) Rumor had it that Harvard's president had named Bishop to the deanship a decade ago because he had wanted someone more or less controllable on the Business School side of the Charles River. It hadn't worked. The president, mistaking subtlety for docility, had wound up with a subordinate who was a grand master at the game of intra-university politics. What Bishop wanted from the university, he almost always got, although it was hard to see him getting it. What the university wanted from Bishop, it almost never got.

Closer to home, Bishop ran his school in similarly oblique ways. Under his seemingly mild gaze, things somehow *happened,* almost always producing an outcome that he ultimately declared to be satisfactory. "Very good," he would say in a tone that implied that the news he was receiving was unexpected but relatively unimportant. (Neither was true.) But if you tried to trace a particular outcome back to Bishop's hand, you would be frustrated. In most cases, it seemed, his agents didn't even know they were his agents.

Ordinarily, the faculty might have rebelled against this kind of leadership by prewiring—a style that certainly wasn't advocated in the classrooms of Aldrich Hall. Two factors worked in Bishop's favor, however. The first was that he never took credit for anything. The faculty appreciated hearing, in his quiet tones and full paragraphs, that they were fully responsible for all good things that happened at the school. And the second was that, in fact, good things kept happening at the school. Faculty salaries were among the highest at Harvard. Money for research flowed in a steady stream. Teaching loads stayed reasonably low, and the quality of the students stayed unnaturally high. Creature comforts were well looked after.

Seen against this benign backdrop, did it matter if Dean Bishop chose to do business in impenetrable ways?

The dean's secretaries were still at work. One of the two consequences of tending to the power brokers, Vermeer noted: inhumane hours. The other was the notably stricter dress code that prevailed in the dean's office. Up in the higher reaches of Baker and Morgan, you'd be hard-pressed to find lipstick and hose. In Dean Bishop's lair, though, one dressed for success or one moved on.

"The dean asked that you go right on in, Professor Vermeer," said the more highly polished of the two youngish women who sat behind a modernist mahogany barricade. Vermeer took a detour past the barricade to the large bowl of M&M's that sat on an out-of-the-way side table. He was not a regular visitor to these parts, but he knew about the M&M's. This was how people boosted their blood-sugar levels before venturing into the Den of Inscrutability.

"Hello, Wim," said the dean, waving toward an empty chair on the near side of his huge circular table. Vermeer returned the greeting and sat down. Neat stacks of work were arranged around the perimeter of the table, facing outward, like numbers on a great clock face. "You'll excuse me for not getting up. I played squash this morning with one of our younger colleagues, and I have spent the day getting stiffer and stiffer."

Squash, Vermeer thought, nodding in a way that he hoped looked sympathetic. *Who would be so bold as to tackle this guy on a squash court?*

The dean paused and then continued. "I haven't seen much of you this year."

"No. But then, you keep us very busy."

Bishop smiled: a neutral smile. "Well, very good. And that's all the more reason why I really appreciate your coming over on such short notice."

"No problem. What's up?"

"There's been an accident. You've probably heard."

"Actually, no," Vermeer said. "I've been pretty much out of the loop today. I'm trying to finish an article." This was literally true—it *would* be good to finish that article—but it was not accurate. His class had not met this morning, and he had used the occasion to go downtown and stoke his modest network with some friends in Boston's small financial district. The visit had extended through a discouraging lunch. And his temp, filling in for the secretary who had left several weeks back for maternity leave, was a nocturnal guitar player who dozed by day. No one went to Sam the temp for breaking news.

"Well, brace yourself, because it's unpleasant. You remember Eric MacInnes, who was in one of your first-year Finance sections last year? He drowned in the whirlpool in Shad sometime late last night or early this morning. The time of death is approximate."

Vermeer took in this bizarre news. In fact, he remembered Eric MacInnes quite well. The HBS classroom was a surprisingly intimate setting, despite the ninety-student sections that most classes were taught in, and MacInnes had been a standout in that setting. Not because he had performed at a particularly high academic level. In fact, as Vermeer vaguely recalled, Eric MacInnes was always cutting intellectual corners, always putting himself at risk of being sent up in front of the future-chilling Academic Performance Committee, always skating up to the edge of academic probation and then skating away again.

How? As far as Vermeer could see, MacInnes got through life by charm and seduction. God presumably had shortchanged the hundred souls ahead of and behind Eric in line, just to give extra looks, wit, and spirit to the sparkling-eyed, blond-headed kid up there at the front— just to let him strike those particularly graceful and self-confident poses.

Of course, the fact that MacInnes came from a family that was rumored to be fantastically wealthy only heightened people's interest in Eric, fueled speculation about what made him tick, and cut him some more unearned slack. His classic good looks, overpowered (but dinged and dusty) sports car, and quick wit drew the attention of most of the women in his section—and, Vermeer had noticed more than once, a second look from several male students.

And the kid was a natural-born performer. Vermeer remembered one class in which MacInnes had simply taken over the second half of an eighty-minute class, playing "case method teacher" better than Vermeer himself had ever played the role. It was mainly doublespeak and verbal pyrotechnics—no content, no particular direction— but it was all hysterically funny. One student, Vermeer recalled, breached classroom etiquette by leaving the room suddenly and without explanation. She later apologized to Vermeer, blushing and explaining that she had been on the verge of "sphincter distress."

"Yes," Vermeer said to Bishop finally, "I knew Eric pretty well." He knew that his response should be more compelling, or nuanced, or counterintuitive. This circumstance had the smell of institutional crisis to it, and for some reason he was being invited in. But this only heightened his sense that he was walking on extremely thin ice. What was he doing here in this well-appointed office with the Fitz Hugh Lane oil painting on the wall, and the oversize ficus trees with their relentlessly shiny leaves, and his suddenly accessible dean?

How did Bishop know that Eric MacInnes had been in his Finance class last year? There had been nearly a dozen other such sections running at the same time. And why did Bishop seem to care?

Again Bishop smiled. "Yes. Very good. I thought you did. And the younger brother, too?"

"Yes. I have James this year." James MacInnes was at least two years younger than Eric, but—due either to Eric's forced withdrawal from college for a period of time or (as another rumor had it) a period of over-the-top debauchery in Berlin—James had nearly caught up with Eric in terms of schooling. That was as far as the catching-up was likely to go, however. As a rule, Eric dazzled; James plodded. Eric wriggled through tight crevices solely on nerve and chutzpah; James picked up blunt instruments and chipped tediously through whatever mountain blocked the road ahead. As far as Vermeer had been able to tell, James didn't lack for smarts. But he lacked and even seemed to disapprove of his brother's glibness. Unlike Eric, he seemed determined to earn his way in life.

Their lifestyles, too, underscored their differences. (This had been the subject of gossip in the faculty dining room one day, Vermeer recalled.) Eric lived in high style in Soldiers Field Park, adjacent to the Business School and the most expensive of all the Harvard-owned apartment complexes. James lived in an apartment in a somewhat dicey Cambridge neighborhood just across the river from the school. (Off the record, Business School students were advised not to use the footbridge over the

Charles that connected that part of Cambridge with the Boston campus after dark.) And whereas Eric was conspicuously single, James had been married for several years already.

It was remarkable, Vermeer now realized, that he knew as much about the MacInnes boys as he did. They were, in their own way, campus celebrities. Students and faculty alike lived vicariously through them. And now Eric, implausibly vital even in the high-voltage HBS environment, was, implausibly, dead.

"Let me cut to the chase, Wim," the dean continued. "The school is in a very unusual relationship with the MacInnes family. It would be a shame if this accident damaged our relationship."

Again Vermeer felt his brain working a little too slowly and coming up with uninteresting goods. After what felt like too long a pause, he responded, "I can't imagine how it would *not* damage the relationship, Dean Bishop."

"Point taken." The dean pushed himself up out of his chair. The cushion he had been sitting on gulped audibly for air. He turned three-quarters away from Vermeer and leaned toward the windows, as if to survey the tennis courts just outside the office. In fair weather he would have been rewarded with the sight of graceful young bodies at play. Now the scene was bleak, windswept, monochromatic. A few mock-Victorian streetlights cast light into the gloom. Bishop folded his arms behind his back, cleared his throat, and then continued.

"I'm sure you know, Wim, that we have never been a favorite refuge for old money. I doubt that you have had large numbers of Rothschilds or Rockefellers in your classes. I know I never did, back when I was teaching.

"The truth is," he continued, "that we run a pretty pure meritocracy here. We recruit, we admit, and we train the ambitious and talented. If they come from humble origins, with lots of incoming debt, we loan them most of the money they need to get through the place. We put them under great pressure with the help of bright young people like you. In many cases, we even tear down and rebuild their personalities. This is good for them, and good for us. They learn how they work and how the world works at the same time. And they are grateful to us, eventually, for helping to sculpt and mold them."

He paused, then spoke again in his quiet voice: "But the MacInneses, as I'm sure you've gathered, are a very different kettle of fish. They came here mainly because the father, William MacInnes, became convinced that we could help him prevent the emergence of a generation of dividend-dependent coupon clippers within the family. He believes that a dose of reality here can prepare his heirs to reinvigorate the family businesses. And we believe he's correct in thinking that way."

With long and graceful fingers, he tidied one of the already tidy piles of paper on the table. "So William MacInnes was taking active steps to toss his sons out into the rough-and-tumble of life," Bishop went on, "where few members of the family other than himself have been seen for several decades. He was willing to trade off some of the family's hard-won privacy and insulation in return for a little vigor, vitality, and nerve. In that spirit, he entrusted both of his sons to us. And now one of them is dead on our watch."

Vermeer, although aware of Bishop's reputation for figuring out what made people tick, was nonetheless impressed by the dean's crisp recital. He wondered, irrelevantly, how Harvard's president could have failed to see what he was getting into, ten years back.

"I don't know much about these circles, Wim," the dean continued. "This is not my tax bracket. I *do* know that these kinds of people—very big money, very old money—talk a great deal among themselves. It's possible they have no one else to talk to, or that they can't even understand other kinds of people. The MacInneses took a very visible gamble, and now they have lost in a big way. The next time these kinds of people convene on one of their private islands somewhere, our reputation is likely to suffer some serious damage. Serious and, in my opinion, undeserved damage."

The dean turned toward Vermeer. "Wim, I'm asking you to look after the school's interests in this situation. I want you to serve as our liaison. The rest of the family seems to know something about you, I assume based on what the kids have told them. I need you to help keep the people on this end, starting with Harvard, out of their hair as much as possible, although God knows that's not going to be easy. I will do my best to encourage the good authorities of Boston to get this wrapped up quickly. You might be able to help with that, as well.

"Talk to External Relations and find out whatever they've got on the family. And get hold of Marc Pirle. He's wangled his way onto a couple of their boards. He's offered to get you up to speed. Thanks. Keep me posted."

On that note, as the dean indicated by initiating a handshake, the interview was over. Getting to his feet, Vermeer felt the beginnings of a generalized intestinal dread. Babysitting for the MacInnes family was not how he had planned to spend his time in the next days or weeks. He needed a job.

On the other hand, based on today's lunch, the job hunt wasn't giving him much comfort, either.

"Okay. I'll see what I can do."

"Great. Start tomorrow—no, start tonight. We'll make sure your teaching group gets your classes covered.

"And, Wim, we're in uncharted territory here. Let's be conservative. If you feel like you're going to surprise me, tell me ahead of time."

3

IF SHE COULD AFFORD TO LIVE AT THIS "SOLDIERS FIELD Park," Brouillard observed silently and a little bit sourly, she wouldn't.

The complex's handsome brick exterior promised more than it delivered. The buildings weren't cinder block and wallboard, but they weren't much more than cinder block and wallboard, either. Sharp noises caromed down the hallways and back again. Somewhere in the building, someone was overdoing it with curry powder, no doubt annoying the neighbors.

If you forced me to go to Harvard, she thought, *I'd hold out for one of those Gold Coast apartment buildings over on Mount Auburn Street—high ceilings, walnut trim, the occasional working fireplace.*

Eric MacInnes's apartment was much more than large enough for one spoiled rich kid. In fact, it was just about as big as the apartment in the Somerville two-family where she and her two brothers had grown up. Except that instead of sharing his two-bedroom suite with a noisy bunch of Irish–French-Canadian family members, Eric had lived with a treadmill, a Nautilus machine, a StairMaster, and other shiny fitness equipment in his spare bedroom.

Brouillard took a notepad out of her pocket. "Nice work if you can get it," she scribbled. It was understood around the department that nobody else looked at her notepads, ever.

The same police photographer who had shot the Jacuzzi was now looking for something to photograph here. There wasn't much. The dusting team looked busy, but they were only going through the motions. Whatever had happened hadn't happened here.

More notes: "Fastidious kid. A priss. Creature comforts. Silk sheets." On to the closet, where several collections carried the silk motif forward. A remarkable collection of ties, she thought, diamond-racked on an expensive-looking tie holder. "Top drawer, bureau," she wrote, "neatly folded silk handkerchiefs many matching ties in closet."

"Health nut," after surveying Eric's private gym. As she prowled in and out of additional corners of the apartment, this became a column heading with a growing list of entries: "treadmill. natural toothpaste. vitamins. magnifying mirror: pore check!" Based on a quick scan of the refrigerator and pantry, she added: "careful eater. no booze." "Fruit bowl, full, on table," she noted during one pass through the living room.

"Hey, Captain," called out one of the uniformed policemen, out of sight in the bedroom. "Here's something you'll want to look at."

Patrolman Offner sat cross-legged on the floor next to Eric's computer station. The computer was on, displaying a spinning HBS shield screen saver. Onto what might have been a clean sheet from Eric's closet, he had dumped the contents of a stylish white trash can. There were two small piles of trash: one getting smaller, the other getting bigger. With one rubber-gloved hand, he was holding the smallest possible corner of a slightly wrinkled piece of paper. "This was near the top. So far, nothing much else."

Brouillard gestured with her fingertips for him to spread the note out on the desktop. There was a tight band of type across the top fifth of the page, looking as if it had fallen into some standard default margins: an inch at the top, left, and right. *Nice black type,* she thought in passing. *Nice to have a high-speed HP laser printer around, just in case you need it for your scribbles.*

This is now that was then, the scrap of writing began as if in midthought. *I live in this winter that you have conjured up and coldly it infuraites me. What scent eminates from love that can't be satisfied? Your scent. Our scent. Whatever we build together falls down collapsed flat. We are those inflatable structures, a tennis bubble, crushed under the snow. I wish we were there. I wish you were dead and sometimes I think you are.*

Captain Brouillard read the note quite a few times. Quickly, then slowly, then quickly again. "You're right, Patrolman Offner," she finally said. "That is an interesting piece of work. Please get a couple of copies for me after the dusters look it over. And tell the medical examiner that we're very interested in the autopsy results."

4

THROUGH INTERMEDIARIES, WILLIAM AND ELIZABETH MacInnes turned down Dean Bishop's invitation to stay at the dean's house while they were in Boston claiming the body of their son. Instead, they let it be known, they would stay at the Four Seasons, downtown.

This was a bad sign. Most visiting dignitaries felt honored to be put up at the dean's house, which one of Bishop's predecessors had transformed from a down-at-the-heels brick pile (where deans no longer chose to live anyway) into the equivalent of a four-star inn.

"Perhaps you should pay them a call at the Four Seasons," Bishop had instructed Wim Vermeer by voice mail, filling him in on these developments. "You could again express our condolences, offer to cut red tape, escort them while they're in town. Whatever they need. Meanwhile, my office will also be reaching out to them." He left directions for getting in touch with the MacInneses.

Vermeer dialed the number and explained his mission to a Mr. Ralph, who identified himself as a senior member of the MacInnes staff. After a moment's consultation with someone else, Mr. Ralph returned to the phone and suggested a ten a.m. meeting. He would meet Vermeer in the hotel lobby, he said, and escort him upstairs.

Now, fifteen minutes early, seated on a sofa among oversize floral displays in the main lobby of the Four Seasons, Vermeer felt more than a little out of place. His reasons for being here—with the cloying smells of cut flowers putting him in mind of long-ago ordeals at funeral parlors, marking the deaths of various aunts, uncles, and grandparents—were murky at best. He was tempted to leave an excuse with the desk and bolt from the hushed and overheated lobby. He didn't.

The sepulchral quiet was broken when a trio of huge, muscular men in their late twenties swept in through the front door. All had on sunglasses, although the day was overcast. They scanned the lobby as they moved, heads swinging left and right, communicating in terse mutters.

Sandwiched in their midst, swept along with them like a cork on a wave, was a second-tier martial arts movie star, whom Vermeer recognized from an action film he had seen on an ill-fated date a few weeks back. The actor was as handsome in person as he was onscreen. But he was surprisingly delicate—especially in contrast to his bodyguards, all of whom were half again as big as he was. He was younger than Vermeer would have guessed.

As the security wedge snowplowed its way toward the elevators, a tightly packed bunch of about a dozen teenage girls burst into the lobby in pursuit. Giggling and laughing, some even squealing, mostly out of breath, they waved pens and autograph books.

When the celebrity's entourage reached the elevators, the trio of bodyguards shoved their valuable cargo toward the middle door, pushed the Up button, and spun 180 degrees on their heels with almost military precision. They flexed at the knees and leaned forward slightly as the noisy tide of girls crashed up against them. Giving ground by inches, they gradually pinned their employer against the still-closed door of the middle elevator.

Vermeer stared at the actor. As it happened, the young celebrity was staring back at him, mainly because he was crushed against the highly polished brass elevator door and had no place else to look. When their eyes locked briefly, the star shrugged and produced a wan smile. Around the security wedge, the teenagers grabbed at his head and shoulders.

An adjacent elevator arrived with a muted *bong*. Out of it strode a thirtyish brown-haired woman in a trench coat and baggy pants, coat collar turned up against the weather. Looking annoyed at having to make her way through this confusion, she navigated skillfully, fixing a neutral glance on Vermeer as she passed. Behind her came a tall, nondescript man in a funereal black suit, who slid in and took advantage of her wake, a rangy sea bird riding the wind currents behind his vessel.

The beleaguered star and his phalanx of protectors, waiting only as long as absolutely necessary, dived sideways and into the empty elevator, with the muscle fending off the girls behind them. The polished brass door closed again. Several uniformed hotel functionaries, absent during the decisive phases of the battle, now materialized and herded the flushed teenagers back outside. Quiet descended once again on the Four Seasons.

"Mr. Vermeer? I am Mr. Ralph. You can come upstairs now."

It was the funereal man from the elevator, left behind in the silence. Despite his height—at least six two, Vermeer guessed—Mr. Ralph was remarkably insubstantial. He seemed to have only two dimensions: up-and-down and sideways. Vermeer couldn't think of a single thing to say to him, but Mr. Ralph seemed not to expect small talk. They rode up to the ninth floor in silence.

Mr. Ralph tapped discreetly on the door of room 903. When it opened, he stood to one side and signaled with two spare flicks of his hand, as if he were sweeping a dead moth off a table, that Vermeer should enter.

Vermeer walked down a longish hallway and turned a corner into a nicely appointed living area with a spectacular view of the Public Garden. An elderly man was rising to greet him, stiffly at first, but with gathering momentum. An elegant-looking woman remained on the couch where the two had been sitting. The remains of a light breakfast sat on a coffee table in front of the sofa.

"I'm William MacInnes," he said in a deep and slightly overloud voice. "This is my wife, Elizabeth. You are Professor Vermeer from the Harvard Business School. Please take a seat." He lowered himself back onto the sofa and motioned Vermeer toward a chair.

"Thank you." Vermeer, although amused by the old man's peremptory tone, was careful not to smile. MacInnes looked about seventy: balding, with a generous fringe of white hair at ear level. His eyebrows had grown luxuriantly out of control. He wore a blue blazer and gray slacks. His tie matched the handkerchief that emerged in a folded point from his coat pocket.

"Perhaps you should tell us why you are here." William MacInnes's tone, although not unfriendly, had an edge. There appeared to be plenty of wrong answers to his question.

"Certainly," said Vermeer. He slid a business card across the coffee table, dodging the breakfast tray. MacInnes took no notice. "Dean Bishop asked me to convey in person our condolences for your loss. He hopes to meet with you at the school sometime soon, at your convenience. We all knew Eric and admired him very much. I taught him last year, as you may know. And Dean Bishop also asked me to volunteer my services in case you need any help while you're in town."

MacInnes listened intently to this explanation, as if probing for hidden meanings. Elizabeth MacInnes, meanwhile, looked disinterested, distantly studying something on the wall behind Vermeer. She was the most beautiful old woman Vermeer had ever seen. Her hair, mostly gray, still had luster, and the blue of her eyes seemed only slightly diluted. Vermeer was no expert, but he guessed that her gray wool suit—perfectly tailored, with subtle black embroidery around the pockets—cost more than his secondhand Volvo. She continued to stare fixedly. It was not clear that she was even aware of his presence.

"We are in town to claim the body of our son," William MacInnes said. "That's a difficult task, but I don't think it is one that you can help much with."

"Of course you're right," Vermeer agreed. "But sometimes a local contact can make things easier. We have good friends in the city government, as well as at the university. If anything comes up—like red tape to be cut, logistics to be solved, or whatever—we want to make all of our resources available to you."

"In retrospect," MacInnes replied coolly, "it's too bad that those resources weren't made available to Eric when they might have helped."

The harshness of the comment seemed to retrieve Elizabeth MacInnes from her trance. She turned regally, from the waist, toward her husband. "That was uncalled for, William," she declared in a quiet tone that did not invite debate. The old man snorted but didn't otherwise respond.

For the first time she looked directly at Vermeer. "I appreciate your taking the time to visit us. Eric said you were his favorite teacher last year, although I remember that finance was far from his favorite subject."

No diplomat could have intervened more skillfully. Vermeer found it difficult to believe that Eric would have paid him such a compliment, but on the other hand, how else would Eric's mother know who her son's finance instructor was?

"Professors aren't supposed to have favorite students, Mrs. MacInnes," he said, allowing a small smile to creep onto his face. "But I will confess that Eric made a very strong impression on everyone in the classroom, including me."

"I'm afraid I know exactly what you mean, Professor Vermeer," she replied, nodding. "It's entirely irrelevant, but perhaps you can tell me something I've been curious about since Eric first mentioned your name. Are you descended from the seventeenth-century Dutch painter?"

"Yes, directly, but you have to go back a lot of generations to get to him."

"Oh, not that far, surely," she said. "But how wonderful. You must be very proud."

William MacInnes cleared his throat noisily. "Perhaps there *is* something you could take care of for us, Professor Vermeer. We're only in town long enough to talk to the necessary bureaucrats and bring Eric home for burial. It would be helpful if you could arrange to have his personal effects packed up and shipped back to our family home in New York State. I suppose his car should go there, as well.

"As far as I'm concerned," MacInnes continued, "you

can dispose of the clothes and linens and so forth, but I'd like to retrieve any books, papers, and family memorabilia he might have had in his possession. Which I'm sure will have to wait until after the officials finish poking around in there. And I'm told he had some sort of elaborate exercise rig in his apartment that our daughter might have some use for. We should probably get that packed up and sent down to the city. Mr. Ralph can give you the addresses."

Breaking down a dead former student's Nautilus rig was not how Vermeer had envisioned spending the waning days of his academic career. And where would brother James be in all this? Plodding toward the finish line?

Aloud, though, Vermeer was all high service: "Any way we can help, Mr. MacInnes."

The conversation was over. As Vermeer rose to leave, there was a knock on the door. Mr. Ralph slid down the hallway and opened the door, now just out of Vermeer's line of sight. "Okay, Father," a female voice announced. "Time for your shot."

A young woman turned the corner and bounded into the living room at a clip that nearly put her into Vermeer's arms. "Oh! Sorry," she exclaimed, braking and backing up two steps. "I didn't know anyone else was here."

She was compact, a little below average height. A bright purple warm-up suit hugged a trim physique. Her wavy light brown hair was pulled back in a tangled ponytail, more or less held in place by a purple scrunchy. Her face was pretty, in an unformed kind of way. Over her left shoulder was slung a small canvas tote bag with "Catskill Regional VNA" and a stylized stethoscope silk-screened on its side.

"Good morning, Libby," said Elizabeth MacInnes. "This is Professor Vermeer. Professor Vermeer, our daughter, Elizabeth, who lets us call her Libby to minimize confusion."

"Hi," the younger woman said, briefly accepting Vermeer's hand. "I've heard a lot about you from my brothers. Especially Eric."

He hadn't known there was a sister. "I'm glad to meet you. Although I'm sorry it had to be under these circumstances. All of us at the school share in your loss."

She looked down at her running shoes, then back up at Vermeer. "I'm going to miss Eric so much," she said. Now, at this distance, he could see the color of her eyes—deep brown—and also could see that they were red-rimmed and puffy. "He was one of my favorite people in the whole world."

An awkward moment of silence ensued, finally broken by the rumbling voice of William MacInnes. "The professor was just leaving, Libby," he said, "and now we have our little business to attend to."

He swiveled his large head toward Vermeer. "If you need anything else from us, Professor Vermeer," he said in a tone that didn't invite response, "please get in touch with Mr. Ralph."

5

"So WHOSE ARBITRAGE ARE WE ARGUING WITH THIS week? Rhondell's or Schwartz's?"

Marc Pirle, senior professor of finance, clearly enjoyed tweaking his junior colleague. For his part, Vermeer was more than a little surprised that Pirle was conversant with these two obscure quarter-century-old methodologies for balancing pension-plan portfolios with the portfolios of individual plan shareholders—two models that Vermeer had in fact been attempting to improve upon in his stalled research. Up to now, Pirle had not shown any particular interest in, or familiarity with, Vermeer's work.

"I'm hoping that it will soon be the other way around," Vermeer responded. Even to his own ears it sounded lame. "I'm hoping that the Rhondells and Schwartzes of this world will decide that they need to start arguing with *my* arbitrage."

Pirle laughed out loud. "Well, don't hold out for a call from them personally. My understanding is that neither of those two gentlemen is any longer of this world."

He was fiftyish, graying, and slightly overweight, turned out in an extremely expensive and well tailored suit. (A wrinkle, Vermeer decided, would be an impossibility.) His silver hair was combed back, displaying an unnaturally low hairline. The tan on his expansive forehead, though, appeared to be natural, hinting that Pirle had regular access to sunlight in warm climates. And Vermeer knew this to be true: Pirle maintained a villa on an island in the Caribbean, where he sometimes entertained guests who controlled either money or ideas.

His office was more or less the same size as Vermeer's, but it somehow conveyed bigness in a way that Vermeer's didn't. The wood grains on the cabinetry seemed to match just a little better. The paperweight and knickknack collection on various surfaces bespoke Pirle's lofty position as a consultant to the rich and powerful.

Finance, Vermeer knew, was a good field, perhaps the *best* field, in which to establish oneself as an expert. In an economic downturn, the enterprise could always cut back on marketing, lay off production workers, pay less attention to human resource management. But enterprises rarely cut corners when it came to finance—or when it came to the finance professors whom they retained as consultants.

Pirle, it was rumored, *did* cut the occasional corner. He was by all accounts a brilliant financial strategist. His particular interest and talent was in gaining access to capital markets for privately held firms—a skill that not only got him published in the right journals but also made him wealthy.

And there were the hints, too, that Pirle sometimes steered his clients down paths that skirted illegality. This greatly offended his faculty colleagues and, over the years, had located him well outside the generally straitlaced Business School mainstream. But there was never any concrete offense that anyone could point to, nothing much that could ever be said above a whisper, and so nothing had come of the rumors. Belgian by birth, fluent in French and Spanish as well as English, childless and long since divorced, Pirle now floated between Europe and the U.S. when he wasn't teaching, successfully tracking and inhaling the sweet fragrances of power.

He was said to be a ladies' man. This last thought was one that Vermeer, at that moment focusing on a prominent mole on Pirle's neck, found revolting.

"Jim Bishop tells me you're looking after the MacInnes clan," Pirle continued. "That must be an unpleasant task in this particular week."

Pirle was rumored to be one of the more influential members of the Appointments Committee, which would soon be passing judgment on Vermeer. It would have been wise, Vermeer now acknowledged, to have cultivated Pirle over the past few years, but he had never quite had the stomach for it. Pirle had taken to stopping by Vermeer's office frequently in the past several months, ostensibly to advise his younger colleague on the procedural ins and outs of the tenure process. More likely, Vermeer suspected, Pirle wanted to make sure that when Vermeer fell off the promotion cliff, he fell cleanly and completely.

"Yes, it is," Vermeer admitted. "I met them this morning, and they weren't particularly happy to make my acquaintance."

"Under the circumstances, I can certainly see why. A terrible tragedy, no doubt being laid at our doorstep by the family. Even if not on the conscious level." Pirle was famous for enjoying the sound of his own voice. In the café in Spangler Hall, Vermeer had occasionally overheard students doing withering Professor Pirle imitations. "Very sad. But let us get to the business at hand. What do you need from me?"

"I'm not really sure. Dean Bishop told me to touch base with you and get your perspective on the family."

"Perhaps you should have talked with me before meeting with them. I suspect that might have been more helpful."

"I'm sure. But I got the sense that when they called, one jumped. So I jumped. Plus, your office couldn't tell me exactly when you might be available."

"As for my 'perspective,' as you put it," Pirle continued, ignoring Vermeer's veiled criticism, "I've worked with them for a number of years, as I'm sure the dean told you. As a result, I have multiple perspectives on the MacInnes clan."

"Such as?"

"I know something about them as a family, and as individuals. I know a good deal more about their businesses. But for obvious reasons, I am not able or inclined to divulge anything that they may have told me in confidence. And frankly, it seems to me that specifics about their many enterprises would have no bearing on whatever task it is that our good dean has asked you to carry out. In my opinion, if young Eric has managed to drown himself in the bathtub, we all of us will have to deal with that sordid reality and move on."

Vermeer felt impatience welling up: a small geyser in his chest. He suppressed it. "All right, then. Tell me about them as a family and as individuals."

"Well," Pirle began with an unwarming smile, "the first thing you should know is that I *love* working with this family. They live beautifully. Unlike most wealthy

Americans, they are not afraid of their resources. And they understand that wealth is nothing if it does not leverage the future. They apply that lever with considerable relish."

"Who is your principal point of contact?"

Pirle looked as if he resented the interruption, and paused pointedly. "I've worked with William, the patriarch, for nearly a decade," he continued. "He is far from brilliant, but he is broad-gauged and determined. He rules his realm quite effectively. I think it's fair to say that he is quite worried about what will happen when he dies. That will not happen soon, I think, although he has a moderate case of diabetes, for which he receives treatment."

This time Vermeer chose not to interrupt, so Pirle, free to embroider, continued with his recitation. "His wife, Elizabeth, is a remote and somewhat regal figure, in my limited experience of her. She plays no formal role in the family enterprises, although I suspect that she exerts a conservative influence that can be quite powerful. There have been times when William has reversed himself quite abruptly and inexplicably. Since he is not given to whimsy, my theory has been that these are the cases in which Mrs. MacInnes has asserted herself.

"I gather you know the boys as well as I do, or perhaps better. They have not yet played any serious role in any of the family's businesses. You should understand, by the way, that I and others who advise the family are grateful for that fact. I don't think the death of Eric, bright and charming as he was, can be construed as a commercial setback. The father had more or less faced up to the fact of Eric's irrelevance. If I had been pressed, I would have predicted Eric's death by dissipation on a Greek island perhaps twenty years hence. Excuse me, did I say something offensive?"

Vermeer realized that his distaste for Pirle was showing up on his face. "No. Maybe a little cold."

"Maybe so. But I prefer not to engage in family fictions. On beyond Eric, we have James, of course, for whom I hold out some hope. He is duller than Eric, although perhaps the equal of his father. He has traditionally been more willing than Eric to shoulder some of his family responsibilities, however ineptly. For that I give him credit.

"And last and least there is the sister, Libby, whom you have not met?"

"This morning. But only in passing."

"Another unknown, although totally unlike her mother. My sense is that young Libby is extravagant in her affections, and that her affections run in many directions at once. She has not thrown herself at me, which may put me in the minority of eligible males. I believe she suffers from being a female in a quite traditional family. She pretends to be duller than her brothers but may well be the smartest of this somewhat limited brood. To her I give credit for plunging into a tedious and plebeian profession—nursing—and sticking with it. I believe she is active in her professional circles, whatever those might be. And I have seen her administer insulin to her father when the visiting nurse was unavailable. Having met him, you will appreciate the challenge of sticking needles into the veins of Paterfamilias. Oh, yes, and she is some sort of feminist, as well."

The MacInnes family, Pirle continued to explain with increasing self-importance, now split its time between two residences: a brownstone in Brooklyn Heights—one of only two remaining single-family houses in the borough's only good neighborhood—and an estate in up-state New York, where much of the family's business was now headquartered. (In the age of the modem, the century-old suite of walnut-paneled midtown Manhattan offices had become an anachronism; it had been sold off a few years earlier.) The upstate residence, according to Pirle, was the "stuff of fiction": three thousand acres, a private lake, and a rambling baronial home perched atop a cliff overlooking the water.

"The MacInneses were granted the land by Charles the Second in the 1660s," Pirle continued. "Normally taciturn, they will tell you this story in excruciating detail if you bring up the subject. The grant once comprised what is now most of two full counties, spanning a large piece of central New York State. Much of the land was sold off or set aside as nature conservancies long ago, but the family has held the lake and the surrounding acreage for more than three centuries.

"They have never chosen to behave as if they were residents of the small towns that had the effrontery to become incorporated around them. I doubt that they have any contact with the local population beyond the obligatory. I've been told that there used to be two manor homes on the property, one on each side of the lake, but the family tore one of them down as a protest against a proposed increase in local real estate taxes. They will recite that story with some urgency, as if it were something that happened yesterday. In fact, it occurred more than a half century ago. In any case . . ."

Pirle apparently was preparing to wind up his impromptu lecture. Over the course of his monologue, Vermeer noted, Pirle's soft accent had thickened a bit, reinforcing the European formality of his speech.

"I repeat that last story to you, Mr. Vermeer, to make two points. The first is that this is not a family to be trifled with. And the second is that young Eric's death will be viewed as part of a bigger picture that most people, probably including yourself, will not comprehend easily. Many other bright and charming young MacInneses have died before their time, and this family can tell you when, where, and how, going back several centuries to rude episodes in the Scottish highlands. Eric's unscheduled departure is a tragedy, but it is certainly not a calamity. Assuming James stays healthy and procreates, the continuity of the bloodline is assured. The family will go on; its business will go on.

"And that is what this family believes is important."

6

BROUILLARD FOUND HERSELF AT HER SECOND HARVARD housing complex in two days. This time it was Peabody Terrace, a tired-looking clump of buildings alongside Memorial Drive, just across the Charles River from the Business School. From the upper floors of the Peabody Terrace high-rises, you could look across the Charles River to the Business School campus.

And if you did, Brouillard thought to herself, you would also be looking up the social and economic ladders of life. The footbridge over the river—spruced up a decade or two earlier for a visit from Prince Charles that somehow had never come off, and now reassuming its mantle of spalled concrete and general seediness—did little to close the gap between the two worlds. And although Brouillard was now officially off her own turf, a Boston cop in Cambridge, she felt much more at home here than at Soldiers Field Park. Here the winter grit was never swept off the sidewalks. Instead, it was tracked in large quantities into a drab and uninviting outer lobby, where it mixed with crusts from the salt that people's boots had dragged in.

How did the old joke go? "What's Cambridge without Harvard and MIT? Summahville." Some Somerville natives took offense at this putdown of their small and crowded city on the other side of Cambridge. Brouillard did not, because it was simply true. Cambridge was a city like any other in eastern Massachusetts—worn out, scrappy, hidebound, intensely political—except for its peculiar academic overlay.

The town-and-gown tensions that waxed and waned over the decades led to some moments of low comedy. Once, not long ago, as a Cambridge cop had told her with obvious pride, the homegrown mayor took offense at some Harvard insult, real or imagined, and renamed Boylston Street "John F. Kennedy Street." Because the street passed through the Harvard campus, this arbitrary executive act forced Harvard to reprint untold reams of letterhead, envelopes, campus maps, and business cards. The mayor was quite pleased with himself.

———————

Brouillard pushed the buzzer for apartment 11B— "MacInnes"—and awaited the metallic response.

"Yes?" A female voice, presumably Elaine MacInnes.

"Captain Brouillard, Boston police. I have an appointment with James MacInnes."

"I'll buzz you in. Wait by the elevators, and I'll come get you."

Brouillard leaned on the glass door when the buzzer sounded, stepped inside, and walked over to the elevators. A few long minutes later, one of the elevators shuddered to a halt, the doors opened, wobbling a bit from front to back, and a painfully thin young woman stepped out.

"Hi. I'm Elaine MacInnes." She extended a frail right hand limply, palm almost horizontal, as if she wore a ring that expected to be kissed. On the other hand she wore the narrowest of gold wedding bands and what looked to be a very expensive watch. "Welcome. Please come up." Out of the corner of her eye, Brouillard thought she saw a discoloration—a mole? A bruise?—where the arm of her right sleeve had ridden up slightly.

Riding up in the elevator, the two women exchanged a few small-talk sentences while Brouillard, mostly from force of habit, scrutinized James MacInnes's wife. Five six and barely north of a hundred pounds, Brouillard guessed, looking through the young woman's designer sweats. Her unnatural thinness shoved out her cheekbones and made her deep-set hazel eyes even more prominent than they would have been if they were used to surveying a normal diet. Her blond-frosted brunette hair was gathered in several places, up high and then again down low, in a way that was calculated to look casual. She spoke breathlessly, finding her voice high up in her throat, reinforcing her ethereal appearance—something like the taped phone conversations of Jacqueline Kennedy Onassis that Brouillard had once heard on the radio. She looked as if she might blow away in a light wind. Or worse: She looked as though, if her shoes fell off, she might just float away.

"We decided to live over here, rather than Soldiers Field Park," Elaine MacInnes was saying, "because it seemed like a good idea to get a little distance from the place." She nodded her head in the general direction of the Business School. "Also because it just seemed a little more, uhm, *real* here, if you know what I mean."

The conversation trailed off as they made their way down to the far end of a surprisingly dim hallway. MacInnes opened the door to apartment 11B and motioned for Brouillard to step inside. "Jim," she called out, "your detective is here."

It was a friendly enough living room, Brouillard noted to herself: decorated expensively but not ostentatiously. The workhorses of graduate-school existence—cinder blocks and planks, assemble-it-yourself Ikea furniture—were nowhere to be seen. And the rugs looked to be real Persians—perhaps the only ones in this entire housing complex, Brouillard thought. (Working alongside Customs on the docks, Brouillard had learned to tell a good rug from a bad one, even without turning it over.) Brouillard guessed that interior decorating was how the wife of James MacInnes expressed herself.

Across the room, James MacInnes himself was slowly climbing out of a black leather lounge chair that looked too comfortable to leave behind. "Hardly *my* detective, Elaine," he said. Unlike his wife, he spoke from down in his chest. On his first few steps toward Brouillard, he rolled his shoulders and bent his neck left and right, moving like an overmuscled batter approaching the plate.

"Hi. I'm James MacInnes."

MacInnes was just over six feet tall, brown-eyed, with a free-hanging helmet of light brown hair. Once in motion, he appeared to be fit and agile. His handshake was just right: short and to the point.

"I'm Captain Brouillard. We spoke on the phone. Thank you for agreeing to talk with me."

"You're welcome. Although I don't have much to tell you about Eric's death. You probably know a lot more than I do at this point."

He waved Brouillard toward the couch and, almost

imperceptibly, indicated with a nod to his wife that she should sit in the overstuffed armchair to Brouillard's left. He sat in a less comfortable-looking chair opposite Elaine and perched a sock-covered foot on the edge of the glass coffee table. Good housekeeping, Brouillard thought, when you can walk around your house and your white socks stay white.

"I'm sorry for your loss," Brouillard began. "I know this is a difficult time for both of you, and I'll try to keep this brief. But it's important to talk to people as soon as possible after an incident like this, while their memories are still fresh."

"We're ready. Fire away." It was clear that James intended to speak for both himself and Elaine.

"Okay. When did you last see Eric or talk to him?"

"We had dinner on Friday night with him and his girlfriend."

"How would you characterize his mood?"

"Normal Eric," James replied. "But normal for Eric is not normal for most of us. He's—" He caught himself. "I guess I have to learn to start talking about Eric in the past tense. He *was* a charming, funny guy. A showboater. I loved Eric. My wife loved Eric. Everybody loved Eric. Among other things, he was a fabulous mimic. Well read, despite his limited attention span. A great conversationalist. The first guy you'd invite to your party, if you were a smart hostess. He was an insurance policy for a social event. Never a dull moment. Guaranteed."

"Excuse me for asking," Brouillard said, "but it sounds like maybe you didn't approve of this—what did you call it?—showboating."

"Eric and I are very different kinds of people."

"How so?"

"It hardly matters now, I'd say," James replied. "But what the hell. My family always called us the tortoise and the hare. No secret: I'm the tortoise."

"But the tortoise wins the race, right?"

"In the fairy tale, yes. I'm not so sure about real life. It seems to me that people like my late brother, God rest his soul, get by on a song and a smile. Without ever actually doing much work or committing themselves to much of anything. Well, that's just not the way I am. I worry more about the content than the packaging.

"And by the way, just so you don't send a report into some filing cabinet about how disloyal I am to my dead brother, I'm not telling you anything I didn't tell Eric lots of times. Or discuss with my whole family, for that matter. We talk about this kind of thing all the time. We are very self-conscious on the subject of responsibility. Comes with the territory."

"You mentioned Eric's girlfriend. What is her name, and where can I find her?"

"Jeannette Bartlett. She's in Eric's section. I don't know her number offhand. I'm sure the school can tell you where to find her."

"How would you describe their relationship?"

"I'd rather not."

"Why not?"

"Because I think she should describe her own relationship."

Brouillard turned toward Elaine MacInnes. "Okay. How would *you* describe the relationship between Eric and Jeannette Bartlett?"

Elaine looked surprised to be called upon to speak. "Well, uhm, I'd say very affectionate," she chirped.

"They'd been going out since last spring. They enjoyed each other's company."

"Was there any indication of trouble between them? Any evidence that they'd had a falling out recently?"

"Oh, please," James broke in. "Are you suggesting that my brother's girlfriend dragged him into the men's locker room at midnight and drowned him in the pool? That's a little far-fetched."

"No, Mr. MacInnes, I'm not suggesting anything. I'm asking questions, which you have volunteered to answer. But we can always continue this at some other time. Downtown, if you want."

"Frankly, I'd prefer to get this over with as soon as possible."

"Good. Then I'll ask again: Did Eric and Jeannette seem to be getting along all right, or not?"

"Oh, like two lovebirds," James said with overdone sarcasm. "Just this past Friday, in fact, they cooed and pecked all the way through dinner."

"Oh, James," Elaine quickly interjected, her thin eyebrows jumping. "Let's just answer her questions." She turned again toward Brouillard. "We used to have dinner together on Friday nights a lot. Maybe two or three times a month. Otherwise we didn't see them much together. My own sense is that Jeannette loved Eric deeply. Maybe more than the other way around."

"And this past Friday night?"

"Things seemed perfectly normal between them. Jeannette mentioned at one point that she felt a headache coming on—sometimes she had migraines—and they left a little earlier than usual. I assumed it was because of the headache. But that was it. Nothing else unusual."

"Thank you, Mrs. MacInnes. That's helpful. Now I have to be a little more direct. Were they lovers?"

Elaine blushed slightly and crossed her arms in front of her modest chest. James made a small snorting noise. "I never asked them," he said.

"But you assumed so?"

"They're grown-ups. Sure."

"And to your knowledge, did Eric have any other romantic interests? Anyone else, past or present, who might still be playing a role in his life?"

"I wasn't his babysitter," James said. "If there was anybody else, he wasn't talking to me about it. But I assume not. I assume he would have told me, if there was."

"What about you, Elaine? Anything to add?"

"No, not really. I think James is right. The MacInneses know one another pretty well, too. Better than the average family. But it's possible that James's and Eric's parents would know more than we do about Eric's . . . love life. They are very interested in having grandchildren. We hear about that subject a lot, so I assume that Eric must have, too."

"Did Eric have other close friends? People he hung out with?"

"No," said James. "Eric felt he was different from other people at the school."

"Different in what way?"

"In many of the same ways that I am," James replied a little slowly, as if he were talking to a child. "Our background. Our prospects. Our responsibilities, as I've implied."

"Uh-huh," Brouillard said blandly, scribbling notes with a distracted look on her face. "Just a few more questions.

James, I wonder if you know who stands to benefit financially from Eric's death."

"I do not know."

"Did he have a will?"

"I hope so. I assume so. Our family has ready access to good legal advice. Although I'll admit that I didn't write my will until I got married, and Eric was obviously a freer spirit than I am."

"I know your family is very well-to-do. Was Eric personally wealthy? Are you and your sister personally wealthy?"

"Yes and no," James responded, drumming on his watch face with his right middle and index fingers. "Eric, Libby, and I have had enough money given to us, on a prearranged schedule, so that we're more than comfortable. And we certainly stand to inherit substantial assets from our parents, although I have no idea how much. For tax purposes, much of the family's wealth is tied up in trusts, of course. But day to day, money is not an issue."

"How are in-laws handled? Are they cut in?"

"Is that your business?"

"Either now or later, yes."

"God, this *is* unpleasant," James growled. "Okay. My wife signed a prenuptial agreement that limits her involvement in the family's financial affairs. This sort of thing has gone on for several generations at least. It would apply to anybody Libby might marry, or anybody Eric might have married."

"And how did you feel about that, Elaine?"

Elaine exhaled audibly through pursed lips, halfway puffing out her cheeks. For the first time, she didn't look at James. "I objected to it."

"Why?"

"I thought it implied a lack of trust. I thought it cast doubt on my feelings for James."

With that, James again rose up out of his chair, and stood with his fists planted on his hips. "I think this has really gone far enough," he said, his face flushing with anger. Brouillard was glad the coffee table sat between them. "I think this is just gossiping," he continued, "and I hate gossip. Do you have any more questions that might be relevant to Eric's death? If not, I'll ask you to leave."

"Just one more," Brouillard said. "Where were you Sunday night between, say, nine p.m. and dawn?"

Although the untrained eye might have missed it, James's bravado took a hit. His shoulders sagged just a little. Now he looked as if he wished he were sitting down again. "Excuse me," he replied, "did you just ask me for my alibi?"

"Not exactly," Brouillard said blandly. "I asked where you were late Sunday night and early Monday morning."

"What does that have to do with my brother drowning in a hot tub?"

"Well, I'd say 'nothing,' unless you tell me otherwise. All we know is that Eric was someplace he shouldn't have been, and that something happened that shouldn't have happened. We're trying to figure out what and why." She made a little show of poising her pencil expectantly, just above her notepad.

"When do you read me my rights?"

"Oh, that wouldn't happen until we arrested you for committing a crime. And we don't even have a crime. As far as we know."

"Oh, all *right,* then," James said. "We were here. I studied all afternoon that day; then we had dinner. Then we cleaned up, watched part of a bad movie, and then I studied again, and then we went to bed. This morning the phone started to ring. Yours was the fourth call, I think, after the school, my parents, and my sister. Not a lot of people have this number. Unlisted."

"So neither of you went out?"

"I didn't. Elaine went up to the Square right after dinner. We had run out of coffee. After that, we were both in."

Brouillard glanced at Elaine. "That's right," Elaine confirmed in her vanishing voice.

"What was the bad movie?"

"Sabrina," James said. "The remake, with Harrison Ford. Bad as it is, you should see it. It depicts a psychological struggle between two rich brothers, one of whom is a solid citizen and the other of whom is a lovable flake."

His sarcasm hung like a fog in the air, almost wanting to condense on the carpet. He was still standing on the far side of the coffee table, glaring at Brouillard, who showed nothing back to him. Elaine, seated, studying the floor, looked miserable.

"Well, I don't have any more questions for now," Brouillard said brightly, snapping her notepad shut, putting the pad in her bag, and then putting her coat and bag on the glass tabletop. She leaned toward Elaine. "I couldn't help noticing your watch. It's quite beautiful." She leaned forward expectantly.

"Oh, it's nothing special," Elaine said, slightly embarrassed, obligingly extending her left arm. "Although the band is antique."

"Can I see the clasp? I have sort of a thing for antique clasps." Which wasn't true, of course. But by now, she had Elaine's hand in her own. Gently she turned the sparrowlike wrist over, so that Elaine's palm faced upward. She reached out with her other hand and gently pushed the cuff of Elaine's sweatshirt up her arm an inch or two. And there, on her unnaturally pale forearm, were three ugly oval-shaped bruises, like slightly flattened quarters, lined up in a row: one, two, three.

"Quite beautiful. And fragile, too. Be careful with that, Mrs. MacInnes."

7

JEANNETTE BARTLETT WAS NOT WHAT BROUILLARD WAS expecting. A bit on the plump side, she had shoulder-length brown hair and a round and plain face. Her upper front teeth were a little oversize, and her upper lip pulled upward, tentlike, at the center, as if it were determined to stay out of the way of those teeth. She was wearing a lavender cotton fisherman's sweater that had begun as too big for her. Since that time, it had been stretched out at the bottom, front, and back by just the kind of nervous downward tugging that she was now unconsciously engaged in.

For Jeannette Bartlett, Brouillard guessed, body image was a problem. Butt image appeared to be a particular problem.

They were seated at a black oak mission-style table at the far end of the café in Shad Hall. Eric had died the day before—and only a hundred yards from here, Brouillard was thinking: one floor down and a few long rooms over.

Bartlett had suggested the meeting place on the phone. ("My dorm room is too small and messy," she had explained in a distracted voice.) Brouillard had been surprised at the proposed setting—it seemed a little ghoulish—but had agreed to it.

Now she was kicking herself for not insisting on a different locale. If Bartlett was really as upset as she seemed—and if she wasn't, Brouillard concluded, she was a hell of an actress—this was a terrible place for an interview. Aside from the proximity to the Jacuzzi, it was a fishbowl. And although the room was getting crowded, the other students were instinctively steering away from the two intense-looking women in the corner. Word was getting around.

"I know this is very difficult for you, Jeannette," Brouillard began, "and I do appreciate your willingness to meet with me so soon after Eric's death."

"No, it's good to be able to talk to someone," Bartlett said with a slight catch in her voice. "It really helps. And it feels more useful than just going and crying in the counselor's office. I want to help you catch the person who did this to Eric."

"Just a sec, please, Jeannette," Brouillard said, fishing her notepad and pencil out of her shapeless canvas bag. She put the pad down on the table, opened to a clean page, and wrote BARTLETT, JEANNETTE in block capitals, clearly visible upside down from the other side of the table. She definitely wanted to control the pace and pitch of this conversation. "Okay. All set. Now." She looked up again at Bartlett's forlorn face. "What's this you just said about someone 'doing something' to Eric? I don't mean to sound unkind. But on the face of it, couldn't you conclude that he just made a series of bad choices? That he took a bottle of whiskey into the whirlpool, got drunk, and drowned?"

"Bullshit." Bartlett didn't swear easily. The expletive fell, rather than rolled, off her tongue.

"Why do you say that?"

"Because I knew Eric. He would never have killed himself. He was one of the happiest, funniest, sweetest people I've ever met. And besides that, he didn't drink."

"Maybe he fell off the wagon. It happens all the time. Believe me."

"*No*, Captain," Bartlett said forlornly. "You don't understand. He wasn't on or off the wagon. He just never drank, period. He gave it up a couple of years ago, the way some people give up smoking. He didn't like the taste, didn't like having his mind get dulled. And he said it makes you fat. He was terrified about getting fat. He worked out all the time. He simply wouldn't go drinking in the whirlpool at midnight. Never."

"Let's back up a bit. How long had you two known each other?"

"About a year and a half. Since we got here two falls ago."

"And how long had you been going out together?"

Bartlett hesitated, sucking on her upper lip. "Well, I don't know exactly what you mean by that. I guess—do you mean, like, officially 'dating'?"

"Yes."

"Well, we were spending time together since the first week of classes, and we just spent more and more time together, I guess, after that."

"Were you lovers?"

Bartlett blushed. "Do you need to know that?"

"Yes."

"We were very affectionate, including physically. But we weren't sleeping together, if that's what you mean."

"Forgive me, but can I ask why not? It may be relevant."

Bartlett didn't answer, intent on studying the tabletop.

Putting her pencil down, Brouillard pressed the point, although gently. "A case of principle? Other people in the mix? Whatever you say is okay with me."

When Bartlett finally looked up, her expression included equal parts of pride and defensiveness. "There was no one else for either of us. I was raised a Catholic, but I wasn't saving myself for marriage or anything. But you need to understand that Eric was a gentleman, in the old-fashioned sense of the word. He came from a very unusual family. He had a very strong sense of values. Not religious values, exactly, but, like, more a sense of what was fair. What was right. I always felt that if he didn't want to rush things, well, that was perfectly all right with me. Or even a relief. It wasn't an issue, really. We were both getting what we needed from each other."

"What were you expecting from the relationship, over the long run? Like, what did you think was going to happen when you graduated this spring?"

"I think he was going to ask me to marry him," Bartlett said, her voice thickening. She furtively eased a tear out of the corner of her left eye by sliding her left forefinger up the side of her nose. Another tear came right up behind the first. It slid down her cheek unhindered. "And I was going to say yes."

"I talked to James and Elaine MacInnes this morning. They told me that the four of you had dinner on Friday night."

"Uh-huh."

"How was Eric's mood? During dinner, after dinner?"

"He was fine. Normal. I think he was making an extra effort to tease his brother. Maybe you noticed that James is, uhm, a little bit stiff. Eric loved poking at him, getting him going. Some of that was going on. Maybe a little more than usual."

"And you had a headache?"

"It felt like the beginnings of a migraine, which I sometimes get. But that was an excuse, mostly. I mostly wanted to get out of there and get some sleep. I don't really like socializing with them that much. Poor Elaine has to hop around James like a little bird, whispering and peeping. I don't like to watch it."

"Uh-huh. I saw some of that. Funny, James referred to you and Eric as lovebirds."

"Well, for sure, *he* wouldn't know." Now a tear began wending its way down her other cheek.

"How do you get along with the rest of the family?"

"Have you met them?"

"No."

"Well, as they say, there's a first time for everything. They're a unique bunch. I went out to their place in New York State for a weekend once. Which is definitely something you should do, once, if you get the chance. I haven't been back since. I think that's been okay on both ends."

"Why?"

"For one thing, I'm not very comfortable with the concept of servants, and they've got a ton of them. As for the MacInnesses, they were like most families with sons— like, 'nobody is good enough for our little boy,' except maybe more so. Maybe there was a hint of the gold-digger thing in the air." She shrugged heavily. "I don't know. Maybe I was being too sensitive. Usually it's the mom who's on guard; in their case it was the dad. Or seemed to be. I don't know. Maybe they didn't even notice that I was there. But I don't think they were all that eager to welcome me into the clan."

"Let's go back to Friday night. Eric dropped you off at your dorm room, and—"

"Yeah."

"And when did you see him again?"

"Oh, God," Bartlett said miserably. She slumped back in her chair and raked the fingers of both hands backward through her hair. "I never did. The next morning I went skiing with my girlfriends in Vermont. I came back late on Sunday night. I expected to see Eric on Monday."

"No contact during the weekend?"

"He called me on Saturday at the condo where we were staying, and left a message on the machine. Nothing unusual. He teased me about my Vermont headache remedy."

"You erased the message?"

"Yeah." Her lips were pursed together, evidently to stop their trembling. "A condo. You wouldn't leave a personal message lying around. Now I wish I had it."

"Jeannette, do you have any idea what Eric might have been doing in this building in the middle of the night?"

"Oh, God," she said again, mournfully. "I do. Yes. But I don't want to get anybody in trouble."

"What do you mean?"

"He had a pass card."

"He had a key to this building?"

"One of those plastic card thingies. Yes."

"Not something that students are supposed to have?"

"No."

"What about the alarm system?"

"That, too. He knew how to shut it off. I'm sure he paid somebody something to get all this stuff. That was something he would have done without thinking twice. But I never wanted to know about that."

"Why go to all that trouble just to get in here?"

"Oh, I don't know," Bartlett said, guilt now sweeping across her face and mixing with the grief there. "God. It all seems so dumb now. But Eric really liked to be able to get into the Jacuzzi at all hours. He even got me to go in once, in the middle of the night. But I didn't like it. It was like a tomb, except hot. Dark and hot." She shuddered. "He thought it was exciting. A 'guilty pleasure,' he called it. I think he liked the breaking-the-rules part as much as he liked sitting in that whirlpool. Maybe more. I told him I hated it. I never went back. But I know he did. He used to joke about 'getting in hot water.' His code phrase for coming over here in the middle of the night. Oh, shit. Now my damn nose is running."

Brouillard already had a tissue at hand. She passed it across the table. "Did he tend toward a particular night of the week?"

"Sundays. Sundays only, I think. His way of starting the new week off right."

"Was it just you, or did he take other people with him?"

"I can't say for sure, but I don't think he would have taken other people. That would have been too risky. He could have gotten thrown out of school if he had gotten caught."

Brouillard pondered these odd revelations for a moment. "Jeannette," she finally continued, "now I have to ask you a really tough question. You've been very helpful, and I don't want to make this any harder for you than it needs to be. But I want to show you something."

She pulled a photocopy out of her bag. "This is a copy of something we found in Eric's room yesterday morning. What do you make of it?"

She handed Bartlett the scrap of writing:

This is now that was then. I live in this winter that you have conjured up and coldly it infuraites me. What scent eminates from a love that can't be satisfied? Your scent. Our scent. Whatever we build together falls down collapsed flat. We are those inflatable structures, a tennis bubble, crushed under the snow. I wish we were there. I wish you were dead and sometimes I think you are.

Bartlett's face turned gray as her eyes leaped left and right across the lines with increasing speed. "Oh, God. Oh, God. This is . . . Excuse me. I think . . . I think I'm going to be sick."

And then she climbed to her feet, both hands over her mouth, and lurched unsteadily from the room. As she left, her heavy oak chair, put in play by her abrupt departure, teetered on its rear legs for an instant, thudded backward onto the carpeted floor, bounced once, and came to rest.

Now the room was absolutely still, except around its farthest reaches. Dust motes rose slowly in a column of sunlight that perversely had begun to spotlight the center of Brouillard's table. The detective was aware of dozens of pairs of eyes in the room flitting back and forth: from her to the upturned chair and back again. After a few long seconds, an embarrassed-looking young man with oversize red ears glided over like an undertaker. "Let me get that," he offered, without looking at Brouillard. Fluidly he righted the chair with one pass of an arm and then slid back over to his own table.

———————

By the stylish clock on the wall—skinny hands, no numbers—a full five minutes passed before Bartlett returned. She reentered the café flanked by two other women who kept their fingertips very close to her elbows. They glared pointedly at Brouillard—there was a lot of that going on recently—and melted away just before they delivered Bartlett to the table.

Brouillard smiled sympathetically and gestured toward the empty chair. "How are you feeling?"

"Not so good." As Bartlett sat down, she pushed the offending photocopy toward Brouillard with her forearm. She avoided making eye contact with it. "Sorry."

"My fault," Brouillard said. The detective was blessed, or cursed, with an acute sense of smell. She detected the acrid smell of vomit, seeming to roll off Bartlett in pulses. "I didn't know how rough that would be for you. Sorry."

"No, it's okay. Listen, Captain Brouillard," Bartlett said, now leaning forward with an unexpected gray-metal flash in her eye. "Eric didn't write that horrible thing. All that note does is prove what I tried to tell you in the first place. Eric was killed. And that wasn't enough. Now some person who's very sick is trying to cover his tracks."

"Why are you so sure that Eric didn't write it?"

"Because it has nothing to do with him. Or us. That's not what our lives were about. I already told you, we were happy. Plus, it's terribly written. It's full of cheap sentiments. Words that are spelled wrong. Eric would never have produced something like that. Never."

"Jeannette, is it possible that Eric was struggling with trying to tell you something? That he was having trouble expressing something painful?"

"Eric didn't have trouble when it came to expressing himself. He was proud of his ability to express himself, and had good reason to be. And we didn't have any painful things between us. We talked to each other, all the time. We never wrote each other notes. We didn't have to."

"Okay," Brouillard said, "let's assume he was writing the note to someone else. Was there anybody else in his life who might have been making him feel this way, giving him this kind of trouble?"

"Oh, God," Bartlett said again, but this time in a forlorn, plaintive kind of way. "Don't you see? There was nobody else. That's the whole point. I was Eric's only friend in the whole world. He was rich and smart and good-looking, and he was the loneliest person I've ever met."

She shook her head as her eyes welled up again. "So now you tell *me,* Captain," she said just before her voice broke. "Why would anybody want to kill such a lonely person?"

8

THE NEXT MORNING, VERMEER WAS ONCE AGAIN WAIT-
ing in the sitting area outside Dean Bishop's office. The
summons from the corner office had been on his voice
mail when he arrived. One of the dean's highly polished
secretaries, a young woman named Maude with plucked
and perpetually startled eyebrows, brought him coffee
and then retreated back behind the mahogany ramparts.

Waiting to be called in to Bishop's inner sanctum, he
weighed the pros and cons of dipping into the M&M
bowl just down the hall. He was still drowsy, and his
mental dialogue was proceeding a little too slowly. Was
eight a.m. too early for M&M's? Probably. Did M&M's
go well with coffee? Possibly. But if he didn't finish them
before the meeting started, what would he do with the remaining half handful? Toss them into his computer bag?
If he slipped them into his pants pocket, how long would
they have to heat up against his thigh before real trouble
began?

The glass door to the outer hallway opened and in
walked a vaguely familiar-looking woman. "Rumpled"
was the first word that popped into Vermeer's head, although on balance, her clothes were probably less wrinkled than his own. It was the world-weary look around

her eyes that projected dishevelment, Vermeer decided. She nodded once to Vermeer in the short interval between when a secretary took her trench coat and when she returned with a mug of coffee. Then the woman sat down in a chair at right angles to Vermeer's, cradling her coffee with both hands and ignoring Vermeer.

An image popped into his head: *the elevator woman.* The purposeful-looking woman who had skirted the mob of teenagers at the Four Seasons, with the insubstantial Mr. Ralph following in her slipstream. Up close, it was an interesting face. The look of weariness gave her some appealing depth. Her clothes were resolutely baggy, discouraging any further scrutiny.

Resting her mug on the table in front of them, she checked her watch and *foof*ed a little puff of air straight up her face to redirect a wandering sprig of brown hair. Not satisfied with the result, she then attacked her hair with a quick rake of both hands across the top of her head, from her forehead backward, shaking her head quickly from left to right as her fingers plowed from front to back. Vermeer, out of the corner of his eye observing this ritual only a few feet away, was relieved that he was not munching on peanut M&M's. At this distance it would have sounded like a gravel quarry at work.

———————

"Professor Vermeer? Captain Brouillard? Dean Bishop will see you now."

The tousle-haired woman, now identified exotically as a captain, stood up, collected her coffee and handbag, and walked in ahead of Vermeer. Bishop greeted them with a smile and a handshake and motioned for them to sit down in the welcoming leather chairs at the large round conference table in the center of his office. This time the table was absolutely bare.

"Well, Captain Brouillard," Bishop began, "it's good to see you again, even under these circumstances. Were you introduced to Wim Vermeer? I've asked him to sit in with us, since he's serving as the school's informal representative in the MacInnes situation."

"Nice to meet you," she said, extending her hand. Everything about her—body language, expression, inflection—conveyed the opposite.

"This is your meeting, Captain," the dean continued. "But of course, we're eager to hear what you've learned and get some sense of how and when this is likely to get wrapped up."

Brouillard frowned as if debating something mentally and then removed a dog-eared notepad from her pocketbook. She turned a half-dozen pages of the pad slowly, silently reviewing the scrawled handwriting on them. She was not concerned about keeping the dean of the Harvard Business School waiting, Vermeer concluded. By all appearances, she would not be easy to stampede.

"Unfortunately, Dean Bishop," Brouillard finally responded, "we're not anywhere close to having all the answers. In fact, I'm still figuring out what questions to ask. Like, for example, I need to know what kinds of security systems Eric had to get past to slip into Shad Hall undetected. What kind of pass card let him into the building? Do your systems keep a log of after-hours comings and goings? Were there alarms he had to shut down? All that kind of stuff. I assume your B and G people can help out there."

"Of course. I'll have my assistant, Maude, ask them to call you. The person you want to speak with is Alonzo Rodriguez."

"I'll also need access to his student records," she said, scribbling.

"I assume our registrar can release them to you in confidence. There may still be some privacy issues at this point. Maude can set that up, as well."

"I've already requested his phone logs. I assume that e-mails, even deleted ones, stay on your server for a certain amount of time," she continued, still writing and not looking up. "I'll need access to all traffic to and from his account."

"That's not something I know much about," the dean confessed. "Maude can tell you who to talk to in IT. I suggest you try starting with John Matteson, but Maude may know better."

"Counseling?"

"That would be Wilkinson. Dr. Brian Wilkinson."

"Is there a central record of any other services that the deceased might have used at the school? Physical trainers? Masseurs? Tennis instructors? Tutors?"

Bishop thought for a moment, seeming to phrase his response so as not to give offense. "Captain Brouillard, our students are all grown-ups, in their twenties, or in some cases their thirties, and we treat them as such. We really don't track their activities outside the classroom."

"Well," she said, glancing up from her pad to look Bishop in the eye, "that's certainly one approach."

"There was alcohol involved, I understand," Bishop said, choosing to ignore the implied criticism. "What have you learned about the alcohol level in his blood?"

"I'm waiting for the lab results. Why do you ask?"

"Again, I'm no expert," the dean said mildly. "But alcohol and a hot tub in the middle of the night seems like it would be a lethal combination. One gets reckless or sleepy; one slips and falls. That could be the end of the story."

"That's one scenario," she conceded. "We're working on a couple of scenarios. I'm not prepared to talk about them at this point. But there are a number of loose ends having to do with the deceased's personal life."

"Such as?"

"In a nutshell, Dean Bishop, I'm developing two pictures of the deceased that don't fit together very well. Eric MacInnes number one is a happy playboy who almost always gets what he wants. Eric MacInnes number two is a frustrated loner who is under some kind of serious pressure, of an unspecified but possibly sexual nature."

She paused, staring hard at Bishop. "So I haven't even figured out which kid died in your whirlpool yet, Dean Bishop. But I will."

Looking slightly sideways, Vermeer watched Bishop's face as Brouillard talked. The dean had maintained a generally bland countenance, but it had now taken on a stoic cast, as if frozen in place. Bishop was accustomed to structuring things to his satisfaction, and this process didn't lend itself to that. Any structuring, it seemed—any spinning or tweaking of scenarios—would be performed by a detective with a hatful of attitude.

"Well," Bishop said after a pause, "no one has any interest in dragging this out. Not us, not the MacInnes family, and not you. So of course we'll do what we can to help you get your questions answered."

"Good. And there's another line of inquiry that I need to follow up on. I need to understand who stands to benefit from the deceased's death. I'm having some trouble getting a handle on the MacInnes family's finances. And my conversation yesterday with Mr. and Mrs. MacInnes wasn't very helpful, probably because I wasn't able to ask the right questions. I'm a little out of my depth when it comes to the ownership of large and complicated businesses."

"So am I," he said disarmingly. "How can we help with that?"

"I understand from the MacInneses that one of your professors, Marc Pirle, is a longtime adviser to the family. I'd like to have a conversation with him."

"Of course," Bishop replied, "although Professor Pirle may well decide that there are things he can't tell you without the family's permission."

"Fine," responded Brouillard. "And as we both know, sometimes those rules get bent a little bit. Let me put it this way: The sooner I get what I need, the faster things go."

"Fair enough. And in that spirit, I suggest you bring Professor Vermeer along with you when you have your conversation with Professor Pirle. Professor Vermeer is an expert in finance himself, and he's worked with Marc Pirle for a number of years, so he could prove to be very useful to you. Perhaps even beyond that one conversation, if you were so inclined."

Brouillard looked sideways at Vermeer. As one corner of her mouth turned down, she barely arched one eyebrow—gestures that were visible only to Vermeer. She was signaling disdain and skepticism in equal doses. "Ordinarily, Dean Bishop, I'd say no to a suggestion like that. I don't like being bird-dogged. But since I seem to be crossing paths with Professor Vermeer anyway, and since there's a chance that he may be able to help me understand what I'm hearing, I'll go along with it—for the time being. The minute he gets in my way, he's gone."

"Fair enough. Anything you want to add, Wim?"

Vermeer had yet to utter a word at this meeting. He was savoring the little ironies that were washing over him. Two days ago on the verge of being out the institutional door, today he was the finance expert that most of his senior colleagues didn't think he was. Two days ago nowhere near the middle of the institutional deal stream, he was now being called upon by the dean to help manage important relationships. Nearly anonymous for three years, he now had a first name.

It was flattering, but it wasn't good news. Now, in addition to packing up jungle gyms, he had to hold hands with a hostile detective. His job hunt, more pressing with each day that came and went, was receding into the distance.

But he had picked up on Brouillard's reference to crossing paths with him. That meant she had remembered him from the hotel lobby, as well. Which was at least a little interesting.

"I'm happy to help in any way I can, Jim." It was fun, this first-name game. "Maybe Maude can help us get Marc scheduled for later today."

9

Brouillard was the first to arrive at the Charles Hotel. Ten minutes early, she waited at the maître d's stand, refusing more than once to give up her trench coat. "I'd hate to have it get stolen," she explained. The maître d' looked from Brouillard's eyes to the coat and back again—more than enough to convey his sense of how absurd the notion was.

The lunch crowd looked extremely well heeled. Except for a few conspicuous tourists, one actually wearing a belly pack, people conversed quietly. In the parts of Boston that Brouillard most often frequented—Back Bay, the South End, the student ghettos along Commonwealth Avenue and Huntington Avenue—the professional lunch bunch also dressed the part but mostly played at thinking big thoughts and cutting big deals. She suspected that here at the Charles, strategically positioned on the Business School and Kennedy School side of Harvard Square, there was less smoke and more fire. At the Charles, business really was getting done.

Professor Marc Pirle had suggested the place and time for the meeting, once the dean's secretary had succeeded in tracking him down. Brouillard had found it odd that a professor would be somewhere other than his office or a classroom at nine o'clock on a Tuesday morning, and that no one was particularly surprised by his unexplained absence. Her watchdog, Vermeer, had shrugged it off while Maude made her series of calls. "He obviously doesn't have a class this morning," Vermeer had said. "He's probably got a consulting gig downtown, or maybe somewhere out on Route 128. He'll beg off of lunch with his client, rush over here to meet with us, and then hurry back out and spend the rest of the day there."

"For money?" Brouillard asked.

Vermeer laughed. "Absolutely for money. In his case, big money."

"How big?"

"Let's see. It would depend in part on who the client was. Let's have him teach a case in the morning and then follow up with some small group work and then a couple of one-on-ones with the honchos in the afternoon. I'd guess at least ten thousand."

"You've got to be shitting me!" Brouillard blurted out, astonished, then instantly regretting the lapse. In her business, it paid to act surprised when you weren't and unsurprised when you were. It did no good to look small-town in front of watchdogs and other strangers.

She saw Vermeer striding into the restaurant before he spotted her. In his slightly saggy gray suit and yellow paisley power tie, he looked as if he could fit in here when he needed to. But there was something a little off kilter in his walk and his posture that suggested that he might feel more at home at Eddie's Kitchen, the cholesterol shop a half block away where that guy on the Cambridge force had taken her on a date. (The date hadn't gone well.) Vermeer had a roundish but not unattractive face. His shoulders were a little rounded and unathletic-looking, but he looked like he kept himself up. His blond hair, falling into his eyes, wasn't long, but it was starting to curl around the fringes. Brouillard speculated that he had to get frequent haircuts in order to fit in at the Harvard Business School. From the looks of it, he didn't like haircuts.

"Hi," he said, coming up alongside her. "Let me guess. Pirle isn't here yet."

"No sign of him."

"Well, let's claim his table before someone else does."

The maître d' led them to Pirle's table (but only after asking if they wouldn't rather wait at the bar for the "third party"). They both ordered coffee. It came in thick white mugs with oversize handles. Sipping the dark brew, Brouillard instantly forgave the restaurant for its fake-Vermonty decor. Coffee like this, in mugs made for holding, made up for a lot of sins.

"Nice place," she said. "I especially like the chickens roasting on an open fire." She pointed at a slowly turning rotisserie next to the grill, where several chefs in spotless white aprons barely avoided colliding with one another as they prepared meals. Three birds, stretched out and impaled on a horizontal stake, were achieving a nice golden brown.

"Ducks."

"Excuse me?"

"Those are ducks roasting on an open fire."

Now that she looked more closely, she had to agree that they weren't chickens. "Okay," she conceded. "Make way for ducklings. Maybe you should be a detective."

Vermeer laughed. "I've eaten here before. They're on the menu. Can I ask you a question?"

"Sure. I'm not promising to answer."

"How did Eric die?"

Brouillard frowned. "Maybe you should tell me first exactly what your role is in all this," she said.

"I would if I could," Vermeer said. "I'm mostly making it up as I go along."

"Well, if you want to get me talking, you need to give me a little more than that."

He smiled. "Okay. As far as I can tell, the dean wants to try to salvage whatever remains of the relationship between the school and the MacInnes family. He settled on me to serve as his representative mainly because I've taught both Eric and James. If that was his notion, it turns out to be a good one. Mrs. MacInnes told me that I was Eric's favorite first-year teacher."

"What did you talk about with the parents?"

"Almost nothing. What you'd expect, under the circumstances. I told them that we'd help them in any way we could. The old man complained that we should have taken better care of Eric, which is probably true. Mrs. MacInnes seemed a little dreamy and disconnected—"

"Sedatives," Brouillard interjected, as if she had been called upon in class.

Vermeer blinked, then continued. "Right. Sedatives. But anyway, she got focused enough to make it clear that she knew who I was. Then the old man asked me to box up and ship Eric's personal effects to various mansions after the police—you guys—are finished poking around. And finally, the daughter, Libby, showed up to give him a shot."

"Excuse me?"

"An insulin shot. Pirle explained this to me. The father is diabetic, and she's a nurse. When she's around and his regular nurse isn't, she gives him his shots."

"Anything else you learned that I should know?"

"Don't think so. Let's face it: I was mostly ornamental. I *am* mostly ornamental."

She paused to sip her coffee. "And do you do this sort of thing regularly?"

"No," he said. "We don't have a lot of students die on us."

Brouillard nodded. "Okay, Professor. I'll be sure to speak more precisely from now on. Does the dean call on you for lots of troubleshooting help? I assume he has a team of cronies that runs the place. You're one of them? You're in the loop?"

"No. Not even close. But yes, he has his close advisers on the faculty, and I'm sure that if one of them had taught both of the boys, I wouldn't be involved."

"Would you rather not be involved?"

Vermeer looked up from his coffee cup. There was a wisp of a smile on his face. "Pass," he said.

Brouillard nodded. She didn't know a lot of college professors, but the ones she had run into loved to hear themselves talk. Maybe this one didn't.

"And now," Vermeer said, "I think you owe me an answer to my question."

"Actually, I don't," she replied coolly. "Investigations are confidential."

"I answer a whole string of your questions, and you don't answer one of mine?"

Again she nodded. "Welcome to police work." After a long sip on her coffee, she spoke again. "I'll tell you what. Let's use the Dirtball Theoretical."

"Does it give me my answer?"

"Of course not. The Dirtball Theoretical is a way of talking around a subject. A trick I learned from a dirtball lawyer. He'd be in court, and he'd go down a particular line of questioning, implying more and more terrible things, until the opposing counsel finally objected. He'd make a show of looking like a bad boy, and then he'd go down exactly that same road all over again, only this time saying that everything was 'theoretical.' Same questions, same answers, same impact on the jury. He got away with it more often than he didn't.

"So." Brouillard paused. "The Dirtball Theoretical. When you find a body floating in water—or not floating—you ask whether the victim had water in his lungs. Let's assume it's a he. Then you ask whether it's the right kind of water. Say he drowns in a Jacuzzi. You want to make sure that it's Jacuzzi water, right?

"Okay. So assume it's Jacuzzi water. Then you want to figure out if anything else was going on. Any bumps or bruises? Let's say, using the Dirtball Theoretical, that there's evidence of a severe blow to the back of the head, say, just about where the head and neck come together. Well, then you want to know what might have caused this blow. A two-by-four? The edge of the Jacuzzi? Sometimes the answer's obvious. Sometimes it's not. When the victim spends some time soaking in water after the blow, it's harder. Let's assume inconclusive.

"And meanwhile, you look at toxicology—drugs and alcohol. Assume they're there. Or more specifically, assume alcohol is there. How did it get there? If there's a half-empty bottle of something nearby, do the blood alcohol levels correspond to having consumed that much of whatever it is? If they're high, but maybe not high enough, was someone else sharing the bottle? Or maybe we didn't start with a full bottle.

"Then you mix in your background interviews, which give you some idea about whether your victim is a tippler. Let's assume he isn't. In fact, let's assume he never touches the stuff. So what happened in the Jacuzzi? A party of one, made special by some booze? Some kind of suicidal gesture? If so, a plea for help, or the real thing?

"And that, Professor Vermeer, is my personal version of the Dirtball Theoretical. For what it's worth."

10

A SMALL STIR ON THE OTHER SIDE OF THE RESTAURANT announced the arrival of Professor Marc Pirle. He walked so purposefully across the room, with the maître d' struggling to keep ahead of him, that heads turned in his wake. "Sorry I'm late," he said, still ten feet from the table but closing quickly. "The traffic was unforgivable. Grotesque." He tossed his silk-lined black wool overcoat onto the waiting arm of the maître d', who seemed to know the drill. "Thanks, Henri. I'll hold on to the briefcase today."

He extended his hand across the table to Brouillard. "You must be Captain Brouillard. Marc Pirle. Very nice to meet you. Hello again, Mr. Vermeer."

"Thank you for agreeing to meet with me on such short notice, Professor Pirle," Brouillard began. "I'm sorry to drag you away from your meetings."

"I've found that meetings can usually wait if there are other meetings to attend." He sat down as if he owned the chair, and the table, and perhaps the restaurant. "And Dean Bishop has strongly encouraged me to cooperate in any way I can. So how can I help you?"

"I understand that you're close to the MacInnes family."

"On a strictly professional basis, reasonably so."

"It's a formality, really. We're looking into the circumstances of Eric MacInnes's death. I need to get a handle on where the family's money comes from, and who stands to benefit from Eric's death."

"Certainly," Pirle replied. "To some extent, I can assist you with the former. As for the latter, I am certainly not privy to the contents of their individual wills."

"Fine. So we'll start with the money."

Pirle paused as a beige-aproned waiter who had been hovering in the background, looking for an opening, jumped in to take their lunch orders. Brouillard and Vermeer ordered sandwiches and more coffee. "Just a seltzer with lime for me," Pirle said, looking at his watch.

"So," he continued after the waiter departed, "a primer on the MacInnes fortune. This would take a while to do properly, and of course we don't have time for that. In any case, the MacInnes empire is like a lot of old family enterprises: some of this, some of that, and some other things, too. That's mainly because opportunities show up in different places over the decades. If a family stays in business long enough, and if it includes the occasional competent person from generation to generation, its portfolio becomes more and more diversified. And as things get bigger and more complicated, new functional organizations get set up to keep track of and service the various businesses. Sooner or later, for example, a financial group gets created. Maybe a transportation enterprise, if one or more businesses need things to get moved from here to there.

"Going back to specific origins: the MacInneses hit these rude shores in the mid-seventeenth century with more than ample resources. Why they came is a small mystery. They don't appear to have been under a cloud. They don't seem to have had any particular religious motivations. My best guess is that they were unnaturally ambitious, especially in light of their aristocratic background, which is not normally a spur toward entrepreneurship. When the king of England granted them a substantial piece of what is now central New York State, this was probably no more than a small token of His Majesty's esteem. After all, how valuable could a trackless forest populated by hostile savages, too far from the navigable Hudson and St. Lawrence Rivers, turn out to be?

"The answer is, *very* valuable, but you had to wait a century or two. Meanwhile, the first New World MacInneses exploited the raw materials that God had given them: pelts, some iron, wood for charcoal, ice for transshipping to the south, and so on. As they had back in England, these MacInneses encouraged tenant farmers to clear and farm the flat lands. This was wealth-building the old-fashioned way: by the sweat of other people's brows.

"Anyway," Pirle paused, briefly interrupting his own lecture as he caught someone's eye at a far table and nodded in that direction, "you get the picture. Then came capitalism. The arrival of the canals and the railroads in the mid-nineteenth century raised the stakes considerably. Gradually, the MacInneses' remote landholdings came within reach of the largest metropolitan area, the biggest market, in the nation. The timber from their forests became more valuable, as did the produce from their farms.

"More and more money flowed in. When the surpluses started to pile up, they founded the MacInnes

Bank of Commerce, serving commercial accounts only. They bought the railroad that serviced their various valleys. They set up a real estate arm to manage their lands. Originally, they were probably worried about poachers. In recent years, they've involved themselves in a housing development on the periphery of the one reasonably vital college community within their sphere of influence. Meanwhile, they shipped in engineers, who built dams on their rivers to provide power for their gristmills, and later for their textile factories. When the time was ripe, around the beginning of the twentieth century, they rebuilt the old dams and started selling hydroelectricity. Several of their friendly little freestanding hydro plants helped jump-start the regional grid in the wake of the most recent regional blackouts. A little-known fact, but true.

"But like many wealthy families," Pirle continued, "the MacInneses have been better at getting into things than at getting out of things. Business is oftentimes a very emotional pastime, and family businesses often exaggerate this problem. It's not just 'that tired little railroad that we own a large piece of'; it's 'the pioneering railroad that Great-Grandfather built.' Obviously, this creates difficulties over the long run. As I've told them many times, if you're going to be undisciplined about going into things, you have to be extremely disciplined about getting out of them.

"Think of the MacInneses as both a relic and a portent," Pirle continued ponderously. Vermeer recognized the cadence: Pirle was winding up toward his finale. "They are antiques, curios, and perhaps also omens. They are the people who financed the explorations of the New World. They tolerated the excesses of the Napoleons and

Bismarcks, mainly because their assets were beyond the reach of tin-pot despots and their wars. They paid for Queen Victoria's empire and King Edward's steamships. Through syndicates, they probably bankrolled both the *Lusitania* and the kaiser's U-boat that sank her. In all of these ways, you could say that they are as irrelevant as yesterday's dust.

"And in a real way, they are also tomorrow," he went on. "They are the families of Asia and South America who are building extraordinarily powerful business networks. They mix family issues and business issues without a second thought. The family is in business—it doesn't much matter which business—and this is the certainty as far out as the future stretches. They think of the fur trade and the semiconductor industry as points on a continuum of opportunity. I, for one, find all this endlessly fascinating."

As he reached for his water glass, Pirle looked as if he expected a spontaneous burst of applause. Brouillard, Vermeer noticed, had not taken a single note. "Right," she said. "Fascinating. So what does it all mean for today?"

"About thirty years ago," Pirle responded, happy to expound further, "when William MacInnes was still fairly new to the job of family patriarch, he followed the advice of his financial advisers and took the family enterprise public. The whole thing: real estate, transportation, timber, construction, the finance operation, and so on. I was thoroughly astonished to discover recently that there are even a few fairly tired consumer brands in the mix: haircare products, teeth whiteners, and so on.

"In any case, public they went, and the results since then have been less than compelling. In retrospect, the whole idea of becoming a public corporation was ill conceived. I became involved perhaps a decade ago. Since that time, I've been telling William MacInnes that he needs to make significant changes in the structure of the empire. And until very recently, he would tell me in so many words that he was sick of hearing these arguments from me."

"What kinds of changes?"

"Ruthless changes," Pirle said, smiling malevolently. "Revisions to the company's ownership structure. Wholesale prunings. In other words, things that families generally aren't good at."

Brouillard had begun taking notes. She acknowledged Pirle's last comments with a nod, still scribbling, and then looked up. "You said, 'until recently.' So did he agree recently?"

"As a matter of fact, he did."

"Was this something the family would have debated?"

"Debated, yes," Pirle said. "Whether that debate would have affected what the paterfamilias ultimately did, I don't know. I would doubt it. William and Elizabeth together own enough stock so that he could have imposed his will in any case."

Brouillard nodded again, scribbling. "Uh-huh. That's helpful. Tell me: Who owns what, and how does all that change as a result of Eric's death?"

"Well, the stock ownership is public information, of course. Today, the MacInnes family owns fifty-one percent of the common stock of MacInnes Incorporated. I may have the breakouts wrong, but I believe William MacInnes owns fourteen percent, Elizabeth owns thirteen percent, and the three children own eight percent each. The parents were gifting shares to the children for many years, but that stopped a few years back. The current structure seems to be the one that William was aiming for, at least for the time being."

"Except that Eric's dead," Brouillard said without looking up.

"Of course," Pirle acknowledged. "Except that now Eric is dead."

"What happens to his stock?"

"I have no idea what will happen to Eric's stock, since they have wisely declined to involve me in their estate planning. I think it is unlikely that they would allow that stock to revert to the older generation and therefore become subject to estate taxes in the not-too-distant future. If there were grandchildren available, I would expect to see generation-skipping trust devices, but for better or worse, there are not. Most likely, the stock will go to the remaining son and the daughter, probably in equal amounts. So far, William MacInnes hasn't shown the backbone that would be required for him to be nonegalitarian."

"So," Brouillard said slowly, doing some quick calculations on her pad, "nothing much changes, right? The parents still have twenty-seven percent between them, and if your guess is right, James and Libby go from eight to twelve percent each. The surviving kids get fifty percent richer. But from what I've seen, they were already rich enough."

"As you say," Pirle replied, effectively conveying his disapproval of the concept of "rich enough." "And there are many other MacInnes assets that exist outside the corporation. So if anything, if you consider that stock alone, you risk understating the children's real wealth rather substantially."

The waiter arrived with their lunches. While Vermeer and Brouillard began working on their sandwiches, Pirle speared the thick wedge of lime in his seltzer and wrung it out vigorously, sending a shower of juice and pulp into his glass. At his request, the waiter returned with two more slices of lime in a small dish, and he treated them similarly.

Watching Pirle watch them eat, Vermeer was reminded of his younger sister's bout with anorexia. She used to love to watch people consume, because, as she later explained it when freed from her illness, the process was so manifestly disgusting that it reinforced her resolve to starve herself. On holidays and at other family gatherings, she always brought a camera to the table. She took pictures of people putting food in their mouths. Then she ordered up oversize prints of the worst shots and sent them to her victims with cheerful cover notes about nothing in particular.

"You're welcome to my pickle, Marc," Vermeer said to Pirle. "I'm not going to eat it."

His senior colleague failed to suppress a shudder. "No, thank you, Mr. Vermeer. I only take two meals on the days that I don't get a chance to work out."

Brouillard seemed absorbed in her note taking, so Vermeer decided to poke at his prickly colleague. Pirle's condescension had finally gotten to him. And, Vermeer admitted to himself, he wouldn't mind if this Captain Brouillard stopped treating him like spoiled produce.

"Marc," he began, "you focused on ownership. But obviously ownership and control can be different issues. Maybe you can give Captain Brouillard an idea about who actually controls the MacInnes assets."

Pirle sighed just audibly. "Certainly, Mr. Vermeer. And

again I'll assume you're talking about the corporation, as opposed to other family assets about which I have chosen to learn very little. As things stand today, there is a single class of stock. If the family acts in concert, which to date it always has, it can use its fifty-one percent stake to steer or override the nonfamily shareholders. It could actually get by with a significant minority interest, as I've pointed out to Father William several times, but this is a manifestation of their fundamental conservatism. And although there have been a few contested directors' elections, those nonfamily shareholders have been more or less satisfied with the MacInneses' management of the business. Rather inexplicable, in light of the mediocre performance of the stock. Foolish people can be very patient, I suppose."

"Have they considered multiple classes of stock?" Vermeer remembered that this was a fairly common strategy among privately held companies, but had no idea if the tactic would work for a publicly held business dominated by a single large voting bloc.

"As a matter of fact," Pirle replied, "they have, although I'll ask you to keep this confidential. Before Eric left this world, William MacInnes was contemplating a move to create different classes of stock in the company, only some of which could be voted. It would basically convert certain larger holdings to preferred stock, which would be nonvoting except under extraordinary circumstances. The net result would be that the operating managers, who might or might not be family members, would be able to exert more effective control over the affairs of the company. Not an elegant solution, but a functional one."

"Was this restructuring your idea?"

"It was. And *is,* Mr. Vermeer. It will solve a number of problems that the overall business will face in the next few years, beginning with the succession issue."

"What other kinds of problems does the business face?"

"A lack of synergy among the various parts. I've already described the state of the enterprise to you. It is a hodgepodge, however well intentioned. Certain things need to go. Other things may need to be acquired. Concentrating voting rights in the hands of the managers will make that process vastly easier."

"Does the rest of the family know about this plan?"

"I have no idea. I am careful to talk business only with the senior Mr. MacInnes."

"Which family members were supposed to wind up with this voting stock?"

"Our discussions were still on a general level. But knowing William MacInnes, I suspect he intended to split the voting stock with the two boys. His wife, Elizabeth, is not a player, except insofar as I explained in our previous conversation—as an intermittent influence on her husband. The daughter, Libby, has never expressed much interest in the business. She's a nurse, as I think I told you earlier."

"And what happens to this scheme now?"

"You will have to ask the MacInneses those questions. I have no idea. My role was simply to advise William MacInnes as to what would be best for the business. At the risk of restating the obvious, I have tried very hard to stay out of family matters, which sooner or later almost always degenerate into the illogical."

Brouillard, who had been alternating between her sandwich and note taking, picked up her pencil. "Very helpful, Professor Pirle. If I may say so, you certainly seem to lead an interesting life."

Pirle puffed up a little bit. "Hard work and good luck. They have combined to put me in the right places, I suppose."

"But one more time, for the benefit of a Boston cop who doesn't get out much," she continued, "who comes out ahead as a result of Eric's death?"

"That depends entirely on those wills that I haven't seen. Assuming, of course, that Eric was clever and focused enough to have written one. But as I've already implied, rich families with good lawyers never let assets flow backwards—that is, from younger generations to older generations. I have to assume that lacking representatives from the next generation, Eric's assets will be divided between James and Libby. So they benefit. James is married, so I suppose his spouse, an elegant but inconsequential young thing, benefits indirectly.

"And now"—Pirle arched his eyebrows at Brouillard as he reached for his briefcase—"if there's nothing else?"

"Nothing for now. Thank you for your help. I'll be in touch if I need more insights. Not planning on leaving the country anytime soon, are you?"

Pirle stopped in midrise, looking for an instant like a runner on a starter's block. Then he straightened up stiffly. "No. I'm teaching this semester. I take that responsibility very seriously. So I'll be here until the end of classes. Why do you ask?"

Brouillard, smiling pleasantly, tapped the eraser end of her pencil on her notepad. "Oh, I just don't want to have to call long distance if I have any more questions."

"Of course. Please contact my office."

Vermeer chuckled as Pirle strode out of the restaurant, pausing only long enough to retrieve his coat from Henri. "That was funny," Vermeer said. "Well worth the price of admission."

"Excuse me?" Brouillard, looking slightly irritated, stuffed her pad and pencil in her bag.

"Watching you drop that old film noir line on him: 'Not planning on fleeing the country anytime soon, are we?' He looked like you'd pulled your gun on him."

"Oh, just standard operating procedure. I want to know where my sources are, especially if they seem like the globe-trotting type. And the department doesn't like getting bills for overseas calls."

"Look me in the eye and tell me you weren't busting his chops."

Brouillard smiled slightly as she asked a passing waiter for the check and a refill on her coffee. "Pass."

"Lunch is on me, by the way," Vermeer said. "Or more accurately, on Dean Bishop."

"Yeah, okay," she replied distantly, all at once again preoccupied. For a long minute she looked over Vermeer's shoulder, at a point somewhere out in the windswept brick courtyard. When the check arrived, Vermeer handed the waiter a credit card. Brouillard, mug in hand, now staring in an unfocused way at the wall behind him, somewhere near where it joined the ceiling, didn't seem to notice the transaction. He decided to wait her out.

"Okay, time to talk some turkey," she said finally. She looked around to confirm that she couldn't be overheard. Even then, she lowered her voice slightly. "I told your dean that I wouldn't put up with being babysat. There are good reasons for that. This is a formal police investigation. It's not a sandbox for civilians. And furthermore, it's *my* investigation. Nobody else's."

"Okay, but—"

"Let me finish. I don't want you underfoot. I don't want you running back to your boss every five minutes telling him what I'm up to. That is unacceptable.

"On the other hand, I can see ways that you could be helpful to this investigation. You have good access at your school. You have at least some access to the MacInnes family, at least as long as they need you to run errands for them. And you seem to know enough about high finance and voting blocs and so on to fill in some of the blanks for me. Not that I couldn't get there myself sooner or later, but you could probably get me there a lot faster."

"Probably."

"Don't interrupt. So here's the deal: I tell you what I need to know, and you either get me the info or you tell me how to get it. If something that doesn't make sense to me makes sense to you, you explain it to me.

"I also tell you what *you* need to know, and nothing more. I give you enough so that you can reassure your boss that I'm moving as quickly as possible—which I am—and that I'm not out to drag anybody through the mud. Which I'm not.

"And finally, as far as the rest of the world is concerned, you and I have no deal. You're doing your job, whatever the hell that is, and I'm doing mine. If you claim this conversation took place, I will call you a liar. And believe me, they'll take my word over yours."

"I believe you."

"So, do we have a deal?"

11

Alonzo Rodriguez was late.

Brouillard sat alone in a conference room adjacent to Dean Bishop's office, fiddling with her Swiss Army wristwatch—a surprisingly nice and useful gift from an otherwise forgettable boyfriend. With nothing else to do, she looked at the framed prints on the white wall closest to her. After a minute of study, she realized that they were different architectural schemes for the campus. Judging from the fussy lettering and some dead-giveaway details—the occasional old roaring-twenties-type car penciled onto an imaginary street—she guessed that they dated back to the Depression or earlier. Most of the designs showed a quiet little country road hugging the riverbank—no resemblance to today's impassable traffic canyon alongside the Charles.

She spotted the winning design. To her eye, it was no better than most of the others, and nowhere near as interesting as one or two of them. But then, she didn't pretend to be an architect.

She would give him five more minutes. Then she would go back to her office and invite him to visit her there. When that happened, experience suggested, he would wish he had not blown off this first appointment.

There was a tentative knock on the white wooden door, which then swung open. "Excuse me," the voice arrived before the face. "Sorry to be late, but we had a small emergency. Burst water pipe. The cold." Rodriguez pushed the door shut behind him, then came forward to offer his hand. "Alonzo Rodriguez. But please call me Al." He spoke with a very slight Spanish accent.

"Captain Barbara Brouillard, BPD. Please sit down."

He sat down after carefully placing his coat over the back of the chair. As he did so, Brouillard sized him up. Dark gold skin, black hair, and slightly oversize ears. He wore a standard-issue white-collar crew boss's uniform: khaki pants, white shirt, plain tie, unscuffed work boots. His black winter jacket and black cap, which he was now taking off hurriedly, both sported nice-looking "Harvard Buildings & Grounds" logos. Brouillard guessed he was an up-through-the-ranks guy. If so, she gave him credit for that. Up-through-the-ranks couldn't be easy at a place like Harvard.

"The dean's secretary said you wanted to talk to me," he said, looking concerned. "I don't know how I can help you, but I'll try."

"Good." Brouillard wasted a few seconds going through her preliminaries slowly: pad out on desk, pencil poised, and so on. Then she looked hard at him. "Well, Al, here's the situation. I really *do* expect that you can help me, because this is right up your alley. You've heard about Eric MacInnes?"

He nodded, his eyes widening slightly. "The boy who died."

"Exactly. So this is a police investigation. I need to ask you to keep this conversation confidential. Okay?"

"Sure. Yes." Anxiety mounted on his face. "But is this—am I . . . ?"

"Are you in trouble? No. This is just a conversation between you and me. I don't want to talk about you. I want to talk about your buildings."

"So it's okay? To talk to you?"

Sighing inwardly, she wondered if detectives fifty years ago, before people watched all those cop shows on TV, had to answer these kinds of questions. She doubted it. "This is just a conversation like any other conversation. Entirely voluntary. You want to stop at any time, you stop."

He nodded, eyes still wide.

"Good," she continued. "So let's start with security at Shad Hall. All I know so far is that during business hours the front door is open, but you need a pass card to get through the inner doors."

"Correct. Your student ID. Or if you forget it, sometimes you can get the front-desk people to buzz you in. If they recognize you."

"Other doors?"

"Yes. Mainly for emergency exit. The maintenance crew and deliveries come through the back. Mostly during the early morning. Never at night."

"So no other doors are ever open?"

"They are not supposed to be."

"The building closes at—what?—ten p.m.? What happens after hours?"

"It's, uhm, eleven p.m., I think," Rodriguez said, obviously reluctant to contradict her. "After that, no one is supposed to be in the building. The front door lock is on a timer—once it locks, you can get out but not in. The staff people do a sweep of the building to move the stragglers out, set the alarm with the keypad, and go out the front door. That's about it."

Brouillard took notes. As always, she liked the scratching noise of the pencil working its way across the paper. It made her feel as though she was making progress. "And how do they open up in the morning?"

"Well, just about the same thing in reverse. The custodians get there at around four a.m., swipe a pass card to open the back door, hit the keypad to turn off the alarm, and go to work. The door locks behind them. By six the front desk is manned, and the front door automatically unlocks."

"One alarm for the whole building?"

"One perimeter alarm, yes."

"Motion detectors?"

"No. We decided against it. Too much air exchange, pushing the drapes and potted plants around, sending in false alarms. Plus, there's nothing much to steal in a gym."

"Uh-huh. How about the tunnel system?"

"More or less the same thing. The tunnel access to Shad comes out in the building lobby. That door locks and unlocks on the same timer as the front door."

"Al," she said, jotting notes, "I have to say, you do know a lot about the security systems in your buildings."

"Not all of them as much as this one," he said, deflecting the compliment. "I was, uhm, involved in its design. When the building was built. We had lots of discussions. The architects told us that the real experts are the people who actually work in the building, and that our opinions counted. It's a management theory."

She nodded. Her pencil on the pad made a *scritch, scritch* sound, like mice in the walls. "Okay, got it. So unless the deceased managed to hide out in the building during operating hours, which I take it you don't think is very likely, then he had to have a pass card that opened the back door. And he had to know the code to turn off the perimeter alarm. Any way his student ID could have gotten him in? Any way he could have gotten extra privileges coded into it, or something like that? Obviously, Al, I don't know what I'm talking about, here."

Rodriguez looked a little more uncomfortable. "Well," he said, "I can't say that's not possible. It *shouldn't* be possible. But I don't know much about that coding technology. Which is changing pretty fast, as I understand it. So what I know is probably out of date."

She nodded. "And, of course, he could have gotten a hold of one of those special custodian's pass cards for the back door."

"I don't see how such a card wouldn't be missed. There are only a few, and they're assigned to specific people."

"Coded to those individuals?"

"Yes. Or at least distinguishable—you know, like 'number one,' 'number two,' or whatever. We know who's got number one, and so on."

"Same thing with the keypad codes? Or does everyone use the same one?"

Again he hesitated. "Uhm, well, before I tell you something that might be inaccurate, Captain, I'd like to check that out. I think we have a system that lets us know who opened the building on a given morning. But that kind of system is only as good as you are willing to maintain it. You know what I mean? Sometimes, people get lazy. Or careless. Maybe more than one person winds up using the same code."

"And do you recode on some regular basis?"

"Sorry, but I don't know that. I should know that."

"Actually, Al, as I said, I'm impressed how much you *do* know about this building." As she changed her tone, she watched his eyes. He was wary. "And I understand that you've got a lot on your plate. You've got how many buildings here to look after?"

Back on familiar turf, he spoke more confidently. He probably even gave tours to visiting buildings and grounds dignitaries. "Depends on what you're counting as a building, and what you're counting as ours. Just shy of thirty. Plus the grounds, and a lot of the operations, too."

"Like I said, a full plate." She put her pad and paper away, pushed back her chair, and made moves toward gathering up her coat and bag. As she rose to her feet, Rodriguez rose along with her. He started putting on his coat, reaching for his hat, obviously eager to get out of this white room.

"Even so, Al," she said. He stopped in midsleeve. She thought of freeze tag—did kids still play freeze tag? "I need you to put me at the top of your list. You've seen the papers, right?" She reached into her bag and pulled out a copy of this morning's *Herald*. A BAD BUSINESS, blared the huge headline. The accompanying story was painfully thin, since she wasn't releasing much—yet.

"I have seen them, yes."

"The point is, Al, a kid died in *your building* the other night. He wasn't supposed to be there. In your building. He shouldn't have been able to get into your building, Al.

"So obviously, Al, somebody screwed up. And chances are, that somebody works for you. So now you have to go find the right people, and ask them the right questions, and come back, and tell me, what happened?"

12

M*Y DEAN'S PEOPLE MOVE QUICKLY,* VERMEER THOUGHT
to himself as the truck approached Brooklyn, *when the
task is clear and the incentives are strong.*

The ride down from Boston had been uneventful.
Paleologos Trucking had seemed surprised at the idea of
a passenger traveling in the nearly empty moving van,
along with the small load of boxes and partially disas-
sembled workout equipment. The driver, Leon, spoke
heavily accented English—somewhere from central
Europe, Vermeer guessed—and doled it out only when
absolutely necessary. Otherwise, he chewed on his
droopy mustache and listened to recordings of what
sounded like gypsy music on a boom box that he kept on
the bench seat next to him. On the few occasions that
Vermeer tried to engage him in conversation, Leon nodded and turned up the boom box.

As Leon worked, the gearbox made scary grinding
noises. Either this truck had serious mechanical problems, or Leon didn't know much about standard trans-
missions. Or both.

Vermeer had agreed to the nondeal that Brouillard had
proposed. The detective would continue to follow up on
threads in the Boston area. Vermeer, meanwhile, would

use the excuse of returning Eric's belongings to the MacInnes family houses in Brooklyn and upstate New York. At those two locales, he would once again convey the school's deep regrets—and, without being obvious about it, pursue some of the questions that were on Brouillard's mind.

He had no illusions. If Brouillard had thought there were promising leads to be pursued out of state, she would have done it herself. Based on her comments about babysitters being close to her investigations, she was happy enough just to get him out of town.

On the other hand, he saw no reason not to take her up on her offer. Aside from his job search, there was nothing particularly pressing on his plate. He guessed that the MacInnes family would rather deal with him than with a Boston detective. And, he admitted to himself, he found Barbara Brouillard an interesting challenge. She seemed to stay a full step ahead of him—and most other people—without particularly exerting herself.

Dean Bishop, for his part, approved of the plan, although with his accustomed tone of calm and reserve. "Very good," he had said on the phone. "Take whatever time you need. We're covering your classes. Keep me posted."

Now, as the moving van left the Brooklyn-Queens Expressway and made its way down clogged and double-parked Prospect Street, Vermeer was struck by the absurdity of today's mission. Mr. Ralph, the ghostly family factotum, had warmed up slightly on the phone. (Everything was relative, of course; Mr. Ralph started at below the freezing point of salt water.) Although he was cooperative in giving Vermeer directions to both locations, he had made it clear that no family members would be "in residence" at the city home. Yes, he had confirmed, Miss Libby maintained her principal residence there, and therefore it made sense to move Mr. Eric's fitness equipment there. But at the moment, Miss Libby was in seclusion upstate with the family.

A small domestic staff managed the city residence. Ellie Donahue, Mr. Ralph had said, ran the household. Her assistant, Dan Beyer, was most qualified to decide where to put the fitness equipment: His primary responsibility was security, but he also doubled as Miss Libby's personal trainer. Vermeer thought he detected a hint of disapproval of Dan Beyer somewhere in Mr. Ralph's voice. Vermeer also guessed that Mr. Ralph was paid not to have opinions.

As they made their way slowly through Brooklyn, the Manhattan skyline rolled out from between local buildings and then disappeared again. It was an enormous, dense, piled formation of concrete and stone, and it never failed to impress Vermeer. Nothing in his life experience—growing up in a small Midwestern town, attending school and graduate school in the Ivies, and even spending time in Boston's tallest buildings—permitted him to become jaded toward New York. Sometimes, on business trips to the city, he slotted in a few covert extra hours just to amble around the canyons of Manhattan.

With a final scream of gears, the truck came to a halt outside a four-story building. "Tree, four, tree Atvater," Leon announced. He opened the door and slid out of the cab.

Like all the other buildings on the street, 343 Atwater featured an oversize front staircase bordered by ornate black handrails, leading up to a massive door that was elevated a half level above the street. Tucked in well below street level, on either side of the stairwell, were small windows covered by heavy iron grates. A well-tended plot of ivy, punctuated by flagstones leading to an armored doorway under the stairs, sat between the house and the street. Unlike most of its neighbors, which were constructed out of pinkish-brown sandstone, the facade of the MacInnes residence gleamed in what appeared to be white marble.

The heavy front door swung open almost as soon as Vermeer rang the bell. The doorway then filled up with one of the most dramatically muscled men Vermeer had ever seen in real life.

"Professor Vermeer? I'm Dan Beyer. Welcome to Brooklyn." He extended a large hand and then applied a handshake of bone-crushing force.

A second and third look at Dan Beyer still revealed mostly muscles. Even his jaw sported extra muscles, flexing back by his ears and neck and running in ropes down into his sculpted neck, making him look as if he could bite lampposts in half. Oblivious to the cold February wind blowing down the street, he wore only a form-fitting T-shirt, warm-up pants, and running shoes. His very light, yellow-blond hair was closely cropped on all sides, although it was long enough on top to stand upright above his forehead like a well-cultivated hedge. He spoke in a flat, high-in-the-nose voice that Vermeer associated with Buffalo and the vast, boring expanses of western New York State. He looked twenty but could have been pushing thirty.

"Sorry that we're a little late. We seemed to be trying to stay well below the speed limit, especially on the larger highways."

"Not a problem." Beyer did not appear to be amused.

Down at street level, Leon, who had indeed refrained from pushing any envelopes in the preceding four hours, now was wasting no time. He had already pulled a retractable steel walkway out from underneath the truck and opened the cargo door. Now he reemerged into the thin sunlight pushing a two-wheeler that was heavily loaded with boxes. He steered his cargo down to street level, turned his back to the house, hefted the two-wheeler up onto the sidewalk easily, and looked up at the front door.

"Looks like he knows what he's doing," Beyer said. "I'll go open up the basement. We'll put the equipment down there for the time being. We can put the other stuff in Mr. MacInnes's study upstairs."

Vermeer soon found that he was more or less irrelevant to the unloading process. Beyer's muscles weren't just for show; he was astoundingly strong, hefting heavy and bulky objects with ease. And for his part, Leon had years of practice working in his favor. A far better mover than a driver, he knew how to make weight work for him. He also had an eye for figuring out how to fit ungainly pieces of workout equipment through the relatively unforgiving basement doorway—a half turn here, a jog there, now straight up to take advantage of the higher ceiling just inside. When a two-person job came up, he directed Beyer with purposeful jerks of his head, punctuated by an occasional approving or disapproving grunt.

Vermeer took the opportunity to poke around. The basement, which extended from the front of the house to a hidden garden at the rear, was mainly the servants' domain. It was essentially an open space, with boxed-in columns demarcating several zones of activity. Roughly the front third of the space housed mechanical systems:

water heaters, oil burners, tools of all sorts. All appeared to be relatively new and high end. The middle area had been transformed into a well-equipped fitness center, which clearly didn't need the additional treadmill, rowing machine, and weight-lifting equipment that Beyer and Leon were now moving into it.

Toward the rear of the house, walled off by shoulder-high partitions, was a large and surprisingly sunny kitchen. Judging from the oversize ovens and stoves and the large dumbwaiter door recessed in one of the walls, this was the mansion's main kitchen.

There wasn't much more to see here. Waiting until Beyer was outside with Leon, Vermeer picked up a box marked "papers" and quietly climbed the stairs. When he pushed open the door at the top, the stairwell emptied into a high-ceilinged entryway dominated by an ornate chandelier, a huge gilded mirror along one wall, and a grand white-marble stairway that looked a little oversize for the relatively narrow house.

"May I help you?"

Vermeer turned to face a stocky, stern-looking woman who appeared to be in her late fifties. Her graying hair was tied up in a tight bun, and she wore a chest-to-knee white apron, starched and spotless. Around her neck hung a chain with what looked like a blank ID card on its end. "Oh, hi. You must be Ellie Donahue. I'm Wim Vermeer, from Boston." He made a show of putting down the box, which wasn't particularly heavy, and shook her hand.

"Yes, of course. Mr. Ralph told us you'd be arriving this morning."

"Dan said that the boxes of papers were supposed to go into Mr. MacInnes's study." Not the whole truth, but true enough. "Maybe you could show me the way?"

"Certainly. Follow me." She led Vermeer up the staircase and into a gloomy wood-paneled hallway. The only light came from a skylight high above the stairwell; the far end of the hall, where they were now headed, was obscured in shadows.

The heavy wooden door to William MacInnes's study was locked. Donahue bent forward from the waist and put her badge in front of a small plastic panel next to the door. There was a heavy click, and a red light on the panel turned green. She pushed the door open.

"Nice system," Vermeer said. Bank-quality locks.

"The family pays attention to security, if that's what you mean," she replied sparely. "And I certainly find it preferable to carrying a set of keys all over the house."

The study felt neglected, as if it had once been a favorite lair but had fallen out of favor. Dominating the room was a massive wooden two-sided partners desk with a heavy oak swivel chair on one side. Vermeer remembered that he had once seen a picture of a very similar desk that John D. Rockefeller had shared with his original business partner as they invented the oil business. The carpets on the floor, probably magnificent in their day, looked comfortably worn and faded. Floor-to-ceiling bookcases lined two of the four walls. Judging from the acrid perfume that hung in the air, the clear plastic humidor on the desk was an old friend of the owner. Now, though, it was nearly empty, with two lone cigars on its bottom shelf.

"That corner, I think." The housekeeper pointed at a spot on the floor.

He put the box down.

As they left the study, Donahue gave a small tug, and the door swung shut. The lock clicked, and the light winked red again. Vermeer noted that several of the other doors leading off the hallway also had tiny red lights at the ready. One door, at the far end of the hall, was slightly ajar.

"You know," he said, "if you just want to prop that door open, I can just bring the rest of the stuff up without bothering you."

She looked appalled. "No. That wouldn't be possible. We keep these doors closed at all times."

"Well, there are a lot of boxes. And it doesn't make much sense to have you running up and down twenty times with me. Why don't I bring all the boxes up here and stack them up in the hall? When I'm done, you can come up and open the door for me."

Fingering her passkey like worry beads, Donahue looked at the stairwell and then back at the now closed door, calculating the trade-offs involved. "Well," she finally said, "I suppose that would be all right. Just come find me downstairs as soon as you're ready." When they reached the ground floor, she disappeared behind a door leading to the back of the house.

In fact, there weren't more than a half-dozen boxes, the last of which he soon had piled up outside the door to MacInnes's study. But he had bought a little time to reconnoiter. He paused at the top of the stairwell to make sure that no one was approaching.

Then he walked to the unlocked door at the end of the hall.

Stepping inside, he had no doubt that this was Libby MacInnes's room and had been for many years. *Palimpsest* popped into Vermeer's mind—a hundred-dollar word favored by humanities graduate students: *a parchment with several generations of writing on it,* from back in the days when paper was too precious to throw away. The room looked like it had been overwritten many times, with traces of a former life surviving each time. In one corner was a custom-built set of shelves displaying a large collection of toy horses. (One long row of Appaloosas had fallen over like dominoes; it seemed unlikely that anyone would ever stand them all up again.) Some tattered wall posters testified to Libby's past infatuations with long-disbanded boy bands. The lavender window treatments—badly overdone, to Vermeer's amateur eye—matched the pale satin wallpaper as well as the dust ruffle on a large four-poster bed. But at some point, Libby had moved on to bolder colors. Now the primary colors of throw rugs, bolsters, and other knickknacks overwhelmed the original girlish look of the room.

Like William MacInnes's study, Libby's bedroom was dominated by a desk. But the two workstations at the opposite ends of the hall were from different centuries. Libby's desk, a vast V-shaped wedge of white, lurked in its corner like a grounded Stealth bomber. It was burdened with an array of computer equipment, only about half of which Vermeer could identify. Next to one of three flat-screen monitors, for example, he recognized a broadband modem winking green and orange, signaling its willingness to do business, like the one on his desk at home. But Libby had three of these high-speed workhorses parked at various places on her desk. Three separate broadband hookups—one for each monitor? Vermeer wondered. Was Libby running some kind of data-intensive business out of the MacInnes manse?

Moving closer to the desk, Vermeer scanned the tidy piles of papers that surrounded the monitors. They appeared to be articles downloaded from various nursing-related Web sites. Lots of gerunds in the titles, he noted: managing this, understanding that, leveraging this. Vermeer had dated a nursing student, briefly. Passionate and almost universally generous in spirit, she had talked venomously about nursing research.

The wall-mounted white bookshelves above the desk held mostly nursing and medical reference books. One lone knickknack, sandwiched between two stands of books, caught his eye. It was a five-pointed, clear Lucite star, about four inches high, on a black base. On the base was a small plaque with an inscription:

<u>Gold Star</u>
Awarded to Elizabeth R. MacInnes
And the INRR
By the ISMC

Vermeer shook his head, irritated. Someone, somewhere, had saved a buck on engraving. He had no idea what "INRR" and "ISMC" stood for. Whatever the INRR did with Libby's help, the ISMC evidently appreciated it.

Something was nagging at him. It felt as if something was missing. He scanned the desk again and then looked around the edges of the room.

No photos. In fact, other than the taciturn "gold star," no personal memorabilia, mementos, or keepsakes of any kind. No family.

"What the hell are you doing in here?"

The sharp-edged voice caught Vermeer by surprise. He nearly jumped off his feet, like a cartoon character. In the doorway—in fact, completely filling the doorway—was Dan Beyer. He looked like an aroused guard dog behind a fence. Except that there was no fence.

"Oh, hi, Dan." Vermeer flashed back through what he had been doing in the past several seconds. He decided that it was bluffable. "Just finished moving those boxes up here and really needed to find the head."

"This isn't a bathroom. It's a bedroom. A private bedroom."

"Yeah, I can see that now, but it was the only door that happened to be open. I gave Ellie a yell, but she didn't answer. And things were getting a little urgent. Still are, in fact."

Beyer calculated the plausibility of this. His face softened slightly. It was plausible. "Uh-huh. Well, now that you've discovered your mistake, I think you'll want to be heading downstairs." He stepped into the room and swept both overmuscled arms toward the door.

"You bet. Just point me toward the bathroom, and I'm a happy guy."

13

ALTHOUGH THERE WASN'T ANY UNUSUAL ODOR IN THE air—just the airborne molds from behind the walls of the tired-out station house, the smell of too many bodies at close quarters over too many years, the smell of generations of floor wax—Barbara Brouillard was wrinkling up her nose.

This was a habit of concentration that dated back to when she still wore cheap glasses that tended to slide down her nose. She had been unaware of it until a few months earlier, when Dick Davidson, at the next desk, picked up on it and started riding her. Ever since then, when she surfaced from one of her reveries, she was likely to find her colleagues, seated at their desks, wrinkling their noses in exaggerated ways. Then, likely as not, someone would start to snort, piglike. And things would go downhill from there.

Not today, though. The bullpen was quiet. Davidson was on vacation. The other self-appointed chief tormentor, Buzzy Silver, was still out on an extended medical leave. Silver had been involved in an embarrassing hunting accident in the White Mountains—alcohol was rumored to have been a factor—and had caught a fellow hunter's .22 rifle slug in a particular part of his anatomy with lots of nerve endings. He was still receiving a steady stream of interesting get-well gifts, mostly prostheses of various sorts, from his colleagues at District 11.

Brouillard had sent a card, but she didn't miss him.

She was taking advantage of the relative silence to think through the MacInnes case. And her nose was wrinkling. Because, if this was a puzzle, the pieces weren't adding up to much. At the same time, it felt as if the pieces *might* fit together if she could just look at them in the right way.

A couple of months earlier, she had attended a rubber-chicken luncheon—some sort of cops-and-community goodwill get-together; she had drawn the short straw—and found herself sitting next to an archaeologist from Boston University. As he described it, his job was heaven on earth: the occasional lecture and obligatory faculty meeting sandwiched between digs in New Mexico. There, he said a little dreamily, he and his graduate students hunted Native American artifacts by day and drank jug wine under the big sky by night.

To Brouillard's ears, most of his chatter was boring and self-serving. But he captured her imagination when he described the nitty-gritty of the dig: the careful delineation of zones of excavation, the hot sun and dry desert wind, the small shovelfuls, the sifting of reddish, bone-dry desert soil, the painstaking numbering and recording of objects and pieces of objects. In particular, she found herself responding to his description of the challenge and frustrations of trying to assemble a complete ancient clay pot from a small mountain of shards. "Maybe the pieces were all there," he had said, "and you just hadn't found the right combination." Or maybe the pieces weren't all there, and you had to go back to the earth. All the while knowing that you might *never* find what you were looking for.

"That's interesting," she had said, as much to herself as to him. "That's kind of what I do, too." She briefly described how she assembled clues and nonclues, rearranged them in multiple ways, some of them unlikely, and went back out looking for the missing pieces of the puzzle. *Back to the earth.*

The archaeologist mistook her interest. Maybe she'd like to talk further over dinner sometime, maybe this week? The slightly more aggressive pitch in his voice wasn't well concealed. In her experience, lots of guys, especially middle-aged guys and *especially* middle-aged guys leading quiet upper-middle-class professional lives, found the idea of a female detective intriguing, or challenging, or whatever.

"I don't know," she had said in a matter-of-fact tone. "Will you be wearing that nice gold wedding ring, or will you be taking it off before dinner?" The professor made a little show of being offended, then quickly showed her his back. He spent the rest of the lunch deep in conversation with the person on his other elbow. So much for community goodwill.

Her phone rang. Brouillard picked it up warily. She hadn't touched it yet this morning. Sometimes the frat boys on the evening shift did silly things to her handset. That was definitely something she was going to attend to one of these days.

"Brouillard."

"Hi, Captain. Art Deming here."

"Hi, Art. Got anything for me?"

"I think so, yeah."

"I'll be over."

Pulling out of the car pool in an unmarked Taurus—reasonably new and not yet overwhelmed by the stale residue of smoke or the inevitable little green Christmas tree air freshener hanging from the rearview—Brouillard knew that this in-person trip was probably unnecessary. There wouldn't be much to look at; a phone conversation probably would accomplish just as much.

But the long drive would give her a chance to wrinkle her nose in private. And she could also take a detour through the old neighborhood, where she hadn't been in a couple of months. And finally, Art liked the attention.

Art Deming did business a block away from where Brouillard had grown up. The neighborhood had gone way upscale since then, of course. A former mayor of Somerville had detoured the Red Line way off its natural route, blocking the extension of the line until he got a subway stop in Davis Square. That, combined with Tufts University's expansion and its long, slow climb into academic respectability, had pushed property values out of sight. Her parents had sold their triple-decker just before the boom, convinced they were getting an amazing price, and had moved to Florida. Today the house was full of graduate students and was worth ten times what her parents had sold it for. Meanwhile, down in Clearwater, they called her every week, speaking mournfully of the heat and the bugs and talking of how much they missed the changing of the seasons.

The puzzle pieces, Brouillard reminded herself, heading over the bridge that linked Boston and East Cambridge. It featured huge decorative pillars of cast concrete that looked like the salt and pepper shakers in a cheap restaurant. Probably not the effect that the bridge designer had been aiming for, she said to herself. It was not the first time she had made that mental comment about the Salt and Pepper Bridge.

Bear down, she scolded herself again. *The puzzle pieces.*

Eric's cause of death: drowning, but with an asterisk. Water in the lungs, consistent with drowning. But bruises and contusions at the base of the skull, consistent with a blow to the back of the head. Or consistent with whacking your head against the tiled rim of the Jacuzzi if you staggered, slipped, and fell.

Blood alcohol levels that were probably high enough to make you stagger, slip, and fall, especially if you weren't much of a drinker. But not high compared to your average patron of the Black Rose at Quincy Market on your average Friday night.

One odd fact that she wasn't sharing with anybody, even in the Dirtball Theoretical: a single tiny puncture wound midway up Eric's left arm. Overlooked at the crime scene because it sat squarely in the middle of a mole straddling a prominent vein. The medical examiner had spotted and flagged it, although toxicology didn't show anything other than alcohol.

Eric hadn't visited University Health Services. Wasn't known to have seen a physician in the Boston area. Didn't have allergies. Wasn't a skin-popper. Wasn't the type to spontaneously start tattooing himself.

So what, Brouillard wondered, was the little hole in his arm all about?

Clothes carefully hung on the wall pegs of the shower stall nearest to the Jacuzzi. Nothing unusual in the pockets of the pants or shirt. A wallet with ten crisp twenty-dollar bills in it, suggesting that Eric had recently visited an ATM. The bank had confirmed the transaction. For what it was worth, there hadn't been a robbery.

Another odd note: a missing pass card. In the pocket of Eric's pants, hung carefully near where his body had been found, was the pass card that had gotten him into the fitness center. The thoroughly intimidated Alonzo Rodriguez had promised to find out how he had obtained it. Most of the possible answers weren't very compelling. Brouillard wasn't much interested, for example, in hanging some cash-strapped custodian out to dry. (That was Harvard's issue, if it came to that.) But if other people had pass cards like this one, that was worth knowing about.

Oddly, though, there was no pass card for Eric's apartment. And despite a careful search, none had turned up in his apartment. Had he lost it? Loaned it to someone? Hidden it under a doormat somewhere? Dropped it down a storm drain as a symbolic gesture on his way to committing a lonely suicide?

Suicide. The crumpled note in Eric's trash can certainly hinted at some kind of deep trouble, even desperation. But not necessarily a self-destructive streak. Jeannette Bartlett's anguished testimony, too, argued against suicide.

The thought of Bartlett prompted Brouillard to run through the cast of characters. Again, there wasn't much to work with. The thuggish brother with the wispy wife. The sister, mostly an afterthought. Both sibs would benefit from Eric's death, going from real rich to *real* rich. The angry father and the sedated mother. The Harvard crowd, deans and professors, playing their institutional roles, covering their institutional butts, mainly wishing that she would disappear from their busy and important lives. And Bartlett herself, either legitimately torn up or going for her first Oscar.

Brouillard's thoughts drifted back to her meeting with Bartlett in the fancy lunchroom. Bartlett's hasty departure, and the chair thudding heavily on the carpet in the sunlight.

The fact was, Brouillard knew, she would never get the full picture of what Eric MacInnes was all about. She could only get inside the head and heart of this dead rich kid vicariously and selectively, through the eyes of people who didn't think like she did or ask the kinds of questions she asked or sift information the way she did.

But Bartlett, distraught as she appeared to be, had more insight than most. More than once, Brouillard had reviewed her notes summarizing Bartlett's version of Eric MacInnes. It fit with all the physical clues he had left behind: self-absorption, tidiness, an obsession with life as a sort of continuous performance. And loneliness. That fit, somehow.

Had Eric been planning to marry that drab classmate of his, so far "beneath" his appointed station in life? Brouillard doubted it. Had he confided in her? Brouillard was sure of it. Bartlett knew Eric—at least Business School Eric—far better than did the members of his clannish, above-the-fray family.

And this brought her thoughts back to that crumpled note in the trash can, the note that had sent Bartlett rushing to puke in the bathroom.

What was it about that note that felt wrong? The introduction of some love angle that no one seemed to know anything about? The misspellings? The effort to wax poetic? The bare-wire language from a spoiled brat who seemed to specialize in the superficial?

No, she concluded again as she pulled up in front of an ugly one-story storefront on Hillside Street, she didn't like that note.

And that was one reason why she was meeting with Art Deming, deep computer nerd.

In his early thirties, he was some kind of permanent graduate student who was loosely associated with Tufts. And he was more than that.

Here in this crummy storefront, the windows of which still bore sagging vinyl signs advertising the talents of the previous proprietor—who had fixed VCRs until something bad had happened to him or to the business—Deming also ran a one-man data-recovery service.

Deming was very, very good at what he did. He charged his private-sector clients exorbitant sums to grab critical data off damaged hard drives. He probably made as much in a couple of days, Brouillard guessed, as your average Boston detective made in a month.

As a rule, Deming didn't do police work. But Brouillard had helped him out of a minor possession situation a few years earlier—more of a misunderstanding, really. For the rest of his days he was prepared to offer any assistance he could to the rumpled, closemouthed detective who had single-handedly rescued him from what he saw as the black hole of the Boston criminal court system.

Brouillard saw it differently, but didn't always remind him of that.

She pushed open the door of the shop, setting the small bell above the door to dancing and jangling. Moving from bright sunshine to the gloom of the shop, she was momentarily blinded. But she knew from past visits that there wasn't much to see here anyway: waist-high counters along three sides of the tiny shop, mostly bare. Floor-to-ceiling shelves behind the counters—probably original equipment from the turn of the previous century, although recently buttressed with shiny new angle irons to help support the weight of the computers that lined them. Some of these objects looked familiar to Brouillard, as her eyes adjusted. But others looked exotic. She had no idea whether that meant they were very old or very new.

"Hey, Captain." Deming's reedy voice emerged from a room off the rear of the shop. He didn't get a lot of visitors. "Come on back. For you, the inner sanctum."

Although the back room was only a quarter the size of the front, this was where the real work took place. Electronic testing equipment, entangled in great snarls of cables, covered the back half of a huge workbench that spanned the entire side wall. Lights glowed here and there. Fans hummed. Two ugly round fluorescent fixtures with concentric tubes buzzed overhead, throwing down cones of stark, greenish-white light, but the overall atmosphere was still gloomy. A lone window on the far side of the room was completely shrouded by light-tight curtains. Daylight was something to be managed.

Deming was seated at the far end of the workbench with Eric MacInnes's Gateway computer sandwiched between two huge, mismatched monitors. He had wispy black hair and high cheekbones that protruded too far from a pale and gaunt face. His skin seemed to be stretched a little too tight. His wrinkled chinos and clear-rimmed glasses fit the nerd profile, Brouillard noted. His starched blue dress shirt did not.

"So come over and sit down, O my savior," he said, pulling a second chair alongside his own and dusting off the seat with his shirtsleeve.

"For the record, I think we should just agree that you saved yourself," Brouillard replied.

"Yeah, yeah. Except for the fact that you told me what to say and when to say it."

"Well, then, it's our little secret." The truth was that Brouillard couldn't even remember the specifics of his drug bust, beyond the fact that he had been in the wrong place at the wrong time with a satchelful of someone else's goods: quantities sufficient to get him into some serious trouble. He had been overwhelmingly contrite and needed a break. She had given him one.

She draped her trench coat over the back of the empty chair and sat down. "So what can we learn from Eric MacInnes's computer?"

He looked sideways at her. "A lot. Or at least enough to make you want to learn more."

After an exchange of e-mails the day before, she had retrieved Eric's computer from Evidence and sent it over to Deming's shop. In a follow-up phone call, she had described to him the cast of characters and asked him to keep an eye out for anything out of the ordinary. If there were any Word documents, spreadsheets, or other files that didn't seem to be strictly routine, she wanted to know about it. If the computer had been tampered with in any way, she wanted to know about that. If he could retrieve anything that Eric might have tried to get rid of, she wanted to know about that, too.

To the side of the computer, she had taped a manila envelope, sealed with strapping tape, with Deming's name on it. Inside the envelope was a photocopy of the crumpled note from Eric's trash can. "You haven't seen this," she cautioned him on the phone. "But I want you to find it. And anything else that feels anything like it."

She knew she didn't have to tell him the rest of the things she was interested in: the great motivators of sex, money, and power. She knew she didn't have to ask him to review Eric's e-mail. He would do that as a matter of course.

Most of this work, especially the reviewing and sampling aspects, was far below his skill levels. In addition to being extremely systematic in his thinking, he had surprisingly good people instincts. He was at the same time nosy and discreet—two qualities that Brouillard rarely found in the same package. And, of course, he believed that he owed her big-time.

Deming now waved at his electronic array. "Basically," he said, "there's a couple of levels of intervention that are possible. I've done the easy stuff—top-level content and first-line technology tricks. You could dig a lot deeper on both fronts. On the content side, if you had a couple of days or weeks, you could read everything on his machine. That's not what you pay me for." It was a lame joke; she didn't pay him.

"On the technology side," he continued, "if you decide you want to go further, there's ways to do that, too. I could do some of it, but at some point I'd have to start charging you for it. There are other people out there who could go down even further, and they'd charge you way more than me. If you went that route, it would take time and it would get expensive. You're looking at a whole lot of ones and zeros. And at the end of the day, you might not learn anything more from them than I'm about to tell you."

"So tell me first what you've got, Art, and then we can talk about what else might be needed."

"Right, right," he said. "Getting ahead of myself, as usual. Okay. So, the first thing I did to Electronic Eric"—he nodded toward the machine—"was to check out his e-mail situation. I just did some sampling. Nothing much to report there. I printed you out a complete log, in and out, and also a representative batch of some incoming and outgoing. Long story short: He likes his family but doesn't go out of his way to hook up with them. He seems pretty tight with sister Libby. He has a pal with the lame screen name of 'downhilldave13740,' who comes to him courtesy of AOL, and who I take to be a guy who he's known forever. Maybe a drinking-buddy type, a ski bum, whatever. They confide in each other, but within solid guy boundaries. Eric complains to him that his finance elective is boring, worries that there's a little too much hair in the shower drain—that sort of stuff. Not a high emotional quotient."

Art, on a roll, moved along. "What else? He likes this woman Jeannette, but maybe not as much as she likes him—hey," he said, noticing Brouillard's raised eyebrow, "just a guess. Whatever. He bids on the occasional *tchotchke* on eBay, but good stuff—no junk. The average number of spammed e-mails slipped through his filters, including some pushing porno sites and member enlargers, but there's nothing to indicate that he's paid any money to slobber over or buy any kinky stuff.

"And his housekeeping isn't too great. There's quite a backlog—more than a thousand e-mails in each direction. So you can go back more than a year, if you're so inclined. I mostly sampled stuff that looked promising."

Brouillard quickly scanned the sheaf of printouts. Deming seemed to have summarized them accurately. On first blush, Eric appeared to be a careful and competent writer. No misused words. Very few typos, even on notes that appeared to be dashed off. Later she would work through this cache more carefully.

"What's your confidence level," she asked, "that you're seeing the whole volume, incoming and out-going?"

Again he shrugged. "Hard to say. I thought about that. There's little things that might raise a question. Like, sometimes there's days missing, and occasionally a whole week. But he could have been out of town; it could have been school vacation. You'd have to sync all that stuff up. And I didn't see any conversations with obvious holes in them. When he says, 'Got your note,' the note seems to be there. But no way did I match 'em up one-for-one. That's a drudge job, frankly—not my thing. And again, we're talking days to do it right."

"Let me ask it a different way. If messages had been deleted, could you tell? And could you reconstruct them?"

"The short answer is no. E-mails aren't saved as sepa-rate files. They're part of a database that's accessed by your e-mail program. When you dump data from a data-base, that information is gone. Period. It's like a sentence in the middle of a Word document—you decide you don't like it, and you delete it? It's gonzo. The document is there, but that little piece is gone."

"That's the short answer. What's the long answer?"

He smiled. "Yeah, well, I was pretty sure you'd ask.

The long answer is only a little better, for your purposes. The basic thing to remember is that there's more
than one machine involved when you do e-mail. Say
you send a message to your girlfriend. It goes to the out-
going mail server, which packages up the message and
sends it off to its destination. On the other end, you've
got your girlfriend's incoming mail server, which receives the message and delivers it to your girlfriend's
machine.

"Every server administrator configures their system
differently. But most systems are set up to keep a log of
the network traffic. On the other hand, they don't generally keep the body of the message you send to your girlfriend. Nobody wants all that junk lying around in their
systems. And anyway, there are some privacy issues,
right?

"But they *do* tend to keep track of the sender's name,
the recipient's name, the subject of the e-mail—assuming you bothered to write something on the subject line—
and the date and time you sent it."

"So," she interrupted, "I need a copy of the server's
log of e-mail to and from Eric. Which Harvard is supposed to be pulling together for me."

"Right. Well, you can bet that Harvard's intranet has
enough bells and whistles to give you at least the stuff I
mentioned. And at the same time, I'd bet that Mother
Harvard isn't storing private e-mail messages. Too
messy. Too many liberals and law school professors in
the neighborhood with time on their hands."

She pursued her own line of thought. "And then I sit
down and compare that log with these printouts, and see
if they match up."

"Well, yeah, but like I said, that's a truly crappy job.

Especially since this kid hasn't dumped much of anything for more than a year. Aren't there police cadets, or something like that, who you could hand this kind of stuff off to?"

"That would be nice," she said dryly. "What else? What about spreadsheets, Word files, and so on?"

"No spreadsheets, databases, or exotic stuff, beyond what he needed for school. I'm no expert, but I don't think he knew a spreadsheet from a bedsheet."

Nerd humor. She smiled. "So far, Art, you're not telling me much I don't already know."

"Yeah, but the best is yet to come. I went spelunking for that little 'tennis bubbles' note you sent over. And what do you know?" He paused for effect. "It wasn't there."

When she didn't respond, he continued. "Okay, not too surprising, right? You figure Eric writes it, prints it out, decides for whatever reason that it's a really bad idea, crumples it up, and deletes the file. What he doesn't know is that we can come along behind him and get it back."

"It's deleted, but it's not gone? How does that work?"

"Because he hasn't really deleted it. Word files are different from e-mails. They're actually pretty hard to get rid of. Of course, he could sit down and reformat his hard drive. That would get rid of the document more or less permanently. But it's also the most drastic way imaginable. It's like burning down your house to solve your cobweb problem. You basically only do that if you want to start life over again, and reload all your software, and re-create your Internet preferences, and so on, and so on. It's the get-a-new-life mode. Very bad.

"The other way to make a document go away

permanently," he went on, "is the way most of us do it—gradually. We just keep adding stuff to our hard drives, and sooner or later, the computer decides it needs that disk space that has a big 'Available' sign hanging over it, and overwrites it.

"So anyway"—he saw the impatient look on her face—"I ran a utility that looks for ghosts—the afterimages of deleted documents. That program turned up thirteen ghosts, including the one you were specifically interested in. I can call them up for you."

He pointed to the monitor closer to her. She watched as he clicked open a folder. She saw only a list: "Document 1," "Document 2," and so on, up to "Document 13."

"Again, most of these files aren't very interesting," he continued. "Schoolwork. Ho hum. Blah, blah, blah. Reminds me that I'm glad I never went to business school. I can print them out if you want. But Document 11 is the one you were looking for. There." He double-clicked. Up it came. "Same as the photocopy you sent over."

She could see that. "What do we know about when the document was created?"

"Unfortunately, nothing. Deleting the file doesn't necessarily get rid of it, but it usually strips the date and time stamps off. That's what it did in this case. Gonzo."

"Is Document 11 newer than, say, Document 10?"

"Not necessarily. Luck of the draw."

She pondered the screen for a minute. "So what you're telling me, Art, is that there's not much to learn here."

He grinned. "So far, all we've learned is that there's not much to learn from the tennis bubbles note. Which, as you say, I haven't seen. But there's one other thing." He pointed to the icon for the recycle bin. "Let's look in here and take a peek at the trash that he hasn't even bothered to take out of the house yet."

This time a series of Word and Excel icons came up. There appeared to be about two dozen of them. "Again," he said, "mostly boring stuff. Odd that he doesn't empty the trash for weeks on end, but I guess that's consistent with how he handles his e-mails. Memory is cheap, right? You get a big enough hard drive, and you're a low-level user, you almost never have to clear it out.

"This one here," he continued, tapping on an icon and talking a little faster, "this one I think you'll like." He dragged it onto the desktop and double-clicked to open it. "I printed you out a copy." He handed her a single sheet.

Interesting that you set yourself up as a knowitall, it began. The typeface and margins appeared to be the same as on the crumpled-up note. *When in fact you know almost nothing. It just means that you fall from a higher place when you fall. It means that those of us who you try to doninate and intimidate are less likely to reach out to you as you head for the rocks. Which your about to hit in a big way.*

"Ugh," Brouillard said.

"Yeah. Nice imagery from the pampered rich kid. And stay with me, because there's another little thing going on here."

She wanted to savor this new scrap—to roll it around in her mind, hold it up against its predecessor, probe for nuances. But Deming was opening something up on the other monitor.

"What we have here is the computer's operations log. You wouldn't have this on an older machine, or on a Mac.

Okay, so you and I are now officially glad that Bill Gates's dark legions out in Redmond don't have enough to do with their time, and that they keep adding all this unnecessary junk. And we're also glad that young Eric's family bought him the latest version of Windows, which includes this particular junk.

"Basically, this log tells you everything that's been done to this machine, dating back just about as far as you want to look. And trust me, I went back farther than you want to look. The interesting thing happens right here, right down at the end of the log."

He tapped the screen once again, like a geologist tapping a revealing seam in a rock face. "Somebody went in and changed the computer's clock. They backdated it a day. Then they reset it to show the right date again.

"Now, you have to ask yourself: Why would somebody want to do that? Somebody just playing around, to see how the date and time function works? Maybe. But not likely. It doesn't feel like our Eric, right? He's got better things to do with his time. He doesn't *do* housekeeping. And anyway, there's still more to this little mystery."

Deming, rolling out the details, was showing a little flair for the dramatic. And now, he knew, he had an attentive audience.

"What you discover when you line things up," he continued, pointing back to the monitor closest to her, "is that *that* little story, and *only* that little story, was written in the window created by the bogus time stamp."

Brouillard shook her head. "I'm sorry. Try it again."

"Okay," Deming replied. "It's Sunday night, 'long about midnight. Eric sits down at the keyboard. At twelve fourteen a.m., for reasons known only to himself, he changes the clock on his computer, turning Sunday into Saturday. He then writes his little haiku about Humpty Dumpty heading for the rocks, and saves it. Then he changes his mind about the whole thing and throws Humpty Dumpty in the trash. At twelve twenty-one a.m., he changes Saturday back into Sunday. And as usual, forgets to take out the garbage."

"And then," Brouillard said slowly, nose wrinkling, "he goes out and dies."

14

It was Vermeer's idea to meet at the Stockyard for lunch.

"Doesn't exactly strike me as your kind of place," Brouillard said skeptically on the phone.

"See how little you know about me?"

It was a former train station on the once-proud Boston & Albany's main line—an impressive heavy granite-and-sandstone Richardsonian edifice with lots of dark brown gingerbread, from back when railroads were the dot-com equivalent. Most of Boston's slaughterhouses, Vermeer had been told, used to be located in this vicinity. Cows came east in their boxcars, got off the train in what was then rural Brighton, and got turned into hamburgers.

The Stockyard had excellent hamburgers. It also had a kind of cheesy red-Naugahyde decor that appealed to Vermeer. And best of all, it was the kind of place where, despite being only a few miles from the Harvard Business School, you were absolutely guaranteed never to run into anybody from the Harvard Business School. Guys with thick necks, yes. Thoroughly guilty-looking couples, almost always. But never any senior professors of finance.

Brouillard was late but unapologetic. Sliding into the booth across from him, she looked more frazzled than usual. She took off her trench coat, *foof*ed her hair out of her eyes, and looked disapprovingly at Vermeer's beer.

"A little early in the day, don't you think?"

"In this place, a beer is simply camouflage. Helps you blend in. A mixed drink works even better."

"Not for me, thanks. I'm sometimes called upon to fire a weapon."

Waiting for their food, they made small talk. Occasionally a commuter train rumbled by, shaking the foundations of the building and releasing a few bubbles from Vermeer's beer. Brouillard told a colorful story, involving a container ship and one Tony "Carbine" Carbone, from her days in East Boston.

Vermeer couldn't think of anything comparable in his own background. So he challenged the detective to a game of snapshot.

"Don't know it."

"Easy. We pick someone nearby. But not so close that they can hear us. We each make up the guy's life story. Then we compare stories."

They agreed on a victim: a fleshy-looking character in his late fifties at the end of the bar. He looked prosperous but not healthy. His silver hair, combed straight back from his forehead, had an odd yellowish tinge. He was drinking shots.

"You're up first," Vermeer said.

"Okay." She thought for a minute. "His name is Joseph D. Whitelawn. He wants to be called Joseph, or at least Joe, but everyone in the world calls him 'Whitey.' It bugs him. He was born and raised in the D Street projects. Comes from a family of six kids; on-again, off-again father. Fell in with a bad crowd. Did just enough time to scare himself straight. His family pulled some strings in their state senator's office and got him a job with the Edison. Been there ever since. Started on a line crew thirty years ago, and now he supervises a couple of line crews. Except that they don't really need much supervision from the likes of Whitey. He doesn't bother them; they don't bother him. Three years from retirement, and counting the days."

Vermeer was impressed. "Excellent. But no. In fact, his name is Michael Maffeo. He tries to get people to put the accent on the second syllable, but everybody calls him 'Mike Mafia.' Which is completely unfair, because in fact he's an aluminum-siding salesman from Fitchburg, with almost no connections of any kind, good or bad. He used to have a couple of strong commercial accounts in this neighborhood, and he started bringing customers here twenty years ago. It got to be a habit. He's nervous about using the company card for a liquid lunch, but so far, nobody in Accounting has objected, so he's still doing it. He doesn't like the way the neighborhood around here seems to be heading. Too upscale. Too much glass and brick. Not enough siding."

They played a few more rounds as they ate their hamburgers. Brouillard's characterizations always drifted into life on the edge of the law, although usually with some kind of redemption involved. Vermeer's characters were all strivers, salesmen, ladder climbers. He didn't redeem any of them.

"Okay, time to talk business," Brouillard said, signaling the end of the game as their coffee arrived.

"That's what this place is all about. Here, even love is business."

"Right. So tell me what you learned down in New York City." She took out her notepad and pencil.

Vermeer gave her a brief rundown of his visit to 343 Atwater. There wasn't much to tell, he admitted. He described Ellie Donahue and Dan Beyer. He described the passkey security system. He described Libby MacInnes's room, its lone knickknack, its high-powered computer setup. And he described the fury on Dan Beyer's face when he caught an intruder in Miss Libby's private bedroom.

"Interesting," Brouillard responded, jotting some notes. "So she knows her way around computers. The systems looked like they might be used to run a business?"

"Just a guess. In any case, there was way more there than you'd need to order stuff from L.L. Bean online or look up nursing trivia."

"And you have no idea what the award was all about?"

"None. The something-something recognizes Libby and the something-something for all their good work."

She sighed and tapped the rubber end of her pencil, slowly but forcefully, on her pad. "These are the kinds of details you're supposed to pay attention to. They may be important."

"Well, I was going to write them down. Then I got interrupted by a mountain on its way to being a volcano."

She snapped her notepad shut and reburied it in her oversize bag. "Well, under those circumstances, I guess I can't blame you." She paused as the waitress refilled her coffee cup. "So now what? You're heading for the hills?"

"Tomorrow. I'm driving Eric's car and some knickknacks back to the country house. In a town called Middleford, somewhere out west of Albany."

"What time are they expecting you?"

"Midafternoon. It's about a five-hour drive."

"If you're willing, I want you to do something for me out there."

"Okay. What?"

"I want you to have a conversation with a guy who lives in the same town—Middleford. His name is Dave Westerling. A pal of Eric's who turned up on Eric's computer. Here's the info."

Vermeer looked at the page, obviously torn from one of Brouillard's notepads and written out for his benefit. Name, phone number, and screen name. "AOL nickname downhilldave13740," he read out loud. "You wouldn't think that there were 13,000 guys out there who wanted to call themselves 'downhilldave.' "

"There aren't. That's a zip code. Middleford."

"Huh. Your powers of deduction at work?"

"Yeah, that," she said. "Plus, he was in Eric's address book. Plus, it's the same zip code that shows up on Eric's checkbook, bank statement, passport, and so on. Middleford seems to be one of those little towns they own out there."

15

Brouillard STOOD MORE OR LESS HALFWAY ACROSS the broad span of the Lars Anderson Bridge, leaning against the chest-high wide concrete sidewall and looking over the edge. The streetlights on the bridge didn't cut very far into the winter darkness. She suppressed a shiver. *Yeah, it's cold up here in the wind,* she scolded herself. *And it's a hell of a lot colder down there.*

The vista below her had a ghostly, otherworldly quality. The ice on the Charles River was translucent rather than transparent. The flashlights of the divers below it sent out cones of light that the slow-moving water beneath the ice grabbed and distorted, then briefly set free, and then distorted again.

The divers had slithered their way out onto the ice from the Harvard boathouse on the Cambridge side. Jurisdictional issues would be addressed later. For the moment, the Metropolitan District Commission police, who in warm weather patrolled these waters in high-speed powerboats, were working with the staties, with Cambridge and Boston (including herself) just as happy to watch from the sidelines.

As a result, much of what Brouillard knew came third-hand. The state police sergeant in charge of the scene, recognizing "Ms. Biz," had taken a few minutes to brief her. Apparently, Jeannette Bartlett had left the Cambridge bar by herself shortly before midnight. She had seemed increasingly disconnected and subdued in the previous day or days; her friends had decided to take her out to get her mind off her troubles. Yes, some drinking ensued, but not so much that anyone's judgment was impaired. Not so much that anyone worried about Bartlett walking back across the river by herself.

Three hours earlier—at exactly 12:16 a.m., according to a passing motorist with a digital clock readout—the dark form that shouldn't have been perched on the bridge wall midspan suddenly stopped perching there. Yes, he might have had a few pops himself, but not so much that he wasn't aware that something *odd* had just happened. He put his flashers on and pulled over. He found a wallet and a woman's wristwatch on the cold concrete surface.

He looked over the edge, more or less as Brouillard was doing now, and saw a hole in the ice. He dialed 911. Several police forces arrived; he told his story a dozen times—no, he hadn't touched either the wallet or the watch; did they think he was *stupid?*—and was finally allowed to head home, with the promise of more interrogations to follow. People wearing plastic gloves examined the wallet, which turned out to belong to one Jeannette Bartlett.

Brouillard guessed that unless the divers got real lucky, unless the body had snagged on some obstacle near where it had slammed its way through the ice, Bartlett would not be found until the ice broke up in the next thaw. Right now, that increasingly rigid mass might be only ten or twenty feet away from the wet-suited divers. Or it might be well on its way to the dam down by the Museum of Science. A messy case. Brouillard sighed. Like a sword hanging over the head of the MDC police. All you could hope was that *you* found the body, rather than some family of tourists picnicking on the Esplanade in May.

"*You* did this."

She had assumed that the dark form approaching purposefully from the Cambridge side of the river was some sort of cop, since it was well within the cordoned-off perimeter. But now she recognized the gait and voice of James MacInnes. He had on a down coat but no other winter gear.

"You're not supposed to be here, Mr. MacInnes. This is a crime scene. You need to get back behind the yellow tape. Better yet, you should go home."

He was flexing his bare hands. It didn't look as though he was doing so to keep his fingers warm. "You're damn right it's a crime scene. A crime committed by *you*." He came closer, index finger jabbing toward her chest.

Not giving ground, she watched the finger. "Mr. MacInnes, you don't want to get any closer to me. And you certainly don't want to lay that finger on me. If you do, you're going to get a free ride in one of those patrol cars. And they won't be taking you anyplace you want to go."

"Oh, yeah, you're tough, all right," he snarled, now stopping short. "You're especially tough on young women who can't defend themselves from your assaults."

Of course, the thought had occurred to her. Standing in this biting and unforgiving wind, exhausted enough to let her mind wander, she had already replayed the encounter in Shad many times over, wondering whether her questions had helped push Bartlett to this miserable end. But she didn't want to hear the same possibility raised by the likes of James MacInnes.

"Judging from those bruises on your wife's wrist, Mr. MacInnes," she said evenly, "I would have said that assaulting young women was your specialty."

"Who the *fuck*—"

"Shut up and listen to me very carefully," she interrupted, loud enough to get his attention but not loud enough to further fuel the fire. "You've now accused me three times of causing Jeannette Bartlett to do this to herself. I don't like it. In fact, it really pisses me off. So if I hear it from your rich-boy mouth one more time, I'm going to put a pair of handcuffs on your rich-boy wrists and run your rich-boy ass in on a spousal abuse charge. And Massachusetts takes that kind of thing very seriously. Okay, so maybe the charge won't stick. But it will take days to sort it all out. I can guarantee that.

"So get off my bridge," she concluded. "Now."

Now the cold seemed to be catching up with him. He shoved his fists into his coat pockets and hunched his shoulders to cover his neck. But another kind of cold was coming out of his eyes. She could feel it washing over her, challenging her, on its way to the frozen ground.

"Captain Brouillard," he said, just before turning on his heels, "you don't have the slightest idea who you're dealing with."

16

THE FIVE-HOUR RIDE OUT FROM BOSTON WAS UNEVENT-ful, but only because Vermeer had resisted his impulse to put the car through its paces.

The Acura NSX, teal green, with two seats and an excess of swooping body angles, was unlike anything Vermeer had ever driven. The dings and scrapes in its fiberglass body were merely protective coloring: This was more a projectile than a car.

The car's true nature began to become clear in the Business School parking lot, when he happened to glance at its overwide tires. No treads. Then there was the front seat, which urged you into a semirecumbent position. And once ignited, the car made two noises at once: a throb and a whine. When you stepped on the gas, the throb got bigger and the whine got higher. And because the engine was right behind you, almost square in the middle of the car, it seemed to be taunting you, behind your back. Egging you on.

Turning left onto Western Avenue and tapping the accelerator just a little too heavily, Vermeer learned what the no-tread tires were all about. They allowed the car to talk back from street level: *Really? You want to do that? Well, okay.* On the next right-hand curve, he tromped on the gas pedal going into the turn. Centrifugal forces mushed him against the driver's door. The car hugged the pavement.

Several miles later, as he reached up far above his head to pull his ticket out of the machine at the Mass Pike tollbooth, he was reminded that his butt was only inches above the road surface. And well before the Newton exit, he found out how quickly this car could hit 120. He now understood the voice behind him: *The faster you go, the happier I am.*

And that was when Vermeer decided that he wouldn't get into a conversation with this car. His quick riffle through the minuscule glove compartment before blastoff had turned up no registration papers. Although the registration tag on the New York license plate was current, the inspection sticker on the windshield had expired months earlier. Vermeer imagined explaining the whole messy situation—dead rich kid, Harvard, and so on—to the state trooper who flagged him down doing 120 through the moneyed western suburbs.

Reluctantly he slowed down. He had had a motorcycle once that talked to him in the same kinds of ways. He had finally had to get rid of it.

Mr. Ralph had not seemed surprised or even particularly interested that Vermeer would be driving the Acura to New York State himself. It would be no problem, he said on the phone in his abstemious way, to get Vermeer to the Albany airport afterward. From there he could catch a flight back to Boston. Given the distances involved, however, Vermeer should plan on spending the night at the estate. "As for getting here, I'll fax you a map and written directions," he continued. "My understanding is that Master Eric's car isn't particularly well suited to winter driving. But the roads here are clear, and I believe the weather looks good for the next several days. So we will expect you the day after tomorrow—say, midafternoon—unless we hear otherwise from you."

Vermeer figured out the cruise control, set the Acura at a boring seventy-two, and settled down into his leather hammock. He remembered Mr. Ralph's mixed assessment of the car three hours later, when he turned off the thruway and headed west on Route 23. This was an old two-lane state highway that soon attacked the eastern flanks of the Catskills. Although the road was bare, there were patches of dirty snow in the shady gullies of the road cuts, and—toward the tops of the mountains—bigger and cleaner white patches in the woods. No, he thought; you wouldn't take this car, with its treadless tires, oversize engine, and racing transmission, over these mountains in a snowstorm.

Gradually, the landscape settled down again, although the road never quite gave back the altitude it had captured over the previous twenty miles. The tourist traps and three-state views disappeared. The radio stopped playing Top 40 rock; it was now dominated by country music and white evangelicals. Pickups and SUVs now populated used-car lots. Slowly, the scrubby and overgrown fields of eastern New York gave way to working farms— mostly dairy, Vermeer guessed, judging from the occasional black-and-white herd huddled together in the corners of frozen fields, using one another as shelter against the winter wind. Now and then, a gray-sided barn, complete with vented cupola and green-copper rooster weather vane, pushed up to the very edge of the blacktop.

The town of Middleford believed in marketing. A roadside sign on the edge of town described Middleford as A GREAT PLACE TO LIVE. In smaller letters, the sign claimed a population of 8,240. A second sign, partially obscured, pointed out that the posted speed limit was thirty. Vermeer slowed to what felt like a throbbing, rumbling standstill.

The farms stopped and the town started. Middleford was all of about ten blocks long, perched alongside and only slightly above a fast-moving river, which in this season had fringes of thick ice along its banks. There wasn't much traffic, and there were no parking problems. *Middle-ford,* Vermeer thought to himself. No doubt there was a Northford and a Southford, or maybe an Eastford and a Westford, somewhere on this river. Today, of course, there were bridges. But in its day this little river had been a formidable obstacle to commerce. There had been ferries and tolls. There had been frustrations and fatalities.

On the far side of the river, away from the town, a single set of train tracks hugged the riverbank—the MacInnes Railroad? Up from the river and the tracks rose a small mountain, the town-facing side of which had been denuded of its trees to create a short but very steep ski run. Those who ventured down that slope, Vermeer guessed, didn't worry much about finesse. They worried about stopping.

Town Hall was an ornate, late-nineteenth-century affair, cream colored, with lots of heavy black trim and the date "1887" prominently displayed in black wrought-iron letters just below the peak of the roof. Two doors down, the Middleford Cinema appeared to be permanently closed. THA K YOU FO YOUR PATRONAGE, read the remaining letters on the marquee.

The Rope Toe Café, on the far side of town, wasn't

difficult to find. Even in midafternoon in the middle of the week, the bar was the biggest draw in Middleford. A nondescript one-story structure, it was surrounded on three sides by unlined blacktop, with its fourth side backing up against the river. A large rooftop exhaust pipe toward the rear of the building, listing to one side but propped up by numerous homemade braces, emitted a plume of heavy-looking smoke. More than half the vehicles in the parking lot were pickups, many sporting multiple bruises. These were work vehicles: in their scraped-up and dented beds, they carried scraps of lumber, or locked-down tool chests, or hay bales, or cinder blocks, or portable generators. Feeling conspicuous, Vermeer parked the Acura between two of them. He locked the car—understanding that this was a silly habit of the city—and moved quickly down the long sidewalk to get out of the greasy wind.

Inside, though, the same grease hung in the air undisturbed. So did the ripe smell of beer spilled long ago and never quite cleaned up. A massive carved wooden bar ran almost the full length of the building, its impact doubled by a wall of mirrors behind it. The bar, Vermeer thought, was probably worth more than the building. There was a brass rail near the floor, but no stools. Several dozen men, and here and there a woman, stood in knots along the bar. Almost all were dressed in some combination of jeans, quilted vests, flannel shirts, and muddy work boots. Bud, in bottles, was the beverage of choice at the Rope Toe.

Several patrons looked over their shoulders to check out the new arrival; not recognizing him, they went back to socializing. A dusty deer's head mounted above the mirrors trained its glassy eyes on the far wall. On one antler hung a Yankees baseball cap.

A piece of floor space adjacent to the bar was reserved for a heavy-looking pool table, its green felt surface, not currently in use, brightly lit by a low-hanging fluorescent fixture. Beyond that was an even larger space, empty at the moment. Vermeer guessed it might be used for dancing and, sometimes, fighting. And around the edges of the room were about a dozen sturdy-looking picnic tables, covered by red-and-white-checkered plastic tablecloths. The tables came equipped with bolted-on benches. In the whole place, there wasn't a stick of furniture that was available for throwing. The ketchup, the salt, and the pepper were served up in plastic bottles.

At one table at the far end of the room sat a youngish-looking man in a plaid flannel shirt. He nodded and beckoned Vermeer with two fingers crooking in tandem.

"Hi. Dave Westerling. You'll excuse me if I don't get all the way up," he said, half rising and extending a hand. "Once you get parked on one of these benches, you tend to stay put."

"Wim Vermeer. Nice to meet you." Vermeer sat sidesaddle on the facing bench, then swung his legs into position under the table. The goal was to avoid hooking the checked tablecloth and bringing the cluster of plastic bottles into your lap.

"Welcome to Middleford and the Rope Toe. Rustic, sure, but the best beer in town."

Ironic but not nasty, Vermeer decided, scrutinizing his tablemate. Up close, Westerling looked even younger than he had first appeared—barely twenty, it seemed. He had big shoulders attached to muscled arms, light brown hair, and a wide-open face. As he folded his arms on the table, Vermeer sneaked a look at his hands. Like the trucks outside, these were country hands: callused, banged, bruised. At the moment, they were nursing a Bud.

"I'm told that a Bud is a Bud, everywhere in the world," Vermeer replied.

"True. Except in Germany, where Budweiser is actually a type of beer," Westerling said with a slight smile. "In fact, Eric told me that."

The bartender sidled over. He had an aggressively low hairline, which pointed down at the center, toward his eyebrows. His three-quarter-length white apron was clean except at waist level, where it rubbed against the back edge of the bar. At that latitude, there was a broad gray smudge. "What'll it be?"

"Bud," said Vermeer.

"Dave? You fixed?"

"All set for now, Nick." Nick nodded and withdrew.

"Thanks for agreeing to meet with me on such short notice," Vermeer said, not sure where to begin.

"I should be thanking you. When you called, I realized that I really wanted to talk to somebody about Eric. He and I were close."

"I know." Although he was under orders not to say *how* he knew. He had a fib prepared, if necessary, but Westerling didn't ask. "How long had you known him?"

"Most of my life. My family used to have a dairy farm on the Delphi Turnpike—the last turnoff on the right before you get to the MacInnes place, coming from this direction. I'm sure if you looked back a few generations, you'd find that my family worked for Eric's family. Maybe they were even indentured servants. It goes back that far, I think."

"So you and Eric played together as kids?"

Westerling smiled. He began slowly shredding the

label on his beer bottle. "You mean, like two kids on the same block in the suburbs? Not quite. The distances were a little too far. And the MacInneses don't mingle much. And you don't exactly ride your bike over to the MacInneses' house and ask if Eric can come out to play.

"So, no, I didn't play with him like normal kids play. They had a cook named Ellie—a real nice old Irish lady, big as a boat—who believed in the curative powers of unpasteurized milk. Sounds quaint today, with all the hoopla about mad cows and salmonella and hoof-and-mouth. But she'd bring a five-gallon tin over to our milking parlor and sweet-talk my dad into selling some milk to her, fresh from the holding tank, before the company truck came to take it away. Looking back, I suppose she paid good cash money for that milk, since my dad was always glad to see her coming. To a farmer in these parts, cash money is gold.

"Anyway. Sometimes she'd bring along this little pudgy kid. He'd hide behind her skirts and refuse to make eye contact with anybody. That was Eric. Eventually, somebody decided that Eric needed some exposure to kids his own age. They would send a car for me. A big old black Lincoln. God, I remember scrubbing myself with a bristle brush on the days when I knew that car was coming, trying to get the smell of cow shit off of me."

"What was it like, going over there? Did you have fun once you got there?"

"I never had so much fun in my life," Westerling replied. The pleasure of the recollection shone from his eyes. "You haven't seen the place yet? Well, when you do, imagine seeing it through the eyes of an eight-year-old. It was like Disneyland and *The Addams Family*, all rolled into one.

"The four of us—Eric, James, Libby, and me—we'd go exploring in the attics of the mansion. Sometimes, if we thought we wouldn't get caught, we'd ride bikes in the ballroom, scuffing up the floor something terrible, leaving black skid marks. Or we'd play in the carriage house. Which, by the way, was still full of antique carriages last time I looked, probably worth a fortune all by themselves. In the summer we'd swim or go fishing in the lake, which they used to stock with trout each spring—and still do, for all I know. In the winter we'd ride their Flexible Flyer sleds down their driveway, which seemed to go downhill forever. And of course there'd be a truck idling at the gatehouse, waiting to pick us up.

"And sooner or later, some servant would show up with a tray of goodies. Hot chocolate in the winter, lemonade in the summer. Fresh-baked cookies. Ladyfingers, with a little crust of sugar on top. Have you ever had a fresh-baked ladyfinger?" He smiled at the memory. "So yes, Professor Vermeer, I loved going over to Eric's house. It was our very own theme park, right here in Middleford. And kids like me never got to go to theme parks."

"Did you go to school with him?"

"No way. The MacInnes kids all had tutors when they were young. Then, one by one, they went off to boarding schools—first Eric, then James, then Libby. Meanwhile, I was getting on the big yellow school bus every day and heading off to the local elementary school. Then the regional schools. I lost touch with Eric for a couple of years in there, somewhere during middle school.

"We hooked up again a few years ago. By then, of course, things were very different between us. He wasn't the pudgy, shy kid anymore. He had slimmed down, shaped up, seen the world. Drunk Budweiser in Berlin, and so on. Meanwhile, I was still the hick from the small town."

"But you still had enough in common? Despite the changes?"

Now a guarded look came into Westerling's eyes. "Well, for sure, we had plenty of memories. And I think as Eric started to understand his, uhm, unusual place in the world, he tended to circle back to the few people who knew him and loved him for himself, way back when. Before the money and the power meant so much. And it didn't take him long to circle back to me. Because there weren't very many of us, frankly. Poor little rich kid, in a sense. So he taught me things. I reminded him of things. Maybe I taught him things."

The small red and silver shreds of the beer bottle's label were piling up in a small mound below his fingers. Vermeer wasn't sure where to go next. A random image of Barbara Brouillard, scribbling on one of her ever-present notepads, came into his mind. "Did you ever meet his girlfriend?"

"Girlfriend?" Westerling's face was blank.

"Jeannette Bartlett. His classmate from Harvard."

"Oh. Well, sure, I know Jeannette." He put a little extra emphasis on her name. "She came out here once with him. And we had dinner together a couple of times when I visited Eric in Boston."

"I had the impression that they might be planning to get married, after business school."

Westerling pushed some stray label bits back toward the main pile. "Well, that would have surprised me."

"Why?"

"Because I wouldn't have guessed Eric to be the marrying type. James, yeah. Libby, for sure. Not Eric."

Again, Vermeer wasn't sure where to go next. He decided to push a little harder. "I have to ask you a tough question. Back in Boston there's some sense that Eric may have been very unhappy during the last couple of months. The police seem to think that he may have killed himself, or at least put himself in harm's way."

Westerling exhaled slowly, through pursed lips, making his cheeks puff out briefly. "Well, if that's what they're thinking, I'd say that they're way off base."

"You think he was reasonably happy?"

"I don't think he had ever been happier, at least since he was a kid."

"You sound pretty sure of that."

"I am sure of that."

"Why?"

"Because he *told* me, in so many words," Westerling said a little curtly. "As recently as a week or two ago. We talked on the phone. He had come to terms with a lot of things, starting with himself. He felt he had paid his dues. He had lived up to everyone's expectations of him. He was prepared to take control of his life, live it on his own terms. He talked about moving to California, starting over. He even asked me if I wanted to go along."

"And you said no?"

"I said no."

"Why?"

"Because it wasn't *real*. Although of course Eric wouldn't have thought in these terms. Trust funds are portable. My life isn't."

"How do you mean?"

Westerling sighed. "Okay. You really want to know?

Two years ago my father had a bad stroke. A real bad stroke. He's in a local nursing home, more or less paralyzed. We sold the farm, but the proceeds weren't enough to keep his bills paid and support my mother at the same time. I'm their only child. So I'm needed to stay here and keep an eye on things. And chip in when I can. End of story."

"What do you do here? What's your job, I mean?"

"I work at the Agway. This time of year, I sell bags of feed to those guys at the bar. In planting season, I sell them seeds. In growing season, I deliver liquid fertilizer to them, and sometimes even apply it if they ask me to. I do some contract pesticide work when something gets out of control. I moonlight a lot.

"And just so you understand," Westerling continued in a flat tone, "I count my blessings, in part because my crappy job comes with health insurance. It's one of the few jobs around here that does. And I count my blessings because my boss is clever enough to let me duck out for a few hours on a slow February afternoon to talk to some professor from out of town who I describe as being in tight with the legendary MacInnes family. Which might somehow be good for business, although he can't quite figure out how."

Nick approached the table again. He looked disapprovingly at Westerling's scrap pile and then at Vermeer's bottle, which Vermeer had barely touched. Without even slowing down, he swung a wide arc back to where the customers were drinking—and paying.

This time, Vermeer didn't attempt to break the silence.

"You know," Westerling finally said, looking sideways out the window, "you're not at all what I expected."

"What did you expect?"

"I guess I expected a little more . . . insight. Sorry. But I thought you and Eric were close at one point."

"I was his favorite teacher last year. At least according to his mother."

"I thought you were closer than that."

Now it was Vermeer's turn to be baffled. "Did Eric tell you that?"

"No. Eric was never comfortable talking in those terms."

"So who did? Who was?"

"Does it matter, Professor Vermeer? If it's not true, it's not true. And I could tell the minute you walked through that door that it wasn't true. So why don't we just let it go at that?"

17

THE MATCHED GRANITE OBELISKS, EIGHT FEET TALL AND more than two feet across, with pointed caps, were more than up to the task of supporting the pair of massive iron gates that spanned the driveway leading to the MacInnes estate.

The gates were painted in high-gloss black. When closed, as they were now, they defined a classic bell curve: low toward the edges and tracing a steep curve up to the peak, where they met. In the dead center of each gate was a large gilded "M."

It reminded Vermeer of a high-end cemetery.

The slate-roofed gatehouse to the right of the driveway, which straddled a heavy fence, was unattended. Vermeer sat behind the wheel of Eric's Acura, waiting for something to happen.

Nothing happened.

There didn't seem to be a doorbell. He decided that he wasn't getting out into the bitter afternoon wind any sooner than he had to. He honked once, politely. Nothing happened. But no particular rush: The car had a powerful heater and bun warmers.

Finally, there was some activity in the driveway, uphill from the gate. A small white pickup truck turned the last bend, going a little too fast, and came to an abrupt halt next to the piece of the gatehouse that was safely inside the fence. A man in a heavy knee-length coat got out, held up a gloved index finger to Vermeer—*one minute!*—and ducked into the building. Slowly the big, black gates opened inward.

The attendant reappeared and hurried over to the Acura. Vermeer lowered the window. "Sorry, Professor Vermeer," he said breathlessly, taking off his right glove and extending his hand. "Patrique Talley." Pronouncing his first name, he put the accent on the second syllable and rolled the "r" a little bit. "We expected you earlier. Mr. Ralph figured that you must have changed your plans. When it gets this cold, we usually close the gatehouse in the late afternoon and bring the guard up the hill."

"So what does the pizza guy do?"

Talley, who looked to be in his late twenties or early thirties and sported a thin Gallic mustache, missed a beat. Then he chuckled. "Well, eventually he realizes he's got the wrong house. And then he goes away.

"No, seriously," he continued, as if he didn't want to leave misinformation floating in the air. "Usually we monitor the gate from the house, when we're not down here in person. But we're a little understaffed today. That's why we didn't spot you. Why don't you follow my truck? The driveways can be a little confusing, if you haven't been here before."

It was a steady climb through manicured woods. The Acura complained noisily about the slow pace, growling to be let loose. "No chance," Vermeer said out loud to the car, breaking his no-conversation vow. Dusk was gathering. Here and there an unmarked road dipped off to the left or right. As the minutes went by, Vermeer was increasingly glad that he had a guide. He expected each turn to reveal a building, but the turns kept coming, each presenting more forested hillsides. Now and then the occasional antique stone wall, blotchy with lichen and moss, ran alongside the road, suggesting that there had once been farms and fields here.

Finally, after what must have been more than a mile, the MacInnes mansion came into view. Looked at a little sideways in the twilight, lights ablaze on three levels, it could have been a small passenger liner afloat on a great gray ocean of lawn. Turrets and towers poked up as silhouettes against the sky. It was impossible from this distance to see exactly where the ends of the building were.

Talley drove under a stone porte cochere and pulled over, motioning for Vermeer to do the same. Up close, the house turned out to be an immense pile of cut red sandstone, with occasional punctuations of granite. Up close, it looked even bigger than it had from a distance. There was a focused kind of echo under the stone overhang when they closed their car doors.

"You need help with your bags?"

"It's just this one. I can manage, thanks." Feeling both relief and reluctance, he handed over the keys to the Acura.

Talley pushed open an ornately carved front door— heavy, judging from the way he leaned into it— and waved Vermeer inside. Vermeer's first impression of the front hallway was that he had walked into an oak cathedral: oak floors, oak-paneled walls, oversize oak furniture. It was an enormous vaulted space, rising several stories toward what appeared to be a skylight far overhead. A massive staircase yawned open at the right side of the foyer, ascending a few steps to a landing the size of Vermeer's kitchen, then turning again to begin the climb to the second floor. The same thing appeared to happen at least twice more in the darkish regions far above them.

Everywhere along the paneled walls—on the main floor, up the staircase, and as far above as Vermeer could see—hung oil portraits, ranging from large to immense. Many had small lamps at the tops of their frames. These lamps, already lit—or constantly lit? Vermeer wondered—provided islands of light in this great, dark, mock-Gothic space. Here and there, Vermeer thought he spotted a portrait that bore more than a passing resemblance to William MacInnes.

"Ah. Professor Vermeer. We had nearly given up on you." Mr. Ralph's flat tones came from the far end of the entrance hall. He crossed the room almost noiselessly, accompanied by a younger man who walked a few steps behind him. When Mr. Ralph slowed down, so did his shadow. Vermeer guessed that this was a Mr. Ralph in training: succession planning at the MacInnes estate.

"Sorry to be late. It was a little tough getting out of Boston, and I decided that I should drive within the speed limits." And, there was that little off-the-itinerary stop at the Rope Toe.

"The car didn't give you any trouble, I hope?"

As if on cue, the Acura came roaring to life outside, although its throbbing din was now much reduced by the great stone barrier of the mansion's walls.

"No. Although it did tempt me."

"As it tempted Master Eric, I'm sure." Mr. Ralph paused, then gestured at his shadow. "This is Benton. He'll show you to your room. We've put you on the lake side, although I'm afraid there's not much to see so late in the afternoon." He glanced at a nearby grandfather clock. "It's now five fifteen. Dinner is served at seven in the dining room. Mrs. MacInnes hopes that you'll dine with the family."

"It would be my pleasure."

"Excellent. It's that door, over there." He gestured. "Mr. MacInnes will be wearing a jacket but not a tie. And now I will leave you in Benton's most capable hands."

———————

Benton deposited him in the second-floor suite almost silently. He insisted on putting Vermeer's overnight bag on a folding furniture rack, like an ambitious bellboy, but he did not pause to be tipped. On his way out the door, he pointed at a call button. "Please do ring if you need anything," he said in a passable monotonic imitation of Mr. Ralph.

Even in the now dim twilight, Vermeer could see the benefits of a room "on the lake side." The mansion was startlingly close to the lake; in fact, one wing off to the left, supported by a system of trusses, appeared to be straddling a small inlet. Judging from the nearly dark sky outside his window, Vermeer guessed that he was facing more or less east. So the sun would rise over those MacInnes hills on the far side of the lake, then illuminate the peaks and parapets of the MacInnes mansion, and then make its way down to the MacInnes lake. Where, depending on the season, it would either make the MacInnes ice glisten or warm the blood of the MacInnes trout.

Vermeer snooped long enough to get a feel for the amenities extended to MacInnes guests. Satellite TV.

High-speed Internet access. The furniture was high end but definitely not heirloom quality. The bathroom boasted an impressive array of soaps, shampoos, slippers, hair dryers, shower caps, and shoeshine and sewing kits. It felt less like a home and more like the Four Seasons—and to some extent it probably was a place of business. He checked for a monogram on the plush white terry cloth bathrobe that hung on the back of the bathroom door. There it was, on the left breast pocket: a miniature reproduction of the black "M" from the front gates.

He showered, puttered, and channel-surfed until it was time for dinner. At 6:55, he made his way back down the grand staircase, wondering how this cavernous space with all its hard surfaces managed to absorb noise. Where there should have been ricocheting echoes, there was only silence.

The dining room door was ajar. Light was spilling out into the dim hallway. He wondered if he should knock, then decided that he had already been invited. He pushed the door open.

"Professor Vermeer," said Elizabeth MacInnes, from what sounded like a great distance. "How good of you to join us for dinner."

The family—father, mother, and daughter—was clustered at the far end of an endless mahogany table with at least a dozen chairs lining each of its sides. William MacInnes sat at the head, with Elizabeth to his left and Libby to his right. Two matching chandeliers hung from the twenty-foot ceiling, casting down dim pools of light. The room carried forward the decor of the front hallway and stairwell: oak everything, and oil paintings of MacInnes forebears—almost all men, looking more or less dour.

William MacInnes nodded heavily and waved his hand at the empty seat next to Libby. Libby, wearing a skirt and sweater but otherwise looking frumpy and ill at ease, extended her hand as Vermeer sat down. "Nice to see you again," she said. She didn't sound as if she meant it.

"Thank you for having me," he said, addressing himself to Elizabeth. Again he was struck by her immaculate silver-haired facade and her regal bearing. He wondered, irrelevantly, where someone like William MacInnes went looking for a wife when the appointed time came.

"Well, we do appreciate your help in this difficult period." She appeared far more alert than she had in Boston. She picked up a small silver bell and rang it gently. A door swung open, and a sixtyish woman in a black uniform and white apron came in carrying a silver tray with four soup bowls.

"I hope you like pea soup, Professor Vermeer," rumbled William MacInnes.

"I do, sir," Vermeer replied. He hated the stuff.

"Good winter fare. Sticks with you."

"Absolutely." He was served third, after the two women. Just looking at the filled-to-the-brim bowl of thick green goo made his stomach flop. Gamely he picked up his soupspoon. The spoon was very heavy.

"Thank you, Mrs. Talley," Elizabeth said. "Give us a few minutes; then feel free to bring the main course whenever you're ready."

"Yes, ma'am. Thank you." The servant disappeared through the swinging door.

"Mrs. Talley," Vermeer repeated out loud, delaying the inevitable plunge of the spoon. "Any relation to Patrique?"

"She's his mother," said Libby, who didn't appear to like pea soup, either.

"Interesting."

"It's actually not that unusual," Libby continued. "There aren't all that many jobs in Middleford and the other towns around here. We don't pay much, and the benefits are lousy, but it's steady work."

William cleared his throat and glared at his daughter. "If you please, Libby," he said. "You're really not in a position to assess the pros and cons of serving on our staff."

"Well, respectfully, Father, I think I am."

"We'll agree to disagree, then. But the truth is, my girl, that even the MacInnes family can't suspend the laws of economics. If people choose to work here, they obviously think that's in their best interest."

Libby had defiance all over her face, but seemed to choose her words carefully. "If you own the only gas station in town, Father, you can charge pretty much what you want for a gallon of gas. And if you have the only payroll in town, you can pay as little as you want."

"Oh, please, Libby. This isn't the only payroll, and payrolls aren't the only option. And even if one insists on joining a payroll, there are lots of other places in the world to find one."

Elizabeth broke into the conversation like a linebacker. "Mr. Ralph tells me, Professor Vermeer, that your drive was uneventful."

"Yes, ma'am, it was. And I've never seen this part of New York before, so it was quite an interesting ride. I was quite glad that it wasn't snowing, coming over those mountains."

The rest of the dinner proceeded along these lines. Father and daughter disagreed urgently on issues that neither seemed to be passionate about, and Mother monitored the low-grade combat, occasionally swooping in. Daughter drained her wineglass several times. Vermeer made small talk with Mother, struggling first with his soup and then with a beef stroganoff that seemed to be made mostly of mushrooms, another least-favorite food. Mrs. Talley came and went, speaking only when spoken to. She looked surprised when Vermeer asked if she had made the lemon meringue pie that she sliced and served from a massive carved sideboard.

"Oh, no, sir," she replied. "The pastry chef made it. This afternoon."

Finally, William MacInnes signaled the end of dinner by taking his napkin off his lap and depositing it on the table. His wife and daughter re-created his gestures almost exactly, pushing back their chairs only an instant after he did.

"Professor Vermeer," William said in an overloud voice, "please join me in the library for brandy and a cigar."

"That would be a pleasure, sir."

Libby waited until her father had turned his back and begun his long walk out of the room. Then she touched Vermeer's elbow lightly. "Don't leave tomorrow without saying good-bye," she said quietly. "I'd like a minute to talk to you."

"Why not later, after brandies and cigars?"

She shook her head. "No, Professor Vermeer. That's not the way it works. The gentlemen are having their cigars, and the ladies are retiring for the evening." With that, she caught up with her mother and hooked her right arm into her mother's left, and the two left the room together.

By the time Vermeer found the study, William MacInnes had placed two black cigars on a sturdy-looking coffee table and was pouring a generous dollop of a thin, honey-colored liquid into two large brandy snifters. Vermeer had seen this brandy ritual in late-night movies. He took the snifter proffered by MacInnes between his ring and middle fingers, swirled it gently, and sniffed. He wasn't much of a drinker. It smelled far better than he expected.

Cigar rituals, though, were foreign territory. As a rule, smoking cigars made him feel a little green. Which made him think again of the pea soup. He watched MacInnes carefully and more or less did what his host did. MacInnes extended a lighted match. As the cigar reached full ignition, Vermeer remembered that he had been in a very similar room in the Brooklyn mansion: the master's lair, also thoroughly permeated by the smell of tobacco burned over the course of many years.

The master now sat heavily in a well-worn leather chair on one side of the coffee table. Vermeer sat opposite him. They puffed, swirled, and sipped. MacInnes's eyes moved slowly from the cigar to the brandy to his guest. Finally, he broke the silence.

"I know a lot about you, Professor Vermeer."

"Really?" Vermeer, surprised, wasn't sure whether he was supposed to respond. "How? And why?"

"I make a point of knowing a lot about my adversaries."

Not for the first time on this long day, Vermeer felt as if a fist had connected with the side of his head. "Well. Am I your adversary?"

"As it turns out, no. But that was my understanding when I began my inquiries."

Vermeer focused on the brandy. He could do without

the cigar, and he certainly wouldn't miss William MacInnes's mind games. The brandy, however, he could get very used to. "I'm curious, Mr. MacInnes. Is this a particularly good brandy?"

MacInnes laughed—a fundamental sort of snort. "Of course."

"You didn't say how you learned about me."

"Believe me, you don't want to know how. All the usual ways that are available to someone like me."

"Nor did you say *why* you thought I might be your adversary. An idea that totally astonishes me, by the way."

MacInnes simply shrugged.

"What was your focus?" Vermeer pressed on, feeling as if he were playing a corrupt game of twenty questions. "Personal? Professional?"

"A focus would have been premature. Would have risked excluding things. Therefore, no focus."

"Okay. So what did you find? Tell me about myself."

MacInnes scratched his chin contemplatively, weighing the notion. "Most important, I found that you weren't involved in any sort of improper relationship with my late son. That was important to me. For a whole host of reasons, only some of them having to do with morality and the abuse of authority.

"I found," he continued, "that you are a first-rate teacher but only a second-rate scholar, which is why it's unlikely that you'll be considered for tenure this spring. Or, if you do put yourself forward, you'll be unlikely to get promoted.

"And I found that you lead a surprisingly boring life." The old man was now warming to his task. "That you are attracted toward the opposite sex, but you are consistently unsuccessful in love. That you don't manage your money particularly well. In fact, surprisingly badly in light of your finance background. That you have only a few close friends, none in the Boston area, and not much contact with your family. And that you may have an enemy or enemies. That part is still a little bit murky."

This room, Vermeer noted as his eyes strayed from wall to wall, didn't have a single portrait on its walls. Maybe this phlegmy, rheumy old man didn't want his distinguished ancestors looking over his shoulders as he conceived his plots. Although those forebears surely had their own little plots to conceal. "I don't think you got your money's worth, Mr. MacInnes."

"No?"

"All that effort, and you didn't even discover that I can't stand pea soup. Or mushrooms."

"Ha." MacInnes snorted again. "Or maybe I did, Professor Vermeer. Maybe I did. Maybe I drew up this evening's menu very carefully." He appeared to be smiling.

"Mr. MacInnes, you'll excuse me if I don't find any of this amusing. Unsettling, but not funny. This is the second time today that I've been accused of being in a homosexual relationship with a young man I barely knew, and whose death is now the subject of a police investigation.

"So I'm the first to admit that I'm out of my depth here," Vermeer continued, trying to remain cool on the surface. "But if I'm not your adversary, as you seem to have concluded, then maybe I'm your ally."

"Exactly. The old, often misquoted Arab proverb: The enemy of my enemy is my friend. Or at the very least, an ally of mutual convenience. That's why I arranged to have this conversation with you. And by the way, I did not know about the pea soup or the mushrooms. Just plain bad luck."

Vermeer pondered the metronomic pendulum of yet another grandfather clock, this one working away in a fairly well lighted corner of the room. The face read a few minutes after nine. He realized that the clock hadn't struck the hour. In fact, none of the many clocks in the house seemed to have rung.

"None of your clocks sound."

"Excuse me?"

"That clock in the corner didn't sound the nine hour. The clock in the dining room didn't ring, either. And I don't recall the clocks in the hallways making any noise, either."

"Very good, Professor. Very good." MacInnes nodded his great silver-and-gray head approvingly. "The clocks that didn't strike. Like the dog that failed to bark in the Conan Doyle story. Very observant. Well, they've been rigged not to sound. You can imagine the din, every quarter hour. And the ruckus at noon and midnight."

"But it wasn't really that, was it?"

"Excuse me?"

Based on personal experience—his family had a houseful of striking clocks when he was a boy—Vermeer felt he was on firm ground. He also felt it was time to stake out some territory. "No, I'd say that someone in your house suffers from insomnia. Someone can't stand to hear those sleepless quarter hours slipping by, hour after hour. Someone with the power to wave his wand and make all these heirlooms go mute. You, for example."

The old man waved his cigar hand impatiently. "We're not here to discuss my sleeping habits."

"Nor my sex life. I hope."

"Fair enough. So let me get to my point, Professor Vermeer. As you say, there is a police investigation under way. I'm told that Captain Brouillard is both competent and tenacious. That's good. I'm guessing that your role, whether you know it or not, is to make this investigation go away. That's *not* good. So I want to change your incentives.

"I have no idea if Eric was murdered," he went on. "If he drowned in a drunken stupor after some illicit tryst in a building where he had no business being, well, that's for our God to pass His judgment on.

"But if he was murdered, there's some chance that was a purposeful blow against this family. Or against its enterprises.

"Which is entirely unacceptable.

"Which is why I am offering a reward of one million dollars for information that leads to the arrest and conviction of Eric's murderer—if, indeed, he had one.

"And believe me, Professor Vermeer, if it were legal to offer a bounty for a head on a plate, I would just as happily do that. In either case: one million dollars."

18

BREAKFAST, FORTUNATELY, WAS NOT A GROUP AFFAIR. Mr. Ralph, who evidently rose and set with the sun, was hovering in the front hall when Vermeer came down the grand stairway shortly after the clocks failed to strike 8:00.

"You slept well, I trust?"

"Yes, thank you, Mr. Ralph." There was no one within earshot. "That is, once I stopped worrying about the fact that until very recently, my host suspected me of seducing his son."

"Ah, well, I would know nothing about that." His face was pleasant stone. "Do come into the kitchen for some breakfast. I should warn you that it's rather informal."

"That will be a relief."

The kitchen, as full of sunlight as the rest of the house was gloomy, was a living museum of cooking paraphernalia. There was what appeared to be a functioning, or at least scrupulously maintained, oak ice chest. Next to it was a Norge refrigerator, at least a half century old, with a compressor on top. It was definitely in use. And next in line was a sleek new Sub-Zero refrigerator-freezer combination. An enormous gas stove, with a dozen burners and some other elements that Vermeer didn't recognize, squatted as a massive island in the middle of the room. A brightly polished copper exhaust hood extended all the way above the island, just out of forehead-bashing range.

Mrs. Talley and Patrique nursed coffee mugs at an enamel-topped table in a sunlit corner. They floated away from the table the moment they saw Vermeer enter. Despite his protests, they refused to sit down again.

"So what can we get you to eat?" At this time of day, Mrs. Talley wore a white uniform under her white apron.

"Uhm, let's see. How about toast, orange juice, and black coffee? If that's not too much of a bother."

"Not at all, not at all. Although it doesn't sound like enough. It'll be just a moment." She bustled off.

Vermeer looked around. In the instant that he had been placing his order, both Mr. Ralph and Patrique had disappeared, Cheshire cat–like. He wondered if the MacInnes staff practiced their appearances and disappearances.

"Mr. Ralph asked me to tell you that he has booked you onto a noon flight from Albany to Boston," Mrs. Talley called from across the room. "He suggests that you plan on leaving here no later than nine. Patrique has volunteered to drive you."

"Perfect." At this point Vermeer was not eager to spend any more time than absolutely necessary at Castle MacInnes. And if two hours in a car was the price of an exit visa, Patrique seemed like the most affable of the bunch.

"Mr. and Mrs. MacInnes send their regards," she continued, reappearing with his coffee and juice, "and also their regrets that they won't be able to see you off this morning."

"Sleeping in?"

"Oh, goodness, no," she said. She seemed astonished at the notion. She offered no further explanation.

On her next trip back to the table, she carried a plate of toast and a tray of jams, jellies, and two kinds of butter. And a small white envelope with precise-looking handwriting on it.

"Oh, and before she went out, Miss Libby asked me to give this to you."

"Thank you, Mrs. Talley." He dropped the envelope casually on the table and picked up a knife. "I would call this a perfect breakfast."

"Well, thank you, sir."

"Will Libby be back this morning? She told me last night that she wanted to talk."

"I don't think so, no."

The envelope had his name written on the front. He turned it over. On the back flap was the "M," this time embossed. Sealed.

He used a spare butter knife—heavy, lots of tooling—to open it. Inside was a single sheet of notepaper, folded in half. He unfolded the note. He scrolled past yet another embossed "M" to the four words on the page.

"Please be careful," it read, in the same studied handwriting. "Libby."

19

A<small>RT</small> D<small>EMING HAD BEEN ABSOLUTELY RIGHT</small>, C<small>APTAIN</small> Barbara Brouillard noted silently and grumpily. Reviewing several months' worth of e-mail, matching up incoming and outgoing messages, was a crappy job. A drudge job.

Especially because she wasn't learning anything. She already knew that Eric MacInnes was a very bright, superficial, and overprivileged young snot. Almost two thousand e-mails later, coming and going, she knew exactly the same thing, although now there was a lot more embroidery around the edges.

Maybe the kid had had it drummed into him: Don't commit anything important to writing. It was a lesson that she herself had certainly learned, in a very different context. And Eric MacInnes probably had far more to hide than she did.

She got up from the Formica-covered table in her tiny kitchen, rubbing her temples. She had taken the pile of work home, on the theory that it would go faster without the distractions of the office. It wasn't going fast.

Rummaging in the refrigerator, she wound up digging deep into the fruit drawer. Time to go to market. Thank God for Granny Smiths, down there at the bottom of the drawer with the last shriveling lemon, dependably immortal.

———————

Her tiny apartment, referred to by unembarrassed real estate agents as a "one-bedroom," looked out over an alley off Commonwealth Avenue in the student ghettos of Brighton.

The previous tenant, a nursing student living alone, had been burglarized. To Brouillard's eye, this should have come as no surprise. The fire escape outside the third-story window went all the way to the ground, in the alley, where no one would be keeping an eye on it after dark. The nursing student was the third tenant in a row to be burglarized and to move out in a hurry.

Brouillard had moved in happily, celebrating the artificially low rent. On her third night here, while she was dozing off in the dark in her oversize wingback chair with the ottoman—a technique she had discovered for relaxing after a bad day at the office—there was a light scuttling on the fire escape. She came wide awake instantly. Then there was some probing of the first of the three windows that opened out onto the fire escape. Then the second. And finally, the third, which soon gave way to the burglar's determined nudging and poking.

Up went the sash, slowly and quietly, until it stopped at about two feet, where Brouillard had nailed in some homemade stops. So that there would be enough of an opening to squeeze through, but it wouldn't be easy. She heard a whispered *"Shit."*

Into the dark living room came a foot, toes pointed upward. Then a second foot. She waited until half a torso, topped by a gaudy silver-plated belt buckle, was inside. A hand gripped the windowsill on either side of the torso.

"Police. Freeze."

The torso froze.

"Okay. Now. Bring the rest of you in through the window, nice and slow. But keep both hands just like they are, right there on the bottom of that window where I can see them. But before you do, listen carefully, and tell me what you hear."

She cocked her automatic, which she had kept at her side for just this eventuality. A quavering voice, youngish, came through the window: "A gun. A gun being cocked."

"Right. So you're ready to do what I say. Come on in."

A quaking body, topped by a head in a ski mask, squeezed its way in feetfirst, knocking over a potted plant on the way. The clay pot shattered on the window seat. The body flinched.

Now she turned on the light next to her. It was very bright. "Don't worry about the plant," she said. "Keep sliding in. And keep those hands right out in the open. Like you're doing the limbo." She doubted if her intruder knew what the limbo was, but she liked the analogy.

Body and masked head were now totally inside the room. His heels touched the floor, and the small of his rigid back was arched against the edge of the window seat. He looked like a kid sliding feetfirst down a slide. Except for the mask, of course, and the fact that there was no slide. Brouillard guessed that the edge of the window seat was now digging deeply into the kidneys of her visitor. There might well be some clay shards wedged in there, too.

"Very good. Now. Right hand stays right where it is, and left hand moves to the head and takes off the mask."

He did as he was told. Off came the mask. He was twentyish, of mixed backgrounds: a little of this, a little of that. He was shaking visibly. Gold post in his left ear. A gold tooth. Prominent mole on his cheek.

"Excellent. Now. Whole body stays very still while you pose for a picture." Keeping the .38 trained on him with her right hand, she reached for the Polaroid camera standing at the ready on the side table. *Flash.* Out rolled a white square. *Flash.* Out rolled another white square. They fell on the floor as she put the camera back down.

"Okay. Now you're going to tell me your name. Don't even risk making me think you're lying, because I'll shoot you. Home invasion. Self-defense."

He was twitching now—a combination of fear and muscle fatigue. "William L. Busby, ma'am! Don't shoot me!"

"You pretty sure that's your name?"

"Ma'am, yes ma'am!"

The telltale response, inscribed so deeply into every young soldier's and sailor's brain that it reemerged under stress, like hives, forever after. "Which branch of the service were you with?"

"Army, ma'am!"

"What part of town you from, Private Busby?"

"JP, ma'am!"

"Jamaica Plain. So you're pretty far from home. You're the same guy that did the last three jobs here, too?"

"No, ma'am! Al Dunphy, he done the others. He's doing time at Cedar Junction. He told me about it. His idea. Please don't shoot me."

"Well, maybe I will, and maybe I won't. But for now, I want you to reach up as high as you can on my window with your left hand, spread your fingers, and push those fingers against the glass. Roll 'em from left to right, like you're taking your own fingerprints. Which you are. Nice and slow. No smearing. Very good. Now the right hand. By the way, didn't Al tell you to wear gloves?"

Rolling his fingers, he didn't answer. He was shaking violently.

"Okay, Private Busby. Here's the deal. I have two nice pictures of you here, and a full set of prints." No matter that the Polaroids didn't actually reveal very much. "I'm going to take one of these pictures to the police station where I work, and put it up on the bulletin board. And I'm going to send the other one over to my friends at District 12, in JP, and they'll put it up on their bulletin board. And I'm going to run your prints against the government's central file, and I'm going to check whether your name is really William L. Busby. But that won't matter a whole hell of a lot, because everybody will know that the guy in the picture with the gold tooth and the nasty mole on his left cheek tried to rob a Boston police detective. Get it?"

"Uh, yes, ma'am!"

"And one more thing."

"Yes, ma'am!"

"I want you to tell all of your friends—every one of them—to stay clear of the thirteen-hundred block of Commonwealth Avenue. If there's even a whiff of trouble around here, William L. Busby, I'm going to hunt you down like the flea-bitten dog that you are. You got that?"

"Yes, ma'am!"

"And meanwhile, you're going to hope that nothing bad happens to me personally, right? With your picture hanging up in two station houses?"

"No, ma'am! I mean, yes, ma'am!"

"Okay. So go on; get the hell out of here."

———

She hadn't heard from William L. Busby since. In fact, her impression was that her whole neighborhood had quieted down a bit since that encounter.

She sat back down at the table, crunching on the tart green apple. She had finished the worst of her homework: reconstructing multiple electronic dialogues between Eric and his e-mail correspondents. Art Deming, of course, had summarized the chitchat accurately. Nothing strange, nothing obviously missing. Of all the people in his world, Eric seemed closest to "downhilldave13740," the guy that Vermeer had been assigned to check out. Then came sister Libby. In distant third place came alleged girlfriend Jeannette Bartlett, now of the Charles River.

In none of his notes did Eric aim for dramatic effect or reveal any particular emotion. He was often funny, sometimes very funny. He even made Brouillard laugh out loud more than once. This was a feat, given her deepening headache. But he didn't come across as tormented, or even particularly thoughtful. No deep grooves in the ice, as her hockey-playing brother used to put it.

The second task of the afternoon, which had now turned into evening, was to compare the e-mail logs from Eric's machine with those that Harvard's central tech-support group had finally coughed up. Getting Harvard officialdom to go along with her request hadn't been easy. She had had to go up the BPD ladder several rungs, eventually threatening to involve the mayor. Even then, getting the Harvard mainframe to generate the data turned out to be a troublesome process.

But now, two days later, she had the lists. Under the heel of her left hand was what Eric's computer remembered about his e-mail activity: dates and times, to and from addresses, and subjects. And in her right hand, once she had discarded the remains of the Granny Smith, was what the server remembered about that activity.

The two lists were supposed to be the same. And no doubt, she grumbled, they *were* the same. The fact that Brouillard was even bothering with this step was overkill. Her colleagues, the Dick Davidsons and Buzzy Silvers of the world, would think she was nuts. Maybe they were right. Maybe she *did* need to get a life.

Arbitrarily she started six months back. This cut the task in half. (At her request, Harvard had provided a year's worth of data, making a matched bookend for Deming's work.) She folded both lists in half vertically so she could put the columns of tiny type as close together as possible. She sighed out loud: The formats were slightly different. That meant that she couldn't just look at the last line on each page to see if they tracked. It meant she had to go more or less line by line. She got out a long ruler and started with Eric's outbox.

An hour and a half later, eyes almost completely blurred over, she blinked in astonishment. She backed up a few lines and retraced her footsteps. She was now in December, two months ago. According to Eric's computer, there was no activity on the nights of the twelfth and nineteenth. And according to Harvard, Eric had sent out a small blizzard of e-mails. Just before and just after midnight. No "subject" included.

All to the same address: wvermeer@hbs.edu.

She put the out-box logs to one side and picked up the in-box logs. She went to December 12. Nothing on Eric's machine. But according to Harvard, Eric had received one e-mail.

From wvermeer@hbs.edu. No entry in the subject line.

Now that she knew what she was looking for, it was easy. Except for the occasional bit of spam, these messages, to and from, were the only ones with no subject listed.

Same thing on the nineteenth.

Same thing once in the first week of January. She grabbed her neglected checkbook from under a pile of bills and squinted at the tiny calendar. All Sunday nights. All late at night.

Same thing last Sunday night—the night Eric MacInnes died. Two messages to wvermeer@hbs.edu. And one back. From wvermeer@hbs.edu.

And then nothing more.

20

THE DIAL TONE STUTTERED AGGRESSIVELY IN VERMEER'S ear. Verizon—or whatever his phone company was currently called—had messages for him. He punched in his code. *"You have three messages."*

As Central Office (or whatever it was called now) queued them up for delivery, he looked at the dark landscape outside his kitchen window. He wished he had gotten home earlier, early enough to go for a quick run, sweat out his extended stay at the Albany airport, and shower away the residues of aristocracy and airports. A nice enough little airport, Albany, with some interesting historical exhibits that demonstrated that Albany—or at least the broader metro area—was once important. Like woeful Schenectady, up the road, which Vermeer had once visited on business. But after the third mysterious hour of ground delay, and full of the fizzy guilt associated with a twenty-ouncer of a local brew (a "big boy," in Albany), Vermeer had been more than ready to leave Albany behind.

"Hi, Wim, it's your mom." She talked in an armor-piercing voice for a few minutes about what was on her mind. Her central theme today was that *other* parents' children called *them*, like, for example, the children of

these particular parents, and the children of those nice people who lived two houses up, and who had the good job with Bell Labs, and so on, and so on, until Central Office cut her short. Vermeer punched 3. Deleted.

"Hi, Wim, me again." Mother resented being cut off in the middle of a thought. Sometimes when this happened, she started the thought all over again, from the beginning. This time she did not. She merely elaborated. Dutifully, pacing into the living room and back, he let the tape run until she got cut off again. Three. Deleted.

"Yeah, hi, Vermeer." Not expecting the deep male voice, Vermeer stopped pacing and put the phone closer to his ear. *"Dan Beyer. In New York. Call me when you get in."* Then a ten-digit number. Then a click.

Vermeer played the message again, this time with a pen in hand to pick off the phone number. He dialed it. A female voice answered by repeating the last four digits of the number—like an extension in a bank. Vermeer thought he recognized Ellie Donahue's voice. "Hi. Wim Vermeer returning Dan Beyer's call."

"Hold, please, Professor Vermeer."

After a few minutes, Beyer came on the line. "Hello."

"Returning your call, Dan."

"Yeah. Thanks." He didn't sound thankful. "I have a message for you from Libby."

Vermeer waited. If Beyer wanted to deliver this message, he was concealing it well. "Well, fire away, Dan. What's the message?"

"I'll just read it to you. She says, 'I'll be in Boston at the end of the week. Really need to talk with you in person. How about dinner at the Four Seasons on Friday, at eight? Let Dan know if that works for you.' "

"Sure. Works for me, Dan. Please let her know."

"Yeah, okay."

"Hey, Dan, tell me something."

"Maybe."

"Why didn't Libby just call me herself? Why put you in the middle of it?"

"I don't ask her questions like that. She wants help, I help her. That's my job."

"Is she there now? Can I talk to her?"

"No."

"Can I talk to her before Friday, if I need to?"

"No."

"What if something comes up?"

"What's going to come up? You don't seem busy."

"Hey, Dan, out here in the real world, things tend to come up. What if I have to cancel?"

"Simple. You call this number. You leave a message."

Vermeer didn't enjoy Beyer's tough-guy act: doling out little thuggish syllables as if they were precious stones. He decided to tweak him. "Great," he said. "So it's not really like going out to dinner with a beautiful young woman. It's more like going to the dentist to get my teeth scraped. So, Dan, will someone call the day before and confirm my appointment?"

There was a pause. "Let's get something straight here, Vermeer." Beyer's voice was calm and cold. Vermeer imagined him flexing a sequence of muscle groups as he talked. "I don't like you much. I don't like what I've heard about you. I don't like the fact that you were snooping around in Libby's room. Looking for the bathroom, my ass. And I don't like the idea of her going out to dinner with you—or being anywhere with you, for that matter. I don't trust you, and I don't trust your type.

"I'm going along with her on this trip to Boston, to

keep an eye on things. So I'm going to be in the vicinity, Vermeer. So I recommend you don't pull any of your tricks."

Hanging up now would be a good idea, Vermeer knew. There was nothing to be gained by baiting the bodyguard. Nevertheless . . . "Listen, big Dan," he replied. "I don't do tricks. If I did, I wouldn't do them with you in the room. But unless I'm guessing wrong, you aren't going to *be* in the room on Friday night. No, sir, big Dan. You're not an out-in-the-public-eye kind of guy. You're an under-wraps kind of guy. You're going to be upstairs, ordering up a cheeseburger and a side of steroids from room service, right? All by yourself, while your Miss Libby and I are downstairs, drinking expensive wine and having a nice evening together. And then, of course, there's the rest of the evening—"

"Fuck you." *Click.*

Hanging up, Vermeer wondered why he had gone out of his way to clatter his stick up and down the sides of the gorilla's cage. That wasn't like him.

21

BROUILLARD KNEW SHE WAS STALLING.

What she needed to do was pick up the phone, call Vermeer in for questioning, and move things along, toward some kind of resolution.

A quick check with Art Deming had confirmed what she already suspected: There was no way that a "false positive" could have been created on either Eric's computer or Harvard's server. The most likely explanation, the *only* likely explanation, was that Vermeer himself had sent the self-incriminating messages. Of course, as Deming had pointed out, assume the computer in his office is always on or isn't password-protected. *If* somebody had access to that office, again it would be no big deal to impersonate him. And the trail, although still circumstantial, would be pretty hard to deny. Of course, if somebody then responded to the "planted" e-mail, Vermeer would have known something odd was going on. *Unless the impersonator was clever and lucky enough to pick off that response before Vermeer spotted it . . .*

Jeez, Brouillard said to herself, wrinkling her nose, *why am I fighting so hard to avoid reaching the obvious conclusion?* Why didn't she just go to the DA with the evidence she already had, which was strong enough to pull some warrants and build the case against Vermeer? The answer was, she decided, that she had a feeling about this case—a feeling that things were more complicated than they seemed. And this didn't fit together well with her sense that Vermeer, although now in the thick of things, was not particularly complicated. Smart, yes. A good talker. Seemingly interested in helping with the investigation in his limited ways. But not especially complicated.

Or maybe he *was* deep. Maybe he was one of those disturbed characters—cunning, detail oriented—who hangs around the fringes of an investigation, chumming it up with the police and eventually making a surprisingly on-target observation about a crime of his own commission, pushing the cops a little closer, but not too close, to the truth. She didn't have much experience with those types, and she wasn't sure she'd recognize one if it came her way. Once, on a rotation with Arson, she had sat in on an interrogation of a fire starter who had miraculously pulled people out of two different burning buildings. He must have calculated that it would be seen as a coincidence. It wasn't.

She looked around the station house. The tired old building, with its aged fluorescent light fixtures on long stems, its tan paint peeling in large leaf-size sheets off shiny damp walls, and its grubby brown linoleum floor with underlayment starting to poke through in high-traffic areas, didn't provide much motivation. And although there were lots of blue suits in evidence out in the public areas of the building, she was the only plain-clothes in today so far. Most of the empty desks around her looked far messier than hers. They were all behind in their paperwork; she was not. She was tempted to give in to the headache that had come back behind her left eyeball, turn off the gray metal lamp on her desk, whose low buzzing she only heard when she was grumpy—like now, for example—and go home to bed.

Instead, she shook two caplets out of the oversize bottle of Advil in her top drawer. She washed them down with the lukewarm remains of her coffee. Then she reached for the phone.

The desk sergeant led Vermeer to Brouillard's desk. She got up as she saw them approaching. "Thanks, Jack," she said. Then, turning to Vermeer: "Thanks for coming in. Let's find someplace to talk."

After picking up a pad and pencil, she steered him around some cubicles and then down a hallway that was just a little too narrow for two-way traffic. The gallery of black-and-white prints of long-dead officers on both walls heightened the claustrophobic effect. As usual, Vermeer noted, walking behind her, this Captain Brouillard wore resolutely baggy clothes that gave little clue to her shape. From behind, under a gray cotton sweater, her shoulders looked a little squarer than he remembered. The hint of a waistline, introducing black pants that dropped almost directly to the floor. She could be anywhere from well rounded to not much rounded, he concluded. Her brown hair, grabbed down low on her shoulder blades by a black elastic, looked as if it had been taken hostage.

"This'll do," she said, opening a door and flicking on a light switch. A brown plastic sign with white routed-out letters identified this room as Interrogation A.

"Am I being interrogated?" It didn't come out as lightly as he had intended. He followed her inside.

"No," she said, sitting down and waving him toward a second chair on the other side of a battered conference table. "Believe me, you'll know when you're being interrogated."

He scanned the featureless walls. "Isn't there supposed to be a one-way mirror somewhere in here?"

"That's another room. For a different kind of conversation. Let's hope you don't see the inside of that one." She wrote a few words on her pad, drew a line under it, and looked up. "So tell me about your visit to the MacInnes house. Starting with Downhill Dave. Give me all the details, even little odds and ends that you might not think are important."

Starting with his odd encounter with Dave Westerling, Vermeer recounted his trip to upstate New York and continued through to Beyer's recent call and his grudging conveyance of Libby's request for a meeting. He could see no pattern to when she took notes and when she didn't. Several times she put a hand up—*hold it*—and scribbled at length. Two or three times she stopped him and probed for what appeared to be irrelevant details. She seemed most interested in William MacInnes's suggestion that Vermeer might have "enemies," as yet unidentified.

"You buy that idea? About enemies?" she interrupted.

"Not really."

"What do you mean, 'not really'?"

"Nothing. I mean, I give students bad grades when they deserve them. Some of my colleagues don't, from what I can tell. There are a few former girlfriends out there who might still be angry with me. But more likely, they've forgotten all about me. Sometimes I don't call my mother back."

She sighed. "I'm serious here. You should be, too.

How about money? Done anybody any serious damage financially? Stand between anybody and a big pot of money?"

"No to both questions. In fact, in terms of investments gone bad, I tend to be the victim rather than the bad guy. I don't think I'm in line to inherit anything much. I have some investments, some good and some bad. A good life insurance policy with some cash value."

"Who's the beneficiary?"

"The Boston Public Library."

"You took out a life insurance policy to benefit the BPL?" She thought he was joking, and was prepared to scold him again.

"No, no," he said quickly, heading off the lecture. "I took out a policy to benefit my wife and kids, when they showed up in my life. They just haven't showed up yet. Meanwhile, I believe in public libraries. But to be serious, as you say, I don't see any connection between my finances and the MacInneses."

"Did you happen to bring Libby's note with you?"

"In fact, I did." Handing it over to her, he was glad to have avoided yet another of her disapproving looks.

She scanned it briefly, holding it at the corners and along the edges, then placed it delicately back on the table. "Can I hang on to this for a while?"

"Sure. You can keep it, as far as I'm concerned."

"I'll get it back to you. Do you think she wrote it?"

"Well, I assume so. Sure. Although I haven't had any reason to see her handwriting before. Mrs. Talley certainly seemed to think it was from Libby."

He waited for her to follow up on that line of questioning. She didn't. Instead, she put her pencil down, tipped her chair back on two legs, and locked her hands together behind her head. Then she made a strange face: eyes nearly closed, nose wrinkled upward, as if there were a really bad odor in the air.

After what seemed like a long few minutes, she brought her front chair legs back down to earth, picked up her pencil once again, and looked at him thoughtfully. "You know, Professor Vermeer, I've got to point out something kind of obvious here. There's this funny sub-plot that's going on underneath all of this stuff: your conversation with Westerling, old man MacInnes's suspicions, and so on. Everybody seems to be convinced that you and Eric had some sort of thing going on."

He felt his color rising. "Yeah. You noticed that, too. I'm getting kind of tired of it."

"So it's not true?"

"Captain Brouillard, all I can say is, my tastes don't run that way. And even if they did, I hope I'd have the common sense and professionalism—or at least the self-control—to stay the hell away from my students."

"Yeah, well, I'd hope so, too. But there is this thing on the table, and it's coming from more than one direction. You could be lying to me, of course—"

"I'm not," he interrupted coldly.

"Okay, so you're not. Then there are only a few other explanations. One is that Eric misread some signals coming from you and made more of your relationship than was really there."

He realized that his jaw was clenched. He took a deep breath, returning her steady gaze. "Well, he would have needed to do some serious misreading," he finally replied. "Look: I had absolutely no contact with him outside the classroom. Period. I don't remember him ever coming to my office, and I'm sure I would remember that. No phone, no e-mails, no love letters, no nothing. I haven't communicated with him since the last day of class last year, when I'm pretty sure I shook hands with him. And also with about ninety other people, too, on their way out the door. I think I've seen him around campus three or four times since then. We might have waved at each other. Maybe we said hello. Otherwise, nothing. Full stop. Period. End."

"Yeah," she said speculatively, "I was just thinking that. Seems kind of like an abrupt shutdown of your relationship. Haven't we already established that he was one of your favorite students, and you were his favorite professor?"

"Uh-huh, we have. Absolutely. And we've also established that I was James's favorite, too. So how active is *his* fantasy life?"

She shrugged. "I would say, not way active, based on my meetings with him so far." Then she went back to what Vermeer recognized as her standard expression: a mix of skepticism, worry, and contemplation. It suited her.

"One other explanation," she continued, pursuing her former line of thinking, "is that someone is setting you up. Which seems kind of far-fetched to me. And from what you've told me, there's nobody out there with reason enough to set up that kind of elaborate frame job. And at least based on what you've told me, there's nothing that ties you to these people, beyond the classroom link."

"Nothing. Look, Captain Brouillard, the truth is, I feel like there *is* some kind of net being thrown over me. I'm starting to think that William MacInnes is right about the enemies. Even if you don't believe it."

She said nothing, simply looking straight at him, bouncing her eraser off her pad.

"And frankly," he continued, "if you don't believe me, and you think I'm some sort of cold-blooded killer, I don't see why I should help you truss me up like a Thanksgiving turkey. Maybe I should go get a lawyer and refuse to have any more friendly little chats with you."

"Fair enough." She nodded, impassive. "But believe me, Professor, if and when you get to be a suspect, I'll be damn sure to tell you about it. At that point you get Mirandized, and you sit in the other little room—the one with the one-way mirror—and I have a colleague in the room, and also one behind the mirror, and the tape rolls. And at that point, I'll be *insisting* that you have a lawyer. And if it comes to that, you'll need a *real good* lawyer, Professor Vermeer, because I almost never bring the wrong person into that little room.

"Meanwhile," she continued in the same flat voice, "I can promise you that for the time being, it won't hurt you to continue to be helpful. Which you have been, by the way, and I appreciate it. Sure, if I decide you're a suspect, we'll have to play by a different set of rules. But obviously, nothing you've told me up to that point could be used against you. Nothing you've said today, for example. All off limits."

She registered and acknowledged the expression on his face: confusion, skepticism, a touch of fear. "Look, Professor Vermeer. The way I see it, you don't have a lot of choices. If there is some sort of conspiracy being played out here, you're going to need me to help figure it out. Trust me: I'm way better at this than you are."

Feeling a little bruised, he saw no particular reason to trust her. But a dubious ally looked better than none at all. "Okay. For the time being."

"Good choice, Professor Vermeer. Believe me."

He tried to lighten the mood. "First name's Wim, by the way. Feel free."

"Thanks, but I find that formality—titles and last names—is very useful in situations like this. Keeps everybody focused on the stakes of the game. Which in your case are very high."

"Okay."

"One last topic," she said, picking up her pencil again. "Tell me about the computer setup and e-mail system at Harvard."

Somewhat surprised at this shift to the mundane world of PCs and electronic housekeeping, Vermeer answered her questions as best he could. Yes, you needed a password to get onto a Harvard computer, unless you left it on all the time, which most people tended to do. In his case, he locked his office door whenever he wasn't there, so leaving his computer on—which he tended to do—wouldn't be an issue. No, you didn't need another password to pick up and send your e-mail, except, of course, from remote locations, when you had to go through another ISP. Yes, people tended to tell their administrative assistants their passwords—it was hard to do business, otherwise—but for the most part, people were careful about that. Harvard discouraged people from picking passwords that were obvious, and he hadn't done so and hadn't told anyone other than his secretary his password. Once his succession of temps had started arriving, he hadn't given out his password to anyone. But of course, the door was open during the day, and there were several people out there who knew his password.

"So why all this interest in passwords and e-mail?" he asked.

She shrugged lightly but caught his eyes and held

them. "Too early to say. But when I come across Word documents and e-mail logs, it's helpful to know what I'm looking at. Some places tend to be more careful, and some places tend to be less careful. Sounds like Harvard is on the more careful end.

"Well," she said, snapping her pad shut and pushing back from the table, "that's all I've got for now." She stood up. Taking her cue, he did the same. "I've got a lot of stuff to catch up on," she continued, "although it's mostly routine. Forms and follow-ups. You're having dinner with Libby on Friday?"

"Yeah. But hopefully not with big Dan."

"Good. I want to hear about that. My sense is that she was pretty close to Eric. Maybe she can shed some light on some of this stuff."

Again their eyes met as they shook hands, and remained locked for a few seconds beyond the handshake.

"And, Professor Vermeer," she added, although nothing in her tone suggested that this was an afterthought, "I think Libby's advice is good advice. Be careful."

22

LIBBY WAS SITTING AT THE BAR—MODERNIST BUT WITH some soft edges—when Vermeer made his way into the Four Seasons restaurant. Next to her, overwhelming his bar stool like a toad on a stubby stick, was Dan Beyer. She waved at Vermeer and then motioned for him to come and join them at the bar.

"Hi, Miss MacInnes. Dan."

Libby got up, took his extended hand, and surprised him by extending her left cheek for a kiss. Beyer, who evidently found it easier to rotate his body than turn his head on his neck, watched Vermeer close the distance, with obvious disapproval. His blue blazer was too tight in the chest and shoulders—purchased in some earlier stage in his physical development program, Vermeer guessed. Beyer nodded once, like a hatchet chop, implying that he had finished sizing up the situation. Then he slid his mass off the stool and drained the bottom half of his beer glass in one long swallow.

"So, listen, Libby, I'm heading upstairs," he said, pointedly ignoring Vermeer. "Call me when you turn in."

"Dan," she started to object. "What could possibly—"

"No argument, please. Not under the circumstances. Call me." He pushed past Vermeer.

Vermeer watched her reaction, which shifted from amusement to worry to frustration, all in a few seconds. As her eyes followed Beyer's broad back out of the room, Vermeer took the opportunity to examine her in profile. It was only the third time he had seen her, but each time she looked completely different. Tonight she wore a black cocktail dress that somehow seemed prim, even though it revealed her legs well above her knees and swept downward from her long neck toward her chest. If this was mourning garb, he decided, he liked mourning garb. She was carefully made-up, especially around her eyes. She wore splashes of gold on her right ring finger, on both wrists, and around her long neck. Her brown hair, more or less a jungle the first two times he had run into her, was now beautifully shaped, turned under at the ends to frame her face.

Which was very, very pretty, Vermeer was surprised to find himself thinking. It was as if Libby had made a concerted effort to grow up in the past few days. Had she made this effort for him?

"He's very protective of you," he volunteered, still standing next to her. He considered sitting on the stool Beyer had just vacated. *Under the circumstances,* Beyer had said. Under what circumstances?

She shook her head in a little shiver. "Yes. Even more so since Eric's death. Everybody's on edge."

The maître d' beckoned them, and they made their way to a secluded table tucked up against a windowless wall. Tonight, it seemed, Libby wasn't going to take advantage of one of the restaurant's main selling points, which was a view of the Public Garden that was straight out of the nineteenth century, studded at night by faux gas streetlights. She ordered a particular bottle of French white wine, name and year, without looking at the wine list. The white-coated waiter, who knew her by name, looked pleased at the choice—expensive, presumably. He slid off toward the kitchen.

"Miss MacInnes, I have to ask you something."

She looked up from her menu, seeming startled at the suggestion, and her smile looked a little forced. "We should probably order first, okay? Then let's talk."

The waiter returned with the wine and an elaborate chilling stand with chromed curlicues on its four corners. Libby sniffed the cork, swirled and sniffed the wine, and then tasted it, although looking as if she was just going through the motions. The waiter took their orders, answering a question from Libby, nodding his approval at their selections, and once again backed away from the table, disappearing even before he was out of sight.

"Cheers," she said, raising her glass. "Although maybe that's not the right thing to say under the circumstances."

There it was again. "What *are* the circumstances?" The wine, Vermeer decided, was excellent.

"In what sense do you mean, Professor Vermeer?"

"Please, call me Wim."

She extended her hand, smiling. "Wim. And you should call me Libby. Everyone else in the world does. Except this waiter, who probably thinks that would be bad for business."

He was not going to be sidetracked by her small talk. "In the sense that I don't know why I'm having dinner with you at the Four Seasons. In the sense that when I was at your house in New York State, you told me you wanted to talk to me, and then you disappeared, but not before leaving a note telling me to be careful. Be careful about what, I don't know. In the sense that a lot of people, including people in your family, and maybe including you, seem to have some strange ideas about me. In the sense that the Incredible Hulk who dogs your footsteps has let it be known that if I get out of line, as he sees it, he will throw himself on me and rip my head off. With pleasure. In the sense that I don't even know why you need the Incredible Hulk shadowing you in the first place."

For a long minute she didn't respond. "That's a lot of questions," she finally said. "All at once." She sounded as if she was trying to be light, even frivolous, but was held back by some underlying sense of seriousness. "Some I don't know the answers to. But I can deal with a couple of them pretty quickly, maybe going in backwards order.

"Dan—who actually is a very sweet person, believe me, despite his occasional bad manners—was originally my physical trainer. And still is. We hired him part-time two years ago to come to the city house a couple of days a week to help me with my workouts.

"About a year ago, I started to get anonymous threats in the mail. I didn't take them very seriously, but the family did. The police looked into it but didn't turn up any leads. So the family decided to hire Dan full-time, mainly so he'd be available to travel with me when I went on business trips. The letters stopped coming, so that was starting to die down a little bit in the last few months. Until Eric's death. Since then, he's been my shadow . . . as you say."

"That must sort of cramp your style."

She blushed. "Well, actually, that sort of gets at another one of your questions."

"I just lost you."

"I wanted to have dinner with you because I wanted to talk to you. I *needed* to talk to you. And"—here she stammered a little, looking everywhere but at him—"I also needed a way to get out from under Dan's watchful eye. For later in the evening, I mean."

He felt a little twinge of disappointment. It surprised him. "In other words, you're going to slip the leash and spend the evening with someone else while Dan thinks you're with me?"

"Well, yes. To the extent that he's thinking about it."

Vermeer smiled, without much pleasure. "Oh, believe me, he's thinking about it. He's upstairs tearing the phone books in half right now, just thinking about it. He doesn't like me much. You may have noticed."

"Which I think has something to do with your visit to my bedroom, while you were down in the city. Thanks for delivering that stuff, by the way." So if she objected to his effort at sleuthing, she wasn't letting on.

"You're welcome, of course," he said. He decided that at this point, honesty—at least a limited, modified kind of honesty—was the best policy. "And I admit to doing a little snooping down in New York. But you know, I get paid to think about interesting things. And by any definition, your family is pretty interesting. And by the way, I didn't know it was *your* room. It's just that your door was the only one that wasn't sealed up tight."

She shrugged. "More security. That's a recent development, too. I'm surprised nobody had remembered to pull the door shut. I imagine Ellie Donahue bit the poor cleaning lady's head off the next time she saw her. But in any case, Wim, I don't give a damn one way or the other if you were in my room. In fact, I'm a little disappointed. In the sense that it wasn't your obsession with me that drove you in there." She was trying to introduce a note of flirtatiousness. It wasn't working.

"Well, even if I was obsessed," he said, "I wouldn't tell you. Because you might tell Dan, who would then kill me." He saw her wince. "Sorry. No more jokes about getting dead. So . . ."

Briefly, he drew a blank, trying to think of an alternative topic of conversation. The image of Detective Brouillard, with her pad and pencil and air of purposefulness, popped into his head. "You, uhm, mentioned business trips," he finally said, "and you clearly have some sort of high-powered workstation in your bedroom. And someone said you're a nurse, and when I first met you, you were preparing to give your father some sort of shot. All of which leads me to ask, exactly what do you *do* for a living?"

Now it was her turn to laugh, briefly. "For a *living,* Wim? For a living, I do nothing. I breathe. I call the family office every now and then and plead for an unscheduled funds transfer. Which they always give me."

"That pays the bills, I guess. But it doesn't sound rewarding, otherwise."

"No, it isn't. It tends to make you feel useless. Which eventually got to be a problem for me—feeling useless, I mean—so I decided to go into nursing."

"Why not business?" He was honestly puzzled. "I don't know you well, but you seem to be every bit as smart as your brothers."

"Oh, well, thanks a *lot*—as smart as my brilliant brothers?" She sounded genuinely offended. "And I'll just assume you weren't implying that nursing was somehow less important, or worthwhile, or interesting, than business. But to answer your question, my parents, who control the family business, would *never* let their only daughter get involved. Never, ever."

Their appetizers arrived. Vermeer waited until the waiter had retreated again. "Why not?" he persisted. "Why Eric and James, but not you? Good old-fashioned chauvinism?"

"Well, as you say, we're an interesting family. And it may be a little hard for you to understand, but my parents think dynastically. Is that a word? Dynastically. They think about how my marriage will help or hurt the inter-generational processes of empire building and wealth transfer. And as they see it, having me be in business would take me out of the right circles—the social register circles. Or worse, I might run off with the custodian or the elevator operator or whoever."

When it was clear that she wasn't going to say more on the subject, Vermeer pushed a little harder. "Sorry, Libby, but I still don't get it. How does something like nursing fit into that worldview? Not to be obnoxious, but blood and shit and bedpans? With all those resistant bacteria growing overhead in the hospital's HVAC system? Wouldn't you be better off in a nice little corner office somewhere, wearing a power suit, with your legendary last name on the door?"

She shook her head. "As my parents see it, nursing is okay—for these last awkward years before marriage—because it's God's work. The Florence Nightingale, Clara Barton thing. And the truth is, my parents don't have a clue as to what a nurse really does: blood and shit and bedpans, as you say so colorfully. They don't have any idea how dangerous hospitals are. If they did, they'd be horrified."

"On the other hand, it's got to be convenient for your

father to have someone he trusts on hand to give him his shots."

"No, actually, he barely tolerates that," she said. "The truth is that my giving him the occasional insulin injection mostly just confuses him and my mother. Because I have a skill that they don't have. A skill that's very important to him, and which he can't pay me for. Very confusing all around. So I don't make a big deal of that one."

As their appetizers were cleared and their entrées arrived, Vermeer thought again of her computer array, her Stealth bomber desk, and the Gold Star award on her shelf. "Well, I'm confused, too," he said. "You're a nurse who works with high-end computers with high-speed Internet connections, and takes business trips, and wins awards from grateful groups. What kind of nurse is that?"

"Well, well, you *are* a snoop, Wim." But her smile was warm and her tone friendly. "Okay. I did my hospital time on the pediatric intensive care unit at Mercy, in New York. Emergency care for kids in the Big Apple. Blood, shit, bedpans, and then some. It was very heady and gratifying for a few months. Then it got worse and worse every day. For every little kid we managed to save, two or three others died. I finally realized that I really couldn't stand it.

"So then I went to the other end of the spectrum. I moved upstate to the country house, joined the Catskill Regional VNA, and started making home visits. Which, out in the boondocks, involves a ton of driving. Depending on the season, either through two feet of snow or behind a very slow-moving hay rig.

"Technically, I'm still affiliated with the visiting nurses, working the occasional weekend or holiday when they're short-staffed. But that's gotten tough, too, because thanks to the health care mess, the local hospitals are pushing people out before they're well enough to go home. So that's a huge responsibility. And I've started worrying more about liability. If I ever made a serious mistake, someone would be very likely to go after me. So in that way, at least, I guess I *am* a target. I guess I do need a little protection."

"There's always liability insurance."

"Well, to be blunt, Wim, you shouldn't think of me as a normal person. You have to assume that some different rules apply." She said it not boastfully but matter-of-factly, as if she were describing her hair color.

"So how do the computers tie in?"

"I'm getting to that. A couple of years ago, when I was working at Mercy, I started doing a lot of online research after hours, trying to get a handle on some of the tougher cases that we were dealing with. And two things really struck me. First, there was a ton of stuff out there, focusing on every terrible disease or injury under the sun. Lots of bad stuff, but also some really good stuff. And second, all of this stuff was completely disorganized. No clear hierarchies of information. No obvious way to separate the wheat from the chaff—the good, refereed stuff from the junk. A big goulash, chock-full of bad stuff and good stuff.

"So I started up an online conversation with some nurses who shared my interests. That turned into an interest group, which turned into a Web site, which turned into a 501(c)3. The INRR: the Internet Nursing Research Registry. I fund it myself, although the truth is that it takes a lot more time than money. And now, all of a sudden, I'm starting to get a stream of unsolicited donations, and some calls from interested foundations. Go figure.

You don't need money, and you don't ask for it, and potential donors start to seek you out.

"The business trips are basically about me going to medical conventions—confabs for doctors and nurses—and talking up the INRR and figuring out how we can be more helpful to people in practice, on the front lines. I've also been invited to talk at hospitals, and at colleges with nursing programs, and even at some medical schools. All of which gets me up to Boston a lot."

"Which is a really good thing for your mysterious friend, whom you're hooking up with later tonight. And of whom your family doesn't approve, I'm guessing."

She blushed again. "*Wouldn't* approve of, if they knew about him, no. So that will have to stay our little secret, Wim. Yours and mine. Please."

"Of course. But I'm jealous."

They made small talk while they finished their dinners. Vermeer noted that Libby was putting away the wine at a steady clip. It didn't seem to have much of an effect on her, aside from bumping up her vivaciousness a bit and turning the tips of her ears red. Once or twice she put her hand on his, across the table, and let it linger there. The gesture was warm and sisterly, in a patrician sort of way, although a casual observer might have seen it differently.

And there *were* observers. At several tables around them, well-heeled people were sneaking glances at them. Over by the bar, a lone diner in his fifties surveyed the restaurant occasionally, and his wandering gaze seem to alight on Libby whenever possible. Vermeer didn't blame him.

"So, Libby," he said, as the waiter made yet another round of dishes go away and once again made himself disappear, "we need to talk."

"But we have been talking, Professor Vermeer," she said, covering up a grin with her hand. "And drinking a little bit, too." She had turned down dessert but ordered a glass of calvados for both of them. "Apple brandy. From Normandy," she had explained. From a tedious consulting assignment in St. Louis several years back, which featured lots of long dinners with a lonely middle manager who had nothing else to do and didn't hesitate to chew up Vermeer's evenings, he knew all about calvados. He remembered the morning-after headaches in particular.

"Yeah, but we've been talking about everything but what we should be talking about," he said, hearing the edge in his voice. "I think maybe you're avoiding a couple of subjects."

She sat up a little straighter. The smile was gone. "Like what?"

"Like, you wrote me a note telling me to be careful. Careful of *what*, exactly?"

"I don't know. Exactly."

"Well, narrow it down, Libby." He started using her name deliberately, with emphasis. An old teaching technique. "Space junk falling from the sky? A bus plunge?"

"Of course not."

"Well, then, what?"

"I don't know. I really don't know. But something . . . something just doesn't seem right." Now she was fidgeting, looking off toward the distant windows.

"Right with *what*, Libby?"

"Maybe this wasn't a good idea."

"Maybe *what* wasn't a good idea?"

"This. Meeting with you. I'm starting to think that it might not be."

"Which is why you chickened out, Libby, up at the country place? And why you left the note?"

She nodded, still not looking at him. "I just wanted . . . I just want to tell you that you're sailing in deep waters. That you shouldn't let your—your affection—for Eric put you in jeopardy. God, I'm finding this hard to talk about. But the point is, no one's blaming you for anything, Wim. It just might be better if you could put some distance between yourself and all this mess. While everybody is looking elsewhere."

Now it was Vermeer's turn to look off toward the windows. He didn't know where to start. Once again he felt as if he were taking a fist to the head from a member of the MacInnes family. "My 'affection' for Eric, Libby? Is that the word you used?"

"Yes. Please, Wim, it's not a secret. I know what you meant to Eric, and vice versa."

"He *told* you? Directly? Himself?"

"No. Of course not. He could never tell me about something like that. But I knew. And I understood."

He sighed. "Libby, I feel like I should have a little brochure printed up, that I can hand to every member of your family, like those mutes who used to hand out the little cards in the bus station. That way I wouldn't have to keep giving this speech. *Look at me,* Libby." She did, reluctantly. "I had *no relationship* with your brother," he said, flat but firm. "Ever. In any way."

She watched him warily for a minute. Then she responded. "Wim, I didn't come here to argue with you. I understand why you need to be careful. In fact, I'm encouraging you to be careful. Maybe Eric should have been more careful, too. Well, that's *definitely* true. He should have been. But the family has decided that you weren't involved in Eric's death. So this is a good time for you to get out. Out of the line of fire."

He felt his fight-or-flight instinct kicking in. "One more time, Libby: Not only did I not kill your brother, I never had any sort of relationship with him—good, bad, or otherwise. Or didn't Father William cue you into that part of his investigations? Maybe he would prefer you to think that I'm off limits to you by dint of my unnatural sexual leanings?"

"I don't know," she said after a moment, looking increasingly miserable. "I don't know. I don't care about that. I don't want to talk about my father or what he thinks or doesn't think. I am so tired of all that. But what I *do* know is that you were what Eric needed, at one point in his life. Like Dave Westerling was, at another point." She saw the look of surprise on his face. "Yes, I know that you met with him. I also know that whatever you and Eric had between the two of you was right for Eric, and that's what matters to me. I loved him a whole lot, more than he ever knew, even though he didn't let me into his life very much. I really shouldn't say much more than that. *Can't* say much more than that. Except that I'm worried for you."

He could see that her eyes were welling up. He didn't care, particularly. The tears were for her brother, in any case, or maybe for herself.

"Okay, one more time, Libby," he said. He was angry, and he saw no reason not to turn up the heat. "You and your family are *completely* out of touch. Completely off base. You don't have a clue, any of you. I've never seen anything like it. Maybe it's because you communicate by proxy—by messenger, chauffeur, trainer, butler, bodyguard, and calling card—every which way except directly."

"Please—"

"No, let me finish." He could hear his voice rising, and he saw a couple of heads turning toward him. He didn't much care. "For all your wealth and power, at the end of the day your family is some kind of pathetic cross between an English drawing-room farce and a French costume drama. You hire expensive thugs who don't seem to protect you very well. You send out squads of gumshoes and get back bonehead information, no doubt for big bucks. You see yourselves as superior, above the fray, sophisticated, but as far as I can see, you don't have a damn clue what is going on in each other's heads, let alone my head."

"I don't think—"

"Right. Exactly. You don't think." He dropped his napkin on the table in front of him. Then he stood up, deliberately pushing his chair back from the table. "Meanwhile, by not thinking, and by not seeing what's sitting right there in front of you, you are putting me in a *really deep hole*. I'm talking about *you personally,* Libby. And right now, I don't need your sympathy, or your broad-minded toleration of my alleged sexual orientation. I need help getting *out* of the hole you've helped put me in."

"Oh, Wim, please—" Now a tear had escaped, rolling down her cheek.

"I really don't want to hear it," he snapped. He wasn't playing a part now; now he was fighting for his skin. If she wasn't with him, she was against him. "You call me when you're ready to *help*. And call direct. Don't insert Lurch in the middle."

She sagged. And with that, he got up and stalked out of the restaurant. Passing all those tables, he found it easy to ignore the disapproving looks directed at him by the burghers at the nearby tables. *(He made that pretty girl cry!)* But he found it surprisingly hard to push out of his mind the memory of her miserable, lonely, pretty face, slumped into her hands, eyes covered with the flats of her palms.

That was going to be hell on her makeup, he concluded.

23

OTHER THAN THE PRESENCE OF THE EMBARRASSED faces around her, avoiding her eyes, she saw no reason not to stay and finish her brandy. And then another. So she did.

She got unsteadily to her feet. The waiter appeared, wrapping strong fingers around her elbow. "Shall we put the charges on your room as usual, Miss MacInnes?"

"Yes. Do. Please." She heard herself putting one word in front of the other. Now she would have to put one foot in front of the other. "And of course please add twenty percent. Room . . ."

But here she had a problem. She couldn't summon up the room number to the front of her brain. Twelfth floor, she knew—somehow she always remembered the floor number easily—turn right off the elevator, right again, and then all the way to the end. On the left. She also remembered the geography of hotel corridors. Her brain just worked that way. White plastic card in her purse, with no room number on it, of course. For her safety.

"Don't worry, Miss MacInnes. We'll just send the tab over to the front desk. Do you need any assistance getting back upstairs? I could go get the concierge and ask him to—"

"I'm fine. No. I'm fine." She shook his hand off her elbow. Not wanting to be rude. But definitely not wanting right now to be in physical contact with anyone, either.

Weaving across the familiar lobby, over the garish carpet that she only took note of when she was "tipsy," as she called it in her head, she reflected on the fact that the waiter, whose name she could never quite remember, had simply assumed that she was heading upstairs. As opposed to out to the theater, or the symphony, or something else that would be interesting and glamorous. Why wouldn't she be doing something like that?

But of course, he would have realized that she wasn't carrying a coat.

Which was more than Vermeer had noticed. Bastard. She was only trying to help. To hell with him, if he wouldn't take her help. *But of course, I didn't take help from the waiter, who was just trying to be helpful . . .*

There was the elevator. Up button. Going *up*? Time's *up*. Things are looking *up*. Not really: more like, *the jig is up*. This was one reason why she liked getting tipsy: Things seemed to snap together mysteriously. Patterns popped up where you hadn't seen them before, as if they had been set free somehow. Set free by the wine and the calvados. The French apple brandy that she recently realized that they stocked here just for her. From her side of the bar, she had watched the level in the bottle. It didn't seem to go down much between her visits.

She pressed the round 12 button and watched it turn orange. Reassuring. She half expected something *twelve* to happen. But of course, it didn't. She was not *drunk,* for heaven's sake.

The elevator invited her out. She accepted. And turned

right and walked down the long, long hallway. She drifted past an odd little half-circle table, under the gilded mirror adorned with the beautiful fresh flowers. She could smell them. She chose not to look in the mirror. She wished she knew more about flowers, so that she could ask him if he had noticed the wonderful *azaleas* in the hall. Except she knew, of course, that they were not azaleas. Still moving slowly, she looked back over her left shoulder to admire them once more and bumped hard into a door frame that somehow slid up and caught her by her right shoulder.

Him.

Ouch. That was her shoulder weighing in. Lower down, though, down through her churning middle, she felt mostly anxiety. *Him.* He didn't like it when she got tipsy. He said she was remote, less responsive, less *there.* And of course, he was right. And it didn't make a lot of sense to travel all this way just to *not be there.*

She hated being lonely. One way not to be lonely was to be with him. Another way not to be lonely was to be with the wine, and the brandy. And sometimes she liked to be with them all: with him *and* the wine *and* the brandy.

She and Eric disagreed about how not to be lonely. Used to disagree. Eric was dead. *There:* There was what she had started calling in her mind her Eric pain, which lodged just above her stomach. Tonight it seemed to ride up above her anxiety, like a cruel rider on an ugly horse. She missed Eric dearly. More than she would ever have imagined.

Now she was at her door, fumbling with her purse, fishing for the white plastic card. *Twelve-twelve* was what the door was called. She hoped the waiter had figured that out. But this was a good hotel; they always figured things out.

In some places, you stuck the white plastic card straight in, like a knife between two ribs. (She had seen those ribs on her surgical rotation.) Other places, you plunged it down like a little guillotine. This—she worked it out—was the straight-in kind, which she liked better, because they generally seemed to work better. Or maybe that was just her imagination. Maybe it was just more like a key was supposed to be. The welcome *clud* noise, that you could feel in your bones if your hand was on the handle, and the little green light.

There were no lights on inside as she pushed the heavy door out of the way, stepped sideways, and let it swing shut. Hard. For her safety. No lights was unusual. Usually he liked to start with the lights on and turn them off one by one. He was old-fashioned that way. He was old-fashioned in lots of ways.

She headed straight for the bathroom, suddenly feeling an overwhelming, urgent need to pee. Bathroom light on to get oriented. Rush the clothes out of the way. Sit. Release.

Now with no urgency but with a stronger awareness of her anxiety, she stood up, reassembled her clothes, washed her hands mechanically. One thing that you learned in the hospital if you never learned it before was that the germs find *you*.

She jumped, startled, although she should have *expected* to see that face in that mirror, which was always there and which always ran the whole length of the wall. Where else would it be? And so where else would her face be?

She looked at that face, that silly face, trying to salvage what she could of her eye makeup. Was *she* old-fashioned? Sometimes she thought so. Most of the time, though, she thought she was *un*fashioned. Unshaped. Not well formed. She wondered, for what might have been the thousandth time, what anyone would see in someone who was as unformed as she was. Informed but unformed. She was that. That was all she was.

She glided halfway out of the bathroom. *Glid.* If it went "slide, *slid,*" it should go "glide, *glid.*" But it didn't.

"Turn off the light."

Again she started. Somehow she had forgotten about *him.* The bathroom light, he meant. She had forgotten that she had turned it on. She stopped, slid her hand down the wall until she found the toggle switches. Pushed one and made things much brighter. Not what he wanted. Then rocked both back in the opposite direction. Bringing the darkness back and making it hard for her to find her way into the room. The front room, the one with the glass-covered table over *there* somewhere, and the low coffee table somewhere over *there.* She wished she had looked around the corner and made a map for herself before turning the lights out again.

"Take off your clothes."

This in barely more than a whisper. This was all new, all of it. Maybe on another night she would have been more interested in novelty, in departures, in experimentation. Not tonight. She wanted warmth. Quiet. Reassurance. These were things that he sometimes brought to her. But mostly not.

She reached for the clasp on her necklace.

"No. Leave the jewelry on."

She wondered idly, as she moved her fingers down only a bit to the zipper on her dress, if there was any chance she was going to allow herself to be sick. Sometimes when she got tipsy, and then she got queasy, the easiest thing was to be sick, to get it over with. Usually she did that later. After her stomach had cleared. She was not *bulimic,* for heaven's sake. Also, it was better that he be asleep when she allowed that to happen.

Dimly she could see his outline framed in the chair by the window. The only light came from a crack between the heavy drapes. The light, such as it was, fell only on her. Not on him.

She fished up behind her back from below, found the zipper, pulled it the rest of the way down. Down to the small of her back. Which he had once said was the most interesting part of her. Offended, she was, at first. But then she forgave him when he insisted that he was complimenting her.

Her dress fell to the rug silently. Somehow, she knew she wasn't supposed to pick it up, tidy up, as she went along. This was different.

And the same with taking off her panty hose. She looked toward the couch, wishing that she could perch there, steady herself. She wished they, the two of them, could glide into the other room, the bedroom, and find the bed in the dark, and get under the covers, and enjoy the smell and the feel of the starched white sheets, and maybe enjoy each other, although she wasn't feeling particularly *there.* He would know right away; he would be angry about that. Angry in the bed that she hadn't even sat on since checking in, because she knew he liked the bed to be *unrumpled.* She wobbled as she freed her feet, like shucking corn, regaining her balance on her cornstalky legs. He motioned her closer. With his index finger he beckoned for the hose. She couldn't see his features. He looked blurry, somehow. The dark. The wine and the brandy.

She was very detached now, now that she was taking off the last scraps of her clothes. It was a little too cold to be naked. Her nipples sprouted: a last wall of defense. She was far from comfortable. She now believed that yes, she would be sick, and maybe soon. He was silent, and she wasn't really here for the most part. For the most part she was back in another, less complicated part of her life. Back when she felt as though she knew what was coming next. When people didn't surprise her.

"You first," he whispered, pointing.

She went into the bedroom, too aware of his eyes on her back. *Interesting,* he had called it. The small of her back. Here there was a little more light. The curtains were open a little wider. She was too aware of her jewelry on her naked body. She wondered if she looked foolish. She was proud of her body, yes, but all the same, she so often felt foolish. Did some people not feel as foolish as she did so much of the time?

"Lie down on the bed, Libby."

The sheets were turned down on a broad diagonal. She lay down, wondering if, hoping that, he had remembered to take the chocolates off the pillows. Housekeeping gave her extra chocolates, wrapped in gold and silver foils. Occasionally they wound up getting lost in the bed and getting rolled on and heated up, squashed under knees and elbows and rolled on again, until finally their wrappers gave way and made a terrible, embarrassing mess. The first time, she had made a point of telling Housekeeping that there was a *chocolate* stain on the sheets.

Housekeeping didn't care.

"I'm sorry, Libby." That was all he said. She felt gloved hands around her neck. That was new.

Too late, she panicked.

24

VERMEER WAS SURPRISED, WHEN HE WOKE UP, TO DIS-
cover that he was still annoyed. From what he could remember, his dreams had been grumbly and cranky, too.

Yes, he had been angry enough with Libby for not
telling him what he needed to know. But to some extent,
the scene in the restaurant had been for show. He needed
her to come back to him on his own terms—not as a
representative of the family, but as an ally. As someone
who could help him out of the dense forest he was finding himself in. A low-percentage play, but a play all the
same.

He forced himself to push the topic out of his mind.
No sense in ruining the weekend before it started.
Dressed in his boxers, he made his way into the small
kitchen and turned on the coffeemaker. Through the
kitchen window, over the sink, he had a view of the
Neponset River as it twisted its way through the former
Baker Chocolate complex. Today the river was shrunken
and subdued—a dark, slow-moving mass. Plates of ice
hung like hoopskirts off the boulders in midstream. In a
month or two a hard warm rain would fall, and all the
snow and ice upstream for miles would melt at once, and
this little stream would rage and roar and tumble all over

itself for a week or two. Then it would get lazy and surly again, and in the summer months it would smell bad.

Vermeer had wound up in this odd place by accident. He was new to town. A friend of a friend was moving out. The price was right. And he was a sucker for old industrial sites, and this was surely one of those—the first chocolate mill in America, located alongside the Neponset because at this particular point the river narrowed and dropped rapidly, offering free waterpower opportunities to the first capitalist who could front the money for the necessary dams, spillways, and waterwheels.

The manufacturing facilities huddled around the river had been upgraded and expanded over a century and a half by the clever and aggressive Baker company, which knew as much about marketing as it knew about chocolate. Then the inevitable had happened: General Foods bought the company and, after struggling for a while to work horizontally in a group of vertical buildings, gave up and moved the whole operation to Delaware. The mills were left to the pigeons and the vandals. But very slowly, during the next three decades, most of the little collection of six-story redbrick factories alongside the river had been converted into residential units.

Vermeer quickly discovered that no one else from the Harvard Business School lived here or, as far as he could tell, anywhere near here. He had surveyed the home addresses in the faculty phone book. It turned out that, like other well-to-do professional types, most of his Harvard colleagues favored the western suburbs—the "Ws," as they were known, short for Wellesley, Weston, and Wayland. A smaller group were Route 2-ers, coming in from the northwest, from towns like Lincoln, Concord, Carlisle, Lexington, and Belmont. "A crappier commute," one colleague had told him, "but enough Revolutionary cachet to make up for it." One or two brave souls came into Boston from the north, dealing with the mess of the harbor tunnels mainly because they had boats moored on Marblehead Neck or Nahant.

But if you believed that time is money—as did most people who sold hours, as did most of his Harvard colleagues—then you looked for the easiest route to Harvard and to Logan Airport. So you looked for and paid through the nose for a house in the "Ws." Next time, if there was a next time, he would know better.

With a final purgative hiss, the coffeemaker announced that it was done. Vermeer took his favorite mug out of the dishwasher—favorite mainly because it had an oversize handle, easy to hang on to, large enough to keep the rest of the hot mug spaced well away from his knuckles, which was a good thing if you wound up forgetting about your coffee and reheating it in the microwave two or three times.

Upstairs, someone dropped something heavy. Vermeer had no idea who, or what. He didn't know much about his neighbors. There was something about the massive old walls of this place that encouraged people to stay mostly separate—that and the fact that the developers had been stingy when it came to public spaces.

And finally, the tenants in this particular building were an odd hodgepodge. As far as he could tell, some were there for roughly the same reasons as he was. Others, poorer families, most without fathers in evidence, took advantage of the subsidized units that the city had required the developer to include. Some were divorced fathers (and even a few mothers) from nearby Milton who had to leave the broken home but couldn't or didn't want to get too far away from it. A few were artists, drawn by high ceilings and oversize windows. So when two people bumped into each other here, odds were that they didn't have a lot in common.

He foraged briefly in the refrigerator, not finding much. Briefly he thought about running across the street to the all-too-convenient Dunkin' Donuts, where he could be foolish (bagel), reckless (muffin), or self-destructive (doughnut). But he decided on virtue instead, remembering a baguette in the bread drawer that probably wasn't too hard to consume. He squeezed the paper bag, then dumped the loaf on a breadboard. Edible if toasted.

It was then, unbidden—probably the result of sawing the small loaf of bread in half, much as he had done at one point last night in the restaurant with Libby—that all the sickening twists of his predicament came flooding back into his mind, and into the pit of his stomach. He was in trouble. Serious trouble. Maybe he had guessed wrong. Maybe he should have accepted the few crumbs she had offered him and tried for more help, more information, more hope, the next time.

On the other hand, maybe she hadn't planned on a next time. Maybe she had said her piece and written him off.

His appetite vanished as his anxiety level rose. Would it ever have been possible to take her advice? Was there a point, somewhere earlier in this dark dream, when he could have told the oblique Dean Bishop, the obtuse MacInneses, and the rumpled detective with her tap-tap-tapping pencil, to just go and fuck themselves? Or was the trap already sprung weeks or months ago? Where was the evil emanating from, and why had it chosen to wrap itself around *him*?

His stomach clenched. This time, he knew, it wouldn't

be possible simply to push it all to the back of his mind. He would have to go to the gym and run himself into an endorphin-soaked approximation of calm. And, he thought, looking down at the forgotten French bread in his left hand, better to do that before breakfast.

By an accident of commercial geography, the gym was just about the same distance away from his apartment as Dunkin' Donuts, in the opposite direction. Head north for grease and damnation, or head south for redemption—and, of course, damage to the knees over the long run. The gym, populated mostly by tough-looking weight lifters from the Boston side of the river, was an unassuming little operation, lovable mainly for its proximity. There were no squash courts and never would be. A year's membership cost him less than a month of parking at Harvard.

He put on his version of a workout outfit, which tended to be shabbier and more low-tech than most of the others he saw out in the streets, but which worked well in the unpretentious shop around the corner. His shoes were the exception: He was a sucker for good running shoes. (He had a closet full of nearly new running shoes that had been obsoleted by some new alleged technical break-through.) This shoe fetish was something he had picked up from a consulting client years earlier: "Forget fancy women. Forget traveling. Forget the house on the Cape. The only thing worth blowing a lot of money on is good shoes and a hot car."

Well, at least he had the shoes.

A cold wind hit him as he stepped out the front door, onto the redbrick sidewalk. A nice Boston touch, when they kept the weeds down, which wasn't often enough. He pulled up the hood of his sweatshirt, tugging once on the strings to clench it tight around his face for the short jog to the gym, then stretched his leg muscles just enough to get him to the gym, where he would go through a longer stretching routine.

"Hey, bud."

Just as he pushed off in the direction of the gym, he became aware of a presence off to his left—a burly figure that had moved with surprising quickness out of a doorway just up ahead of him, and was saying something to him as it was enveloping him. A panhandler? Vermeer wondered. Brown overcoat, big hat with a brim bent down and concealing his features. What the bearlike figure was saying in a gravel-coated voice was, as Vermeer's mind sized up and caught up with the situation, *Hey, bud.* Panhandlers weren't all that common in this neighborhood, and they weren't usually out on the sidewalks on an icy-cold Saturday morning. Vermeer thought, *Well, at least I've got nothing to feel guilty about, since I'm not carrying any money.*

He slowed to explain that.

He didn't get the opportunity.

An ungloved fist flashed out from underneath the brown coat and caught Vermeer exactly in the middle of his chest, completely knocking the wind out of him. The first punch rocked him back on his heels, setting him up for the second blow, which smashed into him again in exactly the same spot, midtorso. Vermeer's knees folded beneath him. Around the pain and fear, he thought, gasping, *Someone who knows his work.*

Before he could sag all the way to the ground, the punching bear closed the gap between them, hugging Vermeer and propping him upright. *Why?* Why? Because the bear is steering him toward a car parked at the curb, idling, with the rear right passenger door slightly ajar. To anyone who happened to be watching, maybe it would look as if the jogger were having some sort of problem—the flashing jackhammer punches having been invisible from most angles—and the bear, a Good Samaritan, was giving him a lift.

And now, at closer range, Vermeer could see under the brim of the hat. Could see the contorted face of Dan Beyer—contorted with rage more than exertion. A face of fury, but also of calculation and determination. The balled fists were now clamps, one on either side of his body, steering him as if on an assembly line, raw material heading down the chute for processing. Vermeer knew, absolutely, that he *should not get into this car*, but no part of his body was responding to his brain . . .

Then, from yet another direction, over Beyer's shoulder, came another voice. A female voice, out of place. Flat but intrusive. "Hey. Hey! What's going on here?"

Beyer snarled, just loud enough to be heard, keeping his face concealed, "Back off, lady, if you know what's good for you."

"I don't think so, Dan," the voice said, with command in it.

Barbara Brouillard, now close enough to the action to do business, used her left hand to extend her badge a few feet from Beyer's face, and her right hand to pull a service revolver out from under her own droopy coat. Smoothly rather than quickly. "Boston Police. I say *you* back off. Dan Beyer, right? Well, Dan, I'm an excellent shot from four feet out, plus, I have two officers within thirty feet of your back. Which would be hard to miss in any case, but they're also good shots. So I say you let the professor down nice and easy, and you keep your hands up nice and high, and nobody gets killed. Meaning you."

Even around the searing pain in his chest and the bright lights behind his sagging eyelids, Vermeer could feel Beyer calculating the odds. Could sense that Beyer was deciding whether to simply snap his neck and wait for the hail of bullets to follow. The clamps tightened.

"*Now,* Dan."

Then the clamps relaxed. Vermeer slumped to the ground, watching the dirty snow rush up toward his face, wondering if he would slip under the parked car and somehow die that way. He managed to topple away from the curb.

"Hands where I can see them." He heard Brouillard's cold voice. "Only slow movements. Good. Hands behind your back. Face the car. Good. Now, why don't you bend over and rest that chin right up on the roof of the car. Very good, Dan."

Brouillard snapped on the handcuffs with some difficulty—Beyer's wrists were half again as thick as the average suspect's. On her signal, two uniformed officers stepped forward. They had disbelief on their young faces. Each now reached for one of Beyer's protruding elbows.

"Read him his rights," she said, her voice still hard-edged, "then put him in the black-and-white and keep an eye on him. Meanwhile, call in another unit to come and babysit this car until headquarters can get a team down here to go over it inch by inch."

"Yes, ma'am."

"Don't leave until the babysitters show up, and tell *them* not to leave until after this car is scoured, clean. It's obviously a rental, and I'm not expecting a lot, but that's no excuse for being sloppy. This one goes completely by the book. And tell them when they're done, get it towed to Pier 41, and make sure it's locked up nice and tight. Hertz is out of luck on this one for the time being."

"Yes, ma'am."

"Then you can take Mr. Potato Head here downtown and book him for assault. For starters. Give him his one call. Don't let him talk to anybody else. Keep him under wraps until I get back."

They nodded, still wide-eyed.

"So *go*. I'll tend to the professor."

Vermeer groaned, curbside.

"Who seems to be coming back to life, just a little bit."

25

Brouillard studied the still-gasping figure on the brick sidewalk, calculating how best to get him to his feet. "Not used to taking punches, are we?" Despite the gibe, her voice was not unkind. "He popped you a couple of good ones, that's for sure. One, two. Pop, pop." She squatted alongside him.

"I *think*," she continued in a calming voice, but still with that note of command in it, "that we need to get you back inside so you can count your ribs. Can you stand up?"

He got to his knees and looked sideways at her. He tried to answer but wound up coughing and wincing, and then coughing and wincing again.

"Okay, so maybe you don't try to talk just yet," she said, suppressing a smile. She had seen enough of what she was looking for: alertness, eyes focusing, good color, no blood with the cough, no signs of shock. She reached for the inside of his arm, above his wrist. His hand closed around her wrist. Mountaineering-style. She leaned back and pulled gently, and he leaned into her effort. "Shallow breaths only for the time being, Professor. And meanwhile, maybe what we do is, we just get you up halfway, like so, and then you crouch up on that leg, and then you crouch up halfway on that one—hey, those are some wowza *sneakers*, big fella—and you put this arm over my shoulder. And then we both stand up at once. Right. Very good."

With her right arm around his waist, and his left arm over her shoulder, they shuffled their way back through the front door of his apartment building to the locked inner door. She looked at him and, with her eyebrows, asked for the key. He pointed with an extended toe at the corner of the large rubber mat.

She propped him up against the wall, retrieved the key, and brought it back, shaking her head. "Oh, jeez, the old key-under-the-mat trick. No points for either originality or smarts, Professor, although I guess you know your own neighborhood." She opened the locked inner door and peeled Vermeer off the wall, and they made their way to the elevator.

She deposited him on the couch, stepped back, and assessed the situation again: color still good, minor shakes, voice returning, some healthy signs of embarrassment. She brought him a glass of orange juice—easily accessible sugars—and sat down in a chair opposite him. He nodded, thanking her, wincing again as he stretched to take the glass. She calculated whether, if he passed out and pitched forward, she could reach him before he hit the coffee table between them. She decided she could, just barely, but her odds would get a lot better if she perched up on the forward edge of her seat. So she perched.

"So let's see what we have in the way of reading material here." She picked up two wordy-looking magazines and a tabloid-shaped newspaper from one of the wobbly piles on the coffee table. No, not a newspaper: the *New York Review of Books*. "The *Journal of Finance*. The

Macrame—no, *Ma-cro-economic*—*Quarterly*. None of which looks all that gripping. Beach reading for bachelor professor types?"

He didn't respond. He was pushing on his ribs, one by one, carefully taking a semideep breath for each rib as he climbed the rib ladder up his torso.

She looked at the address label. Then she laughed out loud. "*Wilmer*? Wim is short for Wilmer? Your real name is *Wilmer*?"

Vermeer stopped poking himself, looked up, and sighed. "Yes. Wilmer." He spoke economically but in a voice that was now close to normal. "You don't like that name?"

"Sorry." She laughed again. "It's just such a dorky sort of name. What were your parents thinking of? I mean, I can see Wilhelm, or maybe even Wilbur. But *Wilmer*—that's a terrible thing to lay on a kid."

"It's a family name," he said, gingerly twisting his upper body from side to side, still partly focused on his self-examination. "It got shortened to Wim pretty quick, and I never thought about it much. Except for you, no one's had such a good laugh out of it since junior high school, I don't think."

She could see he was annoyed, but she was not going to let it go. For one thing, she wanted to work him out of his self-absorbed state. And also, it *was* a dorky name, which deserved some abuse. "I mean," she persisted, "I'm trying to think of one cool person whose name was Wilmer. And I can't think of a one. There was the guy who owned the talking horse on TV, Mr. Ed, but I'm pretty sure his name was—"

"Wilbur. An architect. Cool guy. Wrong name."

"Right. And what's the name of the little fat guy with the speech defect who chases Bugs Bunny around?"

"Elmer. Fudd."

"Right." She grinned, enjoying herself, continuing to drag words out of him. "So I can't even think of *any* Wilmers, let alone cool ones."

"Well," said Vermeer, rising to the bait in spite of himself, "you have a very nice city in Texas named Wilmer. Southeast of Dallas."

"Cities don't count."

"Lots of law firms with Wilmers in them."

"Last names, though, right? Last names don't count, either."

"Okay," he replied after a moment. "Here's one that's right up your personal alley. Remember the little hood who trailed Sydney Greenstreet around in *The Maltese Falcon*? The one that Humphrey Bogart proposes to hand over to the police to tie up all the loose ends? Wilmer. No last name. Played by a character actor named Elisha Cook Jr."

"I don't know. Sounds vaguely familiar."

"He's the one who tells Bogart that if Bogart keeps riding him, they'll be 'pickin' iron out of his liver.' " He took a breath. "And then Bogart says, 'The cheaper the hood, the gaudier the patter.' That's Wilmer."

"Well, if that's the best you can do, *Wilmer,* I think you're making my point for me." She put the magazines back on the coffee table, tidying up a few stacks in passing.

"Oh, please," he complained, "don't use Wilmer on me. I already offered you Wim when we talked downtown, and you turned it down. I think I'd rather be Professor Vermeer than Wilmer."

"Yeah, I can definitely see that."

They looked at each other. Both were aware that the conversation needed to take a serious turn. "So," she finally said, "my read is that you didn't need an ambulance ride, and that you don't need a doctor just now, although an X-ray of those ribs might make sense. You tell me if I'm wrong. If I'm not, I'd like to ask you a few questions. Starting with, what the hell was that little scene on the sidewalk all about?"

He shook his head, looking blank. "I was hoping you could tell me. I step outside. I get jumped by Libby's bodyguard. He collapses my lungs with his right pile driver and tries to stuff me into a car. You show up and rescue me." He paused for a moment. His brow furrowed. "And how *do* you show up just in time, by the way?"

"Let me ask the questions for now. You had your dinner with Libby last night, right? Did you run into him then? Did you do anything to really piss him off—I mean, to get him angry enough to come down here and try to wipe you out?"

Again Vermeer shook his head. He noted that Brouillard had produced a notepad and pencil out of some pocket inside her coat, which she was still wearing. "You can take your coat off, if you'd like. I'm not hanging it up for you, though." She shook her head impatiently and tapped her pencil on her pad. He retold the story of his earlier phone conversation with Beyer, in which he had deliberately provoked the bodyguard. Then he recounted the short scene at the bar, with Beyer basically ignoring him. "Less nasty than the phone call," he said. He replayed Libby's confession that she was using the dinner as a pretext to get out from under Beyer's watchful eye. Briefly he summarized the frustrating dinner conversation, ending with him stalking out. "Maybe that was dumb on my part," he acknowledged, seeing the look on Brouillard's face. "But she seemed to think that she could just waltz in, tell me next to nothing—except, of course, reassuring me that my nonexistent relationship with her dead brother was perfectly okay with her—and then waltz out again."

"And then?"

"Then what?"

"Then what did you do?"

"Then nothing. I came home and went to bed."

"No further contact with Libby after you left the restaurant?"

"No, of course not. She was half in the bag at that point, in any case. She wouldn't have been easy to talk to."

"Any sign of her mystery date showing up as you were leaving?"

"Nope."

"Did she have a coat with her? A bag? Outdoor gear?"

"Not that I saw. She got there before me and left after me. I guess she could have checked them in the coatroom. Or she could have been planning to go upstairs and get whatever she needed, before she went out. Why?"

"What kind of shoes did she have on?"

"I have no idea. Black. Fancy. Expensive. Heels, I think, but not too high. Why in the world do you care what kind of *shoes* she was wearing? What does that have to do with me nearly getting kidnapped and killed?"

"What time did you leave the Four Seasons?"

"I don't know. Around nine thirty or so."

"Valet park?"

"No. I'm too cheap. I found a meter about a block away. I'm good at that."

"What time did you get back here?"

"As long as it took me to walk to the car and drive home. I don't know—say, ten o'clock."

She looked down to take some notes. Once she turned the pencil around, erased something, and started over. Intent on her writing, she seemed oblivious to his presence.

"So," he said. "Good thing you were shadowing Beyer. I haven't thanked you for saving my life. So thanks."

Finally, flipping the pad shut, she looked up again. "You're welcome. But frankly, Professor Vermeer, we weren't tailing him. We were tailing you."

She watched his reaction. He sagged a little. He didn't say anything. She took a note. "And it gets worse, Professor. Libby was killed last night. In her hotel room. Too late to be in today's paper, but you can read all about it tomorrow. Front-page news, no doubt."

"My God," he said hoarsely, rubbing his face hard with both hands, as if trying to wake up as somebody else. "My God. Do you know who did it? And why?"

"We don't have a lot so far. We're still checking out the scene, running tests, and so on. These things take time. But put it this way: I'd feel better if we had more to go on."

"Jesus. Poor kid. Does it look like a random thing?"

"On the face of it, no. I'm really not in a position to talk about it at this point." She continued to watch his face, and his body language, intently. He seemed oblivious to the scrutiny, shaking his head slowly, side to side.

Then he stiffened and looked up, his features cold. "So Libby gets killed, and you decide to shadow *me*? And then I step out my front door and nearly get killed, and you want to check out *my* alibi?"

"Actually," Brouillard responded, choosing the question she wanted to answer, "we had a tail on you before Libby's death. One of my colleagues had a very nice dinner last night at the Four Seasons. A rare treat for him, I can tell you. Unfortunately, he was a little too far away to hear much of what you two were talking about. He did see what looked like some signs of passion, though. She cries a little bit; she holds your hand; you get pissed off and stalk out. She finishes her drink all by herself, then orders another, and finishes that one. Then she goes upstairs and dies."

Vermeer got to his feet slowly, corkscrewing his way up and using the arm of the couch for balance. He made his way over to the windows overlooking the river. His back was to her. She could see his hands appear from under his armpits. He was hugging himself.

"So, did your people follow me home? If they did, then they sure as hell know I didn't kill Libby MacInnes last night."

"Well, it's not that simple, Professor." In a matter-of-fact tone, Brouillard sketched out ways he could have accomplished it: sneaking back out of some side door of this hulking building, going back into town, using the second hotel passkey that Libby asked for when she registered but which was now nowhere to be found. And so on. He stood motionless, looking out the windows as she spun the dark scenario. "So it's time to pop the question, Professor. Did you kill her?"

"No. You know I didn't," he said, turning to look at her. "You know I didn't kill Libby MacInnes."

She nodded noncommittally. *I hear you,* the gesture said. Not *I believe you.*

"I had no motive. This is ridiculous. I barely knew her."

"Like you barely knew Eric."

"Yeah," he said icily. "Exactly like that." Then another

thought returned to him. "You were tailing me *before* last night."

"Correct."

"Why? Because I had already killed Eric, or because I was about to kill Libby?"

She was standing up, snapping her pad shut, getting ready to leave. "There's a third possibility," she replied. "Maybe we wanted to make sure nothing happened to you."

"Yeah, maybe."

"Look, Professor," she said, standing up to rebutton her coat and pulling the belt tight around her waist, "let me give you some advice. The proverbial shit is about to hit the proverbial fan. You are about to become famous. It could be as soon as about twenty-two hours from now, when the Sunday papers hit the street."

"Thanks. My friends in the police department, looking out for my best interests again by pointing the media toward me?"

"Actually, no," she said, deflecting his hostility. "We don't talk to the press at this stage of the game, at least beyond the bare minimum. We're certainly not volunteering anything about you, or about anybody, for that matter. I'm telling them the truth, which is that at this point, we don't have a suspect. But based on the questions I'm already getting, I'd say that somebody has tipped off somebody. Your name is definitely floating around. The *Herald* has already connected Libby and Eric and linked you with both of them. The *Globe* won't be far behind. Whether they have the balls to drop your name at this point is anybody's guess. But if not tomorrow, then not long after that, unless we bring someone else in first."

He looked at her from across the room. He was still

hugging himself. "Good to know, Detective. Good to have something new to look forward to. Is that all the advice you've got for me? Get ready to be a celebrity murder suspect?"

"No, there's more. Get yourself a lawyer. A mean one—someone you don't like. Don't take any calls from the press. If they buttonhole you on the street, stiff-arm them. No comment. Take my word for it; you're better off saying nothing. Lay low—someplace other than here; they'll be swarming all over this place pretty soon. Leave your cell phone on, in case I need to find you. And don't leave town."

"Is that last bit 'advice,' or is that an order?"

"*Please* don't leave town."

26

H E WAS SITTING BY HIMSELF IN THE REAL INTERROGA-
tion room—the one with the one-way mirror—but he
wasn't alone. Behind the glass were two officers, keeping
an eye on him. A third waited in the hall outside.

Brouillard entered the room warily, although she took
care not to show any fear. She sat down across the table
from Beyer. His uncuffed hands were folded in his lap,
making him look like an enormous errant schoolboy. But
looking at his upper body, she was glad that the table and
chairs were bolted to the floor.

"This conversation is being recorded," she began. No
response. She took out her pad and pencil. You never
knew when the recorder would break or the tape would
run out. "You've been told that you have the right to have
an attorney present?"

"Yeah."

"And you've decided to waive your right to legal
counsel?"

"Uh-huh." Stretching a little, he moved like a fat snake
on a cold day.

"You're talking to me voluntarily, and you're aware
that anything you say can be used against you in a court
of law?"

"Nothing much to hide, I'd say." He looked her in the eye for the first time. "Did I go after that little fuck-weasel professor? Yeah, I did. I'm only sorry you showed up when you did and I didn't get the chance to finish the job."

"What job? Where were you planning to take him, and what were you going to do with him?"

He looked slightly surprised. "I was going to kill him. I don't know where. Somewhere not in the middle of an intersection, I guess. Find some woods somewhere."

"You were just going to kill him and dump him in the woods?"

"Yeah."

"Why?"

"Because he killed Libby."

"Why do you think that?"

Again he looked a little surprised, although he didn't look particularly interested in what was going on around him. "Why do I think he killed Libby? Because she went out on a date with him and wound up dead. And because he's already killed one of the MacInnes kids, right? Why not kill another one? Maybe he's going for all three."

"Tell me what happened last night."

"He killed her."

"Just tell me what you saw."

"What was to see? When he showed up for dinner, I left him and Libby alone. I asked her to call me before she went to bed. Standard operating procedure. She didn't call. Sometimes she forgets. I called her around midnight. No answer. A little after two, I took the elevator downstairs. Two floors down. Her door hadn't shut all the way. That wasn't too unusual. She was often careless like that. No lights on, I could see. I knocked. No answer.

I walked in. Her clothes were in a pile on the floor. I called for her. Still no answer. By now, I'm getting worried, wondering what's going on. So I walked into the back room, the bedroom, and she was on the bed. I thought she was maybe passed out."

His voice began to get a little thicker. He cleared his throat. "I went over to her. It was dark, but I could see. Her eyes were open. Her neck didn't look right. I could see she was, uhm"—he cleared his throat again—"dead."

"What did you do next?"

He looked down at the table. "What did I do? I covered her up."

"Why?"

"Why? Because she was naked. And I didn't want a bunch of assholes like you coming in and gawking and seeing her like that."

"Then what did you do?"

"I don't remember very well. I was torn up. Mad. I must have picked up the phone and dialed the hotel operator, and told her there was a problem. After that, all hell broke loose. The cops came. I told them what I knew. But you know more about that than I do. I saw you there, right?"

"You were going out as I was coming in. So you went back to your room, and—"

"Yeah. That's right." Now his face began to shift, away from morose, toward murderous. "And I couldn't stop thinking about that little skinny shit-ass, that professor, killing her. Wringing her neck. Squeezing the life out of her. So I decided to go pay him back. You know the rest."

She waited a few beats. "Dan Beyer, did you kill Libby MacInnes?"

His jaw was clenched. She could see the muscles working. "No. You dumbshit cop. My job was to keep her alive. What's his name—Vermeer—he killed her."

"You went from the restaurant to your room"—she checked her notes as she recited—"where you waited, made a phone call to her room, and a little after two, you went down and found the body. Can anybody confirm that?"

"You mean, like the bimbo in my room? No. I was by myself. Room service came, pretty early on. I ordered a movie. Don't recall seeing anybody in the hall when I went to her room. But this is bullshit . . ." He made a move as if to stand up.

"Sit *down*, Beyer. I tell you when you can stand up." He sat. "And," she continued, "I decide what's bullshit and what's not. Got it?"

"Yeah. Whatever. Go ahead. Pin this on me."

"Nobody's going to get pinned. I'm going to figure out who did this. Using your own logic: We caught you in the act of trying to kill one guy. Maybe you also served up the last corpse that we found in your vicinity."

"I sure as fuck didn't kill Libby. And I sure as fuck would have killed Vermeer, if you hadn't gotten in the way."

"How often did you find her passed out?" She intended to catch him off guard, and did.

"Huh?"

"You said when you called her name and she didn't move, you thought maybe she was passed out. Did she pass out a lot?"

"Sometimes she drank too much. Sometimes I made sure she got to bed okay."

"Sounds cozy."

"Fuck you."

"So you weren't her boyfriend?"

"No. Go fuck yourself."

"So why did she ask for two passkeys when she checked in? Why did she *always* ask for two passkeys? When we search your room this afternoon, will we find the other passkey there?"

"No. Fuck you. Search all you want. Maybe she liked to have two in case she lost one of them."

"Think she might have been carrying on with someone else, behind your back? Think she might have been in the habit of giving that second key to that person?"

He looked offended at the suggestion. "What, you think I wouldn't have known about something like that? I practically lived with that woman. No way. You want to find the second passkey? Go search Vermeer's place. Or look in that shitty river behind his place, more likely."

She turned the pages of her pad, as if searching for something missing. A full minute went by. "I don't get it, Dan."

"You don't get what?"

"I don't get what's driving you. Okay, sure, you fucked up—you were hired to protect Libby, and she got killed on your watch. Doesn't look so good on your body-guard résumé—"

"Fuck you."

"Let me finish. Doesn't look so good, but hey, it's only a job, right? You try and draw another paycheck or two from the MacInnes family, who are probably good for it, and then you bail. You walk away. You go looking for the next thing. Maybe you get a job as a stud-muffin on a cruise ship, helping overweight suburbanites keep an eye on their blood pressure while they pretend to tone up, and you just forget about all this crap. What I mean is, you don't risk a life sentence for killing the guy who you think killed your client. Or am I missing something?"

"Fuck you."

She pressed on in the same bland voice, seeming to overlook his hostility. "Actually, you loved her a lot, didn't you, Dan? More than you could stand? And she'd get shit-faced, chasing these losers, and count on you to tuck her in at night. And for a guy like you, she was always going to be out of reach, wasn't she?"

She watched his face purple.

"Fuck you," he said.

27

Vermeer normally went to work on the early side in any case, out of the house by 6:15 in an effort to beat the South Shore traffic into town. This particular Monday, however, he decided that leaving even earlier might be a good idea.

He had chosen to ignore Brouillard's cautions about lying low. There were two possible explanations for why his life was swirling clockwise down the toilet bowl. The first was that this Boston cop didn't know what she was doing. The second explanation was that she *did* know what she was doing.

In either case, following her advice didn't seem to make much sense.

Then the Sunday papers came out.

The *Herald* won the battle for most lurid headline: AND SISTER MAKES TWO, screamed the entire front page above the fold. Below the fold was a blurry photo of a stretcher being shoved into an ambulance on the semicircular driveway in front of the Four Seasons. Several angry-looking uniformed cops with outstretched arms were pushing the photographer away. There wasn't much to see on the stretcher: a blurry black lump poking out at each end of a lumpy white sheet, with two black straps dividing the stretcher's cargo into more or less equal thirds. Ordinarily, Vermeer wouldn't have looked twice at such a picture. He would have sneered at the newspaper that splashed it across its front page. Now he consumed it eagerly—and apprehensively.

The accompanying article, linking Libby's suspicious death with her brother's death two weeks earlier, had Brouillard declining to comment on the case, but "unnamed sources" had told the *Herald* that police were pursuing some hot leads and that they expected to make an arrest shortly. An accompanying sidebar, "Dying Rich," provided a ludicrous, cartoonlike summary of the MacInnes family and fortune. Vermeer breathed a sigh of relief.

Then he read the *Globe*'s version of the same story. What the *Globe* gave up in the headline department (SECOND MACINNES DEATH PUZZLES INVESTIGATORS), it more than made up for in colorful and mostly accurate reporting. The story had a shared byline. One of the reporters was a senior city desk reporter whose name Vermeer recognized; the other was a middle-tier business writer to whom he had provided a number of "sound bite" quotes in the past year or so—not a good sign. Much more than the *Herald* story, their article focused on the Harvard and the Business School connections and even included speculation offered by "well-placed sources" that the two deaths were connected through Harvard. An unidentified source "close to the investigation" identified Libby's dinner companion on the night of her death as a "young Harvard finance professor" who had known Eric.

His stomach flopped.

Again, in print at least, Brouillard declined to comment beyond saying that she and her colleagues would go "wherever the trail of evidence leads us."

It was only a matter of time, Vermeer knew—days, maybe hours—before the reporters laid him out in lavender. They hadn't quite had the nerve to pull the trigger and name him in the Sunday papers, but who knew what Monday would bring?

Which was the other reason why Vermeer had headed to work early this Monday morning. Even though, as he had to admit, it wasn't clear exactly what he was supposed to be doing at work. He had been relieved of his teaching responsibilities so that he could babysit the MacInneses and encourage the police to wrap up their investigations. That hadn't worked out as planned: Another MacInnes was dead, and a second investigation—this time, of a clear-cut homicide—was under way.

Not only was Sam the temp not in sight—not surprising for seven a.m., of course—but his desk in the hallway cubicle was ominously clean. It suggested strongly that Sam the temp was gone forever. A lot might have happened in a week, Vermeer realized.

He dialed his voice mail: "*You have . . . sixty-eight . . . new messages.*" He thought about plowing through them but decided instead to update his voice-mail greeting. Meanwhile, his e-mail finished downloading: 151 messages. Scrolling through the most recent of these, he saw a sudden spike of messages in the past twenty-four hours, many from local media outlets. Yes, there was the *Globe* reporter who had always been glad to get a crumb of punditry from Wim Vermeer. Now, it appeared, he was throwing a noosed rope over the nearest stout tree branch. "Urgent statement from you needed," read the subject line.

Statement urgently needed from you, corrected Vermeer silently. *Unless of course you're hoping I'll confess in an urgent kind of way.*

He trashed the most obvious spam—mortgage refinancings, penis enlargements, "make money from home," and so on—and left the rest unread. The main reason to listen to phone messages and read e-mails at this point was to job-hunt, and no one was going to be putting him on their payroll anytime soon.

He was riffling through the stack of mail and memos in his in-box when the phone rang. Here, well before he was ready for it, was the day's first dilemma: Should he pick it up? Or lie low? Maybe Brouillard was right: Maybe he should hire himself a junkyard dog of a lawyer—a lawyer with fangs and claws—and just hide behind him or her. He could let the machine grab it. He could gather his wits.

He picked it up. "Professor Vermeer's office."

"Professor Vermeer?"

"Who's calling, please?"

"This is Maude Friedman in Dean Bishop's office. The dean thought you might be in early."

"Hello, Maude." He thought he remembered her from behind the mahogany barricade: purposeful, brunette. "What's going on?"

"The dean would like to meet with you as soon as possible. Now, if you're available."

The first two things he noticed, as he was ushered into the dean's inner sanctum and the door clicked shut behind

him, was that there were two people in the room—
Bishop and another vaguely familiar-looking man—and
that neither of them rose or gave any indication that they
intended to shake his hand.

"Good morning, Wim," Bishop said.

"Hello again."

"Please sit down. I'm not sure whether you know John
Eustis, University counsel."

Vermeer nodded at the middle-aged man in the con-
servatively polka-dotted bow tie. Hand tied, of course.
Lean and tanned, with a full crop of blondish-gray hair,
Eustis had the look of old Brahmin money. If he were
decked out in Topsiders and khakis, he would look perfectly at home on the deck of a sloop, cutting through the
wave tops off Nantucket. Vermeer remembered that he
had run across Eustis at a conference on corporate gover-
nance and had wondered what Harvard's top lawyer was
doing in that setting. Now he wondered what Eustis was
doing in this setting.

The answer, for the moment, was, not much. He simply nodded at Vermeer, then looked back down at an open
manila folder on the big round table.

"Well, Wim, we need to have a candid talk," Bishop
continued. "I'm sure you've seen the papers."

"I have."

"It pains me to say so, but in light of everything that's
been going on, I've decided to put you on an indefinite
administrative leave, effective immediately."

"Indefinite *paid* administrative leave," Eustis interjected quickly, addressing Bishop.

"Of course," Bishop resumed with a quick nod toward
Eustis. "That's correct. It appears, from everything we're
reading and hearing, that you've gotten far too deeply in-

volved in the MacInnes situation. That was never my intention. After consulting with Mr. Eustis at the suggestion of the president, I've decided that it's not in the school's or university's best interest to have you involved in what is now an official police matter."

Vermeer felt himself taking shallower breaths. *Fight or flight.* "Frankly, Dean Bishop," he began, in a higher pitch than he had intended, "I'm a little shocked." He pushed his voice down into a lower register. "*I'm* the one who's having all these stories spread about me. I'm the one who got beat up on the sidewalk in front of my house." He saw Eustis take a note. "And now you're banishing me to Siberia because of some newspaper stories?"

Bishop shook his head slowly. His eyelids had drooped slightly, making his face even more difficult to read than usual. "This has become bigger than you, or me, or the school, Wim. I asked you to take on a simple task, and—"

But here Eustis leaned forward, again looking only at Bishop. He put two fingers on the dean's forearm. Bishop stopped talking. Both men sat back in their chairs and regarded Vermeer steadily.

"And you think this is fair, Dean Bishop?" Now, despite his rising anger, Vermeer felt that he was thinking clearly, as if he were watching events unfold from a safe distance. But he knew there was no safe distance here. "Hanging me out to dry just as the jackals are closing in? What about hearing *my* side of the story? Why isn't our Mr. Eustis looking out for *me*?"

"For the moment," Bishop said, "we will await the outcome of the police investigation. With which you will cooperate fully, of course."

"You've *caved*," Vermeer snapped back, not believing what was unfolding before him. "You got a call from Massachusetts Hall, or from the mayor's office, and now you're throwing me overboard!"

The dean reddened slightly. He could have been angry, or ashamed, or some of both. "Maybe, Professor Vermeer, we're all learning something about how the world works. About how—" But once again Eustis silenced him with two extended fingers—a smothering lawyerly blanket, putting out the fire.

"Do I have a right to have legal representation at this meeting?"

This time Bishop did not reply but looked to Eustis. Eustis addressed Vermeer for the first time. "No," he said in a voice that sounded like an ice cube cracking under running water. "You don't. And Dean Bishop has every right to take appropriate administrative actions, especially if those actions entail no financial consequences for you, and if in his judgment your continued presence here presents the possibility of a serious disruption of the educational community. That's what is going on here. In no sense is this a legal proceeding."

"So that's it? I'm just bounced out? And then I sit around and wait for the shit to hit the fan?" Vermeer remembered Brouillard's use of the same phrase only the day before yesterday. It seemed like a long time ago.

"Not quite," said Eustis. "First we have to discuss the terms of your leave."

"Is this a negotiation?"

"No," Eustis said, picking up the top piece of paper from his manila folder. "It's not that, either. First," he began, reading, "we consider the fact of this leave confidential. In other words, Harvard will simply decline to comment if and when we are asked about your current status. And while we certainly can't prevent you from talking to the press, we strongly believe that for you to initiate contact with the media would be ill advised, and we would strongly discourage you from doing so.

"Second, as the dean noted, you will continue to be paid, and your benefits will continue uninterrupted. You will continue to accrue vacation time, and the period of your leave will be counted for retirement purposes.

"Third, you will have no teaching responsibilities, and you will have no other contact with students of this school or of other Harvard departments, on or off campus, until further notice. For now, we are not formally seeking to restrict your access to the campus, but we request that you minimize your on-campus activities and presence.

"In that spirit," he continued, "your mail will be forwarded to your home. You should arrange to forward your office phone to an off-campus number—your residence, your cell, or whatever. You will not have access to the school's intranet. You will not be entitled to administrative support for the duration of your leave, beyond the kinds of support that the institution extends to its employees in the normal course of business.

"And finally," Eustis concluded, "your failure to comply with any or all of these conditions may result in a review of your status, including but not limited to your access to the campus. You are, of course, entitled and encouraged to engage counsel to review your options. The university hopes that this temporary arrangement will meet the needs of all parties at this difficult juncture. I should point out, though, that any decision on your part to contest this course of action may similarly result in a review of your status."

Vermeer wondered if Eustis's inner voice—the voice in his brain—talked in these dry, parsed-out syllables. He suspected that it did. "I hope you don't expect me to *sign* something," he said, trying to match the coldness in the lawyer's voice.

"No, there is nothing for you to sign, Professor Vermeer," Eustis replied. "My office will send a copy of these conditions in a certified letter to your residence. Included in that letter will be the request that you communicate with my office, rather than Dean Bishop's, on any matters pertaining to your leave."

"So Bishop throws me overboard, but you get to hear the splash?"

Eustis had delivered his set piece; now he looked as if he had somewhere else to go. Presumably another murderer, elsewhere across the vast reaches of Harvard, needing to get sealed off like a tubercle in an infected lung. "For the record, Professor Vermeer," he said in a voice as dry as desert sand, "I don't accept your characterization of the dean's action. And I certainly hope, for your sake as well as ours, that there isn't a splash. Of any sort."

On his way out past Maude Friedman and the mahogany barricade, Vermeer spotted a copy of today's *Herald* on a coffee table. It was unlikely, he thought, that the *Herald* had ever been on this table before. Today's headline, only slightly smaller than yesterday's, picked up where yesterday's had left off: A BLOODY FORTUNE.

Below the headline were three pictures. One was an out-of-date yearbook shot of Eric. The second was of a smiling Libby in an evening gown. And the third was a grainy blowup of Vermeer himself, from a picture he couldn't quite place.

But which was far from flattering. Looking unshaved and unkempt. Looking a little like Lee Harvey Oswald in those defiant, gun-toting pre-assassination photos.

In other words, looking guilty as hell.

28

SIPPING ON HER SCALDED COFFEE—THE DREGS FROM the graveyard shift's last pot of the evening—Brouillard wondered where to go next.

The *Herald* sat on the corner of her desk, where she had tossed it. Great headline, she thought—A BLOODY FORTUNE—but a generally crappy write-up. She would have to razz the reporter, a decent enough guy with famous marital troubles, the next time she saw him.

Although she had been late to the scene at the Four Seasons—it took surprisingly long for Homicide to connect this new body with the ongoing investigation of Eric's death—the case had been assigned to her. Everyone up the ladder seemed to think the two deaths had to be related somehow.

She tended to agree. But exactly *how* was a mystery.

The family tie was the obvious common thread. Boston was another, although Libby's presence in Boston—an affair of the heart, if Vermeer's story was to be believed—seemed unrelated to Eric's life or death. Vermeer himself was yet another link, of course, and the one that the newspapers now were pouncing upon. But looking at motive and opportunity, Brouillard couldn't knit the threads together in any convincing way.

The good thing about Libby's death, she decided grimly, was that she would now have the full weight of the department and the city behind her. Eric's death had been clouded by uncertainty, so it had the potential to fall off the radar and get filed away with a thousand other open cases. But Libby's death—her *murder*—was straightforward, violent, ugly, scary, and full of prurient interest. At least for the time being, at least until the next big, bad thing came along, the media would put pressure on the pols, and the pols would put pressure on the police, to *solve this case.*

Pressure wasn't necessarily a bad thing. Doors would open sooner; phone calls would get returned faster. But if the heat got hot enough, the chief, with great fanfare, would put more bodies on the investigation. Which, statistically speaking—she looked up from her desk, surveying the mostly empty desks of her colleagues— wasn't necessarily a good thing.

There was also that irritating fact that she didn't know where to go next. She was still waiting for the coroner's findings and the lab reports on Libby. She didn't hold out much hope for big news from either quarter. Judging from the bruises on the dead woman's swollen neck, she had been strangled. No sign of recent sexual relations, so there was unlikely to be any helpful genetic material sitting around. Nothing under Libby's nails, at least nothing that was visible to the naked eye. No hairs on the sheets that didn't look like Libby's.

And an interview with a Midwestern couple in an adjoining room, in town on a package-deal getaway weekend, had turned up a disturbing fact: Sometime in the middle of the night, maybe two, two thirty, they had been awakened by the buzzing of a loud hair dryer in Libby's room. It went on for a long time, they said. Their impression was that whoever was drying her hair was walking around the suite, since the noise was first loud, then soft, then loud again. But it was *loud,* they agreed with each other in the kind of overlapping sentences that long-married couples tend to fall into—so loud they almost called up the front desk to complain. But they talked it over, and they decided that, well, people certainly had the *right* to dry their own hair in their own hotel rooms, even if it *was* the middle of the night, and then anyway, the noise finally stopped.

Brouillard wasn't thinking hair dryer; she was thinking DustBuster. Tidying up. She didn't like the smell of that. The strong odor of calculation.

Her intercom buzzed. "Captain Brouillard? The mayor's office. Line seven."

Not much surprised, she picked up the handset and punched the flashing button. "Brouillard."

"Good morning, Captain. Hold for the mayor, please."

She *was* surprised at how quickly the mayor got on the line. Usually there was a queue, and usually you didn't jump the queue.

"Captain Brouillard? Pavone here."

The mayor's lack of formality was legendary. In her few dealings with him—a photo op here, a decoration there—she had gotten the sense that Tommy Pavone was a decent enough guy who had wandered into waters that turned out to be over his head. His predecessor had been called to Washington unexpectedly to fill a cabinet post, and Pavone had moved up from a neighborhood-oriented city council job to being mayor of all the city. His street-level training served him well: He knew how to get snow plowed and garbage collected. The financial district types didn't know what to make of him, so they mostly ignored him, and vice versa. With a little luck and a decent economy, he would get reelected.

"Good morning, Mister Mayor. What can I do for you?"

He snorted. "You know what you can do for me, Captain."

"I have a pretty good idea, sir. Arrest somebody in one or both of the MacInnes cases, and make sure the charges stick."

"Right. Preferably both, but I'd settle for this most recent one."

"We're pursuing all leads, sir. We're doing everything we can."

"But reading between the lines, Captain, you don't have much."

She wanted to give him the reassurances he wanted. But as he pointed out, she didn't have much. "Without taking up too much of your time, sir, I'm more optimistic about solving the girl's case than the earlier case." Which was true enough, as far as it went.

He didn't sound comforted. "Captain, do you know what season we're heading into?"

"Baseball" didn't sound right. Nor did "Bruins playoffs." Taxes? Spring? "Springtime, sir. Although it seems like a long way off."

"Yes. Springtime. Which is not that far off, by the way. And in springtime, kids all over the world decide where they're going to go to college."

"Yes, sir. I'm aware of that."

"And in springtime, people from all over the world decide where they're going to go on vacation this summer. Where they're going to honeymoon. Where they're going to have their elective surgeries, which they have postponed through the holidays. Where they're going to hold their conventions in the next fiscal year."

"Yes, sir." It was, she had to admit, a pretty good list.

"So it's important for us to show, you and me, that Boston is the kind of city where you want to do all those things. A safe city. A place where students can take a dip in a whirlpool without dying. Where beautiful rich young women can stay in our four-star hotels without getting strangled in their beds."

"I understand, Mr. Mayor, and—"

"I'm sure you do," he interrupted. "But maybe you don't know exactly how big the stakes are getting. My sources tell me that one of the newsweeklies is thinking about putting this whole mess on its front cover next week. 'Mayhem in Boston,' or some such goddamn thing. I don't see how we can head that off at this point. The best we can do is make sure that the punch line for their story is that we've apprehended the bad guy who did it, and it's *over*. Or that our bad guy has pulled a Charlie Stewart and jumped off a bridge. Saving us the trouble of trying him."

"Yes, sir." The Stewart case had come and gone while she was still walking a beat in East Boston. The guy shoots his pregnant wife, wounds himself superficially, gets rid of the gun, calls the cops, and blames a black guy, whom he describes in great detail. Eventually, the story unravels—the cops never really bought it, anyway—and Stewart winds up throwing himself off the Tobin Bridge. But not before race relations in Boston get set back ten years, with the media fanning the flames of "black man kills pretty, young, white mother-to-be."

"So let's make it happen, Captain. Not necessarily the bridge part. The arrest part."

"Absolutely, sir."

But the line was already dead. Presumably, the next guy in the mayor's queue was already getting his head patted or his butt reamed. More likely reamed. Now, according to procedures, she would have to write up this "m-contact" for the chief's benefit. She pulled up an e-mail form: "Subject: m-contact. Mayor Pavone called Monday at 0930. Wants quick resolution to MacInnes situation. Brouillard." She hit "Send."

The Libby file was painfully thin, so she reached instead for the Eric file. Her filing system was all her own. She used different colored Post-its to signal the age and urgency of an open question. Cool issues got cool colors; hot issues got oranges and saffrons. Hot issues moved to the front of the file. The downside to the system was that it required regular updating—daily, in the middle of a crisis. The upside was that she could carry the hot parts of the rainbow more or less in her head.

Another downside: It looked a little fussy and amateurish. Buzzy Silver, the clown at the neighboring desk, had labeled it "girlish." She had a standing offer from Art Deming to put together a simple computer program, complete with digital blues and saffrons, that would accomplish the same thing. So far, she had turned him down. There was something about moving along those Post-its by hand, every day or two. It *worked*. She didn't want to try something new and find out it didn't work.

Here, in saffron—hot—was her reminder to herself to get some better answers from Alonzo Rodriguez. In her system, you could earn yourself a color. Rodriguez had earned himself a saffron by being several days late in getting back to her.

She dialed his Harvard number. He answered on the first ring. "B and G. Rodriguez speaking."

"Hello, Mr. Rodriguez. This is Captain Brouillard of the Boston Police Department." When she was trying to put people at ease, she used "BPD." In this case, she didn't. She emphasized "police."

"Oh, hello, Captain." He didn't sound happy to hear from her. "I was planning to call you."

"Don't bother. I'll be right over."

"I have a meeting at ten thirty that I—"

"That you may be a little late for. Don't worry about going over to the dean's office. I'll come to your place. I'm there in fifteen minutes."

29

THE SERVICE-ORIENTED PARKING LOT ATTENDANT
pointed her toward an odd little building at the edge of
the lot, which looked like a cross between a toolshed and
a bus stop. "In that door and down the stairs," he had said
crisply after taking a minute to organize his thoughts.
"Head for the chilled-water complex. You turn left at the
bottom when you reach the tunnel. B and G's straight
ahead. You can't miss it."

She didn't like the sound of "tunnel." There was that
thing she had about spiders and snakes, which she associated with tunnels and other dark, wet places. But she
was much reassured when she reached the bottom of the
staircase. This was a *hell* of a nice tunnel, she noted with
admiration: wide enough to drive a small truck through,
with bright lights and bright blue and green accent colors
on the gray cinder-block walls. Cheerful and soothing.
Not urgent, in her color-coding system. The gray rubber
flooring, big-dimpled and shiny, urged a little spring into
her step. No spider webs. No obvious snake pits.

Every twenty feet or so, the cinder-block walls opened
up into broad, four-foot-square glass apertures—like
sidewalk superintendents' perches, only much nicer—
and through the glass could be seen dramatic snarls of

tanks and pipes, all labeled with stenciled words and arrows that indicated what was being transported in which direction. Because of the spider-and-snake thing, Brouillard had never been in the basement of her apartment building. She was sure it didn't look anything like this.

The chilled-water plant, Alonzo Rodriguez's lair, was where all the pipes stopped and started. This was either the mouth of the campus or the butt, or both, Brouillard decided. A dozen people were working at desks or pawing through oversize file cabinets, behind a glass wall that demarcated the end of the tunnel and the beginning of a subterranean office area. All the workers wore the standard-issue khakis and white shirts. She pushed open an eight-foot-high pane in the glass wall, distinguishable mainly because of its chrome hinges.

"Can I help you?" The young woman at the nearest desk asked the question in a solicitous sort of way, with an emphasis on *help,* suggesting that B and G didn't get a lot of foot traffic. That, and also the fact that there was no reception area.

"I'm Captain Brouillard, Boston Police Department, here to speak with Mr. Rodriguez. He's expecting me."

"Uh, okay, I'll just let him know you're here." She punched a few numbers on her phone and spoke quietly—Brouillard distinctly heard the word "police"—and a few minutes later Rodriguez emerged from a rear office. He was not smiling. He motioned that she should walk in his direction. The gesture looked a bit abrupt.

"Please join me in the conference room, Captain."

They walked down a windowless hall—the price of working ten feet underground, Brouillard observed, silently. She wondered if the window cutouts in the fancy tunnel helped keep the people who spent their entire working lives down here from going bonkers.

"You get a lot of spiders here?" she asked, as if casually, as they seated themselves in the glassed-in conference room. The full-spectrum fluorescent lights were bright enough to grow crops under.

"No." His body language was guarded. "Why do you ask?"

"No special reason. Except that I usually associate underground with spiders."

"I associate spiders with bad housekeeping." On his own turf, Rodriguez was more self-confident, more willing to assert himself.

"Well, that explains a lot about the place where *I* work," she said, pulling out her pad and pencil. "So let's get down to it. The last time we talked, you and I were wondering out loud about how Eric MacInnes wound up in Shad Hall after hours. You were going to look into that for me."

"That's correct."

"What did you find out?"

"I'm afraid I couldn't get all the answers you wanted," he began, not looking contrite. "Someone used an unnumbered pass card to access the rear door. Whoever that person was got in just after midnight, and deactivated the building alarm using a legitimate code—in other words, a code that is assigned to a legitimate card. We've gone ahead and—"

She interrupted him. "An 'unnumbered pass card'? What does that mean?"

"It means that it didn't show a registration number when it was swiped through the wall unit. Normally, the system sends an ID number to the building computer to indicate which particular card has been used to open certain doors. In this case, that didn't happen."

"Why?"

Rodriguez had one of those handsome faces that, when put under pressure, got less handsome in a hurry. Tipping back in his chair to the balance point, he shrugged. "That's one of the things we haven't figured out yet. It shouldn't be possible. But it happened."

"So this person with the bogus but functioning card breaches the perimeter and has a certain amount of time to shut off the perimeter alarm, right? How long? A minute?"

"Thirty seconds."

"Gotta work fast. And to shut off the alarm, you need a personal code? Whose code was punched in?"

"That's what I was starting to tell you." He didn't say the rest of the sentence out loud, but she heard it: *before you interrupted me.* "The eight-digit code that was used is assigned to one of our custodians, José Rosas."

"So Eric could have slipped him a twenty to let him into the building?"

"Possibly, yes. But Mr. Rosas lives out in Franklin, out by 495." This was the outer beltway—some thirty or forty miles to the west, and then south. "It's a little hard to believe that Rosas drove in before midnight on his day off, opened the back door to let someone in, drove home, and then drove back in three hours later to open the building. Plus, it looks like the MacInnes boy did this regularly, judging from the computer records. Almost every Sunday night during the school year."

"Same bogus card, same code?"

"Correct."

She took a note, then looked up. "You trust this José Rosas?"

"I do. We interviewed him at some length, and I'm convinced that he knows nothing about any of this. He needs his job and wouldn't knowingly do anything to put it at risk. In addition, I've known him personally for a number of years. In my opinion, he's an entirely reliable person. Which is why he holds the position of trust that he does."

"Uh-huh. And how easy would it be for someone else to get ahold of his code?"

"He says that he's sure he's never told it to anyone. Given the circumstances of opening up the building by himself before dawn, with a card, he's certainly never in a situation where someone is looking over his shoulder when he punches in. Not like a crowded ATM, for example. He has admitted that he wrote his code down and hid it in his wallet—something we specifically tell our people not to do, and for which he has apologized—but he says he was worried about drawing a mental blank early one morning and not being able to shut the alarm down, and I believe him. As you say, thirty seconds isn't a lot of time. He says his wallet is rarely out of his sight, except at home. And anyway, he put a misleading label—'account number'—on the scrap of paper in his wallet. He showed us the paper. There's no way someone could figure out what that number was if they came across it."

"He's legal or illegal?"

Rodriguez stiffened. "He is Puerto Rican," he said, rolling the "Rs" very softly. "Like myself."

"That's how you know him?"

"We grew up in the same town. On an island off the coast. Vieques."

"So, what? You help your hometown people get work up here?"

"Sometimes. Rarely. Is there a problem with that?"

"Of course not. We French Canadians look out for each other, too. Happens all the time. Does he report to you directly?"

The guarded look came back into his eyes. "No. That wouldn't be prohibited under Harvard's rules, but I would be uncomfortable in that situation. Our work sometimes involves assigning unpleasant tasks to people. The way those assignments are handed out has to be viewed by everybody as fair."

She nodded, noncommittal, writing, brow furrowed. "I'm wondering, Mr. Rodriguez," she said without looking up, "how much contact does your staff have with the students?"

"Excuse me?"

She looked up. "How much contact does your staff have with the students here? How easy would it be for a student to make friends with a member of your staff, or vice versa?"

"It would be difficult and, from our side, discouraged. Our job is to take care of the infrastructure here, Captain, rather than to service the students directly. So it would be very unusual for someone on my staff to become friendly with a student. There wouldn't be the opportunity. A food-service person, for example, would have more opportunity. Not only that . . ." He paused.

"Not only that, but . . . ?"

"May I talk frankly, Captain?"

"Please do."

"Well, to my eyes, the young people who go to school here see themselves as the future owners of the world. Or in some cases, like these MacInnes children, the current and future owners. To me they might show some respect, because I wear a tie, speak adequate English, and have some authority over a number of people. I *manage* something, even if it's not something that these young people aspire to manage.

"But our custodians? These young people don't even *see* people like José Rosas, in my experience. And to be fair, I'm sure there's a certain amount of envy that flows in the other direction, which would get in the way of any sort of friendship. When you see the privileges and the advantages that these young people take for granted . . ."

"Not like growing up on"—she checked her notes—"Vieques?"

He suppressed the beginnings of what looked like an unpleasant smile. "Nothing at all like growing up on Vieques," he said, correcting her pronunciation slightly.

"So if anybody in your area were going to have contact with an Eric MacInnes, it most likely would be you."

"Yes. If you phrase it that way."

"So did you?"

"Did I what?"

"Have any contact with Eric MacInnes."

"I did, yes." He put his chair back down onto its four legs but kept his arms crossed in front of his chest. And now he crossed his legs tightly at the knees.

"In what context?"

"He brought a very large amount of athletic workout equipment with him when he arrived on campus. Most of that equipment required some electricity to function, although not necessarily large loads in terms of amperage. He asked us to add several outlets in the spare bedroom, and also asked for help in moving the equipment into that room."

"And you did that?"

"My people did that for a fee that was agreed upon in advance. It was added to his term bill."

"Unusual?"

"Yes," he said, "in those specifics. But not in spirit. Even though our job is to focus on the infrastructure, we try to be helpful when called upon. But the MacInnes boy got no special favors."

"What was your take on Eric?"

"Pleasant. Charming. Not condescending in the sense I was just talking about. But certainly above it all. Not worried much about the things that normal people have to worry about."

"Have you had contact with the other MacInnes siblings?"

"You mean the brother and the dead girl?" He obviously had been reading the papers.

"Yes."

"Why would I have contact with them? The one is off campus, and the other wasn't even a student here." Although he didn't actually answer the question, his tone was sharp. His accent had gotten a little thicker.

"I don't know; that's why I asked. They seemed like a tight-knit family, and this place has a kind of small-town feel. I thought maybe you might have run into them, have some kind of bead on them."

"Well, you were wrong in thinking that."

"So no contact at all with either of them? James or Libby—the 'dead girl,' as you called her?"

"Not that I recall. Nothing of consequence, in any case."

"Waffle words," she wrote down, "re whether knows Eric/Libby." But she couldn't push any harder in this context.

"Are we almost finished, here? I'm already late for my scheduled meeting. So if there's nothing further . . ." He started to push his chair back. He was halfway up before he caught the look on her face. She looked up at him, down at his chair, and up at him again.

"No, we're not quite finished, Mr. Rodriguez."

He sat.

"As I think you guessed ahead of time, I'm not satisfied with some of these answers. I'm not satisfied at all. After almost a week of looking into this, all you can tell me for sure is that you still can't figure out how the hell Eric MacInnes got into your building—not just once, but many times. That's still a problem for me. Which means it's still a problem for you. You're the guy that helped design the Shad security system—"

"I never said that I—"

"Oh, please," she said, with exaggerated weariness. "Please don't tell me again that the fast-moving pace of current technology means that your intimate knowledge of this building is now out of date. I don't buy it. You're in a position to get the answers I need, and you're going to get them.

"I want to know where Eric got that unnumbered pass card, and where he got the code for the panel. I want to know if this went undetected all these months, and if so, how.

"So I want you to call a meeting. I want you to bring to that meeting whoever it takes to answer those fairly simple questions. But for starters, I want to talk to the subcontractor who installed the security system. Tell him to bring along the as-built drawings; that will get his attention. I want the original programmers for that system, and I want anybody who's made any kind of significant coding changes since. I want memos as to who's got what card, and which code is assigned to whom. I want the guy who interprets the security logs for you, Mr. Rodriguez. I want the logs themselves.

"And above all, I want *you*, Mr. Rodriguez, to help me get my answers. Ten a.m. sharp, the day after tomorrow."

He spluttered, just like in the cartoons. "But that's ridiculous! People have schedules; people have—"

She froze him with a look. She was angry. "Don't tell me what's ridiculous and what isn't, Mr. Rodriguez. I'm investigating two deaths, and you're standing between me and the answers I need. Believe me, that's not a place you want to be standing.

"And this time, let's use the dean's conference room. I have a feeling that he may want to join us for this one."

———————

On her way out, fighting a cold wind, she made a long detour by the dean's office. She was sure that there was some way to get to Bishop's office underground, but she didn't want to discover that not all tunnels were as scrubbed as Rodriguez's.

"Oh, I'm sorry," the polished young woman behind the dean's polished wooden wall said cheerfully. "You've just missed him. He's just left for an overnight trip. Usually, it's a good idea to call ahead and make an appointment, especially this time of year, with so much committee work under way."

Brouillard did not want to be rude to this nice young woman. On the other hand, none of these nice people seemed to be getting the message. Maybe it was because none of them had gotten a shot across their bow from the mayor. "Well, Ms. Friedman," she read off the chromed desk plaque, "way back when you were booking today's appointments, I had no way of knowing that the Boston Police Department wouldn't be getting the answers we needed from Harvard. That was a surprise to me."

"Oh, dear," Friedman replied, looking genuinely worried. And then stopped, not sure of the ground she was on. "Well, can I give him a message? He checks his e-mail several times a day."

"Sure. I think I remember the dean saying he wanted a speedy wrap-up of this case. Tell him that that's not going to happen if things keep going the way they are going at the moment. Tell him that if he has any pull with Mr. Rodriguez, this would be a really good time to use it." Maude Friedman was taking notes in what looked like shorthand—lots of loops and swirls. "Tell him he's invited to a meeting in his conference room the day after tomorrow at ten a.m., with Mr. Rodriguez and his associates. And finally, tell him that Mayor Pavone has personally expressed his concern about the situation. And that I wouldn't be surprised if the land deals were on His Honor's mind."

"The *land deals*," the young woman repeated, as she dashed off more swirls and squiggles.

Harvard, always growing, always wanted more land on the Boston side of the river. With the mayor's tacit permission, the university had been buying Allston and Brighton properties through a straw, to avoid paying top dollar. All totally legal, but not a practice that endeared Mother Harvard to the neighborhoods. And this mayor knew it was the neighborhoods that would reelect him.

No, he hadn't exactly mentioned any specific deals to Brouillard that might be hanging in the balance—actually, hadn't mentioned land deals whatsoever—but Brouillard felt she had the authority to improvise.

"Right. Mention the land deals."

She made a mental note to herself to turn herself in to the mayor's office.

30

Brouillard's cell phone started chirping as she made her way back to District—the desk sergeant. William MacInnes was in town—picking up a second dead child in as many weeks, Brouillard realized with a twinge, foolishly scribbling notes with only one eye on the road—and wanted to talk to her.

This morning would be convenient, his people had informed the sergeant. Brouillard remembered the odd character with the sawed-off name: Mr. Ralph. She phoned the number the desk sergeant had passed along.

"Boston Harbor Hotel. How may I direct your call?"

Brouillard sighed. She had been expecting the Four Seasons. A visit to the Boston Harbor Hotel, a huge brick pile on the waterfront, self-consciously designed to look like an old-fashioned ferry terminal, would require her to get to the other side of the Big Dig, Boston's endless road rebuilding project smack in the middle of town. She didn't believe for a minute that the Four Seasons couldn't find space for William MacInnes, even on short notice. So the old godzillionaire must have wanted a change of scene.

"Room thirteen forty, please," she read from her scribbled notes.

Mr. Ralph himself answered on the first ring. "Room thirteen forty. Ralph speaking."

"Captain Brouillard, Mr. Ralph. I got your message. Turns out I can be there in twenty minutes."

"Excellent."

Using shortcuts—and occasionally her removable blue roof light—she made it to the Atlantic Ocean in just under fifteen. But instead of traffic opening up along the waterfront, the congestion got even worse. From several blocks out, she saw why: There was a swirling knot of people outside the Boston Harbor Hotel, and the knot was spilling out into the street. As she approached, this gradually resolved itself into a media melee: trucks, lights, cables running all over the broad sidewalk. A pair of uniformed officers was just now setting up a cordon around the main door into the hotel. TV crews jockeyed for position. One local anchorwoman was already perched on a foot-high crate, looking earnestly at her camera as she spoke into her microphone.

Boston welcomes grieving tycoon. If William MacInnes had been looking for peace and quiet, he wasn't going to find it here. In fact, with the back of his hotel pressed up against the harbor, he was pretty well trapped. At least at the Four Seasons, there were side doors, service entrances, loading docks, and tunnels that could be called into play. Here it was hide, dash, or swim.

Blasting her horn rhythmically, she rolled up on the sidewalk and angled in, helping to define the southern end of the impromptu perimeter. Several pedestrians started to give the nondescript tan Crown Vic a piece of their minds. Then they looked her in the eye, and then they reconsidered, melting back into the crowd. One or two TV cameras swung her way. Either they recognized her—pretty unlikely, despite her recent media coverage—or she had more visual appeal than the revolving door behind which the hotel's uniformed doormen were hiding. Declining to comment, nodding when one of the patrolmen moved a blue sawhorse aside to let her pass, she pushed through the crowd.

"Sit, sit, Captain. Thank you for coming so promptly. It is 'Captain,' isn't it?"

She guessed that this was about as solicitous as William MacInnes ever got. "Yes. It's 'Captain.' " She sat in an overdone, overstuffed easy chair, across a standard-issue glass coffee table from MacInnes, who had sunk deeply into a couch.

"Sorry about the circus outside, sir," she continued. "And of course, I'm deeply sorry about your daughter." She wished she hadn't gotten it backward: daughter, *then* circus.

"Thank you, Captain. Of course I don't hold you responsible for either. I have asked the hotel manager to determine which employee found some personal advantage in calling in the media jackals, and to tell me what sort of disciplinary action he is planning to take in response. As for my daughter . . ."

Here he paused, took a long breath, and put a hand in front of his eyes briefly. When he surfaced again, he was composed. "Libby was always her own person. She lived and died according to her own rules. I'm sorry. Does that sound harsh?"

"It sounds realistic."

He grunted. "My wife is at home. Under sedation. I believe this death is even harder on her than the last one. Or maybe it's cumulative."

"I'm sure this is a terrible blow to you both, sir." She waited a decent interval. "I'm glad you called me, Mr. MacInnes. I wanted to ask you some questions."

"Fine. I'll answer your questions. Within the limits of my ability and willingness. And then you can answer mine, within the same limits."

She smiled. "I hope to get more out of you than you get out of me."

"Unlikely. But fire away."

"Did you know that Libby was a frequent visitor to Boston, and to the Four Seasons? Like, several times a month?"

"No. I did not."

"You weren't aware of her comings and goings?"

"No. She always made herself available for family meetings and other formal occasions. She volunteered to fill in for my nurses as necessary. Even more than was necessary, actually. Other than that, she kept her own schedule. Remember that she tended to operate out of the city house, whereas Elizabeth and I have resided primarily upstate in recent years."

"Do you have any idea why she always asked for two keys to her hotel room?"

"Absolutely no idea. Unless she thought Dan Beyer should have one."

"If she had a particularly close friend here in Boston, do you have any idea who that might have been?"

"None. That's the last thing I would have looked into, or about which she would have wanted me to know."

"Do you know if she touched base with her brothers while she was up here?"

"That's a question for James, I'd say. I never heard either of the boys mention their sister as a frequent visitor, or even an occasional visitor. Not that they would have gone out of their way to tell me something like that, especially if Libby had . . . a swain."

Every once in a while, Brouillard noted, William MacInnes reminded you that he wasn't totally a resident of this century. She had eased out her pad and pencil. She wrote down "swain," not exactly sure of the spelling. "So why *was* Beyer traveling with her?"

"Because that was his job. Libby has been subject to threats in the past. Nothing specific, but credible enough for us to hire a bodyguard. Eric's death redoubled our vigilance. To Libby's dismay."

"She didn't like having protection along?"

"No. She was very clear on that point. We overruled her. For all the good it did in the end," he added.

"Do you think Beyer could have killed your daughter?"

"No. Of course he's strong enough and stupid enough. But no. I believe he was very fond of her, in his own way."

"Do you think she felt the same way about him?"

He shrugged heavily, as if the question either never interested him or no longer could. "I doubt it. Libby was independent, rebellious, and evidently more secretive than I ever realized. So I could be wrong about her. But at the end of the day, I believe, she was one of us. One of our family. For better or worse. No. I don't believe she would have . . . soiled the nest by becoming involved with one of the household staff.

"Nor do I believe that she would have chosen a specimen like Beyer, who was mainly interesting because he was overmuscled, which means he doesn't remain interesting for long. Nor do I understand why she would bother flying up here to be in a relationship with someone who more or less lived under the same roof with her in our city house, as

Beyer does. Or did. That's a long way to go for privacy—how often did you say? Several times a month?"

"Apparently. And for all we know, there may have been other places she traveled to. If you don't mind, we'd like access to her credit card records, phone bills, and so on to check that out."

"Of course. Mr. Ralph can get you whatever you need. I assume you'll protect my daughter's privacy as much as possible."

"We will. As much as possible. And"—there was no easy way to say it—"I'll also do what I can to get her body released as soon as possible. As soon as the medical examiner is finished."

He looked at her impassively. Maybe he was sedated, as well. Or maybe, as that Harvard prof Pirle had said, this family did indeed take the long view. Maybe one daughter, more or less, wasn't going to make the difference. "Yes, do that, please, Captain Brouillard."

She made motions as if to go, but he held up his hand in a braking motion. "I believe we had a deal, Captain, and I don't think you've lived up to your end of the bargain. It's my turn to ask you a few questions."

"Fair enough."

"My sources tell me that Professor Vermeer is your prime suspect in the death of my son."

"Let me just say that he may have had the opportunity. I'm not sure about the motive. And who are your sources, by the way?"

"No, no. You had your chance. But I will tell you that if you're settling on Vermeer, you're barking up the wrong tree. He is nothing in all of this. Although I believe that there are people out there who would have us believe otherwise."

"Who, exactly? And why?"

He nodded unhappily. "All right, I will answer those questions. We don't know who, and we don't know why. Presumably to deflect attention from themselves."

"There are some developments," Brouillard said, choosing her words carefully, "that make us more interested in Vermeer."

"Such as?"

"Such as certain e-mail traffic, although that remains to be sorted out. Such as the fact that he was the last person to be seen with your daughter. They had dinner at the Four Seasons on the night she was killed. Such as the fact that Dan Beyer waylaid him outside his apartment the next morning, apparently with the intention of hauling him off and killing him. We have Beyer in custody. I'd appreciate you keeping all that in confidence, although it'll be public soon."

MacInnes thought through the implications of this news. He didn't seemed rushed. "And yet," he finally replied, "your line of inquiry earlier focused on Beyer. I infer that like me, you're not buying Professor Vermeer as a serious suspect."

She smiled in spite of herself. "I'm pretty sure I said nothing of the kind, Mr. MacInnes."

"I would think less of you if you had, Captain Brouillard. Obviously, you can set a trap and use Professor Vermeer as your bait, if you like. In your shoes, that's probably what I'd do. But I'd recommend that you forget about him as a killer. For better or worse, he doesn't have it in him."

This time she laughed out loud. "I'm sorry, sir. These are serious circumstances, and I'm well aware of your loss. But did you just say 'for better or worse, he's not a murderer'?"

He smiled coldly. "Yes. That would be an accurate re-statement of what I said."

"Nice use of the subjunctive." She said it more to herself than to him.

Now he laughed—thumping, an odd, pneumatic sound, like a tired old steam engine. "What did you just say, Captain?"

"From a Raymond Chandler novel. The private eye gets a walk-in from the street. This visitor is a knock-out, as they always are in those books. Long legs, a throaty voice, and a bust to die for. So she says something 'would be' something, and Philip Marlowe says to himself, 'Nice use of the subjunctive. A Radcliffe girl.' I didn't get it at the time, so I looked it up. A conditional tense."

He nodded, now looking serious again. "Captain, one would make a mistake to underestimate you."

"Yeah, I think so."

"And by extension, it would make sense to be your ally."

"I think so."

"As you know, I have resources available to me that are not available to the Boston Police Department."

"I get that sense, yeah."

"And of course, you have resources that are not available to me. Normally, I would ask for reciprocity. In this case, I will not. For my part, I will let you know as soon as I find out anything that might be helpful to you in your investigation. You can tell me whatever you choose to, all the way down to nothing."

"I appreciate that, sir."

"Is there anything else?"

"One more thing."

"Yes?"

"Professor Vermeer told me that you have more or less placed a bounty on the head of Eric's killer. Assuming, of course, that there *was* a killer."

"Oh, rest assured, Captain, there was a killer. And yes, I have offered a one-million-dollar reward to the person who delivers that killer to me. Or to the appropriate law enforcement agency, I should say. That word is now spreading out across the networks with which my family is in contact. And in my estimation, those are good networks."

She leaned forward, looking him in the eye. "That's exactly what I'm concerned about, Mr. MacInnes. If you put enough money on the table, bad things may start to happen. If the price is high enough, people will start to connect the dots in the wrong ways. There are good reasons why bounty hunters were put out of business."

"Maybe." He didn't look one bit concerned about potential miscarriages of justice. "By the way, Captain, the bounty just went up. For the person who brings in the killer or killers of my two children, the reward is now two million."

31

Back at the chocolate factory, unemployed on a Monday morning, Vermeer thought through his options.

Which didn't take long.

Libby had warned him to be careful, and now she was dead. This constituted a triple, or a quadruple, whammy: She was a sweet kid, who had lost the chance to live out her life. And from a selfish perspective, Libby was someone who could have verified the existence of some kind of plot against him, or at least confirmed some unspecified dangers out there, and now she was gone. In addition, he was now a prime suspect in her death, meaning that Brouillard and her gang hoped to nail his hide to the wall. And finally, his access to the MacInnes family, including the powerful William, was almost certainly gone. Disgraced, suspended, suspected—he was in the deepest of trouble. And who knew what tomorrow's headlines would bring?

What were his options?

One was to do nothing. He could sit back, stop shaving, put his feet up, and wait for the wheels of justice to turn. That would probably require a temporary relocation, as Brouillard had suggested. But where was he supposed to go? He didn't want to impose his growing notoriety on a friend. Plus, he wasn't exactly sure what Beyer's assault represented. Was Beyer a lone nut case? Or was he only the first in a series of paid assassins that the MacInnes family planned to send his way? Vermeer had gotten lucky once. Maybe he wouldn't get lucky next time.

Maybe Brouillard wouldn't be there next time. Or maybe she'd decide not to step in so quickly next time. Maybe the wheels of justice were now working to grind *him* down, rather than the bad guys, whoever they were.

The other choice was to try and help his own cause. And there was only one way he knew of to do that.

He picked up the Boston phone book. There were no listings for "MacInnes, James" in Cambridge. Pawing through an eight-inch pile of unwanted and pristine phone books—business-to-business Yellow Pages, South Shore white pages, and the like—he found what he was looking for: the Harvard Business School student directory. Every year there was a debate about whether to keep printing the directory in hard copy. So far, the older generation—the senior faculty members and administrators who refused to look up phone numbers on the Web—had carried the day. Vermeer had brought it home and never opened it. But he remembered that the book included the phone numbers of *all* students, listed and unlisted alike. And now, of course, there was a new attraction: It kept working even after one's Internet access had been shut off. God bless the older generation. There: "MacInnes, James and Elaine. Peabody Terrace."

"Yes?"

"Hello. Is this James MacInnes?"

"Who's this?"

"Hi, James. It's Wim Vermeer."

There was a long silence. Then: "You've got a hell of a lot of nerve, Professor Vermeer. Calling me, at home, at a time like this."

"James, I need to talk with you. It's urgent. Can we meet for coffee?"

"No way I'd meet with you. Under any circumstances. And I'm going to tell you now not to call here again."

"Wait. Please." Vermeer saw—heard—his last lifeline fraying in front of his eyes. "James, I don't know what you think I've done. But whatever you're thinking, I guarantee it's not true. Any of it."

"Oh, yeah. I've heard about this big plot against you. Sorry. I'm not buying. You're responsible for your own mess. We have nothing to talk about, Professor Vermeer."

Vermeer knew he was sinking. If James MacInnes hung up, there was nowhere else to go. And then the next call to Vermeer would be from University counsel John Eustis, informing Vermeer that he had violated the terms of his paid leave—now about five hours old—by contacting a student. Unlike most of his colleagues, Vermeer actually needed that paycheck. He paid his bills after it cleared.

"James, listen to me." He tried to keep any hint of desperation out of his voice. "I've done nothing to harm anyone in your family. Ever. You may not believe it, but someone has gone way out of his way to hang a whole lot of shit around my neck. Ask your father. He'll confirm some version of that. He told me that himself."

"Professor Vermeer, I may be the most conservative member of my family. So if you're looking for forgiveness, go have another conversation with my father. He's a lot more tolerant than I am. Maybe he'll cut you some slack."

Vermeer knew that despite his mounting panic, he had to listen very carefully. The fact that MacInnes was still referring to him as "Professor" was a good sign: The fraying lifeline still had some life in it. And this issue of "conservative" and "tolerant"—what did that mean? Suddenly, the answer dawned on him.

"James, do you think I killed either your brother or your sister?"

"No."

"Good. I didn't. Do you think that I was Eric's lover?"

"There's no doubt in my mind. Eric was weak and vulnerable, and you abused your position of authority to take advantage of him. And if you try to deny it now, that's even more disgusting to me, in some ways." MacInnes's voice was rising. *Keep him on the phone.*

"James, I have to ask you something. Did Eric tell you *himself* that we were involved? Did you hear it directly from Eric?"

"Why does it matter?"

"Because if Eric told you himself, then that's the end of the story. If it's my word against his, then you'll take his, right? But if someone else told you, then I have to know who. So maybe I can figure out what the hell is happening to me. Please, James."

"No. I don't owe you anything."

"Would it make any difference to you if I told you that I had this same conversation with Libby—almost exactly the same—on the night she died? And that she also told me that Eric himself had never mentioned me to her? That she got this whole idea from somebody else? Somebody that I hoped she would name for me. But she didn't. And now she can't. Only you can."

There was a long silence. Vermeer listened for the

click that most likely would seal his fate. Instead, he heard some rustling and throat-clearing. "Okay," MacInnes finally said. "I'll tell you this much. Eric did not talk to me directly. That wouldn't have been comfortable for either of us. He knew I disapproved of his . . . lifestyle. He talked to someone else. That person talked to me."

"Someone you trust? Someone close to Eric?"

"Yes. Close enough."

"James, listen to me. I have nowhere else to go. I swear to you that I've done nothing wrong. In fact, I haven't done anything at all, including having any kind of a relationship with your brother. My relationship with Eric was exactly the same as my relationship with you. Nothing more serious, nothing less serious. I'm not a homosexual and I never have been, although under normal circumstances I wouldn't give a shit if someone else thought that. What I *do* give a shit about is getting out from under all the other stuff that comes along with that lie. You have to give me the chance to confront the person who's spreading that story, so I can find out why. So I can *stop* it, and fix it."

Silence.

"James, I'm pretty sure that I just lost my job. Calling you probably seals it. I'm about to get blamed for Libby's death, which I also had nothing to do with. In fact, she asked to meet with *me,* to tell me that I was in some kind of danger. That's what the dinner was about. She wrote me a note to that effect. The people at your family's country house can confirm that she wrote it. Mr. Ralph can confirm that. I can *show* it to you, if you want."

Assuming, of course, that he could retrieve it from Brouillard, which at this point seemed unlikely. It was probably exhibit one in the case she was building against him. He wondered if he had blundered by invoking Libby's name, by shooting in eight directions at once, by allowing some of his mounting panic to leak through. By sounding weak.

Silence.

Then: "Okay, Professor Vermeer. Fair is fair." James's voice sounded pained and tentative, as if there was a lot at stake. "I guess you deserve the opportunity to hear the same story I heard, from the horse's mouth. It was Marc Pirle. Professor Pirle. He told me that he and Eric talked about Eric's relationship with you a number of times. Pirle told me that he was thinking of having you brought up on sexual harassment charges, but that Eric had persuaded him to drop the whole thing."

32

SEETHING, VERMEER FLEW ALONG THE BACK ROADS TO Harvard. Driving down the Jamaicaway, with its late-nineteenth-century scenic twists and turns and the occasional ancient and battered tree trunk shouldering its way out into the road, would give him a little more time to cool down. To plan his next move.

His ID still opened the parking lot gate. The oldest corporation in the Western Hemisphere moved slowly. And a good thing, too, since he probably would have had a hard time talking his way past the guard booth. If there was a list of personae non gratae, his name probably was penciled in at the top.

Pirle. It made no sense. To Pirle, Vermeer was less than an insect—not worth slowing down for, not even worth squashing underfoot on the sidewalk and getting the bottom of your shoes dirty. Why would Pirle spin yarns about him and set traps for him? Unless, of course, someone else was feeding Pirle the big lie, and Pirle was merely repeating it. But who the hell would *that* be? Maybe Eric himself, in some sort of confused mental state? But in that case, why wouldn't Pirle talk to him *directly* about it, rather than talking to the brother—and the sister?—of the alleged victim of the alleged harassment?

He walked as quickly as he could across the campus without drawing too much attention to himself. It was possible that James thought Vermeer actually was a crazed murderer. Maybe he had dialed 911 immediately after getting off the phone with him. *Officer! I've just sent a madman to the office of an unsuspecting professor! You have to intercept him!*

But there was no sign of heightened security around Morgan Hall. He climbed the stairs two at a time, then slowed to catch his breath as he approached Pirle's lair. No point in looking deranged under the circumstances.

"Hi, Professor Vermeer! Long time no see!" Pirle's secretary, Delores Adams, gave him a broad smile. He smiled back, relieved. Adams was not complicated. If the cops were waiting in Pirle's office to pounce on him, it would be written all over her face.

"I've been busy as hell, Delores," he said, which was true enough. "And then on top of all the normal stuff, Dean Bishop put me on a special assignment—kind of a hush-hush thing."

"Oh, yeah," Adams said, nodding her head seriously. "I heard something about that. That's why the Finance group had to cover your classes. How's it going? The assignment, I mean?"

"Delores, I wish I could tell you, but it's still under wraps." Disappointment swept across her face. "I'll tell you what, though. When it's all over, I promise that we'll have coffee and I'll give you a firsthand account of the whole thing."

"It's a deal!"

"But meanwhile, Delores, I need about ten minutes with Professor Pirle as soon as possible. Is he teaching this morning?"

"Oh, no, Professor Vermeer. He actually took a long weekend to finish up an article he's working on. Actually, closer to a week. He didn't have any classes today or tomorrow, and Professor Mindich said he could cover his Thursday seminar. So I don't expect him in until the end of the week at the earliest."

"Oh, darn," he said, avoiding profanity. "That's a big problem." He crossed his arms, stroked his chin, and furrowed his brow. The very *picture* of the distracted professor, deep in thought. "A big problem. I really need his signature on something."

"Something related to your special assignment?"

"Well, actually, yeah, Delores, but I really shouldn't say any more than that." He put his index finger to his lips, swearing her to secrecy. "So where is he? Working at home?"

"Not up here, no. He's at his villa. In Puerto Rico. Have you ever been down there? It's a beautiful place, judging from the pictures." She reached up to the cluttered bulletin board on the wall next to her desk and pulled down a snapshot. She handed it to him, a blue pushpin still sticking out of it. It showed a large, blunt beige building, mostly obscured by palm trees, set against a stunning backdrop of blue sky and azure water.

"Yes," he lied easily. "I was down there a couple of years ago. Some Finance-area function. A little piece of heaven, as I recall." He put the picture down on her desk. "Listen, if you give me the street address of the place, I'll see if I can get the document FedEx'd to him down there. It's really a rush. Otherwise, I wouldn't bug him."

She looked uneasy. "I don't know, Professor Vermeer. He really doesn't like me giving out this address." But she was already flipping through her well-worn Rolodex.

She found the card she was looking for, stuck her thumb in the card file, and looked up at him, still hesitant.

"Delores, I know I've got the address at home somewhere, from the last time I was down there, but I'm not sure I can lay my hands on it in a hurry. And this is an urgent matter. Otherwise, I really wouldn't impose on you and him."

She made up her mind. "Well, okay." She started to copy down the address by hand on a yellow legal pad. He had one eye on the snapshot.

"Oh, don't bother with that," he said, extending his hand across the desk, pointing at the Rolodex card. "Let me photocopy it and save you the trouble."

"Oh, you don't have to do that. You probably don't know how to run the machine, anyway." She got up and moved slowly in the direction of the copying machine, fifteen feet away.

Vermeer waited until her back was fully turned. Then he reached across the desk and palmed the snapshot. He heard the copy machine fire up. Out of the corner of his eye, he saw the white light flaring. Letting the pushpin fall to the floor, he slipped the photo into his coat pocket, then nosed the pushpin out of sight with his toe.

"Here you go, Professor," Adams said, walking back toward him and holding out the copy. "Now, you're gonna keep me out of trouble on this, right?"

"You bet. Thanks. You've been more helpful than you know."

33

The big news at District 11 was that Detective Buzzy Silver was "back in the saddle" again—coming back from his medical leave, although not saddling up any too fast. A huge two-sided poster, which looked a lot like a recycled bedsheet, hung over his desk, suspended from the ancient sprinkler system far up in the rafters. It depicted Silver on horseback, wearing a ten-gallon hat. Light brown animals that appeared to be deer were around the edges of the scene, pointing at the mounted figure and laughing. The other side of the poster was more or less the same, except that it featured dark brown animals—perhaps bears. No one knew for sure. And the artists, whoever they were, weren't talking.

Given the nature of the injuries Silver had sustained on his fall hunting trip—that .22 slug to the groin—it was unlikely that he would be on horseback anytime soon. The guys on the night shift had gone to some lengths to hang the poster well out of Silver's reach. Brouillard vaguely remembered a thirty-foot stepladder that the custodial staff used to change lightbulbs high up in the dark recesses of the ceiling. Unless Silver found that ladder, unless he also found someone who was willing to help him—both unlikely—the welcome-back poster would hang above his head forever.

Silver had yet to make his first appearance. It was still early. The room was surprisingly well populated for this time of morning. No one, not even Brouillard, wanted to miss the show.

Her phone rang. "District 11. Captain Brouillard."

"Hello, Captain. This is Dean Bishop."

"Hello, Dean Bishop. Back from your trip so soon?"

"Actually, no," he said. "I'm calling from a hotel room in Chicago. I'm just about to go into a meeting downstairs. But I wanted to get in touch with you as soon as possible about your request for a meeting."

Request for a meeting. That didn't sound right. "You mean the meeting that Alonzo Rodriguez is setting up for tomorrow morning? I hope you can join us."

"Well, that's not the problem," he replied. "Of course I'll make myself available."

"Glad to hear it. The mayor will be glad to hear it."

"Yes. I have a call in to the mayor. But listen, Detective, there *is* a problem. Mr. Rodriguez had to leave town unexpectedly. Apparently, there is some sort of medical emergency involving his father. He had to take a two-week leave, starting today. Under the circumstances, I've asked the assistant head of Buildings and Grounds, Bill Weiskopf, to take over. Al tried to do what he could before he left, but Bill tells me that he really doesn't think having a meeting tomorrow is realistic. For one thing, he says that he hasn't even been able to get return calls from some of the people you want to talk to."

Brouillard reflected on the odd timing of the senior Rodriguez's unexpected illness. She had fully expected

Rodriguez to ask for a postponement. She would have given it to him, after making him sweat for a while. She had not expected him to leave town.

"Has Rodriguez done this before? Taken leaves on short notice?"

"No. At least not that I know of."

"And his father is where? Back home on the little island off the coast of Puerto Rico?"

"Uh, well, yes, that's my understanding. Yes." Bishop sounded surprised that Brouillard could make that leap. "I'm not sure whether he's trying to solve the problem down there or bring his father up here to get looked at in Boston. In any case, it's likely to be a few days before we know much more. Meanwhile, as I started to say, Bill Weiskopf—"

"Dean Bishop," she interrupted, "I have to say that I'm very disappointed. In Harvard. In Al Rodriguez. And in you, frankly."

"Some things aren't in our control, try as we will to control some things."

"I know, I know. We can't control when our aged parents are going to become ill. And when that happens, we have to drop everything and respond. I know that. I've been there myself."

"Then you can understand—"

"What I understand, Dean Bishop, is that the information I asked for a week ago—pretty basic, straightforward stuff, as far as I'm concerned—still isn't available, and now it won't be available anytime soon.

"Let's assume," she continued, "that Eric MacInnes was indeed murdered in your hot tub, Dean Bishop. Statistically speaking, the chances of us finding out who did it go down dramatically with every day that goes by. Now your guy Weiskopf comes in, and starts from scratch. Without laying eyes on this guy, I'm willing to bet that he doesn't know the half of what Rodriguez knows about your building security systems. So we've actually lost a lot of ground. And I have to say, it's kind of odd that when I put a little heat on Rodriguez to help me do my job, he leaves town."

"Are you implying," Bishop interjected, "that Alonzo Rodriguez is a suspect in your investigations? I find that hard to believe."

"If he were, Dean Bishop, I wouldn't tell *you* about it."

"I see no reason for us to be rude to each other, Captain."

"Oh, actually, I see lots of reasons. The dead kid in your pool, for example. The dead kid's dead sister in one of my hotels. A lot of nasty newspaper headlines and TV segments. Have you seen today's *Herald*?"

"No. As I said, I'm in Chicago, and—"

She picked up the paper. "Okay. Picture this. Front page: MACINNES MURDERS LINKED. That's the big type. And then in smaller type: THE B-SCHOOL CONNECTION. Nice picture of your library, with the bell tower. You just can't *buy* this kind of publicity."

"Well, that's another thing—"

"And last but not least," she went on, "I have an angry mayor breathing down my neck. I know you've had some dealings with Tommy Pavone, Dean Bishop. I understand that you and he get along pretty well. But I bet you've never seen him really *angry*. That ain't a pretty sight, as they say."

It was a risky ploy. For all she knew, Pavone and

Bishop talked regularly on back channels, and her bluster would misfire. But Bishop responded in a conciliatory tone. "Well, Captain, neither of us wants an angry mayor. And thank you for reading those headlines to me, because they reminded me of the other reason why I wanted to speak with you."

"Which is?"

"I wanted to let you know that the university strongly encouraged me to put Wim Vermeer on an indefinite paid leave, which I've reluctantly agreed to. He's been relieved of his responsibilities, pending the outcome of your investigations." He paused. It sounded as if he expected her to clap her hands or click her heels. She didn't. "So I just wanted to let you know that in light of recent developments, it was a mistake for me to involve him in the first place, and I do apologize if I've compromised your investigation in any way. Of course, I had no way of knowing that he would become a suspect himself."

"Is he?"

A pause. "*Isn't* he?"

"As far as I'm concerned, he's like everybody else: innocent until proven guilty. Maybe you acted a little too quickly. But I'm sure you followed procedures. Or at least I hope you did."

"Of course," replied Bishop. "Our counsel has been advising us all the way. In fact, it would be fair to say he has taken control of the process. So I can assure you that there won't be any procedural mistakes."

She sighed loudly, putting her throat into it. "Dean Bishop, to tell you the truth, I think that your people have made lots of mistakes, all along the line, and it doesn't sound like you've stopped yet. Tell your guy Weiskopf that as far as the police are concerned, he's already a week late with the answers to my questions. And those answers are getting later by the minute.

"Meanwhile"—she gambled again—"I'll brief the mayor."

34

So where was Vermeer?

Brouillard had tried the obvious places. Judging from Dean Bishop's revelations, she assumed Vermeer wasn't at his Harvard office. The messages on both his home machine and cell phone were similar and vague: *I'll be away for a couple of days. Leave a message. I'll call you back.*

Away where?

On an impulse, she drove down to Dorchester and the chocolate factory. He didn't answer his buzzer. The mailman arrived and, having unlocked and swung the large mailbox unit away from the wall, stuffed little packets of mail secured with rubber bands into the various slots. He noticed her watching him.

"Can I help you, ma'am?"

"Captain Brouillard, BPD." She flashed her badge. He looked mildly interested. "Just wondering if Vermeer in four-D had put a hold on his mail."

"Not unless the hold is scheduled to start tomorrow or later. Because he's got some stuff here today."

An elderly lady banged on the glass outer door, motioning that she needed help getting it open. Brouillard pulled and held it open, and the woman, not pausing to thank Brouillard for her help, pushed a two-wheeled wire grocery cart into the lobby ahead of her, wielding it like an icebreaker. The lobby was now a little too crowded. She plowed past Brouillard, evidently determined to collect her mail. "What seems to be the holdup here?" She was addressing the mailman.

"I'm with the police, ma'am," Brouillard said to the old woman's back. "I'm looking for someone. A tenant here, Wim Vermeer. Maybe you know him."

"I don't know anybody," the old woman snapped impatiently over her shoulder. "Why would I know somebody? The building superintendent knows everybody. You want to find somebody, you talk to the building superintendent. Everybody knows that. Back outside, down the driveway, last door on the left. Did my check come?"

Down the driveway, last door on the left—if she hadn't been looking for it, she would have missed it. The door was below ground level, a few granite-slab steps down from the road surface. An undersize bronze plaque in need of some polishing identified the superintendent's door. It didn't look as if the superintendent wanted to be found. She pushed the doorbell and didn't hear anything. She knocked. No answer.

"No vacancies, lady. Full up."

The voice came from behind her. She turned to see a large man emerging from a matching door, also below ground level, across the driveway. A slow-moving, mean-looking slug of a guy with an unfortunate knot of greasy black hair on the middle of his mostly bald head. Nothing about him looked quite finished. It looked as if his creator had lost faith in this particular project midway through and moved on to something more promising.

"I'm not looking for an apartment," she said, mentally

squaring herself up. "Boston police. I'm trying to find one of your tenants."

He looked at her badge. "Oh, yeah? I had an uncle on the force. Just retired after, I dunno, maybe thirty-five years. Moved to Florida. Bought himself a condo on Vero Beach for ten grand maybe twenty-five years ago. Now he lives down there for free; collects a fat fuckin' pension. You couldn't touch the goddamn place today for twenty times that. Lucky motherfucker. Always got all the breaks."

Brouillard didn't have a lot of patience with this type: purposefully foulmouthed to throw the little lady off balance. Her former auto mechanic had the same bad habits. She whipped out her pad and pencil. "What's your name?"

"Uhm, Castle. Joe Castle."

"Your uncle put in thirty-five years with the police department?"

"Yep. He—"

"Then listen to me, Joe Castle, he earned everything that's coming to him." Before Joe Castle had time to string together his next string of "fucks" and "goddamns," she switched gears. "Look, I'm here on official police business. We can do it here, or we can go downtown. Makes no difference to me."

He snapped to attention. *Behind every bully is a coward.*

"I'm trying to find Wim Vermeer," she continued. "You know him?"

"The perfessor? Sure I know him. What'd he do? He kill somebody? I shoulda known. He sure as fuck took off outta here in a hurry."

"When was that?"

"Yesterday. Came down, told me to look out for any packages he got and take his newspapers in. Then he was gone."

"Did he say where he was going?"

"Nah. Outta state, I think he said."

"Did you do it yet?"

He looked puzzled. "Do what yet?"

"Look out for packages. Take his newspapers in."

"Nah. No hurry. He's outta state, right? Plus, didn't you say he killed somebody? So maybe the guy ain't coming back, ever. In which case, maybe you and I could do business. Maybe even have some fun. If you're lookin' for a place, that is." He made an odd fat face, as if he were in pain. Then she realized that he was trying to leer at her. Her former auto mechanic had this bad habit, too.

"Castle, are you aware that propositioning a law-enforcement agent is a federal offense? Could involve a civil-rights rap?" Complete bullshit, but it had its desired effect. His eyes widened, and his eyebrows shot up comically.

"Hey, lady, I—"

"So we have a bad situation here, right? But let's deal. You let me accompany you when you take the newspapers up there, and in the process, you help me confirm that Professor Vermeer isn't in any trouble up there. And I forget about this bad situation."

He was searching in his memory for something, and it looked like hard work. "You got a—what?—a warrant?"

"Nope. But I've got you."

They went through the front door, and he gathered up the only copies of the *Times* and the *Journal* in the lobby. Then he took her up to the fourth floor on the elevator, staying as far away from her as possible in the small cab. Their elbows touched accidentally at one point. That made him flinch.

"So here we are," he mumbled, turning the lock of 4-D. "The perfessor's house." He let her go in first and then dropped the papers carelessly on the floor. They spread out on impact, like a deck of cards dropped from several inches above a table.

She had no idea what she was looking for, and she couldn't go fishing. She had already put herself on thin ice. A judge might possibly agree that she had reason to worry that something might have happened to Vermeer. *Probable cause.* But no judge would smile on her turning the place upside down.

"You check the bedroom and the bath," she said in her command voice. "Remember: You're just checking to make sure he's not in trouble. Look in the closets and under the bed. Look in the tub. Meanwhile, I'll check these rooms." He grunted, irritated, and shambled off. He had been thinking, *easy boff.* Now, somehow, he was *taking orders* from the easy boff.

Okay, Wim, she said to herself, *just give me one clue and I'll find you. But give it to me quick before your pal Joe Castle comes back.*

Nothing on the kitchen counters. No new food in the fridge since the last time she was here. *Just like my fridge,* she noted ruefully. Two messages on the answering machine—both hers, unless in the interim he had listened to hers and someone else had called in. No time to check that out. She considered stealing the tape and decided against it.

On the coffee table, the same pile of professor-type magazines.

But something new: a world atlas.

Open to a map of the Caribbean.

With a pencil lying on top.

And there, off the eastern end of Puerto Rico, a long skinny island running east-west, called "Vieques." Circled lightly in pencil.

———————

It took the phone companies an hour or two to fax Vermeer's phone records to her office. The landlines showed nothing interesting, to or from Vermeer's apartment. The cell phone records, though, put another puzzle piece on the table. Vermeer had made a number of calls to area code 787: the Vieques area code. He had called a Realtor twice—houseshopping?—and a guesthouse called the Rising Moon Inn. The Realtor was in a town called Isabel Segunda. The guesthouse was in somewhere called Esperanza. She checked the guidebook that she had grabbed at a bookstore on her way back into town. There: basically, the only two towns on the island of Vieques.

AmEx called back next. Yes, there was recent activity on his card: He had purchased a round-trip ticket to San Juan, and a connecting round-trip flight to Aeropuerto Antonio Rivera Rodriguez. U.S. Airways, then a puddle jumper.

U.S. Airways faxed his itinerary: out at dawn this morning, due to return three days from now. A full-fare ticket, which meant he could change his return whenever. Yes, their records showed that Mr. Vermeer had checked in at Logan this morning. The puddle-jumper airline had substantially more trouble pulling up the records, and the person who answered the phone did not speak much English. But *sí*, passenger Vermeer had flown to

Aeropuerto Rodriguez this morning. *Rodriguez.* She knew it was a common enough Spanish surname. Interesting, all the same.

She reviewed her scribbled notes and the various faxes that had come in. *Thank you for not paying cash, Wim.* But cash was what you used to conceal your route of flight. Maybe Wim Vermeer didn't think he was guilty of anything. Or maybe he was guilty as hell, and panicked and wasn't thinking straight.

Or maybe he was about to make a mistake and make himself guilty of something for the first time. She dialed upstairs.

"Chief?"

"Yeah?"

"Brouillard. I need your okay to follow a lead out of town."

The chief groaned. "Who, where, and why?" The chief didn't even like long-distance phone calls. He sure as hell wasn't going to like anything about a midwinter junket to a Caribbean island.

"It's Vermeer, the guy I told you about in the MacInnes cases. The B-School prof who had the ties to the dead boy, and was the last to see the girl alive, and was jumped on the sidewalk outside his house earlier this week. He's flown. Taken off for a remote island somewhere off Puerto Rico." She tried to make it sound as bad as possible without actually pointing the finger at Wim. And at some point in here, she noted to herself, she had started thinking about Vermeer as "Wim."

"Oh, come on, Barbara," the chief said, sounding pained. He had been a decent cop in his day. Now he was playing out the string. In that, he had the mayor's tacit approval, since nobody wanted any turmoil in the department with an election coming up. "You told the guy to hunker down somewhere, right? So now he's hunkering down. He's just being smart. Taking your advice."

"He doesn't take my advice. And there's more." She told him about Rodriguez taking off a day earlier, bound for the same island. "This can't be a coincidence, Chief. We're talking about a dirt island in the middle of nowhere. The two of them—Vermeer and Rodriguez—have got to be connected in some way. I've got to go after them."

"Damn it, Captain," he barked, but she heard the resignation creeping into his voice, "this is the kind of stuff that the newspapers have a field day with. You know what they do with this kind of stuff: 'Top Cop on Fun-in-Sun Junket.' And you *know* they've got their eyes on you. You're investigating the hottest cases in town. Maybe in the country."

"Did you get my e-mail about the mayor?"

"Oh, yes. Goddamn it."

She knew she had him. "Tell you what, Chief: I'll put the ticket on my own credit card. If it's a nothing, it's a nothing, and I won't put in for reimbursement. If it's a something, the department can pay me back. All I need is your okay for an unscheduled vacation. A week. I've got it coming to me."

"Goddamn it and shit, Barbara, I know you have a vacation coming to you—more than one, I bet—but it's gonna look like a damned strange time to be taking it. Okay, okay. Take it. But be careful down there."

"You know I will, Chief."

"No, specifically, what I mean is, be careful you don't get photographed in your goddamn little floral-pattern bikini sucking down a blue drink full of crushed ice with a little umbrella in it. 'Cop Swizzles while Case Fizzles'—that, I don't want to see in the *Herald*."

She laughed. Then, she wondered if she still owned a bathing suit.

35

VERMEER WONDERED HOW LONG IT TOOK A SCREW TO back itself out of the side panels of a two-prop, six-seater Cessna in response to the twin engines' intense vibrations. Several screws near his left elbow were already missing. A couple more had made their way halfway out. Figure the plane was at least thirty years old. Had it taken thirty years? Or did someone maybe tighten up these screws every few weeks, or months, or years?

And was someone paying more attention to the screws that held the outside of the plane together? These were the kinds of calculations that Vermeer tended to make in small, old airplanes.

He had the middle bench all to himself. He and the two passengers in front of him had been stuffed in through a small hatch on the right side of the plane, under the wing. Then that door was closed, and the two passengers on the rear bench were stuffed in through a second hatch on the left side of the plane. On his way in, looking down, he noticed that the threshold of the hatch was made of oak. He had never seen any kind of wood on an airplane before.

This was one of those planes where they asked you how much you weighed and then assigned you a seat. The cast-bronze sign over his head gave him some more material to calculate with. "Maximum floor loading intensity not greater than 120 lb/ft^2," it began. It continued with a series of maximum allowables, from just behind the pilots to the back of the plane. "Area from rear of pilot's seat to front wing spar frame 1000 lbs max," read the first.

There were four such areas blocked out, with a grand allowable total of 2,940 pounds. This crowd, Vermeer guessed, didn't add up to much more than half that. The Spanish-speaking couple on the front bench might tip the scales at three fifty, but no more. He assumed that he himself was still under two hundred pounds, although he hadn't checked recently. And the two kids in the backseat, who couldn't keep their hands off each other, with flushed faces that looked more lustful than sunburned, couldn't add up to more than three hundred pounds total. So even if the engines were old and tired, Vermeer calculated, they ought to be able to move this crowd from here to there.

The plane narrowed toward its nose. As a result, the two white-shirted, epauletted pilots didn't fit shoulder to shoulder. They seemed to love their work, though—something that Vermeer always looked for in people who held his life in their hands. Before takeoff, they joked in both Spanish and English about the little plane, the noise, and the relatively short hop over to Vieques. Once airborne, shouting above the engines, they provided a running commentary—in Spanish; Vermeer couldn't follow it.

The Puerto Rican couple nodded politely, with one or the other making an occasional comment to the pilots. The kids on the back bench, pawing each other energetically, sometimes audibly sucking on each other's tongues, missed the tour entirely.

Vermeer looked out the small window to his left. There were coral reefs along the north shore, which occasionally broke through the wave tops. Underwater, the reefs looked warm and lively; above the water, they looked brown, dead, and dangerous. Windsurfers knifed in and around these reefs. To Vermeer's eye, several hundred feet above them, the windsurfers all appeared to be skirting death. *They must know what they're doing,* he thought. *Which is more than I can say for myself.*

The truth was, he didn't have much of a plan. His white-hot fury toward Pirle had cooled somewhat, which was probably a good thing: Now he was able to think things through a little more clearly. And concentrate on the fact that he didn't have much of a plan.

He could confront Pirle directly.

If he did, one of two things could happen. Pirle could succumb to guilt. He could confess to framing Vermeer, and maybe a whole lot more. Then the two of them could walk down to the local police station together. Pirle could repeat his confession, arms outstretched, hands together at the wrists for the handcuffs, and throw himself on the mercy of Puerto Rican justice.

Not likely.

The other thing that could happen was that Pirle could call the local police and demand to have this madman, this stubble-faced stalker who had trailed him down from Boston, hauled off to some dank jail. The local police would make a few phone calls to Boston—they could call almost anybody—and they wouldn't have much trouble picking sides.

Much more likely.

No, confrontation wasn't likely to accomplish much. The deck was stacked. Pirle was on his home turf;

Vermeer knew almost nothing about this island. He had a vague recollection that the U.S. Navy had maintained some sort of gunnery range here and that local protests had eventually driven the Navy out. Beyond that, nothing.

Pirle spoke Spanish well, Vermeer remembered. Vermeer had made it through his high school Spanish courses, but that was years ago.

Pirle was a wealthy landowner, probably connected to whatever local power structure existed. Vermeer was a nobody.

Pirle was an accomplished liar. Vermeer generally blushed when he lied.

He fingered the snapshot in his coat pocket, looking idly out the window. He needed *evidence*. He needed some way to tip the balance in his favor—to blow apart Pirle's web of deception, to give himself a fighting chance of persuading the world that these deceptions had actually occurred.

So, he decided, leaving the snapshot concealed within his pocket, he needed to take a look inside the villa. He needed to find something that he could use as leverage against Pirle. Something to wave in his face and rattle him with. Anything.

————————

Vieques was given away by a bank of clouds riding above it: a floating skyline. There were clusters of low-rise clouds, then the occasional neighborhood of sky-scrapers. The Cessna, bouncing on some light crosswinds, waggled its wings as it approached a single strip nestled alongside the ocean: prime beachfront real estate, given over to the airport. Through the plane window, the terminal looked whimsical: a beige, green-roofed octagon like an old-fashioned seaside carousel, with covered green metal chutes plunging from its upper level to the ground at steep angles.

Vermeer retrieved his bag from what he guessed to be the world's shortest baggage-claim belt: twenty running feet of sectioned black rubber outside the building, and twenty feet inside. In the parking lot, a dapper gentleman with a deeply creased honey-brown face stood next to a white van. Yes, he acknowledged in formal, accented English, he was the taxi service. Yes, of course, he would be willing to take Vermeer to the Rising Moon, on the far side of the island. That would cost fifteen dollars. But truly, he would prefer to wait until the flight from neighboring Culebra came in. If there was another paying customer on that flight, then Vermeer would pay only ten dollars, and the other passenger would not have to wait so long at the airport. That would be better.

They waited. Fifteen minutes later, the Culebra flight arrived with no paying customers.

Sandy Silva had agreed to pick him up at his hotel after he checked in. He knew that engaging the services of a real estate agent was a roundabout way to scope out Pirle's neighborhood, but it was the best he had been able to come up with on short notice. Hopefully, he looked affluent enough to be a potential villa buyer.

The Rising Moon was an eclectic hodgepodge of connected structures, perched atop a knoll that overlooked green fields running down to the Caribbean. Its owners, Ariel and Rick, had relocated here from California a decade earlier, gradually transforming a seedy dance hall into one of the better places to stay on the island. The walls in his room fairly dripped with California bric-a-brac: several dozen end panels from fruit crates, each decorated with a gaudy, sometimes bawdy, grower's label; and a series of black-and-white pictures of the aftermath of the 1906 San Francisco earthquake.

No doubt Ariel and Rick were happy to be out of the earthquake zone. But the earthquake shots—hollow-eyed survivors looked balefully at the photographer as smoke rose from mounds of rubble behind them—seemed to strike the wrong note for a Caribbean paradise.

Sandy Silva uncovered him in the lobby. "Professor Vermeer? So nice to meet you!" Fortyish, short, and energetic, she sported a helmet of tight blond curls. She pumped his hand energetically. "Ready for your tour?"

He had pulled her name off the Web. His cover story, improvised on the phone, was that he was a professor from the Boston area who had recently come into some money. He was looking to make an investment in real estate. From everything he had heard, Vieques was the hot place to invest, and Sandy Silva was the best person to help him do that. She sounded distracted, almost hurrying him along, until he said that he wasn't interested in spending more than a million. Before renovations and upgrades, of course.

They climbed into her Suzuki Sidekick, which was dented here and there but still new enough to imply that she was prospering. The deal that she had proposed on the phone was that he would pay her a flat fee of sixty dollars an hour. This, she said, helped weed out the window-shoppers and helped keep her available to the *serious* buyers, like himself. She took an imprint of his credit card on a machine that she kept in a gym bag between the front seats.

"So," she said brightly, handing him back his card, putting the car into gear, "which university are you with?"

"MIT," he lied. No sense connecting the dots unnecessarily. "Astrophysics."

"So that's kind of like astronomy?"

He didn't think so. "Astronomy is what you would call a contributing discipline." Sounded about right.

"Oh, well," she beamed, "then this is the place for you. Seat belt, please. Wait until you see the stars at night. Absolutely beautiful!"

She chattered too much and drove too fast for the narrow road, which to Vermeer's eye looked like it ought to be one-way, but wasn't. The landscape *was* beautiful, he admitted: fields and forests descending from a central ridge down to the ocean, occasionally punctuated by a cluster of houses, most of which had farm animals pecking and grazing nearby. Too bad he wasn't a millionaire, and too bad he was on the lam. Whizzing around a blind corner, Silva slammed on the brakes to avoid mowing down three horses standing placidly in the middle of the road, swishing their tails at flies. They ambled away in response to her honking.

"So as I was saying," she resumed, unabashed and again accelerating, "you really *do* have to drive carefully on Vieques, because not only do you have our world-famous wild horses, but you also have our wild cattle and goats, which are less world famous, but *none* of which you want to have running into your car." She gave him a winning smile.

They stopped first at a run-down property on the edge

of Esperanza: an inappropriate color of pink, with a just-barely water view from the second floor. "Not exactly a million-dollar property," he suggested in so many words. She nodded her agreement energetically and suggested that they move on. Their next stop, a half mile down the beach, was an elegant pure-white mansion with its own dock. In the bright sun, set off against the green sea and blue sky, it shimmered and seemed to float.

"*Nice,*" Vermeer finally said, trying to look a little more interested but not interested enough.

"I knew you'd like this one," she enthused. "It's at the top of your price range, though—before you get your heart set on it."

In his hotel room he had studied the snapshot of Pirle's house carefully. The vista behind the house showed a large land mass on the horizon. Looking next at his tourist map, he realized that Pirle's villa had to be facing west, toward the small city of Fajardo on the main island.

"You know," he confessed as they climbed back into the Suzuki, "having seen these two places, I think I might be better off putting my money into a view than into a dock. What are the chances of finding something up on one of those high hills I saw coming in on the plane? Something with a western exposure, so I could kick back and watch the sun go down?"

She arched her eyebrows suggestively. "A romantic, eh? I can just see you sitting there on your deck with your honey, drinking piña coladas and watching the sun set over the Caribbean."

"In my hot tub."

"Oh, *yes,*" she enthused, smiling, lurching into gear and leaving the white mansion in a cloud of dust. "So with that in mind, I think that we should head over to

Bravos de Boston. Especially appropriate for a man from Boston!"

Bravos de Boston, she explained as they bounced along, was a hilly residential section of Isabel Segunda, the largest town on the island. Nobody seemed to know—or at least Sandy didn't know—where the neighborhood's name came from. "But hey, if you buy a nice big house up there," she said, "as far as I'm concerned, you can just say they named the whole neighborhood in honor of you. Nobody's gonna *argue* with you."

To get to Isabel Segunda, they had to go up and over the spine of steep hills that ran down the center of the island. On their way up the eastern slope, with the Suzuki laboring and smelling as though it might be overheating, Vermeer spotted an overgrown complex of what looked like half-finished buildings several hundred yards down a slope, off to his right. A large one-story central building was flanked by two boomerang-shaped arcs of what looked like grandstands. The paved areas around the buildings were sprouting weeds. Sections of roofing above the grandstands were missing, and treetops were poking through the holes.

"What's that? A failed racetrack?" At one point in his life, he had visited quite a few racetracks. This place looked a lot like a certain country track in New England—trotters and pacers only—where he had once lost what was for him a sizable amount of money.

"Ugh," Sandy said, not even looking sideways. "That eyesore? No. Not a racetrack. That was *supposed* to be a children's athletic facility. Never opened. Nine million taxpayer dollars, mostly courtesy of Uncle Sam, down the drain and that's what we're left with."

"What went wrong?"

"Well, what nobody bothered to figure out when they started the thing was that this particular piece of property was right up the hill from the BioBay. One of the main tourist attractions of the island—you'll have to go see it. Full of little sea creatures that glow in the dark. They give tours in these flat-bottomed tin boats. You can get out of the boat and go swimming with the little glowing creatures. Me, I never got out of the boat. It creeped me out. I mean, like, what if you swallowed the things, right?

"But anyway, the environmentalists started saying that the light from the sports complex would wreck the BioBay. Which, if it got wrecked, would be very bad for Vieques, not to mention for the glowing sea creatures. So long story short, they just stopped the thing. Stopped it cold. Never finished, never used. A total waste. And as you can see, a very nice piece of property all chewed to hell."

That, Vermeer realized, would always be Sandy's bottom line: real property removed from her potential inventory, probably forever.

They cleared the top of the mountain and started flying down its western flank. He noticed that Sandy had popped the Suzuki out of gear. She now relied entirely on her brakes to keep the careening car on the twisting and badly banked road.

Isabel Segunda came upon them too fast, announced by a few gas stations and convenience stores. The center of town was a square, with what looked like mostly public buildings huddling around the concrete community space in its center. On one side of the square sat what looked like a one-story public school, but Sandy zipped through the square too fast to let Vermeer be absolutely sure. Aggressively she claimed the tiny two-way streets as her own, at least until the last possible moment. "Shit," she said at one point, as a battered Toyota pickup refused to give way. "Sorry. Bad language." The driver of the Toyota yelled something at her in Spanish.

Then they were past the ferry slip—"a place you want to avoid when the ferry comes in," she complained. Then they shot out the other side of the town, climbing up a tiny winding street to the crest of a hill that overlooked the Caribbean, once ducking off to the right around a blind corner, where they scattered a mother hen and her three chicks, which appeared to be pecking on the remains of a dead sibling. Then a hard left, eliciting an angry yell from someone sitting inside an adjacent house, then two thumps as the Suzuki bulled its way across a drainage ditch, then up another hill. On both sides of the road were modest cinder-block bungalows, mostly nestled in an array of flowering shrubs. Dogs barked. Underweight cats prowled, but the chickens seemed to pay them no notice.

"You see," she said with a note of apology in her voice, "what we have is a bunch of nineteenth-century streets trying to keep up with the times, and not really doing a very good job of it." She pointed at a huge billboard: *Bienvenidos,* it read. *Welcome to Bravos de Boston, a comunidad especial.* "But there are plans in the works to fix all that. And of course, you can go up the back side of this hill, too. From the back side of Isabel Segunda. But that road's a little rough."

"Rougher than this?" Now, in deference to the monster potholes that loomed left and right, even Sandy was moving slowly, rarely getting out of second gear.

"Well, *steeper,* anyway. But rough, too."

His response was cut off: His teeth snapped together

as Sandy blasted her way over yet another drainage ditch. The kind of thing that Vermeer had trained himself to look out for, back in his days as a motorcycle rider. It was set at an angle transverse to the road, so she actually hit it with all four wheels separately: *whunk-whunk, whunk-whunk.*

"So what happens," he ventured, scrutinizing the road ahead carefully, tongue safely away from teeth, "if there's a fire up here? What happens if the fire truck is heading this way and someone is coming the other way?"

She pursed her lips, not welcoming this slightly negative, trouble-in-paradise line of questioning. "Well, what you'd expect. The fire truck comes and puts out the fire. It uses its siren, the people hear it coming, and they pull over. Or more likely, they're up the hill somewhere sipping on a beer, watching the fire. Anyway, I can't remember the last real bad fire we had. These places are pretty fireproof." She gestured at a half-finished cinder-block structure, which looked abandoned behind its chain-link fence. It didn't look as though it would burn under any circumstances.

Five minutes later, they were high in the hills, mostly with their backs to the ocean. The winding road was now little more than a dirt track, sometimes eight feet wide and sometimes less, with the occasional sheer drop on the ocean side. Up here on the hilltops, with expansive views of the ocean, there were no modest shacks or unfinished buildings. Driveways veered off at sharp angles toward mostly invisible homes. Almost all the driveways had motorized gates, on tracks. All were closed tight. "I notice the driveway gates are all closed," he said casually. "Security concerns?"

She laughed, then shook her head. "Horse-poop concerns. People don't like the horses wandering in and tearing up the lawns. Or falling in the pool. Ever wonder how much a dead wet horse weighs? Better to leave the gate shut."

Almost at the top of the hill, he saw it. Unmistakably: the blunt outlines of Pirle's villa.

36

THE REAL QUESTION WAS, WOULD RODRIGUEZ SHOW UP?

He certainly didn't have to. Agente Montoya first had made that point clear to Brouillard. Then, Brouillard could tell, listening hard with her spotty Spanish, he had told Rodriguez over the phone that the detective from Boston was in his conference room and would like the opportunity to ask him a few questions—"*Sí, sí, Isabel Segunda, sí; cuartel de policía, sí*"—but that was entirely up to him, and Rodriguez was not obligated to come in.

Montoya shrugged as he hung up the phone. "He said he will be happy to respond to your questions, Captain Brouillard, but he won't be able to stay long."

"His father is sick, right?"

"He didn't mention that. But he said he'd try to be here within fifteen minutes." Montoya leaned back in his chair and folded his arms above his head. The conference room was the only air-conditioned room in the police station, as far as Brouillard could tell. It looked as if Montoya wouldn't mind passing a quarter hour here. Even in February the noon sun was hot and the weather was sticky.

Her trip down to San Juan had been mercifully uneventful. Not a fan of small airplanes—or any kind of planes, in fact—she had hired a driver to take her from San Juan to Fajardo, on the eastern tip of the main island; from there, she caught the ferry to Vieques. Miraculously, her rental car was waiting at the ferry landing at Isabel Segunda. She signed the obligatory stack of papers, probably buying far more insurance than she needed, and then raised some eyebrows by asking for directions to the police station.

Presumably, not a lot of tourists checked in at the police station first. But this was a necessary professional courtesy. And depending on what happened, she might well need some help from someone with jurisdiction down here.

The *cuartel de policía* was a small municipal building made of cream-colored cinder block, several blocks outside of the congested center of Isabel Segunda. About half the building was given over to a vehicle-maintenance and cleaning shop, mostly open to the weather along its long side. A half-dozen guys of various ages and shapes hosed down vehicles and poked around under hoods. One or two looked up and nodded at her; most simply kept hosing and poking.

Behind the reception desk, a uniformed woman manned the phones and directed traffic. Fans moved the humid air around the station at high speeds. Just behind the desk and slightly to the left was the station's lone cell—the *cuarto detenidos,* according to a plastic sign above the barred door. Brouillard hoped that no one she knew would wind up in that particular cage.

It took a while for the dispatcher to find someone who spoke good enough English to deal with the policewoman who had come from all the way up in Boston. Agente Montoya, who arrived about twenty minutes after the call for an English-speaker went out, had a puffy, saggy copper face, with bags under his eyes that made him look world-weary and skeptical. He invited Brouillard into the sealed-up conference room, steered her toward one of the mismatched chairs around the Formica-topped table, welcomed her to Vieques, and asked how he could help. His English was peppered with out-of-date colloquialisms, as if he had studied a very old English textbook.

Brouillard explained that she had followed an American down here, a man named Vermeer, who appeared to be linked to several deaths up in Boston but who had not been charged with anything. This was an informal surveillance, more than anything, Brouillard said, and the American didn't appear to pose any sort of threat, but of course, Agente Montoya and his colleagues needed to be aware of all this. Meanwhile, she said, another gentleman—a Mr. Alonzo Rodriguez—had been compelled to return unexpectedly to his family home on Vieques. It appeared that Mr. Rodriguez might have some useful information regarding Mr. Vermeer. Or, Brouillard shrugged, he might not. So a conversation with Mr. Rodriguez would be helpful.

What followed was a negotiation disguised as a conversation. If we were to follow the rules *to the letter,* Agente Montoya said, you would *of course* need to work through the extradition unit at Hato Rey, which, of course, would require you to go over to San Juan. If Hato Rey agreed that you needed to talk to Mr. Rodriguez, they would call us, and we would call Mr. Rodriguez, and he could choose to come in or not, and he could choose to bring along his lawyer. All of this would require a lot of *time,* of course.

"So now," Montoya concluded, in a casual-sounding tone, "tell me more about this American of yours—this Señor Vermeer."

Brouillard had thought this through. Vermeer had to sound bad enough to warrant bending the rules and questioning Rodriguez, but not so bad that the local police would feel compelled to act on their own. Although it might come to that. "The fact that I'm here, Agente Montoya, means that my department takes this individual seriously. Very seriously. He had some sort of personal connection to a young man who died under strange circumstances. He also had a connection to the young man's sister, who was murdered several days ago."

"I have heard of these killings," he said. "A bad situation."

"I advised him to get out of the public spotlight, for his own good. The next day, he vanished. Then he turned up here."

Montoya shrugged. "So he is either taking your good advice or he is running away from you. Well. If he thinks he is beyond the reach of the American police here, of course, he is mistaken. If he appears on the Interpol computers as a fugitive, your FBI will fly in and pick him up. He would have been wiser to go to Brazil, I think. There is harder extradition from Brazil."

"*If* he's actually on the run," Brouillard agreed. "Frankly, if he had called me before leaving town and told me that's what he was doing, I probably wouldn't be here."

"And yet . . ." Montoya said slowly. "And yet, he chooses our little Vieques. Not the first place you Americans think of when you want to get away from it all. And meanwhile, as you say, Señor Rodriguez also leaves your town in a hurry, headed for the same small island that most Bostoners—you would say that? Bostoners?—have never heard of. And so you have asked yourself, is this a coincidence?"

"Yes. That's what I ask myself. As a Bostonian."

"Bos-*toe*-nian," he repeated, rolling the word on his tongue. "And you do not think your fellow Bostonian, Señor Vermeer, represents a danger to Vieques? Or specifically, to my Señor Rodriguez?"

"No. I don't think so."

"But you are basically—what is the phrase?—'winging it'? ¿*Improvisar?*"

" 'Monitoring,' let's say. With your awareness, of course, Agente Montoya."

"And are you asking us for our help in this . . . monitoring?"

"Absolutely not. That would be inappropriate." She winged it.

"Good." He nodded. "We could not participate in anything like that without official approval from the mainland. And so the question is, Captain Brouillard, will you conduct yourself professionally on our island, even though you are not here in a professional capacity? And will you call us immediately if there's something we need to know about?"

"Absolutely."

"No guns, of course?"

"I'm on vacation."

"Well, then," he said, reaching for the phone, "let us invite Señor Rodriguez in for a conversation. Did I mention to you, Captain, that he is a cousin of mine?"

Rodriguez showed up looking flushed and a little haggard. He sat down next to Brouillard, nodding at her but not moving to shake her hand. He used the cloth handkerchief in his left hand to dab the sweat off his forehead. To Montoya he said something in rapid-fire Spanish—incomprehensible to Brouillard—and Montoya simply shrugged in response. Finally, Rodriguez turned slightly and addressed her. "I am very surprised to see you here, Captain," he said. "Very surprised."

"Not as surprised as I am to be here," she said. "Thank you for agreeing to come in and talk with me."

"I don't know what more I can tell you. My understanding was that Bill Weiskopf was going to set up the meeting you wanted."

"Uh-huh," she said. "And my understanding is that that meeting will take a while to set up. And without you there, it's going to be much less helpful."

Agente Montoya sat with his arms resting on the rounded shelf of his belly. He appeared to be nodding off.

Rodriguez, for his part, now looked put-upon. "Excuse me, Captain, but as I'm sure you were informed, I needed to return to Vieques. There was not much I could do about the situation."

"Sí, I meant to ask you, Alonzo," Montoya said in a drowsy-sounding voice. "The captain here says Ernesto was taken ill. I hadn't heard of this. How serious is this problem?"

"He's doing fine now. No longer any cause for concern."

With this exchange, to Brouillard's eyes Rodriguez's body language had shifted from annoyed to uncomfortable. He seemed ill at ease talking about his father's illness in front of another family member.

"Mr. Rodriguez," Brouillard said, taking another tack, "I wanted to ask you how well you know Wim Vermeer."

"Professor Vermeer? Not well. I've been introduced to him, and of course, I've seen him around the campus." He dabbed at his forehead.

"Ever invite him down here?"

"To Vieques? Of course not."

"Ever talk to him about Vieques?"

"Never." He was clear enough on that point. He seemed baffled by the general line of questioning.

"Do you have any idea," she continued, "why he might have hopped a flight shortly after you did—on short notice, just like you—and come down here, too?"

"Vermeer is *here*?"

"Assuming that the airlines are telling me the truth, which they generally tend to do. And they've gotten a lot better about checking IDs."

"But . . . but why?" Rodriguez asked hesitantly. "Why here?"

Brouillard shrugged and put her palms up. "I asked you first. Have you seen him?"

"No, of course not."

"So why would he pick *your* island to come visit, of all places? Is he looking for you? And if so, why?"

"No, no," he replied, sounding distracted, as if he were calculating with most of his brain. "No, not looking for me, no."

"Oh, come on, Al. Who *else* on this island would he be looking for?"

Rodriguez glanced at Montoya, who now appeared to be fully asleep, chin resting on chest, breathing heavily. "I really . . . ," Rodriguez began hesitantly, "I really don't think I should be guessing about what is on the mind of Professor Vermeer. I just don't know about that."

"Fair enough," Brouillard admitted. "Let me sharpen up my question a little bit. Do you know of anyone else on this island who has connections to Harvard, or the Harvard Business School, or to the MacInnes family?"

"Well, I told you about the several people whom I've helped to get employment. They—"

"Skip them. Anyone else?"

Once again he passed his handkerchief across his brow, even though the air conditioner had gotten ahead of the heat, and the room was now quite comfortable. "Well, no, other than Professor Pirle, of course. But I wouldn't know if those two are in contact with each other."

Brouillard tried to keep the astonishment off her face. Ducking down, stalling for time, she reached into her bag and pulled out her pad and pencil. She riffled back through her Pirle notes. Vieques? Nothing. She hated shooting blind. "So Pirle is here right now?"

"Well, I really couldn't say," Rodriguez said, obviously not comfortable. "I don't keep track of when he's here and when he's not. You could telephone him at the villa."

"*Pirle = Vieques villa????*" she wrote, small enough so there was no chance of his reading it upside down. "Thanks. I'll give it a try."

"Listen, Captain, I hate to cut this short, but—"

"I know. You have to get back to your father, whom you're taking care of. And who's making a nice recovery."

"Uh, yes," said Rodriquez warily, throwing a glance at his cousin as he got to his feet. "Well, call me if you have any more questions. Although I really don't think I can tell you much more. There is no need to wake my cousin.

Give him my regards." And with that, Rodriguez scuttled out of the room.

There was only a moment of silence. Then Montoya spoke. His eyes opened, and his chin moved—nothing else. "My sense, Captain Brouillard," he said sleepily, "is that my cousin was not being entirely truthful with you. Why, I do not know."

37

BY MIDAFTERNOON, BROUILLARD HAD FOUND HER WAY around the island. She first scouted out Pirle's villa, up in the hills—two cars in the drive behind the locked gate, she noted—and then wound up at the odd place where Vermeer was a registered guest. *The Rising Moon,* she said to herself disapprovingly. No doubt owned by some aging hippie sending out a coded signal to his fellow burnouts.

At first she had had no intention of staying where Vermeer was staying. But in her brief circuit around the island, she had learned that there weren't a lot of choices. The Rising Moon was expensive, but the alternatives ranged from unappealing to scary-looking. Reluctantly she handed over her credit card to the fortyish woman at the front desk. "Do you have anything that's not in the main traffic flow?" she asked. "I'm a late riser."

"Let me see," said the desk clerk. Like her face, her accent was flat and full of the U.S. Midwest. She had a missing front tooth. "Room two-oh-nine is up the stairs and all the way to the back. It's not the nicest view, but—"

"I'll take it."

"Excellent. Since you're a first-time guest, why don't we start with your tour of the Rising Moon, and—"

"No, thanks," Brouillard interrupted again. "I can find my way."

The woman looked annoyed, as if the tour were an important part of her day. "Suit yourself," she said, handing over the room key. "Breakfast starts at eight and ends at ten. It's complimentary." She started to walk to the back of the office.

"But there *is* one thing that you can do for me that would be *very* helpful," Brouillard said. The woman stopped and turned, her face brightening. "Look," Brouillard continued, making up her story as she went along, "I'm something of a hometown celebrity back where I come from—broadcast journalism—and I have reason to believe that there is a photographer who has followed me down here to try to get some unauthorized pictures of me. For money. You know—a tabloid kind of thing." Now she was grateful to the chief, back in Boston, for planting a version of this ridiculous idea in her head.

"You mean, like, paparazzi? Here on Vieques?" Her eyes widened at the thought.

"Exactly. Exactly. So if someone asks after me, could you just . . . you know . . . draw a blank? Not remember me?"

The woman stood up ramrod straight, as if called to attention. "Ms. Brouillard, that is the Rising Moon's policy, in any case. But I *personally* will make sure that your privacy is protected during your stay with us." She leaned forward and spoke in a lower tone. "Just so you know: I've had some trouble with photographers, myself. And if you want a recommendation for some very secluded beaches, you just let me know."

Now, an hour later, sitting under the dark overhang of a mostly open-air restaurant, sipping a lukewarm Corona,

Brouillard allowed herself a smile as she thought back to that moment of false intimacy: two women commiserating about being pestered by paparazzi. She knew she herself was in no danger of being photographed surreptitiously; she doubted that the desk clerk was now or ever had been.

She had chosen the time, more than the restaurant. Even in paradise, the basic rhythms of life would hold, and three in the afternoon would be the deadest time of the day in any local restaurant, anywhere. The last late luncher would be on his way out; the front end of the happy-hour crowd would not yet be on the prowl for free hors d'oeuvres. In other words, a good time to pick up on the local gossip.

The rhythms of life were observed at Amanda's Seaside Café, a brown-shingled affair up a flight of stairs and right off the main street in the little town of Esperanza. Aside from Brouillard, the clientele was down to two tables. At one was a young Spanish-speaking couple, windblown, Brouillard guessed, from a ride on the shocking yellow scooter parked down below on the sidewalk. The boy came up well short of handsome, but the dark-haired girl, tricked out in tiny tight orange Hooters-type shorts and a tight top, was stunning. They were only using one chair: She was straddling him, performing something just this side of a lap dance.

Amanda herself, a tall, thin type in her fifties, with a no-nonsense haircut and a shoulder-to-knee apron sporting a prominent name tag, attempted to take their order. Around the energetic kisses and caresses of his lover, and in a strangled voice that came out in heavily accented English, the boy ordered two turkey clubs and two Dos Equis.

"Anything else?" Amanda rubbed the back of her neck, looking as though she'd seen it all before.

"Both with . . . *extra* . . . *mayo.*"

This last request, gasped out, drew stifled snorts of laughter from two deeply tanned and wrinkled ladies in their late fifties, sitting across the room at the only other occupied table. Chain-smoking and drinking what looked like G and Ts with large slabs of lime, they scrutinized the passionate couple until the turkey clubs arrived and the young lovers disentangled briefly to eat. The wrinkled ladies turned back to their own conversation, now and then still snorting softly.

Brouillard, a practiced eavesdropper, tuned in. One of the two women was recounting what appeared to be the latest installment in the endless saga of her new refrigerator. The fact that it had *actually showed up* on the island, which happened yesterday, was a cause for mock celebration. (The two women raised, clinked, and pulled on their G and Ts.) However, the new refrigerator's owner continued, it was not really clear *where* it was on the island now; it now had to be found again, and then a truck had to be found, and then the delivery had to be made.

"And listen, Sal," said her friend, "when it finally turns up, don't let them just plunk it down on the damn sidewalk. You make sure those guys get it into the kitchen and plugged in, and you make sure it works before they take off on you."

"Hear, hear." They snorted, laughed, and raised their glasses again.

Now Amanda pulled up a third chair and joined them. She had a bottle of beer that must have been ice cold—colder than Brouillard's Corona—which was sweating profusely in the warm, humid air. She wrapped a napkin tidily around its base, and the table conversation drifted from refrigerators to other island chatter. When she finished her beer, Amanda made her way back into the kitchen.

Brouillard felt an odd sensation, a disconnectedness. She wondered if she was coming down with something, or if she was drinking her beer too quickly. Then she realized, with a little jolt of embarrassment, that she was enjoying herself. When was the last time she had sipped a warm beer in the middle of the afternoon? When was the last time she had had no paperwork due, no idiot at the next desk, no gun on her hip?

A warm, perfumed breeze blew in steadily from the ocean, setting the palm trees that lined the ocean side of the road to clattering. Although the little town obviously had some aspirations—someone at some point had constructed an elaborate terrace with a cream-colored, balustraded concrete railing that ran the length of the town along the beach, like something out of Palm Beach—it still welcomed all kinds. Three brown-skinned local kids at the water's edge poked at crabs hiding under worn-out-looking rocks. A strange-gaited character in huge gray dreadlocks accosted an American tourist and his wife—cameras at the neck, belly bags at the waist—and scared them with some sort of mad commentary.

Brouillard refocused her cop's eye, scrutinizing the restaurant's decor. A mass-produced wooden sign nailed to a beam above the two women read, "We will drink no wine before it's time. It's time!" A little farther down the beam she spotted a broken oar with "distance to Halifax, Nova Scotia" hand-painted on its blade: "2,412 miles."

Dumb, she thought, but she could definitely get used to this.

The passionate young couple departed first, leaving half-eaten sandwiches behind them. Next, the snorting ladies weaved out a little unsteadily, leaving separate wads of crumpled cash on the table and yelling good-bye to Amanda, who stuck her head out of the kitchen to wave back. "Walk carefully, girls," she said. This prompted still more snorts and laughter.

Another few minutes went by before Amanda came by Brouillard's table again. "Want another, miss?"

Brouillard didn't, but she nodded yes. Amanda came back with a fresh Corona. "No lime, right?"

"Right, thanks," Brouillard replied. "Nice place you've got here."

Amanda looked around the four corners of the dining room and then around to the L-shaped bar area. She shrugged. "It's a living."

"Got a minute to talk?"

"Sure. Why not? But let me get myself a beer first." When she returned, beer in hand, she pulled out the chair across the table from Brouillard.

"I'm Barbara. From Boston."

"Amanda. From Vieques. By way of Syosset."

"I'm just interested in what it's like to live down here full-time," Brouillard said. "It just seems like such a beautiful place. And laid-back. The people seem so friendly."

"Yeah. It's all of that, and then some. But like every-place else, it's not perfect, either. You thinking of moving down here?"

"I don't know. Maybe. I'm kind of fed up with the winters in Boston. I was talking about moving someplace warmer, and this guy I know said I should look at Vieques. So I sort of combined a vacation and a little exploring."

"Not a new story," Amanda said, smiling. "I did it myself, a while back." She studied her beer bottle, then took a sip. "Well, the first thing you gotta understand is, it's a hard place to make a buck. I've been at this for ten years, and I'm still just squeaking by. It's a tourist economy with not enough tourists. Or at least, that's how *I* see it. Some people here would like no tourists."

Brouillard nodded. "I've thought about the money side. I'm a writer, so a lot of what I do could get done long-distance."

"Well, you know your own business," Amanda replied, "but my advice to you would be, check it out carefully. Doing business down here can be very frustrating. If you can bring the money with you, fine. Otherwise, look before you leap."

Brouillard frowned. "I hear you." She waited a moment. "So is it easy to make friends down here? I really only know this one guy, who's not even here most of the time, and I don't know him very well at all. And I'm not usually this forward—you know, talking to strangers and all."

"Do you mean, make friends with the Americans who live here full-time? The expats?"

"Yeah, I guess," Brouillard said a little haltingly. "My Spanish stinks. So of course I'd want to take Spanish lessons."

"Eventually you would," Amanda agreed, "although I bet you'd pick it up pretty quick. No, actually, that's the good news. Making friends here is a snap. There's a community of, say, between two hundred and three hundred

American expats on the island at any given time. A combination of business owners like me, a couple of trust-funders, and a bunch of American caretakers, who tend to be people who've left their old lives behind. There are local people in this group, too, but they all speak very good English. So Spanish wouldn't be a problem in the social scene, but eventually you'd want to speak enough to keep from getting ripped off by the guy at the gas station, or whatever.

"And it's a real active scene down here. Real active. Of course, I'm stuck here almost every night, so what would *I* know, but my friends tend to eat at each other's houses a couple nights a week—more than they ever did back home, according to most of them. And in general, new people are made to feel pretty welcome, pretty fast. Those two ladies who were sitting over there in the corner, for example? They invite newcomers over for sushi as soon as they find out about them. It's real friendly in that way."

"Sounds great. Sounds better than being single in Boston."

"Yeah," Amanda said, "it *is* great, in most ways. On the other hand, there's never quite enough new stuff to talk about. Too little fresh talent, too many people with too much time on their hands. Sal and Suzie, God bless 'em, being a case in point. There's a huge rumor mill on the island, and when it doesn't get enough raw material, it tends to give itself what it needs. Little stories pop up—who knows where?—and get juicier as they make their way across the island. You can spend a lot of time chasing down rumors, if you worry about that kind of stuff. Me, I mostly don't. I just do my thing."

Brouillard smiled, nodding. "I really appreciate you

telling me all this, Amanda. I feel like I've got a bead on the place already. And you haven't talked me out of it yet."

"Well, I guess if I didn't like it, I wouldn't be in my tenth year of frying frozen powdered potatoes. Don't tell anybody about that." She leaned forward conspiratorially. "So who's this guy you know? Your honey?"

"Hardly." Brouillard laughed. "He's a big professor over at Harvard. My mom worked for him until she retired. He's got some kind of place down here, although I don't know where."

"What's his name? I probably know him."

"Pirle. Marc Pirle."

Amanda made a little noise in her nose, then studied a glossed fingernail at arm's length. "Well, dear," she finally said, "you didn't hear it from me, but with friends like that, you'll need other friends down here."

"Why do you say that?" Brouillard was wide-eyed. "Like I said, I don't really know him that well, but he seems nice enough. He's European, or something. From Europe, I mean."

"Hey, look, honey," Amanda said, shrugging, "I don't want to badmouth your friend. You run a restaurant, you've gotta be *everybody's* friend. You know what I mean?"

"I guess so."

"Put it this way. This is a small community, like I said. Everybody knows everybody. We look out for each other. We sleep with each other and cheat on each other. We lie about each other, and then we stick up for each other when someone else lies about us. We're *tight*.

"Your friend Pirle doesn't choose to be any part of any of that. He stiff-arms everybody that tries to be friendly with him. He won't let any locals near the place—to cut the grass or clean or whatever. He threatens to sue people at the drop of a hat, and he seems to have enough juice to pull it off. He's arranged for special police patrols when he's not in residence—how, nobody knows. Nobody else gets that kind of VIP treatment. His caretaker is someone he shipped down here from the States—a real mean prick; pardon my French. The locals think your friend is a high-and-mighty because he's European, as you say. Me, I just think he's another prick."

Brouillard maintained her wide-eyed look, now injecting a little hurt into it. Amanda sighed, reached across the table, and patted her on the arm. "Hey, look, Barbara, I don't mean to dump on the guy. Maybe he's not as bad as his reputation, you know? I've only run into him a few times myself, and I had no problem with him. Like I said, things get exaggerated here. I will say, though"—and here she brightened visibly, seeing a way out of the thicket she was in—"that a pretty girl like you could do a lot better than him in a *flash,* down here. Guaranteed."

"Thanks, Amanda. And thank you for being so candid."

"You're quite welcome, dear."

"I have one more city-girl kind of question. Is it, well, safe down here for a single woman?"

"Oh, yeah," Amanda said, nodding, "I should have mentioned that. It's very safe. There's a lot of what they call *escalamiento*—petty thievery. A kid with a drug habit breaks into an empty house, takes a TV or radio or whatever. The stuff goes into a closed van, then onto the ferry, then off to who knows where. Unless they open all the vans on the ferry, which they sometimes do. But I can't remember the last violent crime, other than domestic stuff—spouse-on-spouse stuff, or kids mixing it up."

"Can you get your house wired up? I mean, are there ways to tie an alarm system into the police, so they'll come in a hurry?" Brouillard wasn't exactly sure where she was going with this, but it seemed to flow naturally enough.

"Sure," Amanda replied. "My house is tied into the police station, since I'm out a lot of the time. The one time I had a problem, they came quick. They told me they've always got three cars out on patrol, so they can get anywhere on the island within five minutes. You can believe as much of that as you like."

"Wow. I must have picked the best person on this entire island to talk to."

"Yeah, you did"—Amanda grinned—"and most of what I told you is even true. And you seem like a smart person, so I'm sure you'll think long and hard and wind up doing the right thing. And now it's time for me to get back to work. But can I give you two more pieces of advice that you didn't ask for? Girl to girl?"

"Absolutely."

"The first is, hon, don't go falling in love."

Brouillard laughed out loud. "Excuse me?"

Amanda smiled back, but it was clear that she was serious. "There's something in the air down here, Barbara from Boston. Something that gets nice sober Catholic girls saying yes to a second beer in midafternoon, and persuades them that this smooth-talking guy they just bumped into in a no-star restaurant is Mr. Right. I'm not saying you shouldn't have fun, dear. I'm just suggesting you keep in mind what my great-aunt Velma used to tell me: 'Let 'em sleep with you, dear; just don't let 'em put their boots under your bed.' "

"It's a promise," Brouillard said, holding up her right hand, laughing. "No boots under the bed."

"And one more thing, my newfound friend." Amanda put her forearm alongside Brouillard's: mocha next to cream. "You have got to be the *whitest* white girl I have ever seen. So promise me that you'll use plenty of sunscreen the whole time you're here. And wear a hat. Otherwise, you will absolutely burn up. Promise?"

"Promise."

38

THE FIRST SURPRISE WAS THE INTERDEPARTMENTAL EN-velope that somehow had gotten under his door during his travels with Sandy.

He recognized it immediately, even before he saw the words "Harvard University" printed in red across the top. A heavy-duty buff-colored envelope, with columns of spaces for addresses, and perforated by columns of front-to-back holes—the purpose of which had always confused Vermeer. *Ventilation? For memos?* These sturdy workhorses loped from Harvard office to Harvard office, with each new destination added on to the growing ranks of scrawled addresses—first on the front, then onto the back. In a bored moment, he had once read the addresses on a fraying old envelope, imagining it bouncing from place to place like a tired-out dollar bill.

This one, though, bore no addresses at all. It was new. Through the holes, Vermeer could see some white papers. Also, some small marble-size lumps protruding from the package's lower right-hand corner. Like cheap currency, they made a dull jingling noise when he picked up the envelope.

It had an odd little sealing system: a piece of red string mounted on the body of the envelope, which the sender wrapped around a post on the flap. *Good enough to make somebody rich,* he said to himself. He unwrapped the string, lifted the flap, and dumped the contents of the package out on his bed.

First he saw the keys. He recognized them: a pair of keys to a file cabinet. They were threaded together on a bent paper clip.

Then he saw the photographs. A dozen black-and-white prints. In each, a male-female couple engaged in more or less standard sexual acts. Grainy, but the features of the people depicted were clearly recognizable. He recognized none of them.

———————

The second surprise came less than an hour later. He was half lying in a lounge chair on the small terrace overlooking the Rising Moon's broad lawn, a green expanse that rolled slowly down to the edge of the Caribbean. He was preoccupied. As soon as he sat down, he forgot about the beer that sat sweating on the flagstone next to his left leg.

Pondering, he heard the irritating noise of cheap sandals approaching—*flop, flop, flop*—and hoped that whoever it was would head off in some other direction. But no: now, just behind him, and now next to him. The noise stopped.

He turned. For an instant, he didn't recognize her. Then he did. The Boston detective. Brouillard. He gaped, mouth open and pursed like a landed fish.

"We need to talk," she said, easing herself onto the chaise longue next to his. She moved gracefully. She had on a large, floppy sun hat and shades that looked like recent purchases. And a two-piece robin's-egg–blue bathing suit that—while modest enough—revealed more about her various curves than he had learned in all his previous encounters with her, put together. Her skin was alarmingly pale. She kicked off the flip-flops. She folded slender legs under herself.

Too late, he stopped gaping. And said, "So what the hell are you doing here?"

"Pretending to be several people I'm not," she said. "And looking for you. And here you are. No doubt pretending to be someone *you're* not." Locking her fingers on top of her head, and in the process crushing her sun hat, she looked out at the Caribbean. Irrelevantly, he noticed that she didn't shave her armpits. Or at least her left armpit.

"Am I under arrest yet?" He meant it to sound off-the-cuff; it came out sounding surly.

"No. In fact, you're way farther away from being under arrest than you've been in a while." She wasn't looking at him; she continued to gaze at the turquoise ocean.

"Hard to believe. My own personal Inspector Javert hunts me down God knows how many million miles from home and then tells me I'm in good shape?"

She chuckled, remembering the broken oar at Amanda's Seaside Café. "Well, I don't know any Inspector Javert, but assuming that Boston is a couple hundred miles south of Halifax, you're about two thousand miles from home."

They sat in silence for a few minutes. The onshore breeze pushed steadily against their faces, blowing some of the tension out of the air.

"Remember a while back," she finally said, not looking at him, "when we cut our little deal? The deal to help each other out?"

"Yeah. It didn't work out like we planned."

Then she turned her head to look at him. "I think it's working out okay. Even if not like we planned."

He didn't say anything.

"Listen," she continued. "Let's put our cards on the table. I never believed you killed anybody. In my gut, I never believed it. There was something too cute about the whole thing. Something about the way a helpful clue, pointing to you, always turned up just when I needed it. Too cute by a mile. And since I never gave much of a damn about your private life—" He started to interrupt, but she put her hand up. "Let me finish. Your private life is your own business, and I'm not going to help anybody else take you down on that score.

"And so okay, I admit that for a long time I didn't buy the whole someone's-out-to-get-Vermeer thing. It didn't make any sense to me. But at the same time, if it wasn't true, then you looked guilty as hell. So you needed it to be true. And *I* needed it to be true, or else I had to believe that my gut was wrong, and that all these signs of someone being cute weren't really there. And as it turns out, it *was* true. Why and how, I haven't exactly figured out yet, although I'm getting there. But true all the same.

"And so maybe I haven't gotten you off the hook yet, but I haven't done you any harm, either. I think I gave you good advice, all down the line. And if I remember right, I saved your life at least once. So I really don't think you have any good reason to sit there and be pissed off at me."

Now it was his turn to stare at the ocean. He remembered his beer. He decided he didn't want it. "A virgin beer," he said, holding it up. It dripped cold sweat on his thigh. "Want it?"

"Nope."

He put it back down. "I don't think you've told me yet exactly what you're doing here. You don't strike me as the vacationing type. And you've got murderers to catch."

"I came down here for two reasons. Neither of which alone would have been good enough to get me here. First, your B and G guy, Rodriguez, runs away from Boston when I put a little pressure on him, going home to the island of his birth to care for his critically ill father. And at just about the same instant, the mysterious Wim Vermeer takes off for the same little island. So my boss gives me permission to go there, too. On my own nickel, so far. Of course, if I catch a murderer, like you say, they'll probably agree to pay me back."

"I guess I'll let that last part go," he said, allowing a small smile out onto his face. "The bounty hunter part, where you get an all-expenses-paid vacation if you catch me in the act. That sounds kind of bad for me."

"Yeah, it does," she agreed. "When you put it just that way. Which I didn't. And by the way, I'm not a cop down here. If anybody's going to catch you in the act—of doing whatever it is you do—it's not going to be me."

"The part about Rodriguez," he said after a moment. "That part I don't get. I don't even know the guy, beyond waving to him on campus and saying hello, or asking someone in his office to change a fluorescent bulb in my office. I didn't know he had ties to this place. And I have no clue how he might be involved in this mess."

"You're here for Pirle."

He looked at her. "Take off your sunglasses. I want to see your eyes."

She took them off.

"I get the sense that you're a pretty good actress," he said, "pretending to be people you're not, and all. So maybe there's no point to this. But I want you to look me in the eyes and tell me you're not trying to stick a large one up my butt."

"Okay." She held his gaze, with a hint of a smile on her face. "I am *not* trying to stick a large one up your butt. Not in my job description."

"I guess that'll have to do," he said grumpily. "Fine. So let's say our deal's back on: I help you, and you help me. Although as usual, I seem to need more help than you."

She nodded and, a little awkwardly, extended her right hand across her body. She closed up as much of the space that separated them as she could without falling out of her chair. This required her to lie almost on her side, facing him. He tried not to look past her hand as he shook it. He didn't succeed. In fact, he looked all the way up her arm, and beyond. To her well-muscled arms and broad shoulders, and her protruding collarbone. And beyond. To hills and valleys accentuated by her half-turn toward him.

"So as you were saying," he continued a little too quickly, "Pirle. Right. I got hold of James MacInnes on the phone, and he finally told me that it was Pirle who had been concocting this story about me and Eric. So all of a sudden, it all snapped together. The evil bastard is obviously closer to that family than anyone has let on so far. He's some kind of Dutch-uncle figure, as disgusting as that sounds, and he's been pumping them full of lies. I can't stand the son of a bitch anyway, as you may have guessed. My guess is that he's been active in deep-sixing my tenure chances, which weren't great to start with, when he should have been helping me. Then all of this slime pops out. So I decided that I would come down here and do something. Get the goods on him. Maybe break his nose. I hadn't really gotten that far."

She sighed, shaking her head. She had twisted away from him again, rearranging the landscape of hills and valleys. "You should have called me."

"Yeah, well, it felt to me like our deal wasn't on any-more. It felt to me like you were getting ready to haul my ass into jail. In which case I lose my opportunity to help my own cause."

"Not a very good plan, from what you've told me."

"It was the best I could come up with. Plus, I was pissed. Still am."

Unself-consciously she scratched an itch on her chest. She watched her own index finger at work. He caught himself gazing at her again. Some of the same parts of her. *Jesus,* he scolded himself, *keep your goddamn head in the game.*

"It's funny," she said, looking up again. "You scoot down here chasing Pirle, and you don't have a clue about Rodriguez. I blast down here chasing Rodriguez—and you, of course—and I don't have a clue about Pirle. Just found out about him this afternoon, in a little conversa-tion I had with Rodriguez. All in all, it sounds like our working relationship needs some work."

He pulled himself up out of his chair. "In that spirit of cooperation," he said, "there's something else you should know about. Wait here a sec."

———

She was sitting up, cross-legged, massaging the balls of her feet, when he returned. He dumped the contents of the Harvard envelope out on her chair in front of her shins. She picked up one of the prints. Then she put it down and picked up another. Methodically she looked at all of them, registering nothing on her face. She jingled the keys on the paper clip without much interest. "Honey pot," she said finally, more to herself than to him.

"Say what?"

"Sorry. Old cop lingo. You bait the trap with some honey, lure the victim in, and then blackmail him. And it's always a him, of course. Never a her. Guys can't seem to keep it in their pants." But she wasn't really talking to him. She was elsewhere. Calculating.

"It has to be Pirle's place," said Vermeer, wanting her full attention. "And those have got to be the keys to a locked filing cabinet."

She nodded, still distracted.

"So obviously," he continued, annoyed, "I'm supposed to go there and rummage in those files until I find what I'm supposed to find. Whatever that is."

She shook her head slowly, side to side. "No. Too easy. And also too hard."

"What the hell does that mean?"

Now she focused on him. "Look, Wim. This smells bad. This crap came from one of two people: your pal Pirle or my pal Rodriguez. If it's your pal, it's a trap. And if it's my pal, and if it's *not* a trap, you've got five minutes tops to get in there and get back out before the cops arrive. I've seen the jail here. You don't want to be spending time there."

He had turned sideways on his chair, facing her. He rubbed his temples. "Sorry, partner. Gotta do it. I need evidence to nail the bastard, if only to get the MacInneses off my case. If you somehow get the cops interested in what he's doing up there, and he gets wind of it, he might torch the whole thing, files and all. Then we're back to his word against mine. And so far, I lose that matchup." He looked at her. "Tell me that you've got something— anything—that gets me off the hook, so far."

She shook her head.

"Okay, then. I wait until he goes into town for dinner tonight, which, I'm told by my talkative local real estate agent, he does every night when he's here; and I go in and rummage. And get out in a hurry."

"Five minutes. Or less."

"Less."

"Let me make something as clear as I can," she said, packing up the photos and keys as she talked, then handing them back to him. "I want no part of this. In fact, I haven't heard a word you've said for the last five minutes or so. If I had, I'd have to call my friend Agente Montoya and tell him what you had in mind."

"Well, please don't."

She waited, then asked, "You've seen the place?"

"Yeah."

"And if you had just robbed the place, and you had set off the alarm and you knew *for certain* that the cops were on their way, would you go down the front side or the back side of the hill?"

"The back side," he said. "More choices."

"Uh-huh."

They sat in silence for a few minutes. The sun had sunk behind the hills at their backs and was lighting up the tops of the cloud columns in bright pinks and golds. Over on his side of the island, Vermeer thought, Pirle was enjoying a spectacular sunset. Getting on his evening clothes.

"Hey," she said. "One more thing."

"What?"

"In case you hadn't noticed, I don't like loose ends."

"Okay. What's the loose end?"

"Who's Inspector Javert?"

He had to admit it: Risky as it almost certainly was, he liked this strange woman. "The relentless policeman in Victor Hugo's book *Les Misérables*," he explained. "The noble hero, Jean Valjean, steals a loaf of bread to feed his starving children, and the coldhearted Javert hunts him down and sticks him in a stinking French prison to rot forever."

She nodded, taking this in. "There's nothing like a good cop," she finally said. "I guess I'm gonna have to read that book."

39

IT WAS A STUPID PLAN, HE ACKNOWLEDGED TO HIMSELF.
All the stupider because he had rented a car at the last
minute, with his own credit card, in a hurry. The kid at the
rental agency—a glorified shack on the western edge of
town, that looked like it hadn't seen any business that
day—would have no trouble remembering his face.

It was dusk. Parking the car a few hundred feet below
the crest of the hill, on the back side, he slowly walked
the rest of the way up, as if out for a casual evening stroll.
He jingled the file cabinet keys in his pocket as he
walked. He reeked of mosquito repellent. His long-
sleeved shirt and long pants made him a little conspicuous, which was bad. But they concealed his pale skin
from the moonlight, which was good.

He found his hiding place—in a copse of tall bushes
across the street and slightly downhill—and waited. He
thought of the distances he had traveled before and during this haunted part of his life, and wondered what he
might have done differently. The image of Barbara
Brouillard, in her blue suit and shades and floppy sun hat,
and calling him *Wim,* kept coming to mind.

A car door slamming, then a set of headlights. Then
the steel gate rolling open, almost silent, except for the

whir of the motor, until it hit its stop point with a loud *clang*. A car glided out, bigger than most on this island, with a dark, unidentifiable figure behind the wheel, on the far side of the vehicle. The car disappeared down the dark, steep road to Isabel Segunda. The gate rolled back into place, clanging shut again.

Time to move.

After looking up and down the deserted road, he slipped between the gatepost and a high bush, then up the almost grown-over gravel drive. Small lights defined a path up to the front door. He skirted the walkway and also ducked around the well-lighted pool.

He had never broken into a home before, other than his own. But he had seen it on TV often enough: the shielded fist through the glass, the hand reaching in to throw the dead bolt, the door easing open. First, though, he circled the perimeter, getting his bearings on the rambling house, slinking along the ocean-facing deck, feeling scared and foolish, looking in every window he could reach. It was now too dark to see much of anything, but this room, with the floor-to-ceiling bookcases—this was the one he would bet on.

He circled back around to the front door.

———————

Halfway up the hill on the town side road, on a switch-back that had been cut into the side of the hill, she ran through her relaxation exercises to slow her heart. *Breathe in through nose. Breathe out through mouth. In through nose. Out through mouth.*

Her car was parked in the exact middle of the narrowest strait on the tiny road, with blind curves above and below her. The uphill side of the road was demarcated by a deep drainage gully, which gave way to a sharply rising jungle. The ocean side was more or less a cliff, dropping off abruptly to the next tier of houses, fifty feet down below.

She was looking westward, toward town. Her car was about to break down. She was assuming, for no particular reason other than force of habit, that they would come with their lights spinning.

———————

Just like on TV: He smashed a protected hand through a pane of frosted glass alongside the lock. After the glass skittering on the floor, no more sounds—but he wasn't listening. He was fumbling for the lock, finding it, pushing the door open, stepping inside.

There: a low, steady whine. A panel to his left flashing red. Five minutes and counting down.

He walked quickly through the dark house, trying to keep his bearings straight. Left, left, then *right,* somewhere down here. *Here.*

———————

Looking westward back down into the valley, she saw the blue lights, two hills over, coming her way. Coming as fast as the undersize, sinuous roads permitted. She turned the car on and opened the hood. It was still hot from the climb up the hill. Wedging an oversize screwdriver between the snaking, articulated water hose and the engine block, she put her weight on the end of the screwdriver, shielding her face just in case. She was new at this.

The O-clamp that held the decaying end of the hose let go gratefully. There was no eruption. Just a gentle burbling, like a thick soup. An acrid smell as the first thimblefuls of antifreeze danced out of the radiator, fizzed and bounced across the hot metal surface, and hit the dusty road. Then more. Then a good old-fashioned boilover, and then a pretty bad burning smell.

She replaced the screwdriver under the car's front seat.

He was thinking of her caution: *too easy.* Was it a trap? There wasn't time to worry about it—either it was or it wasn't. Four minutes. Less than four minutes. The whine of the alarm was inaudible in this part of the house, but it still lingered in his ears.

The study had file cabinets—lots of file cabinets lining pieces of three walls, in and around the built-in bookcases. Too many. They were labeled. Too dark.

Taking a breath, he walked over to the door and felt for the light switch. *What's the worst that could happen? A neighbor calls the police? They're already on their way.*

He flipped it on.

He pulled the keys out of his pocket. They were different; he had checked. So unless he got lucky, there were twice as many file cabinets: two keys per cabinet.

The labels on the cabinet were laser printed: A over here, B next to it. Z presumably all the way over in that corner. He didn't need Z. He needed M. Which should be somewhere over here in the middle. Here. The top four in this column of five.

Key teeth down, he reminded himself, shoving in first one key in the top drawer of this set, then the other. *No. No. Down one drawer: one key, then the other. No. No. Down another drawer: first one key, then the other. No.* He checked his watch. Three minutes. Minus, say, a minute for actually getting out of here and down the road.

No.

Last M drawer. The first key turned. The little lock popped out a half inch, expectantly. *Now or never,* he thought, sliding open the file cabinet. He wondered what secrets that second key would have revealed.

———————————

They came roaring up the hill in low gear, engine screaming for mercy and blue lights spinning. She stood on the downhill side of her car, waving; her arms crossed and opened in front of her body, as if she were dancing a bad upper-body-only Charleston, even before they turned the blind corner. The doorless Jeep burst into view, nearly slamming into her before the brakes grabbed hold and put the front of the police car into a lurching, gravel-spraying nose dive. A furious cloud of dust billowed forward, turning the twin headlight beams into roiling horizontal pillars and enveloping them.

Frantically they were shouting at her in Spanish. The driver stepped halfway out of the Jeep, putting one foot into the middle of the road and waving back at her, but in his case from left to right with both arms, exaggerated: *Out of the road! Out of the road!*

She pointed over her shoulders with both hands, keeping her eye on the *agente* in the road. *"Agua,"* she shouted, and pointed. *"Agua."*

The driver, and now his partner, jumped out of opposite sides of the Jeep. They sprinted past her, ignoring her. One slammed her hood shut. The other climbed into the driver's seat of her car. Now the first came back and roughly shoved her out of the way. In the direction of the cliff edge. While the second released the parking brake, pushed in the clutch, and rolled her car backward almost noiselessly, gravel crunching under her tires, as he cut the wheel sharply. *Perpendicular,* she noted approvingly, remembering just how deep that drainage ditch was; he was putting himself in no danger of a rollover.

The back end of her car dropped off the edge of the world. There was one loud metal shriek from underneath the car as her headlights shot up into the sky at a forty-five-degree angle.

Then they ran back past her. One hissed something under his breath as he passed; it didn't sound friendly. They took off again in another spray of gravel, pushing back up toward the six-thousand-rpm level as they rounded the blind turn uphill from her, out of sight.

He was on the floor, legs stretched out in front of him, and a pile of folders between his knees. He had grabbed a sequence of three folders out of the drawer. Thank God this Pirle was a compulsive prick: "MacInnes, Elizabeth." "MacInnes, Eric." "MacInnes, James."

He already knew, more or less, what was in them. He hesitated for a precious second, wondering whether, by looking at the photos, he would somehow be complicit— an *accomplice* of Pirle's—in a soiled spiritual way.

Fuck that, he decided. He needed the goods, and he was out of time. Yes, there was Libby, in what looked like sexual distress, with what looked like the saggy backside of the slimy prick himself. He recoiled. *Not a folder to linger over.*

Eric, entwined with his faceless male lover—but male, without a doubt.

James. With the same woman in the pictures that Brouillard had called "honey pot." Local talent.

He scooped them up, stashing them under his arm. And looked at his watch. *Out of time.* If she was right, they were already here, racing up the driveway, maybe with guns drawn. He shoved the file drawer shut and pushed the lock back in. Pirle wouldn't be fooled for long. He would find these files missing. He would retrieve the negatives for "MacInnes, James," and whistle up some new prints. He wouldn't bother with "MacInnes, Elizabeth" or "MacInnes, Eric." Because their voting stock now rested with James.

Because they were dead.

He flipped off the light, for no obvious reason, and started sprinting for the front door. He didn't feel vindicated or exonerated.

He felt nauseated.

40

THE FIRST KNOCK ON HIS DOOR CAME A HALF HOUR after he got back. Vermeer's heart hadn't yet stopped pounding. Now his stomach flopped. He was struck once again at how dumb his plan had been. And continued to be. What if the owner of the stolen property was outside his door, and angry? Did he have a plan for *that*?

No. He didn't.

He grunted. "Yeah?"

"Wim." It was her voice. Low but not urgent.

He opened the door. She was smiling as if she had won the high school spelling bee. Why?

"So. Invite me in."

"Do come in."

"You went out." She was wearing a sleeveless white T-shirt and shorts. And open-toed shoes with no heels. Her hair was dripping from its ends, fresh from the shower. She looked around for a place to sit. The best place was the edge of the bed. She perched primly, straight-backed, crossing her legs at the ankle. He was still standing by the door.

"Yeah. I went to see an old friend. But he was out."

"Too bad."

"Just as well." He shrugged. "He'll know I was there."

"Oh, sit down," she said, thumping the bed, next to her. He sat down.

"I'm wondering," she continued, "whether you're ready to head home tomorrow. Like, on the first available flight. And if so, whether you'd like me to go with you."

He nodded. "Yes. And yes. To both of those."

"We'll have to take your car."

"Sure," he said, puzzled.

"Well, then," she said, standing up, still grinning. She looked as if she had something more to say. The hem of her shorts had ridden up. She tugged them down: first in front, and then in back. "Maybe I'll check on you later. Make sure everything's okay."

———————————

The second knock on his door came only a few minutes later. This time, heart now pounding again for a different reason, he knew who it was. He wondered what more she wanted to say to him. He had more that he wanted to say to her.

But for the second time that evening, he had guessed wrong.

Pirle pushed the long barrel of a sleek-looking pistol against Vermeer's forehead as soon as he opened the door. The barrel got fat toward its business end: a silencer. Pirle had a long finger on his other hand positioned perpendicular against his lips: *not a sound.*

Vermeer backed up, and Pirle pushed the slatted door shut behind him without taking his eyes off Vermeer, or the gun off Vermeer's forehead. He pointed at the bed with his free hand. Vermeer sat. The comforter, he noted, was still warm from where Brouillard had been sitting.

"I think you have something of mine." Pirle's voice was mechanical, with the emphases in the wrong places, like one of those pseudohuman voice-mail systems. "Three things, in fact. I want you to gather them up and come with me. I want you to bring your car keys. If you make a noise, or a sudden move, I will kill you. Happily."

Vermeer nodded as he felt his stomach hollowing out. He pulled open the drawer of the bedside table. He moved aside the pile of publications under which he had buried the files. A thin phone book. A Gideons Bible. A copy of *El Nuevo Vieques,* a local tabloid that he had picked up in the lobby specifically to help create deeper clutter in this drawer.

"You're forgetting your car keys. By the way, thank you for leaving the keys in the filing cabinet. I will have a talk with Mr. Rodriguez about his poor choice of allies. In war, the most dangerous strategy of all is to switch sides."

They walked out into the dark, Pirle trailing a few feet behind Vermeer. Of course there was no one in sight. Of course the ubiquitous Captain Brouillard was nowhere to be seen.

"You're driving," Pirle said quietly. "I'm in back, with this gun pointed at the place where your spine meets your head. Turn right at the end of the driveway."

They retraced the coastal route that Sandy had followed. Only this time the moon was out, and, rather than impersonating a wealthy astrophysicist, Vermeer was playing himself, counting off his last minutes.

"Left here. Up the hill. Stop when I tell you."

And sooner than he wanted to, Vermeer knew where they were going. The failed children's athletic complex.

Which, by the light of the half-moon, would be a terrible place to die.

"Here. Pull over . . . Leave the keys in the ignition. Get out, and step away from the car . . . Lock your fingers on top of your head, nice and slowly."

Vermeer tried to recall some table-turning trick— some quick move whereby he could disarm his killer. Nothing came to mind. He noticed that en route, Pirle had removed the silencer from the gun.

"Okay. Now we're going to walk down this dirt road. You will keep your hands on top of your head. At the same time, you should keep your eyes on the road in front of you. The erosion has been very bad. You will break your ankle if you are not careful."

"Nice of you to worry for me," Vermeer ventured to speak in a low voice. It was the first time he had spoken. He saw the dark shapes of the derelict athletic complex— two boomerangs and a box—looming at the bottom of the road.

"Oh, not at all, Vermeer. You'll be committing suicide down there at the bottom of the hill. A broken ankle doesn't fit well in that picture. Although I suppose I could weave it in, if necessary. Please walk. No sudden moves."

They continued down the dirt road. The deep gullies were nicely profiled by the moonlight, like sinuous snakes. Vermeer stepped over them, with Pirle following in his footsteps, close enough but also far enough behind.

"See that little pile of debris, in the middle of the road?" Pirle posed the question in a jaunty voice, now sounding very pleased with himself. "That's what's left after the happy locals, God bless them, set off their fireworks on one of their innumerable Latin holidays. And when we get down below, I'll show you where some people have set up an impromptu target range. Perfectly safe—there's no one within an eighth of a mile that you could possibly hit with a stray bullet.

"But what does all this mean for *you*? It means that the neighbors up on the hills—those lights you see up there—are totally accustomed to loud noises down in this ugly little valley. They don't even hear them anymore. They certainly don't call the authorities about them."

Vermeer very much wanted to slap the mosquito buzzing near his left ear but didn't want to get shot. "It doesn't make sense, Pirle. I mean, so far, you've made all the right moves, setting me up to take the fall. But me killing myself down here—that doesn't ring true." Maybe aiming for Pirle's ego might forestall his death. There was certainly plenty of ego to target.

"Ah, suicide," Pirle said, drawing out the syllables, practically crooning. "Does it ever really make sense? It runs counter to our every instinct of self-preservation, does it not? Ultimately, the gulf between the person who destroys himself, and the people he abandons by that act, is unbridgeable. And ultimately, the abandoned—the left behind—comfort themselves by saying, 'Of course, he was crazy. We're in no danger of going that route.' They look for ways to distance themselves from what appears to be madness."

There was something in the slow, sick, musical way that he pronounced that one word, "madness," that shredded Vermeer's last vestige of hope. Pirle was completely out of his mind.

"And that's why we, the abandoned, place so much

emphasis on the suicide note," his tormentor continued. "We want evidence that the self-destroyer is different from us—mad. Which, of course, you've been kind enough to provide. It's here in my pocket. Would you like me to recite it?"

Vermeer had no idea what this was about. He didn't respond.

"It's short," Pirle continued, now thoroughly captivated by his own recital. "I've committed it to memory, in part because it conveys such . . . exquisite, utter despair." Now a sort of exultation rose in Pirle's voice. "It reads, in its entirety, 'Make it all go away.' Followed by an exclamation point. And then, of course, by your signature. My guess is that the authorities will conclude that as the noose was closing around your neck, you decided to flee the country. They will discover that you checked in with my Delores, who steered you this way. No doubt you saw me as a trusted counselor, or perhaps an intermediary who could arrange for your surrender to the authorities. But somehow, you never got that far. Sadly, I never even laid eyes on you during your desperate hours here. Too soon, you lost all hope, and you killed yourself in this forlorn place. They won't find your fingerprints in my house, because I will tell them not to bother. A common burglary, a camera and some other valuables taken. Obviously a crime unrelated to your unhappy end on this island."

Make it all go away! Suddenly, Vermeer realized why that sounded familiar. It was the stupid note he had put in his out-box, on top of that pile of memos and junk mail, in an effort to spur Sam the temp into action. His knees weakened, and his sphincter twitched. He was going to die. Pirle was going to get away with it.

"I'm surprised that the MacInnes kids allowed themselves to be blackmailed by you," Vermeer said, still trying to buy time, now trying to rally himself, as they neared the bottom of the hill. Now the abandoned buildings had transformed themselves into dark monoliths—an evil concrete Stonehenge. The jungle foliage on both sides of the untraveled concrete road had closed in, encroaching on half its width. "I'm surprised that they didn't just go to the cops. Or tell their parents, and have you taken care of in some other way."

Pirle snorted. "Not likely. Like most offspring of the superrich, they were paralyzed by their privileges. Eric concluded, I think correctly, that the disclosure of his homosexual exploits would get him run right out of his inheritance. They are a very old-fashioned bunch, very *American*, in that way. In fact, it was only when Eric finally became willing to throw it all away—running off to California, or whatever he had in mind—that other steps became necessary."

"You knocked him out in the Jacuzzi?"

"Yes. A blow to the base of the skull. And held him under, of course. He was surprisingly weak. Actually, the hardest part of it all was persuading him to join me in a few convivial rounds, poolside, before the real excitement began."

"But James—James doesn't strike me as weak."

"James? He is both dense *and* weak. He made the mistake of signing a prenuptial agreement that punished him severely in the case of infidelity. As for 'weak,' I believe his fall from grace came on his third visit here, when his silly wife, Elaine, decided to stay behind in Boston.

"And of course, Libby never grasped anything, poor child. Except toward the end, of course, when she started telling me that we had to warn you about this mysterious danger you were in."

"But why did you need me? Why throw a noose around my neck?"

"At first," Pirle said in an affable tone, as if he were chatting with a neighbor over the backyard fence, "you were just an insurance policy, one of two corollary plans that I would set in motion in the event that Eric's death attracted undue attention. I saw it as painting two alternative scenes at once. You, of course, played the prominent role in the first. I began filling in lots of small, pointillist details for the police to unearth.

"And of course, Libby was front and center in the second picture. Those clues implicated Libby in Eric's death, just in case I needed Libby to commit suicide. The little needle hole in Eric's arm was my favorite." He chuckled. "Suppose someone wanted to inject alcohol directly into the arm of an unconscious young man, poolside? Who else in the neighborhood has a bag full of hypodermics lying around? But I also enjoyed using Libby's considerable computer skills against her. She would show me a trick, and I'd wait a decent interval and then use it. Implicating her, or perhaps you, as the spirit moved me."

Too cute, Vermeer remembered Brouillard saying. But her gut wasn't going to save him now.

"As far as I know," Pirle was saying, "the police haven't even stumbled across most of those clues yet. Perhaps your suicide will prompt them to look a little harder. Your friend, the female detective, seems tenacious, and even a little bit bright. Maybe she'll keep digging. If she does, she'll find you everywhere. More likely, though, they will simply close the case."

"So what happens to the MacInnes businesses?"

Vermeer couldn't have cared less, but he desperately wanted Pirle to keep bragging. "James controls them, and you control James?"

"Yes, assuming the plan to set up voting and nonvoting classes of stock moves forward, and that James winds up holding most of the voting stock. In which case, my influence is immediate. Or if William puts this all on hold—which, of course, he will ask me about, and I will advise against—then my influence will be somewhat attenuated for a few years. Unless something happens to William, of course, which is always possible. After all, he *is* old and tired."

They had reached a flat, open area in front of one of the derelict grandstands—probably intended as a soccer field but now broken up by clumps of small bushes and littered with a random collection of junk, dumped here before the road got too rutted to drive on. Now, evidently confident that the difficult work was behind him, Pirle played the twisted tour guide, pointing out the assortment of objects that people used for their target practice: a huge wooden wire spool with pictures of local politicians taped on it, a row of tin cans perched on a two-by-four spanning two packing crates, a bulls-eye painted on a propped-up piece of plywood, a lidless washing machine peppered with buckshot holes. Vermeer hung his head: the picture of defeat. He watched for an opening, but Pirle kept his eyes on him.

"I still don't get *why*," Vermeer persisted, trying to keep Pirle talking. "You can't need the money. Why take all this risk?"

"First of all," Pirle sniffed, "entrepreneurship consists of taking the risk *out* of a venture, well before you actually take the plunge. And I'm quite good at that. At this moment, for example, I'd say you were at far greater risk than I. Wouldn't you agree?

"And second, why climb Mt. Everest? Because it was there, as George Leigh Mallory supposedly said. Well, I look at this massive old fortune, burdened with all of its anachronisms and deadwood, and I see an enormous opportunity. The opportunity to become one of the most important business figures of the twenty-first century, perhaps, even if my full contributions may never be known. Which will depend in part on whether James keeps his health. He is rather tightly strung, as you may have noticed. But you're absolutely right, Vermeer: Unlike you, I don't need the money. I just love the challenge. But enough small talk, I think. You need to die now."

He raised the gun and closed half the distance between himself and Vermeer. "Put your hands behind you and open your mouth."

"Fuck you, you evil old Continental windbag."

Pirle laughed without lowering the gun. "Prefer to shoot yourself in the heart? Harder to do cleanly. Sometimes there's a lot of bleeding and thrashing and pain. Maybe you would prefer to shoot yourself in the side of the head?"

Now out of options and out of time, Vermeer prepared to throw himself on Pirle, maybe somehow ducking under the gun barrel, throwing up his forearm to try to dislodge the weapon, preparing for the bullet's impact—

"*Freeze.* Police."

But Pirle didn't freeze in response to the female voice. Instead, he slid around to Vermeer's right, placing Vermeer between himself and the voice in the darkness.

"Well, well," Pirle said in a voice loud enough to be

heard in the shadows. "I do believe Captain Brouillard has decided to join us. Amazing. I was just talking about how resourceful you were, and here you are. Step out where I can see you, please. Immediately. Or I will go back to the task of shooting your friend in the head."

Even in the dim moonlight, Vermeer could see her sidestepping out from behind the corner of the grandstand, thirty feet away. She was in a defensive crouch, arms straight out in front of her, aimed at them. "Drop it, Pirle. It's over. You shoot him, I shoot you."

Pirle chuckled, and it was as cold and dark a sound as Vermeer had ever heard. "Oh, really, Captain," he replied. "You should have done better than that. Frankly, I don't believe you have a gun. In any case, I'm an excellent shot, and I have a clear shot, and you don't."

The gun exploded next to Vermeer's right ear. The bullet appeared to catch Brouillard somewhere in her torso, forcing a grunt out of her, spinning her around in a half circle and knocking her to the ground. She lay on her back, motionless.

"Don't worry, Vermeer," Pirle said icily. "If she's not dead already, you will finish her off shortly. After you're dead, of course." He walked back around so that he was facing Vermeer. "So, now would be an excellent time for you to charge at me in fury. I need some close-up powder burns on your clothes for the self-inflicted wound. You *were* fond of her, weren't you? Don't you wish you could have saved her? Or saved yourself? *Do* something, Vermeer!"

The rage came welling up from some depth somewhere inside him, some place he had never touched before. A roar began to take shape in his throat. His vision constricted down to a narrow functional tunnel: from here to there. Almost on their own, for the second time, his leg muscles tensed to spring . . .

Then came a flash and an explosion from somewhere toward the other end of the grandstand. And now it was Pirle who was grunting, turning sideways and collapsing heavily, twitching and shuddering as the gun fell from his hand no more than eighteen inches from Vermeer's feet.

"Señor Vermeer," came an accented voice. "Agente Montoya, of the Vieques Police. It would be most helpful if you could place your hands back on your head—*sí, gracias*—and use your left foot to push the pistol out of Professor Pirle's reach. No kicking the gun, please. Just push it gently with your toe. Don't get between him and me, just to be safe. Of course I will shoot him again if he moves. Although it is my belief that he is either too smart or too dead to move. Good. Now step back again. Thank you."

As Vermeer sleepwalked his way through these little tasks, he heard the purposeful voice speaking again, quietly, this time in Spanish, and then the crackling metallic response of a walkie-talkie. Then a smallish round figure, dressed in black and barely visible in the dim moonlight, emerged from the nearby bushes. He approached Vermeer and Pirle deliberately, pistol in hand. He put his foot on Pirle's gun, eyes flicking from Vermeer to the motionless form on the ground and back to Vermeer. Then, kneeling, his own pistol still at the ready, he put two fingers on Pirle's neck. He appeared to relax slightly. "I also am a good shot," he said matter-of-factly.

"May I go help my friend, please?" Vermeer didn't recognize his own voice. His knees began to knock.

"Not quite yet, please. I first want to make sure that there are no more guns in the area. Turn around so that I

can make sure that you are not carrying one. No. Thank
you. I think there are not any more guns. In fact, I think
your friend is a very brave woman. But please remain
here for a moment. You may take your hands off your
head. And please don't attempt to run away or any other
foolish thing. You would not get far. And I do not think
you have any reason to run away."

Montoya holstered his own pistol, and picked up
Pirle's by the very tip of its barrel. He ambled off into the
shadows, in the direction of where Brouillard still lay on
the ground. Reaching her, he again crouched, fingers outstretched to her carotid artery. "Señor Vermeer," he called
after a moment, "she is wounded, but it appears that she
will live. Please come over here and sit with us while we
wait for the medical assistance to arrive."

Easing down her shoulder strap, Montoya examined
her more closely. The substantial wound in her left shoulder, just below the collarbone, had soaked about a quarter of the front of her white T-shirt, the blood black in the
moonlight. She was still bleeding steadily, still more
black fluid welling up out of the jagged flesh. He placed
his left palm on the wound and applied as much pressure
as he dared, not wanting to push bone fragments into her.

She groaned weakly. Her eyes fluttered open.

He saw that she recognized him. "Stay still and don't
try to speak, Captain Brouillard," he said quietly. "You
and your friend Vermeer are safe. I am sorry for causing
you this pain in your shoulder, but I think you are losing
too much blood."

Vermeer squatted alongside them. Even by moonlight,
he had turned an odd color. He wobbled; he was having
trouble keeping his balance. "If you are going to be sick,"
Montoya said, addressing Vermeer, "please back up at

least a few steps." Vermeer shook his head. He bent down and reached for Brouillard's right hand. He felt her fingers respond.

"Not going to be sick," Montoya continued. "Good. And to prevent fainting, sit down and put your head between your knees. And as for you," he said, looking back down at Brouillard, "you I thought of arresting for the illegal disposal of radiator fluids. But I think instead we will take you to our excellent Vieques community hospital."

41

SHE HAD SUGGESTED COFFEE, MIDAFTERNOON, AT THE Isabella Stewart Gardner Museum, on the Fenway. "Doesn't strike me as your kind of place," he responded, remembering her comment about his choice of the Stockyard restaurant. Which now seemed like years or decades in the past. "See how little you know about me?" she responded in turn.

So she remembered, too.

Now he was waiting in the cramped little bistro toward the back of the museum: the former home of Isabella Stewart Gardner, eccentric grande dame of the Boston fin de siècle art set. He hadn't been here in years—not since a former girlfriend, an art student, had insisted that he come along with her and attempt some sketches. It hadn't worked out, any of it.

He saw her before she saw him. Her left arm was in a sling. Otherwise, she looked surprisingly well turned out: white cashmere sweater, tan slacks, shoes with a slight heel on them, hair down over her shoulders. She had surrendered her trench coat. Today nothing about her looked rumpled. Even the sling somehow looked well put together.

He stood and gave her an awkward hug, around the

edges of her jutting left elbow. But when he bent forward from the waist to give her a kiss on the cheek, she leaned away. "Hey, whoa, big fellow," she said, looking embarrassed. She eyed his half-empty wineglass on the table. "Cops don't drink or kiss on the job."

Somewhat reluctantly, she let him help her push her chair in.

"You're looking rich," he said, deadpan, as he took his own seat.

She smiled. "Funny. I was thinking the same thing about you."

It had been almost two weeks. Vermeer had received a tutorial in the relative status of wounded cop heroes and the people they rescue. She remained on Vieques for only a few hours, just long enough to be stabilized; then a chartered jet—volunteered by a financial services firm thrilled to get in on what looked like a public-relations bonanza—swooped down from Boston to retrieve her. The CEO had made the trip and had elbowed his way into all the pictures that Vermeer later saw: the frantic arrival at Logan, the unloading of the stretcher, the media feeding frenzy. THE HERO'S RETURN, blared the *Herald*. And in smaller type: THIS MS. MEANS BIZ.

No one had thought to invite Vermeer along on that ride. And in any case, Agente Montoya made it clear that he wanted to have a conversation with him before he left the island.

That conversation, actually a deposition, took place at the police station in Isabel Segunda the following day and was brief and cordial. Throwing caution to the wind, Vermeer turned down the offer of a lawyer. With a second policeman in the room and with the tape recorder running, Montoya asked Vermeer to tell him what had happened in the hours leading up to the deadly interlude at the sports complex. Vermeer told a very selective truth; Montoya only interrupted him for an occasional small clarification.

When Vermeer finished his story, Montoya's associate asked a series of questions that appeared to be aimed at determining whether Montoya's use of deadly force was justified. That seemed fair: Vermeer went out of his way to commend the policeman's judgment and professionalism. "I am absolutely certain," he said, "that if Agente Montoya had not done what he did, both I and Captain Brouillard would be dead." And of that, he *was* certain.

In response to a final question from Montoya's associate, Vermeer stated that of course he would be willing to return to Vieques in the event that he was needed at the obligatory inquest. Then the second policeman stated in both English and Spanish that this was the end of the deposition, after which he packed up the tape recorder and left the room.

Montoya, seated and tipping back his chair, seemed to want to linger. "Is there anything else?" Vermeer asked.

"Maybe just one more thing," Montoya said, locking his fingers together across the top of his rounded stomach. "I am wondering if you know anything about a break-in last night at the home of the late Professor Pirle."

No, Vermeer said. He apologized for not being able to be more helpful; he really knew nothing about that. He did not mention his surprise at finding the MacInnes files still on the backseat of his rental car. The car had certainly been gone over carefully before it was returned to the Rising Moon. No one could have missed the files.

And yet here was Montoya, shrugging, slowly rising from his seat, and shaking his hand. "Good luck," he said. "I hope you will come back and visit Vieques again in happier times."

Good luck was not long in coming. As he was packing his bags at the Rising Moon, the phone rang. He tensed: *Who knew he was here?* Then he reminded himself that he could relax.

"Professor Vermeer?"

"Who's calling, please?"

"Thank you. Please hold for William MacInnes." Before Vermeer could respond, he was put on hold. Then came the familiar gruff voice.

"Professor Vermeer? MacInnes. I hear you had some interesting developments down there."

"Yes. But how the hell—"

"Please, please. Don't ask me how I find things out. Suffice it to say that I'm damned pleased with what you and Captain Brouillard pulled off last night. And may I say that I'm happy that Pirle isn't around to stand trial. Got what he deserved, God forgive him. Justice while you wait."

"Not my doing. I mostly stood there and let the bullets fly."

"Without catching one yourself, which is the real trick," MacInnes replied heartily. "But there are loose ends, are there not? I'm thinking of things lying around that might cause disrespect for the dead. So I'm wondering what you think: Would a house fire serve to tie up all those loose ends?"

Vermeer shook his head, amazed. "Is that really a question you want to ask me on the phone, Mr. MacInnes?"

MacInnes snorted. "Oh, don't concern yourself about the security of this phone line. Take that as a given."

"Well, then," Vermeer continued, against his better judgment, not believing that anything in the Rising Moon was secure. "Yes, hypothetically speaking, a house fire would probably help a lot of people, living and dead, including many that you and I have never even heard of. In fact, I had a little fire of my own, down on the beach this morning. But I suspect there are duplicate . . . loose ends . . . somewhere else in the world. Probably in the Boston area."

"Two house fires, then," said MacInnes, chuckling, "more or less concurrent. Hypothetically speaking, as you say. Relax, Professor Vermeer. No one gets hurt in a hypothetical kind of fire."

"I hope not, Mr. MacInnes."

"One more thing, Professor. I've decided to divide the reward money equally between you and Captain Brouillard. A million apiece. That seems like the only fair approach."

———————

"You didn't come visit me in the hospital." She looked at him a little reproachfully. "Although thanks for the corny balloons. Which they made me take home, by the way. A dozen overweight dinosaurs."

"You're welcome. They're Mylar. I'm told that they'll last for months. And actually, I *did* try to visit you. I got within about thirty feet of your room and saw all the reporters camped outside your door. I just didn't have the stomach for it. And I figured you didn't need any more commotion, either. Can you imagine the photographers working the bedside reunion?"

Brouillard smiled grudgingly. "Yeah. With you looking like you, and me in my backless johnny and the dangling IVs and really bad hair.

"But you know," she continued, "you were one of the few people I really wanted to see. Not the mayor or the senator or the other senator, either. My family, of course. A couple of guys from work, although not the other guys. And you. That was basically it."

A waitress arrived and asked if Brouillard would be eating. "No, thanks," she replied. "My friend and I are going upstairs now. Could we have the check?"

He trailed her along the colonnade that bordered the fanciful central courtyard, which somehow managed to be in full bloom in the middle of winter, then up a long flight of stairs to the second floor. They headed to the right rear corner of the building. "Here," she said, stopping to usher him in first. "The Dutch Room. Called that, of course, because this is where Mrs. Gardner displayed her collection of Dutch art."

He looked around the dark, high-ceilinged room. Except for a sleepy-looking guard on the far side, it was empty. Five tall windows along the street side, separated by marble columns, were almost completely covered by full-length rattan shades. They threw the room into perpetual half-darkness, interrupted only by spotlights aimed at specific works of art. The deep maroon tiled floor, worn to an odd shade of pink where the foot traffic was heaviest, accentuated the somber air of the room. Several of the larger frames on the walls were empty.

"Exactly as she left it," Brouillard said, left arm immobilized, waving with her right, "except, of course, for the stuff that got stolen in the 1990 heist."

He remembered: a daring late-night theft of precious

artworks. Then lots of police bluster and art-bureaucrat outrage, but nothing was ever recovered. The stuff was now presumably buried in the windowless vault of some Middle Eastern potentate or Japanese business tycoon, to be enjoyed by only one person forever, or at least until a guilt-ridden descendant fessed up.

She motioned for him to sit in a chair that was not roped off, next to the window, and brought over a similar chair from the adjoining wall. Pulling her own chair up alongside him, she seemed at home. "That was my first year on the force," she continued. "I came down here the morning after as the greenest of green rookies. My job was to keep the gawkers out so that the FBI and everybody else could do their thing. 'Barbie-bar-the-door,' somebody called me. Fortunately, it didn't stick."

He pictured her standing in the doorway in a blue uniform, with cop paraphernalia hanging off her belt. Perhaps standing at parade rest: hands clasped behind her back, feet spread to shoulder width. He couldn't imagine anyone calling her Barbie and getting away with it.

"And let me guess," he said. "You've been coming here ever since."

"Nope," she replied. "Until the day before yesterday, I hadn't been back. Except for one time when we actually chased a bad guy in through the front door and wrestled him to the ground in the courtyard, but I don't count that as a visit."

"So exactly what are we doing here, Barbara?" It was the first time he had ever used her first name.

Now she looked a little less poised, as if she was venturing off solid ground. "Well. See that frame right there?"

She pointed at a fussy-looking dressing table that

backed up against a brown-velvet-draped easel. On the easel was another empty frame, much smaller than its empty cousins up on the walls, although still gilded and overwrought. As a result, it looked as though it was trying too hard.

"The gold one behind the table," he said. "With nothing in it."

"Right." She nodded. "That is where, up until sometime on the night of March eighteenth, 1990, you would have seen a painting called *The Concert*, by Jan Vermeer. Your great-great-great-whatever."

"Uh-huh. Uncle Jan."

She leaned toward him. "So. So I'm lying there in that damn hospital bed, spaced out from all that pain medication they're pumping into me, and suddenly, I remember this exact scene, clear as day, almost from this exact angle, just like I saw it eight hours a day, three days running, more than a decade ago. I'm seeing that empty picture frame, against that desk. And then, after a while, in the hospital, I come back into my right mind, and I'm asking myself, *why that particular scene,* of all the scenes that could have come into my doped-up brain, at that point? Why am I conjuring up a picture of a picture I never even laid eyes on, not even once?"

She looked at him as if she expected an answer. "Uhm, because," he began, "you . . ." He considered making a joke. Seeing the look in her eye, he stopped. "Sorry, Barbara. I don't have a clue."

Disappointment flickered on her face. She pushed her hair back from her face with her right hand, then returned it to her lap. "Well, so," she said, now looking a little flustered, "I get out of the hospital day before yesterday, and I want a quiet place where I can get away from the mayor, and the press, and the agents, and the publishers, and the speakers' bureaus, and all the rest of it. And that same picture comes back into my head—this scene here—even though now, of course, I don't have much in the way of painkillers in my brain to blame it on. So I get a lift down here. And I sit where you're sitting. For about two hours. I just sit and think about things."

At that moment a guided tour flooded into the room: eleven tourists and a docent. Brouillard and Vermeer fell silent as the docent steered their attention toward the Rembrandt next to the doorway. The docent talked about how the sunlight falling on his right shoulder lit up that shoulder and steered the eye toward his face. She explained that this was Isabella Stewart Gardner's first major acquisition, when the grande dame first began thinking about making a museum for the public. The tourists shifted from foot to foot, not answering her leading questions. Then the docent talked hurriedly about the empty frames on the far walls, in which the tourists seemed more interested. She suggested that the reason why the Rembrandt hadn't been stolen was that it was painted on wood and couldn't be rolled up. The group clucked sympathetically, shook their heads, and moved on.

"Sounds like Uncle Jan should have invested in some plywood," Vermeer said into the silence that had gathered again around them. He wondered what she was trying to say. He wondered what he wanted to say. He realized that he was jealous when the tour had come through: He wanted her to himself. He was happy to be sitting alone with her again.

"Look," she finally said, not looking. "I'm not good at this kind of stuff, so I think I've gotta just come out with it and take my chances."